NOT LIKE OTHER GIRLS

NOT LIKE OTHER GIRLS

Meredith Adamo

BLOOMSBURY

NEW YORK LONDON OXFORD NEW DELHI SYDNEY

BLOOMSBURY YA
Bloomsbury Publishing Inc., part of Bloomsbury Publishing Plc
1385 Broadway, New York, NY 10018

BLOOMSBURY and the Diana logo are trademarks of Bloomsbury Publishing Plc

First published in the United States of America in April 2024 by Bloomsbury YA

Text copyright © 2024 by Meredith Adamo

Bloomsbury books may be purchased for business or promotional use. For information on
bulk purchases please contact Macmillan Corporate and Premium Sales Department at
specialmarkets@macmillan.com

Library of Congress Cataloging-in-Publication Data
available upon request
ISBN 978-1-5476-1400-4 (hardcover) • ISBN 978-1-5476-1401-1 (e-book)

Book design by Yelena Safronova
Typeset by Westchester Publishing Services
Printed and bound in the U.S.A.
2 4 6 8 10 9 7 5 3 1

To find out more about our authors and books visit www.bloomsbury.com
and sign up for our newsletters.

To the girl I was when I needed this book the most.

*That girl totally would've rolled her eyes and denied she needed it
and refused to believe she deserved such kindness.*

She did.

I do.

And to all the other girls who need it: you deserve that, too.

NOT LIKE OTHER GIRLS

-1-

So, this is the trouble with girls like me—

I stole that from my mother, by the way. Pass that woman a double shot of whiskey after a long day at the broadcast station, and three minutes later, she'll be sitting cross-legged on the kitchen floor with a shoebox full of photos, searching for the best of me.

JoJo at fourteen, brace-faced but beautiful, a tiara pinned in her sun-streaked hair.

Joey at fifteen, sophomore class president, stunned at her landslide victory.

Joles at sixteen, June's Scooper of the Month at Costello's Frozen Custard, posing a touch too proudly with her bonus check.

No matter how often we repeat this scene—and trust me, it's often—my mother never strays far from the script. "My Lord, Jo-Lynn, just look at you," she likes to say, booze bringing loose the Tennessee twang in her voice. "Look who you could be if you still tried."

Sometimes I fight her on it, like, "Sure is a shame I blew my shot in beauty pageants, high school government, *and* ice cream alternatives."

Most times, I endure her wrath silently until she sighs, not mad, just disappointed, and says, "You won't try. You never do. That's the trouble with girls like you."

She means wild girls. Reckless girls. Difficult girls who talk back and slack off, who tease bright boys with even brighter futures and roll their eyes when other girls dare speak—not in a nasty way, necessarily, but not nicely either.

Or else find a synonym for "bad," and that's the kind of girl I am.

Was, I mean. Past tense. I'm trying—*trying*—to be better, or at least less terrible. But the trouble with girls like me is that screwing up comes to us so easily.

"Okay, it's okay," I say now, alone in my bedroom. "We're cool."

I'm not panicking. Not yet. No, right now I'm multitasking: I wiggle into a pair of black leggings, dig in my hamper for a cleanish sweater, call Miles Metcalf on my flip phone. (I don't use a flip phone by choice, to be clear; this is a *consequence of my actions*.) The line rings once. Twice. On the third ring, I finger-comb a knot from my soaked, snarled hair. The fourth, I tug a turtleneck, drab green and two sizes too big, from the hamper.

The fifth, I heave a sigh and say, "Oh my God, Miles, will you pick up?"

He does not. I drop the phone on my bed as the call goes to voicemail. *Hey, this is Miles Metcalf. Apologies that I missed your call, but I'll give you a ring as soon as I can.*

"Yo, it's Jo." I poke my head through the turtleneck. "You urgently need a new greeting, dude. 'I'll give you a ring'? What

2

are you, ninety?" I stop. Compose myself. Pick up the phone, say, "I know you're probably at school already or en route or whatever, but I need a ride, okay? You'd be my hero forever and ever, love you, bye."

I clap the phone shut, its snap startling my cat, Bay Leaf. She stares, unblinking, from her window perch. She has yet to realize a web of ice crusts the glass, frosting the view of our snowy street. Bay may be beautiful, but she has nothing in that skull but elevator music.

I point a finger at her. "I don't need your judgment, Bay Leaf."

Blame this—the multitasking, the not-panicking—on my broken alarm clock.

Okay, so it's broken in the sense that I forgot to set it last night, despite scribbling *SET ALARM!!!* on a hot pink sticky note and slapping it to my bathroom mirror. The reminder was right there, right in my face as I brushed my teeth before bed, and I thought, *Oh, yeah, I should do that*, and then I did not do that.

But I'm not panicking, remember? I dab concealer on a monster chin zit, hoist my backpack off the floor, hustle into the hall. Bay zooms past me, down the stairs, but I don't follow; I need to make a critical pit stop first.

"Lee!" I pound my fist on my brother's bedroom door. His mattress squeaks, shifts, yet he says nothing. I knock harder. "C'mon, jackass, I know you're awake. I need a ride to school."

"Huh?"

Louder, I say, "I missed the bus," and push open his door. My eyes strain against the sudden dark shift: blackout shades drawn, faded fleece blanket tucked into the curtain rod. I blink my vision into focus. "Cripes, are you on your deathbed?"

"Headache," he says, like the word aches too. Like I'm too clueless to spy the open bottle of Dad's best bourbon on his nightstand. Yawning, stretching, he says, "But I'm good."

"Good, because we need to go." I squint at his alarm clock. 7:04. That means twenty-six minutes until the first-period bell, at which point my ass better be seated in Mr. Chopra's Digital Design II—or else. I swallow hard. "Like, now."

"Ask Dad."

"Dad abandoned us."

"Forever?"

"Worse." I slump against the doorframe. "For breakfast."

It's a bimonthly tradition: Dad and his old chef buddies gather at Flower City Diner in honor of their long-gone glory days, when they'd stumble drunk out of their restaurants at five a.m. in search of black coffee and pancakes.

"Then ask your friends." Lee pauses. "Friend, singular."

Rude, but not incorrect.

It's just that Miles, ever the overachiever, gets to school an hour early each day. Most mornings he marks lab reports for the science faculty or runs scales on his baritone saxophone. Others, he eats his breakfast—an untoasted blueberry bagel with butter—with Principal Lund.

For fun.

I guess being a kiss-ass is why he'll for sure secure the valedictorian title and its $15,000 scholarship, *made possible by the generous support of the Culver Honors High School alumni fund and viewers like you, thank you*, and I will . . . not.

The point is: "Miles is a no-go. Can't you do this one thing for me, Lee? I never ask for anything." I quickly and loudly add, "Except an occasional ride."

"Not happening." He flips onto his stomach. "It's not my fault you're a—"

"That I'm a what?" I say it like a dare. *Go ahead. Try me.*

Lee lifts his head, the movement slow. Pained. He stares at me, his sandy hair flattened on one side, his eyes glassy in the dark of his bedroom. Then he rests his head again. "Shut the door on your way out, will you?"

I could fight him on this. Say, *Don't pretend I'm the only fuckup between us anymore.* But I'm late enough as it is. I abandon his bedroom for the stairs, my middle fingers thrown up, his door wide open. From the landing, I shout, "You're lucky I have a backup plan!"

He's less lucky about what the plan entails. I march into the kitchen, which is thick with the bold, bitter smell of Dad's morning coffee, and snatch Lee's keys off the counter. Just because I've flunked my road test four times doesn't mean I *cannot* drive; it simply means I'm not good at it. Mostly parallel parking and left turns, anyway, and who needs those?

I am, at the very least, capable enough for the two-mile trek to Culver.

Bay Leaf follows me into the foyer and mews as if to say, *Uh-huh, sure.*

"Can it, Bay." I drop the keys on the console table, next to Lee's old senior photo. He's pure golden boy in the picture: the pristine tuxedo and twinkling eyes, a shiny white smile that notches dimples in his cheeks.

My own portrait is *not fit to be displayed*. I keep a copy shoved inside my desk drawer, half-hidden under a dozen stray paper clips, three expired condoms, and a crumpled baggie of weed I mooched off Cody Forsythe last fall, back when I still talked to Cody Forsythe.

Back when I talked to anyone.

More quietly, I add, "It's fine."

That's the trouble with girls like me: we tell ourselves lies until they sound something like the truth. As I lace my boots? It's fine. Zip my parka to my chin, the faux-fur trim tickling my nose? It's fine! Throw open the door and reveal the white winter morning?

"Ah, shit."

Outside, snow falls in fat, heavy flakes, and the sky is a bruised yellow-gray, bright and dark all at once. God forbid the district call a snow day. It's the side effect of a Rochester winter: we're too prepared. The snowplows, salt trucks, unearned confidence behind the wheel . . .

Bay mews again: *Godspeed, dumbass!*

What's my other option here? Call Miles a million more times? Or worse, call my mother at Channel 12 and admit I screwed up, again, and prove I'm exactly the girl she thinks I am?

That's a hard pass.

I reach for the keys and crash out the door in one quick motion. Too quick. The keys fall to the floor, and I end up outside, empty-handed. I sigh, swear, but when I spin back—

"Looking for these?" Lee jingles the keys. He's sick-pale, his face a queasy green. Yet he still manages a smirk when he says, "Nice try, Jo."

Then he slams the door in my face.

The force of it rattles the leaded glass. Clinks the mail slot open, shut. Stuns me so still that I never even think to lunge for the doorknob until the deadbolt latches with a hollow click.

I smack my forehead against the glass. "Kill me."

"Will do!"

I whip my head back. Any other day, and I might joke about it. *Wow, that's quick service, ha ha ha.* Not today. Today I exhale, my breath a cloud in the cold, and I do the one thing I try to never, ever do: I look across the street.

Like a camera finding its focus, there's pretty, nice Maddie Price.

She stands in the glow of the last lingering streetlamp, a golden ray of light shining upon her and—this part is crucial—her stupid white Prius. One gloved hand wields a snow brush. The other holds her phone to her ear.

"I said *fine.*" Her words barely carry, but her tone is clipped. Like she's annoyed, maybe.

Nix that. Now she's giggling. Must be Cody on the other end. They've been dating, what, three months? Four? The way she gushes about him being the best boyfriend on the planet, you'd think she was the first girl to ever fall in love. Never mind that none of what she says is true.

Believe me, I know the real Cody Forsythe. Someday Maddie will too.

For now, she says, "I'll see you soon," and ends the call with a dreamy smile.

Excellent opportunity for me to shout, "Maddie!"

She jerks her head toward me, startled, but looks away just as quick. If I had to guess, I'd guess she's thinking, *Ew, what does she want?* I dash down the snow-packed walkway, up to her.

Maddie keeps her back to me, sweeps the last layer of snow from her windshield. She'd likely ignore me forever, except I skid on a patch of ice and slam into the trunk of her car, hard, which is objectively pretty funny, but Maddie doesn't laugh. Or smile. Or blink.

I nod at her, righting myself. "What's up?"

"Are you lost?" She swipes a snowflake from her cheek, bored with me already.

"Oh, no." I jab my thumb behind me. "I live right over there."

"I was kidding."

"Right. I was also kidding." I fake a laugh. She doesn't seem to find it as funny. "See, the joke is that we're neighbors, so—"

"Did you want something, Jo?" Maddie crosses her arms. Shivers. The air has stung her face a painful pink. The tips of her ears burn even redder. Her outfit of the day—fitted trousers, ankle boots, a soft cream sweater under an unbuttoned wool coat—is both fashion *and* function.

"You look like a dang L.L. Bean catalog," I blurt out.

"That's what you wanted to tell me?"

"Yes. Actually, no. Can I hitch a ride? I was going to commit grand theft auto, but . . ."

What I mean is: *You're my only hope.* Maddie knows it too. Knows the bus schedule by heart from her pre-license days, knows I'll be late without her. She sighs, annoyed, but I swear the edge in those ice-blue eyes softens. I'm positive her posture relaxes. I'm certain—

"No."

I laugh, sort of. "Come again?"

Maddie takes one big step toward me. We're close enough for me to see the smudge of pink lip balm in the corner of her mouth.

To smell her orange blossom perfume. She's a solid five inches taller than me, but I don't shrink back. I refuse.

Not even when she says, "No, Jo. Never," with a grin so big it could split her face in two.

We stand like this—silent, still—for what feels like forever. Then I tuck a frozen lock of hair behind my ear and say, "That certainly sucks."

"I don't know what you expected." Maddie heaves open the car door, fighting a gust of wind that flutters the soft waves in her hair. "Not to be mean, but why would I ever help *you*?"

"Because, Maddie." I'm shameless. Daring her to think back to when this—the two of us, together, talking at the curb—felt so normal only a few years ago. I know she remembers it, too.

For a second, Maddie falters—grin flattening, eyebrows pinching in the middle.

This is pretty, nice Maddie Price, after all. I never meant for the rhyme to stick. To stalk her until our senior year. But it's not like it ruined her life, and it's not like it isn't true. The girl has perfect attendance, top-notch grades, an early acceptance to NYU all but guaranteed. Throw in the soccer star boyfriend, the popular friends, and everything about her is what you'd expect.

No one thinks twice about a girl like that.

Maddie shakes her head, like she's shaking that exact same thought from her head, and drops behind the wheel. "Good luck with the ride."

"Maddie, wait." I wedge my foot in the door. "You know I can't be late. Like, cannot."

Her lips curve. "Why is that again?"

Rhetorical question. I've spent the past six weeks under

academic review, and somehow everyone knows it. But a late arrival would add an extra week to my sentence, which is supposed to expire tomorrow when first-semester report cards post, so again: *I cannot be late.*

"God, Maddie, do you need me to beg? I'll beg." I drop to my knees and spread my arms out wide. "You know I'd never ask if I weren't desperate, but I am beyond—"

She yanks the door shut. It echoes down our street, straight to my bones.

I guess this is how it ends: Maddie, gone; me, alone.

But first, she lowers the window and leans her head out, snow swirling fiercely, furiously around her. "I don't feel sorry for you, Jo," she says, serious as ever. "You have no one to blame but yourself."

I choke out another laugh, but this one hurts. Burns. With one final sweet smile, Maddie shifts into drive, pulls away from the curb—and she leaves me behind.

Something hot prickles behind my eyes. I won't cry. I don't cry. Not when I was nine and tripped on a crack in the sidewalk, my front teeth shattering, mouth slick with blood. Not when I pierced my foot on a rusted nail last summer, and not the summer before that, when the boys got drunk and told me they were the ones who scratched my name onto that urinal that one time, and why couldn't I let it go, it's just a joke, you know?

So, no. Maddie Price will not unravel me either.

Instead, I stand. I wipe the slush from my cold, drenched knees.

And I think, inexplicably, of another photo—one my mother can never see.

Last fall, late October. The night of the bonfire at Durand Eastman Beach. In the photo, I wear tight denim shorts, beat-up white Keds, a black zip-up that isn't mine. It's bad enough how I tilt my head, just so, a hickey bruised on the curve of my neck, but even worse is my smile. Sly. Coy. Like I know more in this moment than some girls will ever know.

I didn't know shit.

I especially didn't know that when the night sky filled with stars, when the fire hissed, half-dead, when every phone pinged with SIX NEW IMAGES, I'd so seamlessly become the worst of me: Jo at seventeen, outcast.

But I guess that's the trouble with girls like me. We always get what we deserve.

- 2 -

It takes less than a minute for my fingers to go numb. Snow slides inside my boot a minute after that. In two more, I round the corner by the fish market and slip on the ice, catching myself on a bus stop sign, whispering, "Shitshitshit."

There's no need to whisper; no one's around to hear me. Even the plaza across the street is dead, from the drive-thru ATM to the 7-Eleven where me and the boys—back when the boys were my buds—used to satisfy our munchies. I'd buy the same assortment of snacks each time: Cheez-Its, a tube of raw cinnamon rolls, and a box of Capri Sun.

My heart pangs. It's such a small thing to miss. How I'd slam six juice pouches in a row. How we'd pop open the rolls and eat the icing with our fingers. How we'd almost choke trying not to laugh, since we were stupid and stoned and certain nothing could touch us.

The digital sign at the bank flicks from 19°F to 7:21 a.m.

My heart pangs again, deeper. Angrier. The extension to my review is all but inevitable, and so is Maddie's delight. I can just see her looping her arms around Cody's freckled neck and brushing her lips to his ear, like, *Jo sure is quick to get on her knees, huh?*

Behind me, a car horn blares. I pull my hand from my pocket, middle finger raised, but the horn *honkhonk*s again. I'm ready to fight when I peer inside the open window to see—

"My hero!"

Miles Metcalf grins, tongue pressed in the gap between his front teeth. "You flatter me."

"Only when you deserve it, and you deserve it, dude."

He shrugs, sheepish. "I was salting the sidewalk for my neighbors—they're elderly; nice folks—and saw your voicemail before I left, but I figured you'd forgotten your phone so I should drive the . . ." He trails off when he sees my face. "Sorry. Rambling. Come on in!"

I tug the door handle, and out roll two empty Red Bull cans. There's another ten in the footwell, plus a dozen cracked candy hearts on the passenger seat.

"Crap, sorry about the crap." He sweeps the shards onto his palm, then stares, like, *What do I do with a handful of broken hearts?* He flings it into the backseat.

"No offense," I say as I climb inside, kicking aside the heap of cans, "but when has your car not looked like this?"

He frowns but doesn't argue the point. How can he? Miles sustains his body on sugar and caffeine, keeps packets of sour candy in his pockets, chugs energy drinks like water. If it'll raise his heart rate and/or turn his tongue blue, he'll consume it.

I pluck a pink Starburst from the cupholder and unwrap it into my mouth. "Drive fast," I say. He waits for me to fasten my seatbelt, and we're off, tires fishtailing, steering wheel wobbly under his white-knuckled grip. My hand flies to the panic handle. "Please also drive good."

"Sorry, sorry, sorry." He pumps the brakes until the tires regain traction. Back in control, he exhales. "Not bad for my first time, eh?"

I steal another Starburst. "First time?"

"First time driving in inclement weather conditions. It's been a mild winter, so . . ." Miles trails off again, pale face flushing. The kid is a ferocious blusher. The littlest things set him off—incorrect test answers, redheads with blunt bangs, the mere mention of S-E-X.

After we read *Romeo and Juliet* in ninth-grade English, Mr. Hardy let us watch the movie adaptation so long as we swore not to lose it during the millisecond you see Juliet's boobs. Most of the boys salivated as they waited for the scene. Not Miles. His knee bounced, rattled his desk. His death grip nearly snapped his pencil in half.

As the shot approached, as we inched forward in our seats, Cody muttered, "All clear, man," so Miles looked up at the exact right (wrong?) moment. He ducked his head, mortified, but he wasn't fast enough. He saw.

Worse, we all saw him see.

We gave that kid hell. The boys cackled, kicked his chair, chucked his pencil across the classroom. I tapped his shoulder and loudly whispered, "Oh my God, do you have a boner?"

He tried to speak, squeak out a denial, but no sound came out. What's a rich red? Scarlet? Crimson? That's how hot his face burned. And the rest of us—me and the boys, *my* boys, boys I thought were my friends—laughed and laughed at poor, shy, innocent Miles.

But just look at us now! Me and Miles, who was waiting right there after everything blew up last fall. My friend, singular.

I pinch his cheek. "I'm honored your first time is with me."

"Yeah, yeah." He swats my hand away. "You think you're funny, don't you?"

"I *am* funny. I wish everyone were as funny as me."

Miles snorts out a laugh. Fusses with his loose curls, flattened from his knit cap. Starts to speak, I think, but lets the words die on his lips. This happens a lot with him: our banter broken, back-and-forth fizzling into a sad, deflated silence.

"Whomp, whomp," I say, and it's a joke. Really.

The quiet hangs between us as he dips through the underpass. When we emerge from the tunnel, the city skyline appears in the distance, jagged and gray against an even darker sky. The snow will lose its charm soon, but right now it's sort of beautiful.

I mean, I still hate it. Rochester is all I've ever known, and I know I want out. Badly.

But sometimes I imagine what it'd be like to stay.

When I do, I think of slow snowfall on cold mornings like this one, when it feels like the world has paused. Like I can just . . . breathe. Then the sky stays gray for six months straight or I hear someone whisper, *See that girl? That's the girl whose nudes—*

My eyes find the dashboard clock. "Miles, I want to ask you something." His thick brows tick up a notch, and I smile in a way I hope is sweet. Helpless, even.

Then I point to his speedometer and say, "Can you floor it, please?"

It shaves a decade off his life, but Miles drives a whopping five miles above the speed limit, breezing through not one but *two* yellow lights to get us to Culver with a minute to spare.

I leap out before the car comes to a complete stop. "Thanks-againfortheride!"

"What?" Miles fumbles his seatbelt. "Wait!"

I don't have time to wait. I dart across the icy lot and into the door by the band room. The din of music—smashing piano keys, wailing violin strings, spit-thick trombone bellows—means no one hangs here much.

Even better, I can avoid Principal Lund. Every morning, she greets students by the main doors with the other administrators, walkie-talkies crackling on their hips. If she saw me now, I bet she'd smile that chilly, unflappable smile and say, "I suggest you hurry, Miss Kirby."

I'm hurrying, I'm hurrying.

I hang a left down the senior wing and bust into the design lab at the exact second the bell rings. It'd be impressive if I didn't heave the door into the wall. Mr. Chopra peers at me over his clear-framed glasses, his marker pressed to the whiteboard.

I gently shut the door behind me. "My bad."

"Thank you for gracing us with your presence." He resumes his self-portrait. "Take your seat—and try not to hurt yourself, okay?"

I shoot a finger gun with a wink and a click of my tongue, and then walk straight into the printer table. No one is subtle about it. Not the twins, Kyle and Tyler Spencer, in a set of identical grins. Not April Kirk, who glares at me through the fringe of her fierce copper hair.

Not Hudson Harper-Moore.

He tracks each step I take to the back row where we sit, an empty chair between us. He's chewing on the plastic stirrer from his to-go coffee cup, but the way he tries to hide his smile is undeniable. The way he eyes me, one corner of his mouth lifting . . .

I mouth: *Do not.*

And yet he does.

He tips onto the back legs of his chair and says so only I can hear, "Comin' in a little hot, don't you think?" I press my hand between his shoulder blades and shove. Hudson rights himself before he falls, the chair crashing into place, metal clattering against linoleum.

Mr. Chopra steps back from the whiteboard. "Why are you still standing, Jo?"

"That wasn't me!"

"Why are you still standing?" he asks again. I sit. He mirrors his cartoon self: arms folded across his chest; mouth set in a thin line, unamused but not unkind. "You good?"

"Yeah, I'm done." I don't mean it as a joke, but Hudson stifles a laugh behind the back of his hand. I shrug out of my parka, suddenly hot. "Shut up, Hudson."

He stretches his arm across the empty chair. "Sorry, did I say something?"

"Nope. Not playing this game with you."

"What game?" He tilts his head, all innocent, a strand of dark, longish hair slipping from behind his ear. The angle gives me the perfect view of his face—the freckles splattered across his nose, warm brown eyes flecked with gold, the small scar on his upper lip.

Then he dares to smile at me.

So, Hudson is not totally terrible. He's nice to look at and mostly a decent guy, but we're not friends. Not anymore. And, fine, there may have been a time (or two) when we'd gotten *very* friendly, but the bonfire, the photos, the fallout—it killed anything between us real quick.

But Hudson never turned on me like the rest of those assholes. He's still fucking irritating, though.

"Know what?" I flash him both middle fingers. "You're the third person I've flipped off today, but I mean it most with you."

"Thanks." He hides another smile behind a sip of coffee, like he's won this round of the game he pretends he never plays. The one that earned us both the Biggest Flirt superlative.

The game I can't play anymore.

I slap my palms on the table and mouth something else. He laugh-chokes the coffee back into the cup. Swiping his chin, he says, "Mr. Chopra, Jo just told me to go f—"

"Two minutes." Chopra pinches the bridge of his nose. "Two more minutes."

I start, "What's in two—?"

Hudson angles his monitor toward me.

DON'T FORGET!! Today is the **last day** to apply for the Senior Experience.

Applications received after **February 5 at 11:59 p.m.** will be returned without review. **No exceptions or extensions**!

To celebrate this exciting day, Principal Lund invites the senior class to join her in the gymnasium during first period for a

SPECIAL SURPRISE from the alumni-mentors! Light refreshments will be served.

Attendance **mandatory** :)

I slouch until my butt hangs off the chair. "That smiley is mocking me."

"You and me both," Hudson mumbles.

The Senior Experience is an annual mentorship program that pairs Culver alumni with the most promising leaders of tomorrow. (Yes, I stole that line from the flyer taped inside every bathroom stall in the building.) From the "invaluable real-world experience" to that sweet, sweet networking, baby, the program is a wet dream for the top students at the top school in the district.

Yet despite the **bolded**, CAPITALIZED letters and two (!!) exclamation points, I did, in fact, forget about the deadline—but I have a valid reason.

And the reason is that I don't give a shit.

"Okay, folks," Chopra says after taking roll, and it somehow counts as a dismissal. Chairs scrape back. Backpacks zip. Then, like an afterthought: "Jo, come here a second, will you?"

"Do I have to?" I ask. His face tells me yes. I approach his desk as the room empties, pick up a pen, and draw a series of sad faces on his attendance sheet. "What's the special surprise?"

"Meet and greet with the mentors," he says. I add angry eyebrows to my latest sad face, so it's the saddest, maddest of all. He snatches the pen from me. "Jo, your layout is late."

"What layout?" I'm deflecting. He means the senior spotlight yearbook layout, my major design project from last marking period. It may or may not be two weeks overdue.

"And you owe me six mini-designs. *Six*. I had to—" Chopra stops, taps the pen on his keyboard. "Conti asked to see your portfolio."

My stomach swoops. "He what? Why?"

I know why. Mr. Conti, assistant principal and pain in my ass, is executor of my review. I've abided by his terms and conditions for the past six weeks: no late arrivals, no detentions, no administrative interventions. We meet tomorrow about the end of my punishment.

The *end* of it.

"I told him I had to convert the file format to send it, but I'd get it to him by Wednesday." Each word is slow and precise. Loaded. Low, he adds, "I can't keep doing this, Jo."

"No, I know. I know." I step toward the door. "It'll be the best portfolio you've ever—"

"Go," he tells me.

I do.

-3-

Here's the issue: I can't finish my portfolio by Wednesday. Not when I've made zero progress on the mini-designs and minimal progress on the yearbook layout. I'd started but stalled after someone submitted "Senior Slut: Jo-Lynn Kirby" as a write-in superlative—thirteen times.

I ripped up each entry and dumped the scraps in the trash, like I didn't even care.

And I *don't* care.

Here's the other issue: I'd rather slam my head into a wall than go to this alumni meet and greet. Even before, I could not care less about the Senior Experience. I'm just not desperate enough to prove I'm the best of the best. To do what it takes to get what I want.

It's unfathomable to me, really. How anyone knows what they want. Like, I barely know what I want for breakfast most mornings. Bacon, egg, and cheese on a sesame bagel? Cereal? Or nothing at all, since it'll be lunch by the time I make up my mind?

"It's fine," I tell myself. Each step I take pounds in sync with my heartbeat.

"Sorry, are you talking to yourself?"

"Shut up, Hudson." I walk faster, but he easily keeps pace. It's not fair. He's so tall that one of his strides equals three of mine. I snap, "Shouldn't you be at the meet and greet?"

"Wow, way to ruin the surprise." He lobs his empty coffee cup into the trash, nothing but net. "One, I had to pee. Two, I'm not exactly the strongest candidate, so."

"Oh. Right." I kind of knew that.

The *strongest candidate* has brains, ambition, and, ideally, plans for college.

It was a genuine scandal when word spread last fall that Hudson Harper-Moore—ranked second, a lock for salutatorian and the $10,000 that comes with it—was applying to zero schools.

Seriously, it got so ugly that an anonymous coalition of students demanded he forfeit his spot. They even ran an open letter in the school paper imploring him to *do the right thing* and to *think of his peers*, which meant *think of their futures*, but what about his?

Those students just want a bump in the rank; the money is nothing to them. (I've never asked, but I sort of get the sense it might be everything to Hudson.) The paper retracted the letter after Lund sent a scathing email about integrity or whatever, but still.

"So, anyway," Hudson says. The awkward silence carries us to the open gym doors.

Not that either of us enters.

The gym drips in black and silver, our school colors: limp streamers twisted in the rafters, confetti-filled balloons, the breakfast buffet. Culver's finest surround a dozen folding tables set center court, the lines extending twenty, thirty students deep.

There's Jack Parker, the most insufferable kid in my AP Econ class, elbowing by the bleachers like he's late for a Young Republicans meeting. There's One-L Daniele de Palma, resident town crier and class photographer, capturing the anxious band girls, flash bright.

The thrum of nerves, the hard-beating hearts of two hundred seniors—it's too much.

I slump against the wall. "I don't want to go in there."

"Me neither." Hudson is quiet a beat. "I mean, we could . . . not."

I roll my eyes up and over to him. Suck in a sharp breath. This is the exact pose One-L Daniele made us strike for our superlative photo last semester: me, back pressed to my locker; Hudson leaning into me with a lazy half smile, his elbow propped above my head.

If I wanted to—which I do not—I could fit myself into the crook of his body. Tilt onto my tiptoes so he can see me clearly when I smile, teasing and sweet, but not that sweet.

I could shrug, coy, and say, "What else did you have in mind?"

Hudson blinks. "What?"

"What?" I clap my hand to my mouth. *What else did you have in mind?*

Those words slipped out of me, and I slipped into the girl I used to be. See, there's a fine line between Biggest Flirt and Senior Slut; I just never knew it existed until I crossed it.

Face hot, I say, "Ignore that," and duck into the gym.

"Jo!" he calls after me, followed immediately by someone else, louder, "Hudson!"

Cody Forsythe. I'd know that voice anywhere—rough and hoarse, like he's forever recovering from laryngitis. He stands under the basketball hoop with Ben Sulkin, star pitcher, next in line for a spray-tanned, silver-haired mentor. His poster reads: Frank Hatch, Finance.

"Over here, man!" Cody shouts, hands cupped to his mouth.

Hudson hesitates. Looks from the boys in their sleek suits to his own outfit: black jeans, ratty high-tops, denim jacket over a white T-shirt. When he lifts his head again, he turns not to them, but to me—and now Cody finds me, too.

My gut clenches as his mouth ticks up, up, up. We had the same orthodontist until tenth grade, but his bite shifted within a year. Now Cody doesn't smile so much as he bares his teeth.

I shoot Hudson a tight grin. "Have fun with your friends!"

He calls out my name again, but I'm already shoving into the restless crowd, trying not to think how those were once my friends, too. Emphasis on *were*.

Here, now, my legs propel me toward the breakfast buffet. I could find Miles, I guess, but that'd mean hanging with his dork band friends who think I'm a brainless blonde. (I mean, come on—my hair is clearly *dark* blonde.) At least back here I can take a breath, even if the air reeks of varnish and sweat. Back here I can be alone.

Plus, you know. Pastries.

I survey the spread: apple fritters, cherry tarts, croissants drizzled with dark chocolate. I reach for a paper plate right as someone—some woman—nabs it first. She says, "So sorry to cut, but my hunger is seconds away from hanger." She clicks a set of tongs together like claws. "Now I feel guilty. What do you want?"

"Uh, a sticky bun," I say. She drops one on a plate and motions for me to take it. "Sorry, are you one of"—I gesture vaguely toward the mentor tables—"them?"

"You sound surprised."

She's just not what I pictured. She's young, for one. Late twenties, maybe? Her hair is knotted in a sloppy bun and her cardigan is stretched, wrinkled, and a run rips her tights from ankle to knee. On *both* legs.

Reading my mind, she says, "I'm only in it for the food." She bites into a turnover, crust flaking down her denim dress. "Why aren't you sucking up like everyone else?"

As if on cue, Cody's loud voice rises above the rest. He's in schmooze mode. Ben Sulkin, too. (Hudson, it seems, has already bailed.) The boys loosen their ties, laugh like old frat brothers reliving their glory days—and Frank Hatch, Finance, eats it up.

The mentor nods in their direction. "Those your friends?"

It's a joke, I think. There's no way she expects me to say yes. I try to see what she sees: the slouch in my posture; my long, tangled hair; the oversized clothes I wear, as if they'd ever hide my body. As if I could ever fully disappear.

I shake my head. "Former friends."

"Yeah? What happened?"

There's no way she expects me to tell the truth, and what could I even say? *Oh, yeah, me and those guys used to be tight, but I pissed off the short one—Cody; ugh, I know, of course his name is Cody—so he leaked my nudes to his entire contacts list.*

That is not a story I tell.

So, I shrug, all casual. Unbothered. "I used to be cool, but now I'm not, so no one likes me anymore." I look down at my plate. "Actually, it turns out no one ever liked me."

"Why's that?"

"Unclear." I pick up the sticky bun and take a big, greedy bite. Mouth full, I add, "I have such a winning personality."

We don't speak for ten seconds. I count. On eleven, she fidgets with her wire-rimmed glasses, like she's bringing me into clearer focus. "What did you say your name was?"

"I didn't, but it's Jo."

"Jo what?"

"Hyphen Lynn Kirby."

She nods once. Twice. Extends her hand and says, "Tess Spradlin."

I stare at her—Tess, I guess—and her outstretched hand. Ew, is this *networking*? There's a non-zero chance I'm eligible to apply if I'm under review, and it's not like I would if I could. All the potential in the world, yet I never seem to reach it. It's the Jo-Lynn Kirby trademark.

I almost say, *I'm in it for the food, too.*

But I keep my mouth shut and take, shake her hand.

"I'm sorry to interrupt—" *Maddie.* Here, beside me, a tight smile plastered on her face.

Something like a laugh, bitter and ugly, bubbles out of me. "Are you sorry? Really?"

Like I never spoke, she says, "It's such an honor meeting you, Miss Spradlin. I'm Maddie Price." She waits a beat after her name, like it could possibly mean anything to Tess. "I, uh, was over in your line, but my friends . . ."

She looks toward the bleachers where they sit, those friends of hers.

The Birds.

Blame the nickname on Mr. Fox, our history teacher sophomore year. Every class he'd tap his pen to his chin, blue ink dotting his skin, and say, "Did I not shut the window? It seems the birds are chittering today," as they giggled, gasped, shushed each other. *Shh, shh.*

Now, Kathleen O'Mara draws the others close, closer, and whispers something mean. I can tell by the way Sara Caruso smirks, her perfect brows arched; by the way Michaela Russell bats Kathleen's arm but struggles not to smile, too. Only when they turn to us all together, all at once, do I realize it's not just mean—it's about *me.*

Heat burns up my neck. I force myself to look down. Look anywhere but at them. Other girls have never liked me, the Birds most of all.

At least the feeling is mutual.

"I, um . . ." Maddie stumbles on the sentence, like she's searching for the last line she read in a book. It's not like she normally exudes confidence or anything, but this is weird. How she's acting almost starstruck. "I couldn't miss the chance to meet you in person, Miss Spradlin."

"What's your thing, Tess?" I ask, then rip off another bite of the sticky bun.

"It's in the program." Maddie shoves a pamphlet from the buffet into my hand.

So helpful, so *obvious*, that Maddie Price. Yet I still open to the mentor bios:

TESS SPRADLIN is a staff editor for *ROC Weekly*. A graduate of the prestigious Arthur L. Carter Journalism Institute at NYU, Ms. Spradlin freelanced in NYC for several years before finding her way home to Rochester. Her writing has appeared in such publications as *The City*, *Chirp*, and elsewhere.

There may as well be a clause that states "anyone who isn't Maddie Price need not apply."

That's pretty much what she tells Tess now. Something about *The Eagle Eye*, the school paper I rarely read. Something about how she's also going to NYU. (No, it's not official yet, but she applied Early Decision II, so she'll hear back soon.)

When Maddie says, "I think we'd be a perfect match," even I buy it.

"Do you write too?"

It takes me a second to register that Tess is talking to me, and in that second, I devour the rest of the sticky bun. I point to my mouth, chew and chew and chew, choke out, "No."

"I'm sort of the writer between us." Maddie flashes her fakest smile, her fingers finding her delicate garnet necklace—an eighteenth-birthday gift from Cody.

I flip my plate into the trash. "You sure are, Mads."

Tess volleys her eyes between us, rapt but pretending not to be. Like me and Maddie are another story to break. "Sorry, one last question." Tess points a chipped black nail at me. "You *don't* write, but can you?"

"I can form a coherent sentence, I guess."

"Then I'd love to see you apply, Jo."

With that—the rapid one-syllable punch of my name—Maddie's face falls. Crumples like a piece of paper in a fist. I'm about to back off (*not interested, sorry*) when Maddie laughs, a low sputter of disbelief, and says one single, simple word: "No."

Two letters, one complete sentence.

But no one tells me what to do.

In one motion, I rip a napkin from the stack, scrounge for a pen in my bag, and hunch to write, *Told you I could form a sentence.*

"Here!" I present the napkin to Tess with a flourish. "Consider this my application."

Then I turn to Maddie and do something truly mean before I go: I wink.

Look, I know I'm part of the problem. How I goad Maddie. Provoke her. But I've tried to untangle myself from this mess countless times, explain I'm not competing with her, not now or then or ever. Sometimes I swear our rivalry exists solely because she can't let it die.

Though I guess neither can I, so what do I know?

-4-

This happens sometimes. I forget I'm no longer the girl who can do and say and get away with anything, forget I have one goal, and one goal alone: getting the fuck out of here.

Here, as in Culver Honors High School. Here, as in Rochester, New York.

So, I recalibrate. I keep my head down and my mouth shut. I tally the days to graduation, which is beyond demoralizing. I focus on tomorrow instead. *One more day.* I loop the phrase in my head until dismissal.

"One more day, right?" Miles fumbles with his coat buttons. "Then you're free!"

"Let's hope." I dig in my locker for my library pass. Per my review terms, I'm required to spend four hours a week in the school library because I guess Conti thinks I'll do homework?

Spoiler: I don't do shit.

"Be positive!" Miles leans against the locker beside mine. Immediately straightens again.

Guess he just remembered who it belongs to: April Kirk.

See, Miles and April dated for a hot minute. It was serious

enough that they went to prom together, but not so serious that it could endure her summer away at band camp. I've never asked about the breakup because I don't care, sorry, but she totally turned on me, long before everyone else did: brutal death glares, a cold shoulder that could give me frostbite.

I don't even know what I did to her.

"Let's celebrate tomorrow." Miles tries to bump my arm. Misses. It's like when Bay rubs my legs but overshoots, her body wiggling. "Celebrate you getting off. Your review, that is."

I slam my locker shut. "Guess we'll see if I fail, huh?"

"You're not going to fail."

"I might." I say it like a joke but . . . I might.

In the weeks after the bonfire, my grades slid with each exam I didn't study for, every essay I turned in late, if I even turned it in—and I watched it happen, like a viewer of my own life. I *let* it happen.

Before winter break, Conti called an emergency meeting to discuss *some concerns*. Dad nodded in the right spots. Frowned during the proper pauses. Then, when Conti announced I'd be under review the rest of the semester, Dad said, "Well, I'm sure she's trying her best."

"You won't fail," Miles says again, peering through the courtyard window. The snow has slowed, but the sky is even darker now. He presses his palm to the glass. The warmth of his skin fans out in rays. "I can help you, you know. If you need it."

The late bell rings, loud enough that I can pretend not to hear him.

I'm in a bad mood when I roll into the library two minutes later. *One more day*, et cetera, but I'm over it now. I shove my pass toward the freshman page. Kathleen O'Mara's little sister. The Irish genes run strong: wide green eyes and fair skin and dark, dark hair.

She stamps the pass and slides it back with a shy smile. "Here you go, Jo-Lynn."

"Jo." Gut reaction.

"Oh. I'm sorry."

"No! No, don't apologize. Thank you, uh. Clare," I say. She smiles, touched I knew her name. (I didn't. She's wearing a name tag.) I awkwardly wave and cross to the dictionary nook, flop onto a beanbag, its corduroy faded and worn and stained with I don't want to know.

Still, I play the part of dedicated student: unzip backpack, find notebook. Honors Physics. Barf. Only Miles, hopeful MIT admit, enrolled in Mr. Holt's AP section. Unless you're a genius like him, no one ever scores above a C—not since my perfect brother with his enviable B-minus.

An unfinished pop quiz and overdue labs spill from my notebook, which is fine. It's fine.

Except a HANG IN THERE! poster crinkles under the vent and some kid reading manga keeps sniffling and I hate how the *J* looks when I write my name, so I snap the notebook shut, then I snap my eyes shut, too. For now, all I want to think about is not thinking.

The peace lasts two minutes at most.

Even from behind my eyelids, I sense the shape of a figure eclipsing the overhead lights, like a cloud slipping over the sun. I hold my breath, hold still, since if I pretend to be dead then—

"Jo?"

"No." Silence drags for two, three, four seconds before I blink my eyes open. Lazily lift my head. Smile my brightest smile at Maddie Price. "Whatever you want, the answer is no."

Maddie licks her lips, chapped not from the cold but from gnawing at them with her own teeth. "I was hoping we could talk. Maybe."

"You were hoping we could talk. Maybe," I repeat. It's not mean—these are her words, her beats—but Maddie flinches. I sit up, the beanbag sinking under me. "Is this about the stupid napkin? Because I'll email that Tess lady if you—"

"No, no. I mean, I need that mentorship, Jo, so you *should* withdraw, but . . ." Maddie lets out a breath, fluttering a hand through her snow-dusted hair. "It's not that."

"Okay, cool, then what do you want from me?"

Easy as that, Maddie Price cracks. She buries her face in her scarf, the sob erupting out of her like it has claws and fangs.

"Uh." That's all I can muster. I hoist myself up and approach slowly, like she's a feral cat in a trap. No one has noticed us yet, and I need to keep it that way.

I cannot—will not—be blamed for making her cry.

Again.

Breathless, she whispers, "I'm sorry. I'm so—"

"Shut up," I say, and take her hand, leading her into the stacks, to the out-of-order staff bathroom. The heat vent is busted, and the toilet flushes on the third try only.

Door shut and locked behind us, Maddie braces her hands on the baby blue sink. Snot drips from her nose and down her lip. She tries to inhale but chokes on it. Gags.

"Ew, Maddie." I pass her a paper towel from the dispenser.

She blows her nose. "I'm sorry."

"Stop apologizing."

"I'm . . ." Maddie takes in a sharp, shaky breath and forces it out again, again, again.

It feels intrusive, in a way. Watching her rebuild the person she pretends to be. I focus on anything but her—the pyramid of toilet paper rolls, the circle of pink soap crusted on the sink, the hard thump of my own heart. It beats a rapid rhythm, uneven, until, finally, her breathing slows.

I take the smallest step toward her. "Maddie?"

She exhales. Holds her own gaze in the clouded mirror. Says, "I think I'm in trouble."

The heat whooshes on, blasting a breath of frigid air from the vent. Chills spike up the back of my neck. "You . . . what?"

"I think that I'm in trouble," she repeats, steady now, "but I think that you can help me."

"Me?" I force a laugh. "Uh, no. No way."

"Please, Jo. I can't go to anyone else. Not my friends. Not—"

"*No.*" I jolt, my elbow striking the sink, pain rattling down my arm. "Like, what does that mean? Trouble?" I flip the word over and over, then gasp so hard I cough on my own spit. "Oh my God, are you pregnant?"

"What? No! That'd be—"

"Immaculate?"

Her face tints pink. "You don't have to say it like that."

This, Maddie being a virgin, shouldn't really surprise me. Cody is her first boyfriend. He may be her first everything. I don't know if she'd ever been kissed before that night at the beach when, in the hot glow of the bonfire, the boy she loved chose her back—but only because he was desperate in a different way.

I heard him say it: *This girl will do* anything *for me.*

But she hasn't done *everything.*

Maddie swipes a hand across her face, her skin tacky with tears. "I'll explain everything, I promise, just . . . not here. Maybe we can get coffee?"

"I'm stuck here until three."

"Then we'll meet at three. By the bike rack?"

"I haven't said yes yet." *Yet.* Maddie catches it, too. I rein it back. Regain control. "Not to be mean, but why would I ever help *you*?"

Maybe that's low of me. To echo her own cruel words from this morning.

Fresh tears dot the corners of her eyes. "Because, Jo."

Somehow this is even crueler.

No. Two letters, one complete sentence. So profoundly easy to say—*no,* just like that—so I don't know why I never do it right. I don't know why, instead, I say, "Fine."

Maddie follows me back into the stacks. "Three, okay?" she says, stepping on my heel. I stop, stoop to fix my boot, and she goes for the unarmed emergency exit. There, she pauses, back to the door—and then she smiles that pretty, nice smile at me.

I refuse to smile back. "This feels like a setup, you know."

For what, I'm not sure. Just call it gut instinct.

Maddie frowns. "I'd never do that to you."

Except she has done that to me. Multiple times. I could remind her of our greatest hits: *The pool party? End of ninth grade? How you made me invite the boys and told your mom it was my idea? What about the time you told Cody about me and—?*

"I'll see you, Jo." Maddie shoves the door but hesitates, half inside, half out. I wonder if she's waiting for an alarm to blare. To get caught. But her face is utterly blank when she turns to me again. Like she'd never been crying at all. "No one can ever know about this."

My breath catches. "What did you say?"

What I mean is: *Why did you say that?*

Those words in that order, the stark blue eyes—

But Maddie is already gone, out there in the cold, hunching into the wind as she walks, a shadow against the fresh slate of snow.

-5-

I wait for Maddie by the bike rack, hands shoved deep inside my pockets, scarf pulled halfway up my face. The layers leave only a strip of skin exposed: eyes, cheekbones, bridge of my nose.

Still, the cold stings.

Three o'clock, right? It must be five after. Last-minute stragglers hustle to the late buses, the ancient engines rumbling, chugging. Black smoke plumes from exhaust pipes.

"Hurry up, Maddie." I bounce from one foot to the other. "Hurry up, hurry up."

I scan the senior lot again, searching for a white Prius. A girl in a black wool coat. (As if that doesn't describe half of Culver in winter.) One girl is headed this way, but it's not Maddie, and she's not alone. I squint into the snow, and then I launch myself behind the nearby trash can, slipping on a frozen puddle of rot, choking back a dry heave.

Only the Birds could bring this out in me.

Kathleen O'Mara leads the way, like always. "Can we move it along, please? Thanks!"

Don't be fooled; Kathleen is the worst, mean and serious and very, very Catholic. I'm not joking when I say I've never seen her smile.

Though she comes close now when Sara eats shit on the ice.

"Get it together, Caruso," Kathleen snaps. I can't tell if she's truly mad or not. It'd help if she had what remotely resembled a sense of humor.

Whatever. Sara is nonplussed. She cackles, head thrown back, her plum-red lips a shock against the snow. "I broke my ass!" she shouts, husky voice even raspier in the cold.

Once, when Miles got buzzed on bad beer at a party last year, he told me and Cody that he finds her voice—no joke—erotic. He used that exact word. *Erotic.* I scream-laughed so hard that I tipped off my barstool, and Cody slurred, "Dude, who even invited you?"

Blushing, Miles said, "Uh, you," but that wasn't the point.

Sara is still wailing about her ass when Michaela Russell drops beside her. "Stay with me," she cries, pressing her hand to Sara's forehead. "I'm here to help, okay? I'm a doctor."

"You're not a doctor," Kathleen says.

"Please give us space, ma'am."

"We're outside. That's lots of space."

"Do I need to sedate you?" Michaela tries to look serious but cracks in about a second. Of the Birds, she's the most tolerable. We were the only girls in our AP Biology lab last year, so she insisted we pair up. We'd shoot the shit about her internship in the local Black History archives, our mutual love of low-quality movie musicals, how Hudson totally checked out my ass when I bent over the microscope.

"Hi, remember me?" Sara raises her hand. "Is it legitimately possible to break my butt?"

Michaela pulls her up but slips herself, the two shrieking, clutching onto each other, and now Kathleen herds them toward her car. Twirling the keys around her finger, she says, "Sorry, so what is Maddie celebrating again?"

"It's a surprise." Michaela consults her phone. "Shoot. She's already there."

Fury flutters in my chest, hot and heavy. If Maddie is *already there* that means she's not here, which means she fucking stood me up. She *set* me up to . . . what, exactly?

"Let's go before she has a conniption," Kathleen says. "I'm not in the mood for this b—"

"Are you hiding?"

I stumble and fall flat on my ass—just like Sara. Hudson holds back a laugh as he holds out his hand. I swat it away and stand, nodding at his coffee cup. "Caffeine is a drug, you know."

"Thanks for the concern. What're you doing?"

"Waiting for—" *No one can ever know about this.* It startles me, the clarity of Maddie's voice in my head. I tuck my frozen hands into my pockets. "Someone."

"That's not cryptic."

"Not cryptic at all. If you'll excuse me, I have a bus to catch."

"Wait!" He reaches for my arm but hesitates, like I'd flinch from his touch. (He's right; I would.) He unlocks his SUV with a quick *beepbeep.* "Do you want a ride?"

God, it's tempting. I despise the bus: the musty heater and smelly freshmen, the way the bus sways as it crawls down ice-slick streets. The ride will make me motion sick. It always does when the roads are like this.

But it's too risky with Hudson. Too something. I can already hear the whispers: *Did you see Jo get in Hudson's car? Where do you think they went? What do you think they did?*

Heat floods my face. I take a step back, away from him. "Not from you," I say, and I bail without another word, not looking back once.

The streetlights are flicking on, pops of orange in the dull light, when I trudge home. I managed not to barf on the bus, barely. The cold is a relief to my clammy hands.

But this heat burns inside me. It simmers under my skin, prickles sweat on the back of my neck. I should know better than to trust Maddie Price, but this—the tears, the lower lip quiver, the insistence that *no one can ever know about this*—is way dark, even for her.

From the house across the street, a burst of light.

Mrs. Price sweeps past the bay window with her arm out-stretched, phone angled toward her beaming face. Video call? Must be Maddie. No one brings her joy like that daughter of hers. She returns to the light switch, twisting the chandelier brighter, brighter, dimmer again.

Then, all at once, she halts. Frowns. Slowly brings her hand to her mouth.

"Quit spying on the neighbors."

I jolt. "Jesus."

My mother laughs from the steps, a cigarette pressed to her

lips. She allows herself two per week. *An ugly habit,* she likes to say. It's the only ugly thing about her. Even like this—no makeup, messy ponytail, yoga pants stuffed into sheepskin boots—she's unfairly beautiful.

The pageant moms used to coo about how much we looked alike. *Those eyes!* (Hers are a stunning cornflower; mine are just . . . blue.) *That hair!* (Hers is a silky blonde; mine is six shades darker and never not tangled.) It was merely a ploy to impress Katie Lynn Springer, former Miss Tennessee Teen, as if their daughters could absorb her prowess through proximity alone.

Joke's on them. I came from her womb, and I've got a regional competition ban.

She nods across the street. "What does that family have against curtains?"

It's not a real question. This is yet another gripe for her List of Price Grievances. Other complaints include: the seafoam color of their house; their elderly dog, Tanner, who has separation anxiety and barks his head off; the four-person gnome family under the hedges, still intact even though Mr. Price moved out of the house and into a loft downtown last summer.

"Those people just want to be seen," she says, and stubs out her cigarette in a coffee mug.

The lingering smoke follows us into the house, or, just kidding, the smoke is coming from inside the house. The foyer is hazy with it. The smoke detector bleats.

I toss my scarf onto the heat register. "Is Dad baking?"

Multiple swear words come from the kitchen, so that's a yes.

Once upon a time, Joseph Kirby was a legend in the local food scene—gruff and tattooed, prone to cussing out customers who disrespected his waitstaff. He was head chef at the best spots in the city, and he still helped in his old man's auto shop, too.

Then, suddenly, he was twice divorced and getting older, getting sick of late nights and the nagging sense that something was missing. Enter the stunning news anchor, new in town and a dozen years younger, who returned her meal to the kitchen. Twice.

Roughly nine months later, he took his paternity leave and never came back.

This is all to say that Dad could fix a meal from literal garbage, but his baking is shit. He crashes out of the kitchen and says, "Hush, bastard," dragging a chair to the smoke detector.

"Who could've seen this coming?"

My mother points a finger at me. "Watch your tone, Jo-Lynn."

"Shouldn't you be at the station?" I snap back.

Kate Kirby is the face of Channel 12. For the past twenty years, my mother has anchored the morning broadcast and cohosted the evening news with various work husbands. If the world is on fire, we can go days without seeing each other—which is fine by me.

"Slow news day," she says, yet she still heads into the den to watch.

Dad climbs off the chair with a grunt. "Hope your brother likes burned brownies."

I follow him into the living room. He goes for the bar cart, but I stop, drop my backpack beside the credenza. His laptop charges, open but asleep, on its surface.

All casual, I ask, "Where is Lee, anyway?" *Also, did he mention I tried to steal his car?*

"I'm out!" Lee shouts from the stairs. His knee buckles on the last step, and he stumbles, his hand flying to the banister. He shoots me a look and says, "Shut up."

"I said nothing." I know better.

This was supposed to be his breakout year at UNC, when he'd harness that *raw potential* and earn a starting spot on the Tar Heels basketball team. Then, four weeks into the fall semester, his season ended before it even began.

Torn ACL. Complete rupture of the left knee.

He moved home for his reconstruction surgery and physical therapy and to finish the year remotely—not that he *really* had a choice. But he'll be back at Carolina next year.

No matter what.

Dad sets down a highball glass. "Got plans?"

"Library. I have astronomy homework." Lee picks up his car keys and rattles them at me, like, *I didn't snitch, but I could. I still might.*

Too loud, I say, "What about a bourbon sour, Dad?"

Lee looks to the bar cart, watching, waiting, before he shoves my arm. Hard. I knock into the credenza, and Dad's laptop wakes, opening to a game of Scrabble and one new email.

SUBJECT: *Academic Status Updates — KIRBY.*

For a second I wonder if Lee sees it, too, but he only flips up his hood and says, "Later."

I find Dad in the reflection of the dusty screen. "How was breakfast?"

"Damn delicious. Flower City is the best, I'm telling you. I got—"

I open the email.

Dear Joseph Kirby,

This email is to remind you of your meeting with Assistant Principal Tony Conti tomorrow, February 6, at 12:30 p.m. Please notify me ASAP if you'll be unable to keep this appointment.

Sincerely,
Dorothy Fitzgerald
Main Office Lead

Shit. Shit, shit, shit.

Did I know Dad was invited to this meeting? Does he? He's still rambling about Flower City—that fantastic diner coffee, the perfect pancakes—as he drops two, three ice cubes into his glass. So subtly, I slide my fingers across the keyboard and smash DELETE.

"There," Dad says, and I spin back, which is the definition of unsubtle.

I nod at the Scrabble game. "Quartz. Triple letter score on the Z."

"Look at that! How did I end up with such a brilliant daughter?" Dad grins at the winning game before turning to me with the same sort of pride. "You have a good day, sweetheart?"

My gaze moves to the window. To the Prices' house, now dark. Sighing, I sink onto the wingback chair where Bay Leaf snoozes, her tiny body curled into a comma. "It was fine."

"Oh, honey." Dad kisses the top of my head. "Tomorrow will be better."

-6-

Today is not better.

If anything, I'm angrier today. Something woke me in the middle of the night. Lee, most likely. His bedroom is bigger, but mine has the attached bath, so I often hear his door open, shut, and his steps pad down the hall during the night. Or maybe it was Bay Leaf romping around the kitchen with an uncooked strand of linguini.

Whatever. The point is, I'm tired and cranky and mad at Maddie for freaking me out and standing me up yesterday for literally no reason, and I'd rather be anywhere but here.

Mr. Conti's office.

Three years of dress code violations means I've memorized every inch of the space. The coffee stain on the carpet. The yardstick propped against the bookcase, waiting.

And, of course, the engraved crystal clock—*Anthony Conti, Ass. Principal of the Year*—proudly displayed on his desk. (It's a fitting abbreviation.) Every second I'm stuck here I spend counting the seconds until I can leave, so I know this clock intimately.

It's how I know Conti has ignored me for the last nine minutes.

He furiously clicks his mouse, but he's watching the clock, too, stewing that Dad is late to discuss my academic status, waiting to complain until the ten-minute mark, which will hit right about . . .

"Dorothy, can you give Joseph Kirby a call?" Conti says into his intercom. Fitzgerald can try, but Dad's voicemail has been full for ten years.

I shift on the stiff leather chair. "I swear I reminded him this—"

"Sorry I'm late," my brother says as he breezes into the office, out of breath and, hold up, my brother? My *brother*?

"You're not the Kirby I expected," Conti says with a laugh. "How the hell are you, kid?"

"Good, good." Lee has ditched his usual uniform (Carolina crewneck, jeans) for a plaid button-up and khakis. *Khakis*, just like the boys we mock from St. Ignatius Jesuit when we spot them in the wild. He points to the chair beside mine. "May I?"

"Be my guest. Your father still signing in?"

"He's not feeling well, so he sent me in his place." His delivery is crisp, the lie effortless. "Didn't he email?"

"Not that—oh!" Conti drags his finger on the screen, mumbling each word. He consults the clock again. "Miss Kirby, what do you think?"

I think Lee needs to cool it with his savior complex. This must break standard protocol, right? Breach confidentiality? Even if he acts like it, Lee is not my parent and/or guardian, and it's not his business if I'm failing. Not that I assume I'm failing. But.

What the hell are you doing here? I ask telepathically.

Lee shrugs, all, *Would you rather call Mom?*

Teeth gritted, I say, "Proceed."

We do, like this is bad dinner theater. Mr. Conti, leading actor, sits taller. "The purpose of this meeting is to assess Jo-Lynn's current academic status. I'm pleased to say she's avoided any penalties that would have extended the length of her review. However . . ."

Conti slides a paper across his desk. My report card. I don't move, so Lee takes it instead, tracking each grade once. Twice. Three times. Then, "She failed?"

I rip it from his hands. "I failed?"

"You failed."

The letters scramble together: F, D, D, F, D, an undeserved C-minus in Digital Design II, an unexplainable A-plus in gym.

For forever, it has both baffled and infuriated everyone— teachers, peers, friends when I had them—that I excel without trying hard. Without trying at all. I have never, not once, been a pleasure to have in class. I talk out of turn, disrupt my peers, squander my potential.

Every report card comment begins: *Jo-Lynn is a bright girl, but . . .*

But now I failed.

Mr. Conti drums his fingers in a non-rhythm. "My primary concern is how these grades affect your overall average." This is it. His grand monologue. "Yes, you failed the semester, Jo-Lynn, but I'm most concerned you'll fail the year."

"Fuck." The word explodes out of me. I duck my head between my knees, dizzy.

Lee grabs the back of my sweatshirt and yanks me upright. "Stop."

"As the top magnet school in the district, we pride ourselves on our rigorous academic standards," Conti says, as if Lee and I didn't veer wildly off-script. "Jo-Lynn, I'm upgrading you to a six-week probationary term. If you show no improvement by then, we'll have no choice but to revoke your magnet status."

"Like, I'd get expelled? *No*. No, I . . . I mean, I knew that I . . . but I didn't expect *this* to . . ."

Lee hugs his arms to his chest. "What *did* you expect, Jo?"

"It's not a guarantee, right?" I ask Conti, ignoring Lee. "I can fix this?"

Conti's mustache ticks up. "I believe that's up to you," he says. My ears feel full, like I dove too deep underwater. Somehow I stand, and so does Lee, but Conti says, "Hold on, kid! I want to hear about UNC, your recovery—tell me!"

I laugh, bitter. "Yeah, tell him, Lee."

Tell him your knee popped when you fled a frat party after it got raided by public safety. Tell him you were shit-faced and earned your second citation of the semester, and it'd mean suspension for anyone else, but you're not just anyone; you're Lee Kirby, point guard. Tell him you were quietly kicked out of your dorm and sent home and promised full eligibility next year—*if* you avoid strike three.

Lee slowly lowers back into his chair. He'll tell Conti none of this. Everyone else thinks it was an unlucky sports injury, too, so why be honest now?

But I don't want to hear it. I step into the office suite and crash straight into Mr. Parrish. (AP English, D.) He grunts, flustered, and fumbles his papers—two take-home midterm packets. The top one has a scribble of red pen in the righthand corner: *Kathleen, please see me.*

Underlined twice.

I'm reaching for it when Lee emerges, mumbling, "Let's go." He shoves a pass into my hand and guides me past the school security guard, out the doors. I'm a half step too slow until he stops dead, spinning back to face me, and says, "Is this for attention or something? Failing?"

"No, it's not for *attention*, asshole."

Not . . . really. I'm not sure Dad ever even told my mother about my review. He shrugged it off as the side effect of a difficult schedule. The thing is, it's *not* hard. I could do well if I tried, but it's astoundingly easy not to try when no one is looking. Not at my plummeting grades or my baggy new clothes or why I have no friends anymore or how it all happened so fast.

Is it that horrible to wish someone—my parents—would fucking see it?

That I'm failing, I mean.

I tuck my arms into my sleeves. "Why did you even come?"

"When I saw that email . . ." Lee shakes his head.

My brother will not let me torpedo my life, no matter how hard I try.

We used to be close, Lee and me. Sometimes I'm still not sure what made us stop. Was it because he'd gotten good at basketball and finally found his way out? Or was it when, seemingly overnight, I became a girl that boys—his friends—noticed?

They'd use that line on me a lot: *I'm friends with your brother.*

There's no way my brother had that many friends.

Quietly, I ask, "Are you going to tell?"

Lee lets out something like a laugh. "What do you think?"

I think this is another secret he'll keep for me.

He sighs out a cloud and looks to the senior lot. Looks again. Stares at those rows of cars, windshields dusted in a fine layer of snow. It's only when he turns back to me that I realize how haggard he looks: eyes sunken, skin pale.

"You look like shit," I say.

"I'm tired." He angles his back to the wind. "*Failing.* Christ, Jo, what happened to you?"

Now I laugh. "You know what happened."

Lee rescued me the night of the bonfire. I sat on the ground, gravel stuck to my thighs, upright only because Hudson let me lean against his legs. The two of them hauled me into the backseat, and Lee kept telling me I better not puke, and what the hell was wrong with me?

I was almost, almost gone, but not far enough to miss what came next: Hudson, pained to tell my brother about the texts; Lee shutting his eyes like he might puke, too.

His old buddies—the ones who eyed me when I was a freshman and they were juniors cruising around in Toyota Camrys and Honda Civics, sensible cars for sensible boys; the ones Lee banned from ever, ever speaking to me, ever—reemerged. They said, *What's up with your sister, dude? How's your sister, bro? Your sister eighteen yet, man?*

None of them even remembered my name.

A few days later, Lee tagged along when Dad dragged me to the mall for a new phone. I told him I'd dropped mine, a believable lie with my history of lost and broken phones. (I'm still mourning that hot pink phone that vanished the summer after ninth grade. RIP.) The truth is, I'd spiked this last one against the pavement, so sick of those DMs and dick pics and midnight texts, like my leaked pictures were an invitation.

Like my body was an invitation.

The flip phone—buy one, get one!—was my punishment.

Dad muttered, "I don't know how you could be so careless," and when Lee glanced at me over the tablets display, I knew he was thinking the same thing.

My face burns now like it did then. "What do I do?"

"You get your shit together. Just keep your head down. Keep it to yourself." Lee nods, agreeing with his own words. "The last thing I need is—"

"The last thing *you* need? Because the world revolves around you, right?"

"I never said that," he says, but I know he thinks it. I know my golden boy brother hates that I'm his opposite: the wild, hellion sister. I know he's embarrassed by me.

I rub the chill from my skin. "I can't fail. I can't . . ."

Get stuck here.

Lee squints into the bright, snowy sky. "Then you better pray for a miracle."

-7-

I don't need to pray for a miracle. I have one already.

My miracle is named Miles Metcalf.

I may be failing but I'm smarter than I look. And I'm smart enough to decode the subtext when Miles says, *I can help you, you know*. He can help me like he helps Cody Forsythe.

Chasing a soccer ball on the field, chasing girls off it, chasing a shot of liquor with a swig of beer—how could Cody find time for school? Find a way into Duke and onto its soccer team?

The truth: Cody cheats. More accurately, Miles cheats for Cody.

The funny thing is, I'd never know if Cody had kept his trap shut. He let it slip last spring when we were at some party at some person's house. He clutched an opened Keystone, the worst of the worst beer, and he kept slurring, "Miles has my keys."

I patted his chest. "You're not driving, buddy."

"Not my *car* keys." Cody threw an arm over my shoulder. He smelled like sweat and beer and smoke, though no one had lit a fire. "*Answer* keys."

All at once, it all made sense. Cody rode his legacy status as the youngest of the Forsythe Four—the super clever nickname given to him and his three soccer-star older brothers—past the entrance exam and into Culver, but he struggled fiercely in class. Then his coach threatened his starting spot sophomore year and, suddenly, he wasn't struggling anymore.

Not since he pulled Miles into his orbit.

Miles became a fixture at parties that year, hovering at the periphery like a bug buzzing around the warmth of a bulb, searching for a way in. I was all nasty about it, like, "Who invited Metcalf?" I never got a good answer, and besides, he was harmless. But this, what Cody said about Miles, the answer keys—*that* was my answer.

The morning after, Cody didn't remember what he'd told me, and I didn't remind him. I filed the information inside my brain to wield if and when I needed it.

And I really, really need it.

The security guard waves me through the metal detector when I flash my pass. I force my way to the band hall, where Miles is feeding a dollar into the vending machine. He nearly drops his saxophone case when I grip his arm and say, "Ineedtotalktoyou," in a rush.

"Oh." The dollar spits out. "What about?"

I rip the bill from the slot and take his hand, dragging him toward the cafeteria. I vaguely register my name as we cross the lobby again and snap, "Not now," not looking back.

But wait. That lilt of my name. Too familiar, too sweet, too—

"Mrs. Price!" My voice pitches up. Miles tilts his head. I squeeze his clammy hand, or it could be mine sweating. "I'll meet you in there, okay?" I tell Miles. Then I muster my fakest smile for Maddie's mom, keeping a few feet between us. "Hey, Mrs. Price. I, uh, didn't know it was you."

"No worries, Jo-Lynn," she says, even faker than me.

From the second the Prices moved across the street on that warm June day—my golden birthday, thirteen on the thirteenth—Mrs. Price hasn't liked me. She spent those early summer days tending the front garden, weeds piled in the grass, gardening gloves black with dirt.

All the while, me and the boys biked lazy circles up and down the block. Mrs. Price and Maddie watched us—watched me, mostly—as my long hair blew behind me and my loud laugh caught in the wind. Once, as I peddled past in short-shorts and a bikini top, she called Maddie to her side and said, "What did I tell you about girls like that?"

She meant for me to hear it. I'm certain.

I readjust my backpack strap. "So . . ."

"Right! I booked a surprise for Maddie," Mrs. Price whispers, like this is a secret only for me. "Mani-pedis at the Del Monte!"

"Oh. Fun."

Nothing has ever sounded less fun. I tried the mother-daughter spa trip before prom last year, and we whisper-fought about everything. My mother thought I should wear my hair up; I wanted it down. She suggested a simple nude for my mani-cure; I picked neon pink, which totally clashed with my dress, a gorgeous beige tulle embellished with tiny daisies.

Then my mother accused me of being contrary to spite her, and I reminded her this was my prom, not a damn pageant, and she said, "Sweetie, you're lucky this isn't a damn pageant," and I stormed out with six pink nails and a pair of complimentary foam flip-flops.

Mrs. Price forces a smile. "I'm sure you heard what happened." I frown. *What happened?* Fast, she adds, "Will you grab her for me? Her phone must be turned off, and it's such a hassle to sign in."

I picture Miles in the snack line, wondering where I am. What I need.

Walking out of Mr. Conti's office, watching my brother get into his car and go, I was so certain this—enlisting Miles—was my only option. But each minute makes me more wary. If I do this, I'll be someone who cheats to get ahead.

I'll be as bad as Cody Forsythe.

"Sure. Fine." I brush back my bangs. "Be right out."

The cafeteria is packed. I step around the trash can heaped with stiff hamburger patties, crushed yogurt cups, and empty pretzel bags, and I look toward Maddie's table. My old one.

The scene is achingly familiar.

At one end, the guys—gifted in academics and athletics, committed to D1 schools like UVA, Vanderbilt, Villanova—toss grapes into Ben Sulkin's mouth, cheering. Along the other end, the Birds: Michaela Russell taps at her tablet screen and Sara Caruso untangles a skein of yellow yarn and Kathleen O'Mara yawns and Maddie . . . isn't there. Maddie isn't there?

Something—a small, tiny something—stings the hollow of my gut.

Miles waves from the snack line, but I hold up a finger. *One second.*

Then I make a beeline for Hudson Harper-Moore.

He sits off to the side, head bent over his phone. He's probably hitting up one of his many fangirls from Our Lady of Lourdes, the all-girls Catholic school. But when I whisper, "Hey," and crouch beside him, his screen displays the *New York Times* crossword puzzle.

He unhooks his earbuds. "Hey, yourself."

"Yeah, uh. Hi. Have you seen Maddie?" I quickly add, "Her mom is in the lobby."

"Isn't she . . . ?" He frowns at her empty chair. Plucks a grape off Ben's tray and flicks it at Kathleen. It pops her on the neck with expert precision. "Where's Maddie?"

"Dunno." Kathleen glares at him, rubbing her nonexistent wound. "Not here."

"Like, not in school?" I grip the back of Hudson's chair. I don't know why. I don't know why each word shakes when I say, "She has perfect attendance."

"Is something wrong?" Hudson asks.

I focus on the floor, littered with popcorn kernels and straw wrappers, streaked with pizza grease, and I try to think, just *think*, for five seconds. Have I seen her today? We don't have class together, and it's not like I seek her out. We're not friends, remember?

These are her friends. Sara, whose knitting needles click unsteadily. Michaela, who stares at her darkened screen. Kathleen, who drags me away from the table, toward the lobby, her nails clawing into my skin. She hisses, "Let me handle this," which is great, because there's nothing I want to do less.

Mrs. Price looks uneasily between us. "Where's Maddie?"

"She isn't here," Kathleen says coolly, tracing her gold cross necklace. "I texted, but . . ."

But. I scratch the back of my neck, the wisps of hair snarled with sweat. "Is she sick or something? Was she okay this morning?"

"I haven't seen . . . she spent the night at her . . ." Mrs. Price tucks her ringless hand behind her back. "She told me she needed space after what happened."

There it is again. *What happened.* Should I know what that means? Does Kathleen? If she does, she doesn't let it show. Instead, she shrugs, says, "Maybe you should call her dad."

"He was on a business trip," Mrs. Price says absently, but then she nods, stepping toward the vestibule. Over her shoulder, she shakily calls out, "It doesn't hurt to check, right?"

I press my palm to my chest. Try to slow my heart. To shut up the voice in my head that goes, *I think that I'm in trouble, but I think that you can—*

"Relax," Kathleen says to me. She picks at her nail polish, a flawless pale pink.

I laugh, not knowing what's so funny. "Can you at least pretend to care?"

Now Kathleen lifts her eyes right to mine. My breath snags in my throat. I used to be the girl who intimidated the rest. One eye roll, one bitter laugh, and they'd cower from me.

This girl was—is—the exception.

"What do *you* know, Jo?" she says.

I know something is very, very wrong.

Even from here, I hear Mrs. Price is getting frantic. Panicked. *What do you mean she never went over? She was never there? How can you tell? So where . . . ?*

The phone slips from her hand. The hope on her face shatters with it. She takes one step back. Another. Then she brings her hand to her mouth and wails.

It's horrible. It's terrible. I've never heard a sound like this.

The security guard abandons his post and yells, "Please calm down, ma'am," but it's too late. Students spill out of the cafeteria, shouting, crowding the lobby. Mr. Conti sprints from the office, past us, and he knocks me back, into—

Cody. *Cody.* His face is a sick, sallow green. He says just one word: "Fuck."

Behind us, someone—or maybe everyone—asks what happened, whose mom is that, shit, what did she say? Did she say *missing*? Missing, missing, who's missing, Maddie is missing, Maddie is gone.

Behind us, someone asks, "Wait, who's Maddie?"

I look to Kathleen again and follow the dotted line of her gaze to the trophy case. To Sara and Michaela in front of it. Eyes wide, horrified, Sara clasps a hand to her mouth. Michaela finds her other hand and squeezes, hard.

"Do you . . . ?" I don't know what to ask.

But Kathleen isn't listening to me. She stares at those girls— jaw set, face serious—and shakes her head the most imperceptible amount. Like it's a warning.

Say nothing.

-8-

2:32 p.m. I ambush Miles in the lobby and tell him that we're hanging at his house, but we have to stop by mine first, and also, sorry, he's not allowed to say no.

Not that he'd ever say no to me.

It's just that I can't be alone right now, not at home, across the street from—

2:41 p.m. Miles idles in the driveway while I sprint inside, up to my bedroom. If my mother were here, she'd follow with a towel and gripe about the snow wrecking the hardwood floors.

But my mother is not here. She probably just got back to Channel 12 to prep the evening broadcast. I can see it perfectly: Kate Kirby brewing a fresh pot of coffee in her dressing room; a producer barging in with this spectacular breaking news.

From the kitchen, Dad laughs. "Whoa, Jo! What's the rush?"

"Me and Miles are going to his place!" I rip open my desk drawer and feel inside, fingers sweeping past the paper clips to find what I want. *Need.* "Just grabbing my, um. Something."

Pockets zipped, contraband secured, I fly back downstairs. Dad waits at the bottom of the steps. Wiping his forearms on an old dish rag, he says, "Slow down, honey. How was your day?"

"Sorry, Dad, but now isn't a good—"

Outside, a police cruiser crawls down the street, tires crunching on snow. No sirens. No lights. No urgency as it slows, stops at that house. *That* house.

"Huh." Dad flings the rag over his shoulder. "Wonder what that's about."

2:54 p.m. Miles doesn't mention the cop car. He's blushing too badly. The flush first bloomed when our hands bumped as we both reached to unfasten our seatbelts.

Now, as he fumbles his house key into the door, his face looks hot to the touch.

It's quiet inside the Metcalf house. Not like mine, with the constant clattering of pots and pans, Channel 12 blaring on TV, Lee's foam basketball thudding against the hoop on his door.

"Your parents at work?" I think his mom is a bank teller, and his dad does . . . a job.

"Until five-ish." Miles glances at his watch and calculates— how much time that gives us alone, together.

"Perfect. Attic?"

Only-child perks: Miles gets the whole space to himself. There's a massive TV, an Xbox, and a hideous purple futon. The first time I saw it, I imagined him unfolding it into a bed for him and April Kirk, and the image was so mortifying that I laughed out loud.

I nod at the TV. "Where's the remote for this thing?"

"What?" Miles unzips his coat, then lowers onto the futon. "Oh. It's right—"

I snatch it from him and turn on News 9, the all-day news channel. (Yes, I'm a traitor to my mother, but I can't wait until five.) I kneel at the coffee table and dump out my pocket.

Miles scoots closer. "Is that pot?"

"You sure are smart, huh?" I pop open the baggie. I've never done this myself.

Before, I always had someone—some guy—to roll my joint and light me up.

Never Miles. He's skittish around the stuff, like MIT admissions will know if he takes a single hit. At parties, he'd nurse a weak beer with a list of excuses ready: *I drove, sorry. Sorry, I took an allergy pill.* No one bothered him about it much.

But sometimes the boys would get too rowdy and try to get him rowdy, too. They'd drape their bodies on his back and shove a sweaty beer in his face, like, "Keystone, buddy?"

I'd say, "Offer him something better," but we never had much better than that.

"I thought you wanted to . . ." Miles scratches his knee, denim torn, worn. "Never mind."

3:01 p.m. I take Miles's phone and search "how to roll joint weed marijuana please."

3:28 p.m. I did something wrong. I'm not stoned at all.

Mostly, I'm cold. (Blame the lack of insulation up here.) I

burrow deeper into my coat, zipping it to my chin, tugging up the hood. The space heater warms only my feet.

I've moved to the futon with Miles, his backpack a barrier between us—one I built, not him. He pulled out his calc textbook while I tried to get high, and his pencil scratch is going to make me scream. I'm almost crabby enough to ask if this is Cody's homework or his own.

But I refrain. Gnaw on my thumbnail. Rip the cuticle between my teeth.

Right as I taste blood, he says, "You're bleeding," the color zapped from his face. Miles is way squeamish, paling at scraped knees and paper cuts. He stands, woozy, and retreats to the bathroom at the top of the stairs. "I'll be, uh. One minute."

"You good?" I call out, but then: *Turning now to a developing story*—

I fumble for the remote. Crank the volume to its max.

The News 9 anchor frowns, grim. "The Rochester Police Department is asking for help in locating a local teenager. Eighteen-year-old Maddie Price has not been seen or heard from since Monday." The screen cuts to her senior portrait and, *God*, maybe I'll faint, too. "Authorities ask anyone with information regarding her whereabouts to call 911. Now, your five-day forecast."

"That's it?" I say. No height, no weight. No eye color (blue) or hair color (impeccably dyed dark chocolate) or special marks (a freckle on her left ear). Maddie is missing, and the story fits into a ten-second snippet. I rewind, watch the segment again—and again, and once more, and then I laugh and say, "That's *it*?"

"How awful," Miles says. I hadn't heard him return. He sits

again, closer, stealing an inch from the gap between us. "Should we turn this off?"

"No." I press play so News 9 resumes in real time. Sabrina Kim, a former Channel 12 intern, interviews a man from Greece (the suburb, not the country) about a snowplow scam.

Miles sets the textbook on his lap. "I just wondered what you wanted. It seemed urgent?"

I mute the TV. I can't think when it's so loud since my brain is loud, too, like I'm dialing a radio knob and the thing won't tune. Every station plays at once: crackling notes of a top pop hit, warbled talk radio, an undercurrent of static.

"Earlier, when you said—"

My report card. It feels like forever ago: Conti telling me I failed; my brother telling me to get my shit together; me telling Miles that we need to talk so *he can help me, you know.*

But I don't want his help, not anymore. Not at all. I just panicked for a second, okay? I'll get out of this myself. Like, I'm better than Cody Forsythe. Smarter, too. Maybe I can weasel my way into the Senior Experience for extra credit and—okay, that sounds worse.

"I don't remember," I lie. "Will you drive me home?"

He swipes his eye, knocking his glasses askew. "Are you, like, mad at me?"

"Why would I be mad?" I stand, stuffing the half-smoked joint in my pocket. He stands, too, ungracefully. He's so gangly, all limbs, like a puppy who hasn't grown into his paws. I say, "Like, Maddie is *missing*, dude, and I . . . I . . ."

"Can I do anything?" Miles asks, sad and gentle and earnest. "To help?"

God, it kills me.

"I'm good, but thank you, Miles. Really," I say, then I turn and immediately trip over the space heater. He reaches out a hand, but I rip my arm back, and I know it's weird, I *know* it, but still I ask, "What did you think I wanted?"

Miles scratches his chin, razor burn red hot. "I wasn't thinking anything."

That might be a lie, too, but at least we're even now.

3:49 p.m. I can't go home. Not yet. Not when Maddie basically shouts in my head, *I think that I'm in trouble, but—*

I walk to the public library.

Inside, two middle schoolers share a chair in the teen zone, blushing and giggling at their steamy fantasy. The children's librarian blows bubbles for the toddlers at story time. An old man browses the new releases. I swipe my library card at the last open desktop and claim my fifteen minutes of browsing.

Then I search "Maddie Price."

So far, News 9 is the only station covering the missing teenage girl: last seen on Monday, eighteen, gone. I wonder what my mother knows, if she knows anything at all. I wonder if she'd tell me the truth or tell me to tune in tonight.

I scroll up, up, and—*shit*—there it is again.

Maddie's senior portrait.

Culver has strict guidelines: tuxes for the boys, with dorky bowties and stiff lapels, and black velvet drapes for the girls. (This, from a school with "inclusivity" as a core value.)

Four days after the bonfire, the portrait studio invaded the gym with its harsh lights and a blue backdrop. The photographer frowned at that hickey when she swept back my hair. Like she was thinking, *This girl let a boy graze his teeth against her skin? Not too hard, not for too long, but hard and long enough?*

Like she was thinking, *Slut.*

Next, she told me to smile, uh, okay, a *real* smile. I refused. In the final image, my jaw is set so tight I have a slight underbite. My too-long bangs fall into my eyes. My glare is deadly.

It'd be funny to me under any other circumstance.

Maddie's picture is, of course, perfect. She smiles a pretty, nice smile that doesn't quite reach her ice-blue eyes. Her hair is flat ironed, tucked behind one ear. Her neck is unmarked.

I zoom in, searching for . . . I don't know what. The frightened girl from yesterday? The girl who ditched me?

Searching for the girl she used to be.

Her voice rings in my head: *Because, Jo.*

Because we were friends once. Best friends.

Not at first. The first year the Prices lived across the street, I thought Maddie was snobby and uptight in her starched Our Lady of Lourdes uniform and patent leather shoes. She thought I was wild and unruly and way too boy crazy.

But neither of us had many—really, any—friends. Yes, I had those boys, but it wasn't the same. They didn't care if I felt invisible, so desperate to be seen, you know?

I practically screamed it: *Just see me!*

Finally, finally, someone did.

And when I looked at Maddie, I saw a girl who needed to be seen as badly as me.

The shift was stunning, sudden but seamless. Enemies, then

friends. It was summer, and I was home alone, and so was she, so why not be alone together? So, I asked if she'd like to take a walk. Talk, maybe. It really was as simple as that.

We'd both be freshmen at Culver in the fall, too, our acceptances a ticket to something better. It sucked that we had no classes together, not even lunch, but we still had the bus and the weekends and the rest of our lives to make up for it.

Then, suddenly, it was summer again, but nothing would be seamless about our undoing.

Losing Maddie was devastating in a way I didn't understand. Not then, not now. At least with romantic love the risk of heartbreak is factored into the equation. It's different with a best friend. That love feels like a guarantee. A certainty.

When I called Maddie my best friend forever, I meant forever in the most literal sense.

No one knows what happened, but everyone still whispers: *Those girls used to be friends, you know.* I'd hear it in our worst moments, like when I chucked that beer can at her skull at the bonfire. Like when she slid her arms around Cody's waist even after what he'd done to me.

I'd had it coming, anyway.

Once, I thought I knew Maddie better than I knew myself. But this girl, the one in the picture—I don't know this girl at all.

– 9 –

News crews from my mother's rival stations crowd the street outside Culver the next morning.

"Vultures." Dad grips the steering wheel tighter as we loop the block a second time. On our third pass, a space opens along the curb. He eases into it, front bumper grinding against the plow-packed snow. But I don't get out. Dad asks, "Want to talk?"

It's not an empty offer. Despite appearances, Dad is gentle. Nurturing. He proudly lists "stay-at-home dad" as his career on social media and keeps a first aid kit with his pocketknife.

But I don't want to talk about Maddie—not yet, not ever.

When the words do come, I ask, "Where's Channel 12?"

Their van, plastered with Kate Kirby's beautiful face, is missing. The other stations have dispatched their fresh meat to shiver in the cold, thrust microphones into stunned faces. Channel 12 should be here, unless—

"You can call her, you know," Dad says gently.

Like, I can call my mother, because a girl needs her mom sometimes? Or I can call Kate Kirby, the star anchor with the latest breaking news?

"It's fine." I force open the door. "I don't even have my phone."

"Hold on, Jo. The phone—maybe it's time we upgrade you. You never have that thing on you, and . . ." Dad fusses with the heat, not looking at me. "We need to be able to reach you."

The cold worms a chill up my spine.

I think it's the cold.

"Whatever," I mumble, and slam the door.

From across the street, Mr. Conti, bundled in a heavy camouflage jacket, is yelling about school property. It's a meaningless threat; no one knows spatial boundaries better than a young reporter starved for a story. My mother would be the first to admit it.

She made a list of rules if I encounter one in the wild: *Do not make eye contact or else . . .*

"Excuse me! Hi there. I'm—"

Sabrina Kim, News 9. I know her better as the Channel 12 intern my mother booted from the annual holiday party. I was a junior, and Lee was home from his first semester at Carolina, and Sabrina *offered* to raid the bar for us, so what were we supposed to say?

I point at myself. "Kate Kirby's daughter. I don't fraternize with the enemy."

"Oh! Tell your mom I said hi."

"No."

It takes approximately two seconds for her to summon someone new—*you, yes, you.* Sara Caruso. *Shit.* Fake cheery, Sabrina says, "I'd love to chat about the missing girl."

"Hey!" I shout. Sara blinks, startled. Her eyes are bloodshot, less like she was crying and more like she didn't sleep. I don't know how she's here today. I don't know how I am either.

Sabrina extends the microphone, like it's so tantalizing. "Change your mind?"

"Yeah, I'll give you a soundbite." I lean into the mic. "Fuck off."

Then I grip Sara's mittened hand and jerk her forward, across the street. She stumbles at first but quickly matches my pace, saying, "Jo," as a dad in a black car beeps at us.

Middle finger raised, I say, "Don't."

I'm not even sure what I mean. Don't mention it? Don't go there? Don't act like we share something now that Maddie—our best friend, current and former—is gone?

Only when we step inside do I drop her hand, but I don't break my stride. Not when the lobby buzzes with *Maddie, Maddie, Maddie, I can't believe she's missing, what do you think happened? Do you think she was kidnapped?*

Do you think she's dead?

"What the fuck is wrong with you?"

The band girls go quiet. I yelled at the poor band girls who have way more of a reason to be upset than me. Maddie plays flute, and she's good, but not the best. That title belongs to April Kirk. Here, she stares down at her scuffed loafers, or maybe the Senior Experience flyer stuck to her heel. Her pale skin is pallid.

"I'm sorry, I . . . I didn't mean anything by it," says Layla Osman, clarinetist. "I'm scared for her. Like, I donated to the fundraiser!" She holds up her phone as if I need the proof. HELP BRING MADDIE PRICE HOME! $5,248 of $25,000 goal met. "And I hope she's alive but—"

I ditch the band girls when I spot One-L Daniele. "What do you know?"

She holds up her hand and says, "Ask again later," like a god-damn Magic 8 Ball.

But I need to know now. I need to know everything about Maddie, missing, kidnapped, dead. Like, what the hell are the donations for? Posters and flyers? T-shirts and a reward and—?

Look.

Cody Forsythe.

He sits on the stairs with Ben Sulkin and . . . not his friends. No, these are sort-of, kind-of pals—lackeys from the soccer team, pretty sophomore girls. His face is vacant. Ben gently rubs Cody's shoulder, the gesture so tender that my throat goes tight. That I almost miss how Hudson lingers at the bottom of the steps, shut out.

But I need to go—down the hall, to the back row of the design lab.

Mr. Chopra watches, swinging his lanyard around his finger. "Happy Wednesday, Jo."

I slam my head against the keyboard.

My portfolio. My portfolio, which is overdue but due today, and which I need to do. Still. Incredible how being on the verge of expulsion isn't the worst part of this week.

When I lift my head, he stands before me, his arm propped on my monitor. I say, "I'll get you the portfolio by—"

"Tomorrow. You'll get it to me by tomorrow."

If I were the crying type, this is the spot where I'd burst into tears. Chopra returns to his desk before I even think to thank him. I rub my eyes, dots of static blurring behind my lids. How did I think I could do this? I can't do this. I—

"Hey." Hudson slings his backpack down at his feet. "How're you doing?"

"Other than the fact that I'm failing and might get expelled and it's my fault since I let it happen and no one even noticed?" I say without thinking. "Yeah, I'm great."

"Expelled? No, I meant about, uh. Maddie. I know you guys used to be friends. So."

Again, if I were the crying type . . .

But I'm not, I'm *not*, so I say nothing at all.

The news vans depart a little before third period. Hurried whispers weave through the halls, pass from person to person like a busted game of telephone.

Something about a senior assembly with the school counselors at noon.

Something about breaking information in the case.

Whatever this "something" is, I don't think it's good.

The auditorium is nearly full when I take the last seat in the last row at two minutes to noon.

I debated skipping, sitting in a bathroom stall until the end of the period, but that seemed somehow worse than this—whatever *this* is. The counselors will probably offer us their sincerest support or a space to share our feelings or something. For now, it's just Conti onstage, fumbling with the microphone. He hisses, "Shit," feedback screeching.

I slouch lower, lower. Look to the doors as Cody enters, stage right. He takes the long, lonely aisle alone, his uncrying eyes fixed on the ceiling. Next, the Birds discreetly slip inside, Kathleen guiding the girls into a row below the balcony.

One seat up and to the left, One-L Daniele watches me watch them—Cody and the Birds, the boyfriend and the best friends—and says, "They were meeting with Lund. Him, too."

"Wait, who?" I ask as Hudson drops into the seat beside mine. He nods at me. I return it with a glare. "What're you doing here?"

He stretches out his legs. "I go here, Jo."

"I'm aware but—"

Someone shushes me. The auditorium has gone quiet, but this is . . . weird. No one dares to break this silence. I missed something. Some interruption that explains why everyone stares at their laps, faces lit. It's like I'm back at the bonfire, and with those six dings, buzzes, chirps, it's me—all of me—on the screen.

My nails cut into the armrest. "What is this?"

One-L Daniele twists toward us, her bob swishing. "Emergency press conference."

I smack Hudson's arm. "Phone. Channel 12."

"You could say please." He navigates to the live stream. (Kate Kirby is blessedly off the clock.) He takes the right earbud and hands me the left. "Ready?"

I'm not but he hits play.

This isn't what I pictured. I don't know what I pictured. A bland conference room? Beige walls, fluorescent lights, a wobbly podium? But the cop stands outside the station like he's off to lunch. He swipes his nose, then begins: "On Tuesday,

February 6, Maddie Price was reported missing after a night away from home." His rhythm is odd; he's reading off an index card. "Her family indicated that this was uncharacteristic behavior. However—"

However.

"—it has now come to our attention that crucial information was intentionally withheld regarding the circumstances of Maddie's disappearance. While we'll still accept tips to our non-emergency line, we have every reason to believe that Maddie left of her own accord."

Off-camera, reporters shout out—*What proof? What happened? How can you be so sure?*

Then the stream goes dark.

In the auditorium, the silence cracks. Erupts. The words knock in my head: *Maddie left of her own accord. Maddie left. Maddie left, she left, she—*

"Maddie . . . ran away?" I don't know how I manage the words. I don't know why I turn to Hudson. His subtle shrug says it without me needing to ask. He knew.

Hudson knew, and I'm getting the feeling everyone else did, too.

"Didn't you hear?" One-L Daniele asks. It's not mean, how she says it. She relays rumors with the patience of a tutor. "So, Maddie got into NYU but—"

"She did?" I can't help the lift in my voice.

Even as friends, I didn't get the obsession. Like, we were *freshmen*; I cared about flirting and forcing myself to like coffee and praying my boobs would get bigger. (I'm still an A-cup, so no luck.) But Maddie knew what she wanted: NYU, NYC. She'd study journalism, maybe study abroad, then live in the city forever and ever, without me—and she's doing it.

One-L holds up a finger, then holds out her phone. It's loaded to an article from the *New York Times*: "NYU erroneously releases more than a thousand early decision acceptances."

I read and reread the headline, not making sense of it. That one word.

"Erroneously?" I repeat, and gasp, smothering it behind both hands.

What was it Mrs. Price said? *I'm sure you heard what happened.* I hadn't heard, but what happened is that Maddie got into NYU, except not, because it was a mistake. It was a *mistake.*

"Poor Maddie, right?" One-L says, and it sounds like she means it. "Those students were marked for rejection, but the admissions portal glitched. She'd already posted her acceptance all over her socials before it got revoked. She deactivated, you know. Everything is gone."

Just like her. Missing, gone.

I sit back. Let it settle. Say it out loud because I need to hear it again: "Maddie ran away."

The speakers pop, sizzle with static. Hudson stares at me. Nods slowly. "That's who you were waiting for. Monday, in the senior lot—it was *Maddie.*"

I shush him, but actually? Fuck this. I climb over his legs and duck out of the row.

He catches up immediately. "Why?"

"Why what?" I refuse to look at him.

The lobby teems with freshmen, laughing, whacking each other with their lunchboxes. I may be short enough to slip into the cafeteria unnoticed, but Hudson is distinctly not a freshman, all tall and built and self-assured. He's so damn confident I follow him—*I* follow *him*—inside.

He steals two chairs from an empty table, the legs wobbly, cracked plastic scrawled with graffiti. There's that cool S thing, a broken heart, a random shape—a trapezoid?

Our knees touch when he sits, but he doesn't move. Neither do I.

Not even when, again, he asks, "Why?"

No one can ever know about this. The last thing Maddie told me—a threat, almost. But I didn't tell Hudson; he connected the dots himself.

No one can ever know about this, only it's not Maddie's voice in my head this time.

"She told me she was in trouble." I grind my teeth, trying, failing to shut up. "She was all upset but told me I could help her." I pluck a cat hair off my knee. "Then she stood me up and ran away, or whatever, so. There you go."

Hudson is quiet. Hudson is never quiet.

Like, yes, I get why the Lourdes girls—why most girls with a pulse—fawn over him. He looks like a boy our mothers would hate, so brooding with those dark clothes, the long hair. (I'm serious, the hair does a *lot*.) But Hudson always has something to say.

Except now. Now, he searches my face so intensely I need to look away. I wonder what he sees. The mess I am today? A girl he thought was pretty once?

Finally, he says, "Huh."

"*Huh*? That's it?"

"What do you want me to say?"

I don't know. I don't know why I said anything to him at all. But this thing is gnawing at me, and it's unbearable. Keeping something so big so close.

"How did you know?" I ask. "That she ran, I mean."

"Lund called some of us to her office before the assembly and warned us about the press conference. I used context clues." He runs his thumb across the scar on his lip. "If Maddie was in trouble, why would she go to *you*? No offense."

"Offense taken." I don't mean that; he has a point. "Who the hell knows what her motive was? Yeah, it was weird, but after she didn't show, I figured it was a setup or something."

Hudson drops his hand to his lap. "She'd do that?"

"Set me up? Uh, yes."

He nods, a quick up, down. "Have you told anyone yet?"

"Um," I say. The truth is, it never occurred to me. That feels stupid to admit, but it's not like I'm in the habit of confiding in *trusted adults*. They'd probably do jack shit, anyway. I add, "You heard that cop. They think she ran away."

The more I say it, the more it makes sense in some small, perverse way. When we were friends, she'd devour books about girls who went on wild adventures and crawled into bed with twigs in their hair. Stuffing clothes into a knapsack, setting out on her own adventure to be like those better, braver girls—it's not impossible she'd try to do the same.

"Maddie ran away," I say again, more certain than ever. "It's fine. It's . . . nothing."

"But what if it's something?" Hudson asks with a lazy half shrug.

I lean closer, heartbeat wild as the distance between us shrinks. "It's *nothing.*"

I repeat those words again and again and again, until they stick in my head like a song.

It's nothing when everyone—*everyone*—turns on Maddie because how dare she scare us like that? How dare that family accept our donations and sympathies, thoughts and prayers, when their daughter never needed them? The fundraiser disappears within the hour, by the way.

It's nothing when the Birds shut everyone out. *No comment.*

It's nothing when the pretty sophomores swarm Cody, the abandoned boyfriend. These are birds of a different feather, small and chattery, annoying and everywhere.

One flutters closest: Alexis Fitch. She has purplish hair and freckles dotted on her nose in eyeliner. Before dismissal, she hugs Cody at his locker and traces her finger down his spine.

Except it's nothing. It's nothing, it's nothing.

Then, like a call and response, Hudson: *But what if it's something?*

I can't think like that.

-10-

The house smells like cinnamon when I get home.

Cinnamon? That can't be right. Dad is a mess of a pastry chef, remember? Mixing up his baking soda and baking powder, burning brownies, forgetting the lemon in lemon bars.

Yet here, on the island, is an apple pie. The crust glitters with sugar, flaky and golden, but the pie plate is cool to the touch. Store bought. Not that I'm picky. I reach for a fork right as Dad materializes, wielding a spatula like a weapon. He says, "Not for you."

"I'm hungry!" My stomach growls on cue. "Hear that?"

"We have food in the fridge." Dad tugs open the door as proof. He pulls out a disposable tray—lasagna?—and sets it on the counter. Next is a plastic salad bowl, a glass jar of vinaigrette, a hunk of butter for the baguette on the island.

I point. "Can I eat *that*?"

"No." He rips a crisp slice of foil. "This is for—"

"What smells good?" Lee pads into the kitchen with a yawn. His eyes are bleary, his face pillow-creased. He had class, I think, or maybe physical therapy, or maybe he put in a few hours at our aunt's auto shop. I haven't seen or spoken to him since the visitor lot yesterday.

Unless you count his pathetic text last night: *Sorry about Maddie.*

"How did I raise such gluttons? It's for . . ." Dad shakes his head, then shakes out a canvas tote. "I'm bringing it across the street."

Lee sits at the counter. "Why?"

"Because their perfect daughter ran away and they 'intentionally withheld' it," I say. Lee flinches, rubbing the sleep from his eyes. I kick his stool. "Hit the bar cart again?"

"Fuck off, Jo. I'm tired."

"Hey! Cool it, both of you." This is as angry as our dad gets. "Pass me that pie."

I break off a bit of crust. "I still don't get why you're doing this."

"To be *kind*, Jo." Dad fits the pie into the tote. "I can't imagine what that poor family is going through. If it were you—"

"I'd never do that to you. Ever. It's nothing, okay?" I don't know how many times I need to say it until I believe it. Until I can quiet that voice in my head: *I think that I'm in trouble, but . . .*

What if it's something? What if it's something, and she's in danger, and I did nothing?

"Wait!" I latch onto Dad's elbow. "Can I? Bring it over, I mean."

This is a weird thing to say. Like, objectively bizarre. But Dad softens, brimming with a type of pride I don't deserve. "Oh, Jo," he says, then to Lee, "Help her with the door."

Lee is no help at all. "You sure about this?"

"Why wouldn't I be?" I sling the bag over my shoulder, staggering under its weight.

"I'm just saying."

"Just saying what?"

He shoves the tray into my arms. "I'm just saying."

"That's what I thought." I nod back at him. "Get the door behind me."

The Prices' doorbell is broken. It rings in the wrong key, the chime haunting.

Inside, a commotion: the dog's tags jangling; someone tripping, cussing. *Shit.* This was a mistake. I don't want to be here. Mrs. Price doesn't even like me, so I'll probably make this—

It's not her mom at the door. It's her *dad*.

Even before the separation, Mr. Price was rarely around: last-minute business trips, late nights at the office. I'm not positive what he does, but I know it requires a suit and briefcase.

I also know he was banging the head of finance at his company. So.

"Hi!" I sound too chipper, like I'm about to sell him goddamn Girl Scout cookies. I fake a cough. Try again: "Uh, hi. I'm—"

"JoJo," he says.

"Oh. Yes." I've always hated the nickname, and I hate that Cody refuses to let it die, but Mr. Price remembers it. Me. I say, "We made food. My dad did. I can't cook." Or shut up. "So . . . if you . . ."

Mr. Price reaches for the pan in my wobbling arms. The tote, too. "This is nice," he says, which means *thank you*, I think. He blinks, dazed, his eyes gray and sunken, then glances warily over his shoulder. "Had you wanted to come in?"

Not even a little. But I need to get Maddie's voice out of my head, like a curse to cast on someone else. So I force a smile and say, "I'd love to."

And, for the first time since I was fifteen, I step inside the Prices' house.

I know its layout like it's my own house, the blueprints etched in my brain. To the right, the dining room; kitchen in back; Maddie's bedroom upstairs at the end of the hall. The decor is as bland now as it was then, better suited for the suburbs than our historic city neighborhood.

The only proof a real family lives here is the wall of photos. So many photos.

Maddie at prom last year. Maddie holding up a lost tooth. Maddie as a toddler in a fluffy dress and feathered angel wings—their miracle baby, conceived long after they'd given up hope on having a second. From the shrine you'd think she was already dead, or at least an only child.

"I'll take this to the kitchen," Mr. Price says. "Lisa's in the den."

The room I know best. Maddie and I spent countless hours in here, doing homework and eating banana bread and watching corny wedding shows sprawled across the couch.

Now, Mrs. Price sits on its uneven cushions, surrounded by even more photos. Hundreds, scattered across the coffee table, tucked under the woven area rug. She looks up, startled, when I knock on the doorframe. Softly, she says, "Oh. Jo-Lynn. Please, come in."

I slowly step inside and kneel on the rug, careful to move a stack of photos. Careful not to look too closely. I mumble, "Sorry," but I don't know what I'm apologizing for.

"I must look pitiful with all these pictures." Mrs. Price rubs her eyes, dry and bloodshot, like she ran out of tears. "I thought we'd need a poster."

Christ. I hate how I can see it: MISSING in fat letters. Maddie's smiling face. Her height, weight, last seen wearing, last known location—what *is* her last known location? I saw her in the library, then she met the Birds, right? Then what?

"Geoff says no posters. No vigils. It'll only push her further away. I pushed her away."

"Oh." I have no fucking clue what else to say.

Like, her mom was (is?) overbearing—tracking Maddie's location, snooping through her drawers, searching under her mattress for a diary. Maddie never even kept a diary. But Mr. Price blaming his wife (ex-wife?) for her running? Jesus.

Sniffing hard, she says, "I came across a photo with you in it, actually. I'll find it."

"No, it's okay if—"

"Here." Mrs. Price passes me the photo, and I freeze. Force myself to breathe because for a second I forget how. "When is this from? Do you remember?"

"I don't know." I do know. I start to pass it back, but she holds up a hand; this belongs to me now. I shove it into my pocket.

She picks up another picture: Maddie in her plaid Our Lady of Lourdes uniform on her first day of eighth grade. It's the worst of her awkward phase—tragic bangs, hormonal acne, a hunch to her posture. Like she was already trying to disappear.

"I never meant to deceive anyone," Mrs. Price whispers, voice rattling. "Her location was disabled when I checked, but I never thought . . . and the note? I didn't see the note."

The note. There was a note. There was a note? Maddie deactivated her socials and turned off her location sharing and left a note, so this must truly be nothing. It must be—

"I need to tell you something," I say, too fast. She doesn't look up, but she doesn't stop me, either. I clear my throat. Clear it again. "The other day, Maddie said—she told me she's in trouble. I don't know what she meant by it, but I thought you should know. So."

Mrs. Price gently sets the photo on the cushion. Even gentler, she says, "How dare you."

I shake my head. "Sorry?"

"How *dare* you." She slams her fist on the coffee table. The photos tip. Spill. I scrabble back, and we both rise to our feet. Each step I take back she matches with one forward. "Is this fun to you? Making up that horrible story? Hurting our family?"

"What?" I shake my head again, whiplashed. "Mrs. Price, I literally don't know—"

"What's happening?" Mr. Price runs from the kitchen. His hand strangles the neck of a red wine bottle, grip tightening when he turns to me. "What did you do?"

I hold up my hands. "Nothing!"

"I knew you'd be trouble," Mrs. Price says. "From the day we moved in." The dog howls, skitters down the hall. "I told her, I said, 'Maddie, you can't trust girls like that,' and then what happened? You brought those boys here—"

"God, that stupid pool party? She *made* me invite them." I've said it for years.

Her eyes have gone dark, pupils huge. "You goddamn liar."

My heart stops, I think.

"Out," Mr. Price growls, so close I can smell his wine, his breath, his sick cologne. Fury cracks his face, those blue eyes burning. He reaches for me, but I wrench back, and again: "Out!"

I'm out. I'm gone.

One step outside, and my teeth start to chatter, the chill slipping under my skin. The door slams behind me, but I don't look back. Not at their house. Not at the side yard where I sat in the grass, my back pressed against the siding, on the night of the pool party all those years ago.

The night we took that photo in my pocket.

The night we stopped being friends.

That night, I couldn't go home. I was too ashamed Lee was right when he said she didn't want me there. Or, she did, but only because the boys would follow. It's the most infuriating thing about my brother. How he is always right, and how I never heed his warnings until it's too late.

He was right about this, too, but I run across the street, up to my room. I'm out of breath when I sink against the door. I told the truth, but Mrs. Price thinks I lied—about this and the pool party, what else? What the hell did Maddie tell her?

The word pings in my skull. *Liar, liar, liar.*

Fine. Here's the real, honest truth: I'm glad that bitch is gone.

-11-

The next morning, it's like Maddie has disappeared in a different way. I search her name on my new phone (thanks, Dad) and read, reread, refresh the few articles I find.

Maddie got that crushing acceptance/rejection to NYU, so she left a note for her parents, then she left, too. That's the story. Not a single article asks more, but why should they when this is so clearly nothing? When it's a boring nonstory about a good girl who made a bad decision?

That cop from yesterday doubles down in his latest statement: "Maddie is, you know, an adult in the eyes of the law. If she wants to get away or take a break or start a new life, so be it."

But I need more, desperately, so I do a hideous thing: I read the comments.

Donna Mariano: How do you miss a freaking NOTE!?!?!?! Then ask for DONATIONS!?!?!?! SICK!!!!!
Jim Sessler: yes . . . agree donna . . . although, maddie is not

innocent . . . all parties should be persecuted for wasting Police time . . .

Silas Ricci: prosecuted* lol

Silas Ricci: lol wait she's cute is she single

Pam Fitch: my niece goes 2 school w/ madison (madeline ???) & says she is dating a boy cory has he been questioned ???

Doug Johnson: prayers. . . . .

Hayden Harbough: My cousin is a cop. That b***h ran.

Blythe Reynolds: your all stupid if u dont think shes dead

I lay face down on my bed for a long time after that.

Later, at school, even the whispers—*missing, kidnapped, dead*—have quieted, because we know the answer: Maddie Price ran away. Everyone else believes it, so I should, too. I *do*.

I want to rub it in Hudson's face, like, *Told you it was nothing,* but he skips first period, and what's the point? I have real shit to worry about. Mainly not failing.

I'm spending eighth period in the design lab with Miles. (He mistook my explanation for missing lunch as an invitation.) I'm about to submit my third mini-design when Chopra steps up behind me and asks, "What am I looking at?"

"Right, so"—I point at the screen—"this is a bay leaf"—I point again—"and this is my cat, Bay Leaf." He's heading back to his desk before I even finish the sentence. I call out, "Art takes many forms, Mr. Chopra!"

Miles snorts out a laugh, scrolling through his phone. "Still nothing on Senior Experience decisions yet," he says, like I asked. (Like I care.) Perking up, he flicks out a hand to nudge me, I think, and says, "Hey, you never told me how things went with Conti the other day."

"Barf, it was . . . fine," I lie. Poorly, too. But maybe Lee was right when he said to keep it quiet. I'm not interested in Miles's "help," and it was reckless to ever consider it, so why tell?

"I knew you could do it!" Miles smiles so sweetly that I want to die a little. "Should we celebrate after school? I'll treat you to a sprinkle cookie. I know you love—Hudson."

"Excuse me?"

Hudson raps his knuckles on the open door. "Hey, Mr. Chopra. Can I print something?"

"Great," Miles grumbles. He and Hudson may be ranked one and two, but it's not really a competition; Miles has an unwavering hold on that top spot. If I were feeling meaner, I'd tell him this rivalry is so one-sided that it borders on embarrassing.

But I really, truly need to finish this portfolio, so help me God.

Hudson takes his usual spot two down from mine. "Is that an herb on a cat?"

"Maybe," I say. "Where were you earlier?"

He keeps his eyes on his screen, but I catch that smirk. "Why? Did you miss me?"

"Shut up, Hudson."

The printer chugs, whirring, barely hiding how Miles sighs again. He shoves a notebook into his backpack. The zipper snags, and he tugs and tugs, but it won't budge.

"Need help, buddy?" Hudson asks.

"I got it," Miles lies, giving up with a huff. Then a slow,

gap-toothed grin spreads across his lips. "Hey, did you see that article in *The Eagle Eye*, Hudson?"

Hudson goes still. Looks from Miles to me to his computer. He navigates to the paper and hovers his cursor on the headline: "Alumni fund unveils revised merit scholarship guidelines."

"Only students enrolling in college will be eligible—effective next year." Miles swipes his brow, fake relieved. "Lucky for you, right?"

"Right. Lucky." Hudson absently presses the scar on his lip before he stands, fetches the printout. "Thanks again, Mr. Chopra," he says, then to me, "See you in gym."

To Miles, he says nothing. I don't blame him. Miles is smart and loyal and mostly a nice guy, but sometimes I remember why the guys knocked him against the lockers in middle school.

Hudson forgot to log out, so I shift to his chair. The cursor blinks on a PDF: *IF YOU ARE A CHILD WHO LOSES A PARENT—Understanding Your Survivor Benefits.* Jesus. Hudson lives with his grandparents, so I obviously know that his mom is, uh. Dead. He mentioned it in passing when we first met in ninth grade, but he rarely talks about it.

"What's that?" Miles asks.

"Nothing." I close out the browser. "Some form."

He rips the zipper free and grins, proud of himself. "So, did you want to? Hang out?"

"Oh. Sorry, dude, but this Maddie stuff—"

"You're still upset about that?" Miles asks. *Those girls used to be friends, you know,* like the past tense means shit. Blushing, he adds, "I didn't know you cared so much."

"Why don't you care at all?" I say it to be mean, but there's truth to it. Why *doesn't* he care? Pretty, nice Maddie Price is unnecessarily patient with Miles—listening to him ramble at parties, refusing to roll her eyes when he preens in class.

He sputters, "I do care! But Maddie is—"

"Enough, Metcalf," Chopra says through a yawn, like he wasn't blatantly eavesdropping on us. "How about you head to the cafeteria and let Jo finish up?" Miles starts to protest but thinks better of it. He stands slowly, reluctantly, and Chopra whistles, pointing him out of the lab like an air traffic controller. Door shut, he says, "That kid's a dick."

"Are you allowed to say that?"

He ignores the question. "Conti emailed. Academic probation? Really?" he says. I hate it. I hate how my name holds so much disappointment. I hate that I let myself fall and fail, and now I have no one to blame but myself. Shaking his head, Chopra says, "You're better than this, Jo."

But maybe I'm not.

By the end of the period, I've done all six mini-designs and started (opened) the layout. It blows, but whatever; Chopra wrote me an after-school pass, so I'll finish once I suffer through gym.

I mean "suffer" literally.

"You're late, Kirby," Coach Burke says, baseball cap shielding his face. He wears a blue tracksuit today. He alternates red, blue, and green, but I've yet to decipher the pattern.

"Sorry." I'm not that late, and I'm not that sorry. I drop on the bleachers with a sigh, then sigh again when Hudson sits on the bench beside me.

"Do these shorts look too short?" he whispers. I roll my eyes, but his shorts are, in fact, a touch too short, showing off his long, toned legs and, okay, why am I looking at his legs?

Coach blows his whistle. "It's a new semester, so you know what that means."

I swallow a groan. It means assessments. Coach points to each station: pull-ups, push-ups, sit-ups. Lots of upward motions. Later, we'll regroup for the pacer test, running back and forth, from one wall to the other, until we fall on our faces.

Hudson, again: "Did I have a growth spurt?"

"Mr. Harper-Moore," Coach says, exasperated, "shut up and pick your partner."

"Oh. Jo."

I search the bleachers for Joey Wilson. Surely—undoubtedly— that's who he means. I didn't know they were friends. Joey is kind of a geek, a trombonist in jazz band, and Hudson is . . . Hudson. But good for them!

Coach snaps his fingers like I'm some untrained dog. "Kirby. Sit-up station."

"No, thanks," I say, and to Hudson, "What do you want?"

"What makes you think I want something?" He follows me across the gym and gestures to the mat. "Ladies first?" I don't move. "Okay, or I can go." He settles onto his back. The hem of his T-shirt lifts, exposing a strip of his stomach, the stripe of dark hair below his belly button.

I look away, face hot.

The whistle sounds—one minute, as many reps as possible, go. So, Hudson goes, then he groans when the timer beeps. Flushed, he says, "You didn't count, did you?"

"Nope." I lay back on the mat and stare at the ceiling, dreading this next part. "I need you to hold my ankles, but if you say a single word about this position, I'll kick you in the face."

Even if he doesn't say it, I bet he thinks it: *This feels familiar, huh?*

The whistle blows again, and I start a steady and miserable down, up, down. The next up, Hudson says, "So, I did want something, actually."

Down. "I knew it." Up. "What is it?" Down.

"You had a weird thing with Maddie the other day, yeah? I did, too."

I sit up too fast, my skull slamming into Hudson's face. Hard. His hand flies to his nose, blood pouring between his fingers. I'm only mildly aware of the pain in my forehead. Everyone scatters, like this thing is contagious. Laughing, he says, "You did that on purpose."

Coach chucks a half-crushed tissue box at me. "Get him to the nurse, Kirby."

Hudson holds a fistful of tissues to his nose and hangs a left in the hall. I say, "Uh, wrong way." He keeps going, like he expects me to follow. (I do, but still.) He goes to the second floor, down the hall, toward—

"I'm not going in there."

"Wait here, and I'll do a sweep." Hudson pushes into the boys' locker room. I glare at the door until it swings open again. Ripping another tissue from the box, he asks, "Did you want to hear about Maddie or not?"

So, fine, I go in there.

It smells horrific—like sweat but worse. I follow him to the sinks, my elbows tight to my body, hands lifted. "I'm definitely going to pick up a fungus in here."

Hudson smacks his palm on the faucet. "Maybe if you hadn't headbutted me . . ."

"Tell me about Maddie."

"Seriously, that is one hard head." He wets a paper towel and swipes his face, blots the stain on his collar. "So hard, Jo."

"*Hudson.*"

He guides me to a row of lockers against the back wall. The metal is painted an obscene yellow, defaced with marker. There are penises, some so specific they must be self-portraits, and this weird wedge shape. The rectangle of a blacked-out name. Tally marks. The word *whore.*

I sit on the bench. "Whose name was there?"

"Huh? Oh. I don't know," he says, and I think it's a lie, but then he peels off his gym T-shirt and my brain short-circuits. Hudson (here, shirtless) passes me his phone, which I fumble, and pulls a clean shirt from his locker.

Then Hudson (here, shirt on) sits beside me, our legs touching. "So, Maddie went nuclear after the decision thing." *The decision thing.* It's such a casual way to say it. "She blamed *me* for her rejection." I'm confused. Hudson can tell, I guess, so he adds, "Maddie is twenty-first in the class. If I'd forfeited my rank, it'd bump her into the top ten percent."

"Does that matter?" I honestly don't know. Before my review, I'd applied to two schools: SUNY Geneseo, which is too tiny, and the University of Rochester, which is here. Then I told my parents I might take a gap year, or whatever, and they were like, *Sounds cool,* and that was it.

He unlocks his phone. "I thought she just wanted someone to blame, but . . . read these."

Monday, February 5

[8:17 p.m.] **MADDIE:** Fuck you, Hudson.

[8:19 p.m.] **HUDSON:** uhhh

[8:20 p.m.] **MADDIE:** I got rejected from NYU.

[8:21 p.m.] **MADDIE:** I missed out on the top ten percent because of you.

[8:24 p.m.] **HUDSON:** oh. that sucks, maddie. i'm sorry.

[8:26 p.m.] **MADDIE:** You should've given up your rank when you had a chance.

[8:27 p.m.] **MADDIE:** You should've given it up before they take it.

[8:29 p.m.] **HUDSON:** wtf does that mean

[8:53 p.m.] **HUDSON:** maddie???

You should've given it up before they take it. I reread it twice before I shake my head, shove the phone back into his hand. "Hudson, that rank is yours."

"Not yet." Panic strains his voice.

Technically true. Back in the fall, we got emails with our projected senior rank, but Lund said over and over that it's tentative until first semester grades get factored in. But that rule exists for students like me, girls miraculously ranked eleventh who tank their grades and their lives.

The top spots never waver, or they rarely do. I think.

"The revised scholarship guidelines—it's because of me, right?"

He presses a scuff in the bench. "After you said Maddie set you up, I thought maybe she did the same to me. But why?"

My eyes flit to *whore* again. "Do you think she was . . . warning you?"

The door bangs, thuds open. I jump up, fast, and Hudson angles his body in front of mine.

"Did you recognize *any* of that shit?" Tyler or Kyle Spencer breezes past us, phone to his ear. "I feel like I failed, man, but that'd be . . ." Pause. "Hold on, I have to take a leak."

"Ew," I whisper, and Hudson says, "Let's go."

The pacer test is about to start when we get back to gym. Coach points us to the bleachers as the buzzer sounds. Two dozen sneakers squeak on the varnished floors. I dig my nails into the bench. Somewhere, I'm sure, someone has carved my name: *Jo is a . . .*

Whore, maybe. *Slut,* definitely. Never *ho,* which feels like a missed opportunity—the rhyme is right there.

"I talked to Maddie's mom yesterday." I don't know where that came from. Why I said it. Why I say, "I told her what Maddie said, but she didn't believe me. She called me a—"

Liar. I've never seen that fill-in-the-blank: *Jo is a liar.*

Hudson watches one back-and-forth of the pacer test. "You talked to her mom."

Duh, I just told you that, I want to say, but that's not what he means. He means to say that I'm still thinking about her, aren't I? I'm still not convinced?

He asks, "What did the cop say again? Her behavior was . . ."

"Uncharacteristic," I offer, monotone.

"Right! It *was* uncharacteristic. Her coming to both of us. Her running away at all." He plants his elbows on his knees. "Everyone just believes it, too. No one is looking for her." The sentence dangles between us. He sits tall again. "I guess *we* could."

"We could what?"

"Look. Investigate."

"Investigate?" I laugh, hard. "Investigate what? Maddie ran away."

Those words get easier to say each time. The truth is, sometimes girls do uncharacteristic things. Even girls like Maddie, who spend their lives doing everything everyone expects of them.

Now I can't stop. "Like, if we investigated—which we're not going to do—how would it even work? No one will talk to me. I'm not . . ." I tighten my shoelaces. "I'm on the outside."

"Then we'd find you a way back in."

"How?" I am genuinely asking. "Her boyfriend is an asshole." *Her boyfriend spread my nudes to, uh, everyone.* "Her best friends hate me." *Kathleen does, anyway, and I hate the Birds on principle.* "I don't even like Maddie!" *Ugh.* "Neither do you."

His hesitation confirms it. "Maddie is fine."

"What a ringing endorsement."

"I don't *dislike* her. Plus, she's dating my friend, so, you know."

"So, you know, what?"

"So, you know, I tolerate her." He stares ahead, but I see it unfold—the gears shifting in his brain, the lightbulb above his head glowing brighter and brighter until I'm certain the glass will crack. He turns back to me, one corner of his mouth quirked up. "You need a way back in."

It takes me a second to get it. To decipher the meaning when he—

"Oh my God, no. Absolutely not."

"Hear me out," Hudson says, sliding closer on the bench. "Us 'dating' is foolproof."

"It's not foolproof! Literally who'd ever believe it?" I ask. He shoots me a *look*. My heart beats the tiniest bit faster. The air has gotten heavier, thick with sweat. I drag my hands down my face. "I've got my own shit, Hudson." Like not failing. Like staying out of trouble. "No. I can't."

"Why not?"

"Because I can't."

"Why not?"

"Because I fucking betrayed her." The words tumble out of me, like a knot in my throat came loose. I wonder how long I kept that thing tied. "There's a reason me and Maddie aren't friends anymore, okay? I'd rather not go there."

I *cannot* go there.

The gym has emptied. I don't know when that happened.

Low, serious, Hudson says, "If my rank is at risk, and Maddie knows something about it, I need to do something. I can't lose this. I can't *afford* to." The scholarship money: $10,000. He props an elbow on the bench behind him, all cool. "I'll do it, Jo. With or without you."

Like a dare.

So, I lean above him, our bodies so very, very close, faces inches apart. His gaze holds steady, but I hear his breath catch.

"Then I guess," I say, "you're doing it without me."

I'm last to enter the locker room.

The other girls have already kicked off their sneakers,

shucked their sweaty tees, swiped deodorant under their arms. One-L Daniele meets my eyes in the full-length mirror. "That was a lot of sexual tension for sit-ups."

"Mind your own business, One-L Daniele." I head to the changing stalls no one uses but me. I found a roach, belly up, under the bench a few weeks ago, but it beats being out there.

Before, I had a brazen kind of confidence. I'd whip off my top, like, *Look at me. See me.* Now it's like my body no longer belongs to me. Like I stopped being a person at all.

Even alone, I can't stand to see myself, so I change fast. The locker room has gone quiet.

Then, low: "Is anyone back here?"

I hold my breath. Step one foot onto the bench, then the other. Right as I peer through the slat, Sara Caruso passes the stall, her combat boots smacking against the gritty tile.

Louder, she says, "I think we're safe."

Michaela comes into view, her neon pink coat tucked into the crook of her elbow. I adore that coat. I told her so when she first wore it last winter, and we joked that she basically invented neon pink, and it startled me how easy it was to laugh with her.

"Make this quick." Kathleen now, impatient. "I want the corner booth."

They must be going to Java's. Culver students get half off with our IDs on Thursdays, only until four. I miss it so much: the mismatched velvet chairs and stained-glass windows and, yes, the corner booth.

"Guys, listen," Sara whispers, frantic. "Her mom sent me, like, five texts last night. She asked if Maddie is in trouble or something?"

I smother my face in my shirt. *Mrs. Price.* She called me a liar but believed me enough to ask Sara if Maddie is in—

"Trouble?" Michaela repeats as Kathleen asks, "What did you reply?"

"Nothing yet."

"Nothing *ever.* Block her." Kathleen peers into the mirror and fixes her part, dragging a nail across her scalp. "Either that, or tell her that bitch isn't our problem anymore."

The girls speak at once again, Michaela hissing, "*Kathleen,*" as Sara says, "But what if she knows we—?"

"She knows nothing," Kathleen whispers, "and neither do we."

-*12*-

I sit on the bench so long the automatic lights flip off.

The Birds denied it, but they obviously know something, right? What happened or where Maddie went or why she claimed to be in trouble? But Maddie couldn't go to the Birds. She said it in the library: *I can't go to anyone else.* Only me. I'm the only one who can—

"Stop," I tell myself, then I do something worse. I think of Hudson. His rank, the money, that form he printed in the lab, the texts from Maddie. That foolproof plan that isn't foolproof at all. But it's nothing.

It's fine.

My legs buckle, stiff, when I stand. I need to focus on me. Focus on not flunking out and fucking this up. *It's fine, it's fine* guides me into the lobby, past students running to the bus loop, past the figure at the security guard desk who calls out, "Jo-hyphen-Lynn!"

Tess Spradlin, no punctuation.

In all this, I keep forgetting about the Senior Experience.

I hang by the trophy case until Tess is signed, scanned, cleared.

She glances at a photo of former basketball captain Lee Kirby behind the glass. She must register our shared last name, so I brace myself for it: *Lee? The would-be (soon-to-be?) star at UNC? You're his little sister?*

Instead, she asks, "Heading out?"

"No, I have a thing due for class. Multiple things due for multiple classes."

"For your academic probation?"

I tilt my head. "How did—?"

"I'm a reporter, remember?" Tess taps her skull with a wink. "Just kidding. Sorry. That's so embarrassing. No, Lund told me when I picked you to be my mentee. But the 'optics' of your probation are 'quite troubling,' so Lund won't allow it. I'm actually meeting her now to drop out of the program."

"Hold on." I need her to rewind. Restart. "You picked *me*? But I didn't even submit a real application. The napkin . . . I was . . ."

Trying to make Maddie mad. It sounds exceptionally petty, but it's true, isn't it? I did the same thing when I ran against her for sophomore class president. I did it again after my victory, when I held up two peace signs and resigned from office, effective immediately.

I did it when I grabbed that napkin.

I did it when I made the choice that would end our friendship for good.

"Let me give you the backstory," Tess says, loosening her scarf. "My mom got diagnosed with cancer last year, so I broke my lease in the city and broke up with my girlfriend." She forces a laugh. "I swore I'd never move back here, but I did, and my mom was dead within a month."

"I'm sorry."

Tess keeps going like I never spoke. "I have nothing left in the city. But I have nothing in Rochester, either, except my underpaid job and a pit bull who still waits for my mom at the door. I haven't written in months. I'm . . . stuck. And I thought the program might get me unstuck, but if I can't have the mentee I want, then I'm not doing it."

"And *I'm* the mentee you want?" I cross my arms. "You don't even know if I can write."

"That's pure mechanics. I care about the story. For whatever reason, I thought you might have a story to tell." Tess holds a silence I don't fill. "Sorry it didn't work out, Jo-hyphen-Lynn."

I'm not sorry, but the words echo in my head: *I thought you might have a story to tell.* As if Tess sees something I can't.

"Hey!" I call after her. "I'm interested."

Tess nods, surprised but not. "Yeah?"

"Yes, and Lund will never go for it, but if she does, then I'll do it. I want to."

Okay, why the hell did I say that? I got possessed by the ghost of someone who cares.

I flick on the lights in the lab. Chopra left me a sticky note— *staff meeting back @ 3*—but I'll be gone by then. My computer is taking forever, so I pull out my phone. I've got a text from Miles asking if I want to hang out in the chem lab before school tomorrow, but only if I want to!

Honestly, I *don't* want to, not after how weird he was earlier. I'll respond later.

Once my desktop finally loads, I print photos from the repository to visualize my design, or whatever, then I draft an undeniably crappy layout and hit submit with seven minutes to spare.

"Thank God," I mumble, and shuffle the printouts into a pile. One photo slips out.

The Birds.

It's from the sidelines of a Culver Eagles soccer game last fall. Kathleen sits front and center on a rumpled blanket, her lips shaped into a smirk. Michaela hugs Sara from behind, both laughing, mouths open wide. And Maddie blurs, unfocused, on the edge of the blanket.

I set the photo down. Pick it up again.

Then I print every photo tagged "Price" in the repository.

Photo #14: The *Peter Pan* pit orchestra from last winter. It takes me a solid ten seconds to find Maddie squished between Miles (so tall) and April (the better flutist).

Photo #26: *The Eagle Eye* editorial staff photo. Maddie, managing editor, is mid-blink.

Photo #35: Maddie in a candid from the cafeteria where her head is turned.

She's a background character in every photo.

Every. Single. One.

What happened is that Maddie lost the one thing she wanted when she got unaccepted to NYU. She held this dream, certain it was hers, and within an hour it slipped from her fingers.

So, she ran. She had to run.

But.

Something is weird with the Birds. Like, Kathleen called Maddie a bitch so easily. (As if I haven't said it, too.) They whispered and rolled their eyes during the meet and greet, but what if it wasn't aimed at me? What if it was at *Maddie*?

There's Cody Forsythe, too. I never watch true crime shit, but even I know it's always the boyfriend. He lets that sophomore Alexis trail him like a shadow, and after what he did to me—

Me. How do I figure into this? Why the setup if nothing came from it?

Unless it wasn't a setup. Unless . . .

I step back, like I can see it if I zoom out. I squint, stare, wait for the photos to take shape, but I must be missing—wait.

The photo still in my coat pocket. Maddie and me at the pool party.

It was hot and humid that June, our first week of freedom after our first year at Culver. But I'd barely seen Maddie. She was too busy babysitting the triplets down the street, too busy with Vacation Bible School and flute lessons and reorganizing her bookshelves and this summer camp at the public library archives.

Now, finally, we were together again.

In the picture, I wear my brand-new bikini top—one triangle striped green, the other hot pink with black seeds. Maddie's ruffled tankini straps poke out of her eyelet dress. She hangs a step behind me, half-hidden, but isn't that because I held the camera?

Or was I the main character in our friendship too?

We both smile, but only mine is real. I didn't know it then. Didn't know how badly she didn't want to be friends anymore.

Know that, in a few short hours, we wouldn't be.

I set the picture in the center of the table. Brace my hands on either side. Every Maddie in every photo whispers, *I think that I'm in trouble, but*—

Maddie thinks I can help her.

"Goddamn it." I slap a palm down, sweep up the photos, feed them through the shredder. Minus the one of us; that, I keep.

Then I run.

Down the hall, out the door, through the cold, the snow, the sopping wet streets. I run all the way to Java's where Cody and the Birds and everyone else—everyone who matters—will be.

I burst through the door, its bells jingling wildly, and shout, "Hudson!" He looks up from the corner booth. They all do. I clear my throat, much more calmly say, "Can we talk a second?"

I go back outside and pace the sidewalk until those bells ring again.

"Hey," Hudson says, so casual. *Hey.*

I take in a breath, take him in—all of him. Black jeans, black tee, no coat. The chill raises goose bumps on his arms. In the glow of the snow, his eyes look less brown than gold.

Maybe he's sizing me up, too. No makeup. Body hidden inside oversized clothes because that's what I want. To be invisible until graduation, and then go anywhere—be anyone—else.

Hudson takes a lazy step toward me. "What's this about?"

"You know what this is about."

"I do?" His mouth tilts into a stupid, crooked smile.

His mouth. I focus on that mouth. His full lips, the scar. I've never asked how he got that. "I'm going to put my hands on your waist," I say. I can feel every muscle, each hard ridge of his stomach through the fabric. He smells good, too, like clean clothes and coffee. "And you—"

He cups my neck, thumbs pressed to my jaw. "This good?"

"Yes," I say, so breathy. "Is everyone watching us?"

He slyly glances toward the window. "Sure seems like it." Back to me. "Is there a reason we're standing like this?"

"You know why."

"You keep saying that but—"

"Kiss me before I change my mind."

It's instant, the muscle memory of his mouth on mine. His hands weave through my hair, tugging me closer, closer. It still isn't close enough.

Even from here, I hear the screams and laughter and whistles, the smack of a palm on the glass. This is what I wanted. I wanted everyone to see this. To see *us*.

Lips close but not touching, I ask, "Is tongue necessary?"

"You liked it last time."

"Oh my God." I step back, away from him. My whole body burns. "Rule number one of this little arrangement is that we never do that again."

Even as I start down the sidewalk, I feel Hudson's eyes on me. I almost expect it when he calls out, "This little arrangement?"

I turn toward him one last time. The snow flutters around us, barely more than dust. Still, it dizzies me. Or maybe it's not the snow at all.

"This is probably obvious," I say, "but I'm in, by the way."

-13-

I'm out. This is—no joke—the seventeenth time I've typed the message. That's not including the number of times I practiced it in the shower (twice) or thought it since last night (a lot).

Yet, for the seventeenth time, I don't hit send.

From downstairs, Dad calls, "Were we expecting someone?"

"Huh?" I shout, and then I gasp, run to the window, rip open the blinds. "No!"

Lee, behind his bedroom door: "Stop yelling."

[7:04 a.m.] **JO**: wait out there or i'm dumping your ass

Because I cannot—*cannot*—explain this to Dad right now. I apply deodorant, brush my teeth, drip toothpaste onto my collar, change, change again, run downstairs.

Dad tips his mug toward the window. "Who's that?"

"I don't know. I mean, I do know. He's not, like, a stranger. So. Bye!"

It snowed last night, the wet, heavy kind that downs power lines, splits tree branches, sets like quicksand. My legs burn when I heave open the passenger door.

Hudson grins at me. "Morning, babe."

"I know I say this so much it's become meaningless, but—"

"Shut up, Hudson." He glances across the street. I follow his gaze to that cherry-red two-seater convertible. Mr. Price's Audi. My mother called it a "midlife crisis car" when he rolled up in that thing last summer, and then he moved out a week later, so . . .

Hudson says, "Nice car."

"It's certainly not as nice as yours."

"Strong statement from someone without a car *or* a license." Hudson balances his coffee cup on his knee and pulls away from the curb, the steering wheel groaning, gears grinding. "Shit, that does sound bad."

I point to the second drink in the cupholder. "What's this?"

"Iced coffee from Wegmans. Cream, no sugar, right?"

"How did you know that?"

"It's not a hard order to remember, Jo."

I swish the cup. Hudson bought me an iced coffee. He bought me an iced coffee from the best grocery store on the planet because he's my "boyfriend," and soon everyone, *everyone*, will know we're "together" and—

"I can't do this." I lower the window, hot. Like, *so* hot. "I'm breaking up with you."

He wordlessly hands me the AUX cord, like it'll distract me. (It will.) I navigate to my saved artists, and Hudson goes quiet, listening. "Is this Billy Joel?"

"You passed me the AUX cord."

"I didn't know you'd pick Billy Joel."

"Precisely why we need to break up." I raise the window, cold. Like, *so* cold. "If I were really your girlfriend, you'd know I love Billy Joel like a damn baby boomer."

Hudson makes a face but lets "Scenes from an Italian Restaurant" play us to Culver. He reverses into a space in the senior lot, his arm thrown behind my headrest, his body tilted toward mine. The car jerks to a stop, and he says, "So, why are we breaking up?"

"Because—"

"Because *I* thought we needed a cover to investigate Maddie," he says. Her name flutters in my chest. Maddie, my ex–best friend, missing four days. He goes on: "I thought we needed to find out what she knew about my rank, and why she claimed to be in trouble. Why she ran away."

"Yes, but—"

But Hudson isn't looking at me. He looks, instead, over my shoulder, out the passenger window at Ben Sulkin and Cody Forsythe. The pitcher and the soccer star. My old friends.

Ben smacks his palms to the glass. "Get a nice ride, JoJo?" he shouts, the glass muffling his voice. "A nice, long, hard—?"

So, yeah, actually only *Cody* was my friend.

This morning he hangs back with this blank look on his face, like he hardly registers Ben or us or anything. Like his mind is somewhere else. Pale, shivering, he types a text for . . .

Hudson skims the message preview. Frantically rips his phone from the dock.

Just like that, the old Cody is back—eyes gleaming, teeth bared in a smile.

My stomach dips. "What does that say?"

"Nothing," Hudson mumbles, shooting a glare at their retreating forms, then shooting off a reply. He tucks the phone into his pocket as he angles toward me, serious. "I want us to try this, Jo. Please. And the second you say so, we'll end it, okay? Just give me one good reason."

"One, Cody. Two, Ben. Three, we basically know nothing about each other."

This isn't true. He knows it, too, but he says, "Then let's exchange pertinent information. I now know you love Billy Joel. I also know that you . . . have a brother."

"Right, and you're an only child." I hesitate. "You're an only child, right?"

"I'm pretty sure. See? This is great. We know so much about each other." Hudson steps out of the car, and I do the same. "What's your favorite color?"

"Green. How big is your penis?"

He slams the door. "Pertinent information, Jo-Lynn."

"I'd say that's more pertinent than my favorite color."

Hudson leads us across the parking lot, our steps grinding on the snow, his hand drifting toward mine but not grabbing it. "Do girls talk that candidly?"

"I wouldn't know. I'm not friends with other girls."

"You were friends with Maddie."

This is bait. He's flinging the line over his shoulder and dropping the lure into the water, waiting to reel me in. I smile up at him. "That ended well, didn't it?"

Then I stop. So does he. This is it. The moment I step into

Culver and sacrifice any real hope for surviving the year unseen, unscathed, the moment we—

"Birds," Hudson whispers. I look to the sky. "No, not . . . the other kind."

Michaela Russell cuts in front of us with a sweep of her arms, her pink coat bright against the gray day. "For the record, I manifested this. You're *very* welcome."

"It's true," Sara Caruso says, so close that I jump. "She did."

Then there's Kathleen O'Mara—head high, arms crossed. This is her tell. Before she gets mean, her body relaxes, like the tight coil inside her unwinds. Monotone, she asks, "How's poor Miles taking the news?"

"Miles?" I echo, confused at first. Then I slap a hand to my mouth, say, "Shit, *Miles*." His text about the chemistry lab, us hanging out tomorrow—today—if I want to. I never replied.

Hudson blinks snow from his lashes. "He knows about us, right?"

Us. I shake it off, look from him to Kathleen to the main doors. "I'll, uh. Be right back."

I rap my knuckles on the open door to the chemistry lab.

Miles glances up from the sink, his hands submerged in the soapy water, suds clinging to his wrists. Beakers air-dry on a paper towel beside him. He looks down again.

"Can I come in?" I ask. He shrugs a shoulder—a yes, no, maybe all at once. I pull the door shut behind me. "Listen, dude, I meant to—"

"Tell me about you and Hudson?"

"Text you back," I say, finishing my original thought. Miles tacks on a laugh, like this is fine, cool, chill. It's none of those things. Not to him.

Look, I'm not stupid. I know Miles likes me. He knows I know. His crush is an unspoken truth with an unspoken rule that he can never make a move. That it's never going to happen.

The thing is, I've *tried* to like Miles. Like during winter break when he invited me over to watch some Marvel movie. I hadn't seen one before—or cared to, honestly—but he insisted I'd love it. Like I'd told him no only so he could change my mind.

But I went, and we were alone in his attic, on the futon, and if I'd scooted to the right, our legs would have touched from knee to hip, and isn't that the first step of a new maybe-thing? The shy smiles, the dumb excuses to "accidentally" touch each other?

As the battle scene raged, I looked up and tried to really, truly see Miles. Not as the dorky kid I've known since middle school, with his graphic tees and a permanent blush, but as someone I could like. Maybe love.

Like he could feel me watching, Miles smiled down at me. "What is it?"

If I broke it down, each individual part was there—his long lashes and loose curls, the gap-toothed smile, the freckle on his lower lip. Miles is cute. He's obviously smart. But when I tried to rebuild those parts into something whole, I felt—

"Nothing," I told him.

I felt nothing.

Here, Miles flicks on the faucet, rinsing a beaker under the stream. "It just sucked to hear it secondhand. I feel like you owed me that much. As a friend," he adds, his face turning redder. "I just don't want you to get hurt. That's it. Guys like Hudson—"

"What does that mean?" I'm too defensive.

"Don't be obtuse, Jo." This is the same tone Miles uses when he helps me with a calculus equation. Like the answer is obvious to everyone but me. "Hudson may act like he cares for you, or likes you, but what do you *really* think he's after?"

This knot of guilt tightens into something else. *Hurt.* That first Monday after the bonfire, Miles found me in the stairwell with my head in my hands—not crying, because I don't cry. He handed me a tissue as if I might, like, *I'm sorry this happened to you.*

Like, *I'd never.*

It felt like a promise.

I try to laugh, but it burns all the way up. "You're a dick, Miles."

His face falls, stricken. "Wait," he says, dropping the beaker. "I didn't mean it like—"

Out in the hall, Hudson is lounging against the windowsill. I wait for it. The taunts about Miles, his crush, and how did I ever think this was any different? That my friendship could ever be enough? But Hudson only holds out his hand.

Every part of me wants to smack it away. End this before we truly begin.

I take it anyway.

-14-

For one brief, startling moment today—when Hudson and I fell into step in a synchronized slow motion, when his hand eased toward mine, when all eyes were on us—I bought it.

I bought *us*: Jo and Hudson, together.

That confidence lasted about thirteen seconds.

It's hard, you know? I've been no one for four months, and now I'm someone. Now, I'm Hudson Harper-Moore's girlfriend. The stares burn into us like the hot beam of a spotlight. Some of the guys keep slapping him up, too, like I'm a thing he achieved.

Like they know what he's after.

God, my fall from grace was so swift and sudden that I never saw it coming. For so long, I was the cool girl. I was loud and fun and untouchable, always hanging with the guys—no girls allowed but me. Then those six photos got out, and I realized real fast how they really see me.

My own fucking friends. Miles now, too.

Hudson at least takes pity on me and agrees to spend lunch in the library. (I'd literally die in the cafeteria.) The second we enter, he sneezes, says, "Pertinent information: I have allergies."

"Bless you," Clare O'Mara says shyly, slipping him the sign-in sheet, stamping my pass. Her elbow bumps a flute case. I didn't know she played, or even why I would. But when Maddie practices hers on warm days, her trills float out her open window.

My ears ring with an off-pitch melody. I shake my head, shake out the music.

Hudson stifles another sneeze. "Ready?"

"Nope." I tip my pass at Clare and, somehow, for some reason, guide us to the dictionary nook. The corduroy beanbag. Hudson squints at its stain. I swipe grime from a cracked book spine and say, "This is where Maddie . . . found me."

"Here? Oh." Hudson nods, almost reverent. "Can you walk me through it?"

I can. I do.

How she came to me with snow in her hair. How she cried: *I think that I'm in trouble, but I think that you can help me.* How I watched her disappear into the cold, not knowing—because I couldn't know—that she'd disappear again, for real, that night.

"Maddie came back for you?" he asks.

I hadn't thought of it like that. "I guess."

Hudson leads me to a table by Fiction: A-L and dumps his backpack at his feet. He fishes out a notebook, says, "Some of us went to Java's that day"—*that day*, when I saw the Birds and him in the senior lot, when Maddie vanished—"and I saw her walking out of school at dismissal. She seemed totally normal. Then you saw her, what, ten minutes later?" He jots down the times. "So, what happened in those ten minutes to make her so upset?"

"She refused to say." I bite my cuticle, ripping the skin. "But she asked me to meet her by the bike rack at three—"

"Right, where I saw you fall into the garbage."

"I didn't fall *into* the garbage. I fell *beside* the garbage *can*."

Hudson sneezes. "Then what?"

"Bless you. Then she stood me up for the Birds." I roll my shoulders up, back, the anger a dull ache days later. "I'm guessing she'd just gotten her acceptance email. And then she posted it on her socials and learned it was a glitch and freaked out and left, the end."

Hudson considers this. "So, it's just a coincidence that she claimed to be in trouble on the same day she got rejected from NYU and ran away? That seems convenient." He sighs, rubs his watery eyes. "And how does my rank fit into it?"

"How do we know it fits at all? Maybe Maddie really did go nuclear and wanted someone to blame," I offer flippantly. "Like, who does it even benefit if you lose that spot?"

He laughs a little. "The person in third. The alumni association. Everyone but Miles."

"Your rank shouldn't have mattered, though. I'm ..." I bite down, weighing how much to tell when I've already told him too much. "I'm eleventh, right? And I don't want to talk about it, but I'm on academic probation, so I'm *sure* I dropped in the ranks. Probably below Maddie."

His brows knit. "Oh, I didn't know you were serious about failing."

"I said I don't want to talk about it."

Hudson rests his chin in his palm, a strand of hair falling into his eyes. "Fine. I'll add it to the list of things we don't talk about."

I match his pose. "Sounds great, thanks," I say. But now all the things we don't talk about scroll through my head. The bonfire.

The prom afterparty. (God.) I change the subject. "Did you tell anyone else what she said?"

"Not the details." The heat flicks on, vent rattling, rustling his hair. He hesitantly adds, "I did text Cody, though."

"Show me."

He extends his phone. Immediately snaps it back. There's a joke in here—*Uh-oh, deleting your dick pics?*—but I'm not in any position to tell it. My phone dings with a screenshot.

Monday, February 5

[8:27 p.m.] **HUDSON:** hey have you checked on maddie?

[8:35 p.m.] **CODY:** y

[8:36 p.m.] **HUDSON:** are you saying yes or asking me why

[8:38 p.m.] **CODY:** why

[8:40 p.m.] **HUDSON:** she's freaking out at me because of nyu

[8:41 p.m.] **HUDSON:** she says it's my fault?

[8:46 p.m.] **CODY:** lol ugh she needs to chill

[8:49 p.m.] **HUDSON:** maybe you should talk to her

[11:33 p.m.] **CODY:** how about u

Tuesday, February 6

[6:14 a.m.] **CODY:** can i get a ride

[6:18 a.m.] **CODY:** nvm

Real contender for Boyfriend of the Year right here. I can't pretend to get what goes on between Maddie and Cody, but his girlfriend is clearly devastated, and he's all put out?

I toss my phone onto the table. "Why is he being so terse with you?"

"I didn't realize he was being terse," Hudson says, sliding his own back into his pocket.

"Oh. Maybe not?" I can't pretend to understand their relationship, either. (Or frankly how boys communicate with each other in general.) He and Cody were the only freshmen to make the varsity soccer team four years ago, so I assumed their friendship bloomed out of convenience.

Hudson has always seemed like the odd one out in that whole crew. Part of it, I think, is that none of us knew him before Culver, since he'd gone to school in a different district. Then he's also just lowkey. Never the center of attention. At parties, he'd drink and/or get stoned like the rest of us, but he'd ditch the second things got too sloppy.

Most nights, he'd head outside, alone, to smoke a joint and stare at the stars. Other nights, I'd join him in the grass, steal his joint, tease him: "You do this on purpose, right? Because you know girls will see you stargazing and think you're all hot and sensitive?"

Then, he'd shrugged, not quite smiling. "Depends. Is it working?"

Now, Hudson runs a hand through his hair. "I think we need to narrow the scope. Focus on one thing." Pause. "Like why Maddie went to *you*."

I roll my eyes, roll them again when he draws two overlapping circles, one labeled *J*, the other *M*. I say, "Wow, a Venn diagram! Did you just pass third-grade math?"

"What's your calc average right now?"

"Can you at least write 'hot' in my circle?"

He adds *annoying*. "We need to figure out what goes here, in the intersection."

Everything I can think of—cheap nail polish and boxed macaroni and cheese, disposable cameras and outdoor naps in the warm summer sun—seems so small now. But it once added up to something. To us, our friendship.

There are two names that fall into the space between us, too, but only one I'd ever share with Hudson, so I steal his pencil and scribble it in.

Hudson peers at the page. Nods, just once. "Probably could've guessed that."

In big, capital letters: *CODY FORSYTHE.*

Nothing happened between me and Cody. Not once. Not ever. It seemed impossible to everyone that we never kissed. That we kept our touching purely platonic: roughhousing, horsing around. But we were tight for so long because we didn't like each other like that. No one believed us.

Especially not Maddie.

"You're *sure* you don't like him?" she'd ask, over and over.

It took everything in me not to go, *Ew, him?* This was the kid who'd eat pizza crust out of the trash, chug orange soda, then belch so hard he barfed. Trust me, I didn't like him—seriously.

But last summer, things got . . . weird. He was touchier than usual, whispering close, hand grazing my hip. He'd pitch times to hang out when the other guys were busy. Late at night, Cody would text: *what are u doing tonihgt?*

I'd reply: *"tonight" is not a difficult word.*

Fast-forward to Labor Day. His three older brothers were back at school, and his parents had gone to Keuka Lake for the long weekend, so Cody was alone in that big house of his.

Halfway through my shift at Costello's Frozen Custard, he texted, *swim?*

Costello's was packed and it was hot as hell and my least favorite regular, Creepy Caleb, was being extra creepy, so I replied, *YES.*

I never thought to ask who else was coming when I went home, changed into my bikini, dug my bike out of the garage. I didn't think it was strange that it was just us when I pedaled up his driveway and leaped into the water, because why would it be? He was my friend.

Cody watched me swim, his legs dangling in the deep end.

"Dare me to dive?" I hoisted myself out of the water, crossed the slick path to the diving board. The heat of the flagstone stung my feet. I stepped up to the edge. "Count me off!"

"Do you think we should have sex?"

"What?" I lost my balance, slipping off the board, flopping into the water. When I came up for air, I was so beyond certain he'd laugh, like, *You fell for that? Literally fell for it?* But his face was serious. I paddled up to the ladder. "Dude, what are you talking about?"

He shrugged. "We're friends. You're attractive."

"Flattering." I climbed out of the pool again, but now I saw how Cody watched, his eyes heavy and dark, lips parted. I wrapped myself in a towel and sat at the glass picnic table.

Cody twisted to face me. "You don't want to?"

"Nope." I unlocked my phone. I had a text from James Quinn,

the quarterback over at St. Ignatius. We made out once (once!) in tenth grade, but he'd send a lazy *hey* whenever his latest Lourdes girlfriend dumped him.

The next was from Miles, asking if I was free and wanted to get ice cream or see a movie but no pressure! We weren't close like that, not then, but he'd just broken up with April, and I'd made the mistake of saying, "That blows."

Then a photo of a Garbage Plate from Hudson. *Don't be too jealous.*

Pretty much all summer, since prom, things had been kind of weird between us. Actually, they'd been so fucking awkward that I could barely look at him without dying inside.

But we'd recently gotten into it about Rochester's foulest delicacy: hot dogs, macaroni salad, meat sauce, home fries, mustard, onions. I find it conceptually horrifying, but I laughed when he said I'm entitled to my wrong opinion. It felt so normal after so long of *not* normal.

"What are you smiling about?"

"No one." I set my phone down. "Nothing."

Cody dropped down at the head of the table. His skin was pink, the type of sunburn that'd peel off in layers. "Ben had sex with that girl."

"What girl?" I couldn't picture Ben Sulkin with any girl. He was shy unless he drank; when he drank, he'd pick fights and/or brag about his pitching stats. "He probably made it up."

"Yeah, probably." Pause. "We should still do it."

"Or you could, I don't know, find a girl who likes you." I never said Maddie's name, but he scrunched his face like I had. "What's your issue with her? She's pretty. She's nice."

"Do you know what else they say about pretty, nice girls? They're *boring*." Cody flicked an ant off his shoulder. "Maybe I know Maddie better than you think, JoJo."

"What does that mean?" I asked, though she and I hadn't been friends in years, either.

He shrugged, disinterested, but his smile betrayed him. "Why are you being so uptight? Everyone knows you'll do everything else. Even if the guys say you never go all the—"

"I need to pee," I said, and I made a critical mistake: I left my phone on the table.

But I wasn't thinking straight. I could hardly think at all.

I was sweating (it was hot) and dizzy (I hadn't had enough water). I collapsed onto the toilet lid and tried to breathe: in, out, in, in, in, in. Of course I'd heard the words guys used for me— *easy, slut, bitch*—as if they weren't doing the exact same things I was. As if they weren't doing them with me. For Cody to wield my reputation against me like that? *He was my friend.*

In, in, in, out. I splashed water on my face until I felt human again.

Then I stepped back onto the deck like nothing had happened. "I'm out," I said blandly, and reached for my phone. Hesitated. Had I left it face up on the picnic table? Was it tilted like that, or was it straight? Had the screen been that smudged with fingerprints?

Later, everyone would say I was asking for it. Why didn't I crop out my head? How come I set my passcode to my birthday— 0613—when it's so stupid easy to guess?

But I didn't know this. Not yet. Not even when Cody grinned, his fierce teeth gleaming, and said, "Let me know if you change your mind, JoJo."

"Don't worry." I slipped on my sunglasses. "I won't."

And I flipped him off.

It doesn't matter now. None of it mattered then, either. I told Maddie again and again that Cody was all hers, seriously, but I think she just wanted a reason to hate me.

As if I hadn't already given her plenty.

Hudson snatches his pencil back and taps the table. "I'm guessing it's not a great time to tell you Cody will be at Ben's party tonight?" *Taptap.* "Or that we'll be there, too?"

"No, Hudson. It's not."

-15-

Like hell I'm going to Ben Sulkin's party.

I pretend I'm down. Tell Hudson, *Sure, eight sounds great.*

As soon as he drops me home, I change into my rattiest yoga pants and an oversized T-shirt from a 5k I never ran. It has a huge hole in the armpit and a bleach stain on the boob, but who cares? No one is seeing me tonight.

Especially not Hudson.

It's just after seven, and soon I plan on developing truly hideous cramps, at which point I'll text Hudson that I'm *so bummed* about missing the party, let's try again never!

The kitchen is my sole destination tonight.

Finding something edible in my ex-chef father's fridge is deceptively risky. I've been burned before: chewy tripe, Bay Leaf's cat food. (That was potentially misguided curiosity on my part.) Once, I confused a ghost pepper for a sun-dried tomato and hurled on my lap.

I'm jabbing at a wedge of cheese (???) when the doorbell rings. I yell, "I'll get it," as if I'm not the only option. My mother probably just left the station, and Dad mans the fryers at the fish market on Fridays. In the basement, Lee is wincing through his physical therapy exercises.

I unlock the deadbolt and—

"Hey, babe," Hudson says, his elbow propped on the doorframe.

"Goodbye." I go to shut the door, but he slips past me, unzipping his coat. The cold sticks to his skin. "Hudson!"

He takes in the house with a whistle, then takes me in, too, looking me up and down. "Is that what you're wearing?"

"I'm not wearing anything."

"I don't think it's that kind of party."

"No, I'm not wearing anything because I'm not going."

"Why do you think I'm here? I knew you'd flake out," he says. Bay Leaf zooms into the foyer and stares with wide, wild eyes. He holds out his hand for her to sniff. "Bay, right?"

"Christian name Bay Leaf."

Bay purrs like a little motor and flops at his feet, biting his shoelaces. "That's adorable. It would be perfect for a chef's cat or—" Hudson straightens, too fast, and sends Bay skittering into the den. "Holy shit, your dad is Joseph Kirby. Holy *shit*. How did I never put that together?"

"Unsure. We literally have the same name."

Hudson lowers his voice. "Can I see his knives?"

"I don't think you can ask a girl to see her dad's knives."

His mouth drops, awed, when he steps in the kitchen. "I can't wait to tell the other cooks I'm fake-dating Joseph Kirby's daughter." Hudson inspects the fridge, then my face. "I'm a line cook at Flower City Diner. Opening shift. Pertinent information?"

"Well, it explains the coffee addiction. Is that why you missed first period yesterday?"

He shuts the fridge. "No, I had, uh. Therapy."

"Oh." That feels like the wrong response. Like, I'm not in therapy, and I don't need to be, but good for him. "Dead mom, deadbeat dad—totally understandable."

Something happens I don't expect: Hudson laughs. He laughs, and it is full and pure, his head thrown back, mouth open so wide I can see the slight overlap of his canine teeth.

From the basement, a dumbbell thuds.

Hudson nods toward the door. "Should we invite Lee to the party?"

I might fight harder if my mother—my *mother*—didn't enter the kitchen. (How did I miss the headlights? Her keys in the door?) Just like that, she transforms into Kate Kirby, Channel 12, with her winning grin. "Jo-Lynn, I didn't know you had a friend coming over."

"He's not my friend," I say. Hudson pops a smile at me. "This is—"

"Hudson?" Lee emerges from the basement, swiping back his sweat-soaked hair.

"Yes. So, Hudson here is, uh . . ." I clamp onto his bicep, startled by how firm it is, and I do something horrible: I squeeze. His bicep. *I squeeze his bicep.* "He's . . . my . . . boyfriend."

Lee makes a face. My mother stays steady.

It takes me four, five, six seconds of silence to realize, horrified, that I'm still clinging to him. I snap back my hand. "I'll meet you upstairs, okay? Lee can show you where my room is."

Hudson nods at my mother. "It's great to meet you, Ms. Kirby. Big fan."

"Kate is fine, sweetie," she says, and sorry, who *is* this woman? Her lovely smile lingers as Hudson follows Lee upstairs but collapses when she turns to me. "That door stays open at all times." I drop my head to the counter. "Sit up, Jo-Lynn. This is your first boyfriend."

An unspoken question lingers: *Is this your first boyfriend?*

Unless you count Gabe Figueroa, editor in chief of *The Eagle Eye*, in eighth grade, then I guess. I am not a girl who has boyfriends. Before, I just had fun. I'd do a lot, but not everything, ever, and I didn't expect anything more than what those guys had to give, which was nothing.

My mother (Kate?) grins again. "He's *cute*. Why didn't you tell me?"

Tell her. I flinch, blinking hard, like I've been struck by an electric shock. We don't talk about this shit. I haven't even thought those words—*tell her, tell her*—in years. It's not like it did me any good back then. "Why would I tell you anything?" I snap. I'm halfway up the steps when she shouts about the open door, like she wants Hudson to hear it, too.

Judging by his face, he does. "Your mom is nice."

I shut the door and flop onto my bed.

"You know, this isn't how I pictured your bedroom."

My bedroom is kind of beautiful, honestly: pale pink walls and a shag rug under the four-poster bed, a peach-patterned duvet, gold lamps that give the space a warm glow. Dad helped me redo it for my sixteenth birthday. I'd been having trouble sleeping, and I was so sick of staring at the stupid glow-in-the-dark stars on my ceiling until two, three, four in the morning.

I sit up. "Why are you picturing my bedroom?"

"No reason. So, what should you wear tonight?" Hudson opens my closet door, and right there, right up front, is my godforsaken prom dress. His fingers graze the skirt. Now I'm thinking about the last time he touched that dress—the tulle, the embroidered daisies.

"I'll find something," I say, strained.

He shuts my closet and tries the next door. "Hold up, you have your own bathroom?" His steps dislodge the showerhead off the hook. He nods back at me. "Overuse?"

"What?"

"Oh. Sorry, it was a, uh, masturbation joke." Hudson blushes, but mine is worse. "That's a thing, yeah? Kathleen has mentioned it. It'll be a bonding point."

I have so many questions. "I'm not going to bond with her over—"

"Jo-Lynn, what did I tell you?" my mother asks from my now-open door.

Hudson smiles. "I'm sorry, Kate." *Kate.* I hate him for it. "Some pals are having a small thing tonight, so we were actually about to head out."

"It's not a *small thing.* It's a party—a big, huge, raging house party," I clarify. "Drinking, drugs. Hudson was going to teach me how to do whippets."

"I don't know how to do whippets," he adds.

To my mother, I mouth: *Say no.* She nods like she gets it. Then she beams at Hudson and says, "Have her home by midnight."

Cars line the street when we arrive.

I take my sweet time toward the door, stepping in Hudson's footprints. He catches on and widens his stride, so I jump to match, saying, "Isn't it profoundly fucked to be throwing a party? Like, Maddie is missing"—*kidnapped, dead*—"and now everyone is going on like nothing even happened"—*because nothing happened*—"including her boyfriend?"

Including us.

Hudson sighs. "It's fucked," he says, and opens the door anyway.

This scene has a funhouse effect, like how the Channel 12 newscasters looked so uncanny at my first holiday party, people I'd only seen on TV come to life.

Here, One-L Daniele captures the scene on her camera. *Click.* Gabe Figueroa making out with his boyfriend by the stereo. *Click.* James Quinn, that St. Ignatius quarterback, pouring tequila shots. *Click.* April Kirk hurriedly talking up at Miles Metcalf, who frowns.

My throat tightens when I see him, his words from earlier still fresh. "Who invited—?" I shut up. I belong here less than they do.

But I *used* to belong. If I squint, I can still see it. There I am, taking aim in a game of beer pong. There, batting my lashes for a hit off a joint. There I am letting some guy—any guy—take my hand and lead me somewhere a little more private.

Here I am, letting Hudson lead me into the living room.

Ben lazes on the chaise lounge with a red plastic cup. I recognize some guys from the St. Ignatius soccer team, and Alexis Fitch, that sophomore who's been hanging all over Cody—the missing girl's boyfriend.

Cody's lounging on the leather couch, his feet kicked onto the coffee table, head bent over his phone. His eyes flick up, fast, then back down to his screen.

Hudson reaches into his pocket and fishes out his own phone. His jaw tenses.

I try to peek. "What did he—?"

"This is why you've been busy?" Cody says it to Hudson but tips his bottle at me. *This.*

Hudson frowns. "I've been busy?"

"Feel like I never see you anymore, man." Cody takes a long sip of beer. "But I'm seeing you now, right? I'm impressed your piece of shit made it over here."

"Bro, I've had to chauffer your ass all week; don't start about cars." Ben snorts, dribbling jungle juice down his chin. He's too drunk to register Cody's glare, but I'm not.

Neither is Hudson. "Something wrong with your car?"

"Routine maintenance," Cody says, yawning. Jesus, his girlfriend is *missing,* and he's—

"—see Jo is here?"

I swivel my head. I don't know who said that. It could be anyone; everyone stares. I hear nothing but whispers now: *Jo. Jo. Hudson. Here. Nudes. Look. Jo. Maddie. Gone. Jo. There.*

"I'm getting a drink," I tell Hudson, and force my way onto the deck.

Trey Gardner, catcher on the Culver baseball team, sits on the railing, off-balance but laughing. He's tall and jacked, with a shock of bleached curls. He tips back farther, farther. Some Lourdes girls shriek until he rights himself.

Wait, is that Jo?

The keg is courtesy of someone's older brother. Doesn't matter whose. What matters is that, undoubtedly, someone has an older brother with a fondness for high school and a fake ID.

And she came with Hudson?

Beer cans spill out of a plastic beach cooler. They stocked the most undrinkable options: Natty Light, Keystone, Labatt. The hard stuff is on the snowy picnic table. I pick up a bottle, the liquor inside a horrific pink.

God, I'd never show my face again.

I take a swig and—watermelon vodka. I *hate* watermelon. Loathe it. I rush to the railing and spit, gagging. Someone says, "That girl is so gross," and I don't know if they mean the spit or the photos or what, but a different word in a different voice rings in my head: *Disgusting.*

"It's so sad about her," another girl says.

I rest my forehead on the railing. It sways with Trey's motion: back, forward, back.

"Did you see her post about NYU? I thought I'd die from secondhand embarrassment."

Not me. *Maddie.*

I lift my head. Two Lourdes girls huddle by the heat lamp, warming their fingers. One is blonde with a beret pinned in her hair. The other is so tall.

"I'd seriously kill myself," the blonde says, laughing. "Wait, I got a screenshot."

Not thinking, I rip the phone from her hand, and there it is: Maddie's Instagram post. It's a picture of Washington Square Park—too touristy, out of focus. The photo a girl would take on her campus visit to NYU. It's captioned, "I took a risk when I applied to one school, my DREAM school, and today my dream—"

The Lourdes girl snatches her phone back. "Manners, Jo."

"I want to see it." I need to see it.

James Quinn appears from nowhere and slings his arm over my shoulder. "I got you," he says, scrolling through his photos. He grins and flips the screen out, and it's—

"Jo!" Sara Caruso turns my face toward hers. "I've been looking all over for you!"

Michaela Russell angles herself beside me. "So glad we found you," she says, tugging me toward the sliding door. I look to the heat lamp—to James and the Lourdes girls laughing, hard.

"Ignore those assholes," Michaela says once we're inside. "Seriously."

I nod, a little whiplashed. "Thanks for the rescue, I guess."

Sara dusts snow from my elbow. "Consider it my gratitude for yesterday. The reporter? Kathleen is always on me for having a big mouth, so that would *not* have . . ." She shuts up, like that reveal revealed too much. "Besides, someone had to be on Jo Patrol."

"Jo Patrol?" I repeat.

Sara cringes, her face scrunched, and Michaela shoots her a fierce glare. She turns to me, sheepish, and says, "It's really nothing. Like, we used to designate someone to be on Jo Patrol at parties and . . . look out for you."

My skin prickles with heat; it could light me on fire. "Why the fuck are you guys here?"

I'm saying it to be cruel. Their best friend is missing, and they're at a *party*. (My ex-best friend is missing, and I'm at a party.) But only now, when their faces fall, do I notice the pajama pants and baggy sweatshirts: SUNY Purchase for Sara; Syracuse for Michaela.

Fast, Sara says, "We were just hanging out, and then Kathleen saw on Instagram that—"

"I *know* he's here," Kathleen says, crashing into us. I've never seen her look so flustered—no makeup, hair mussed. Her eyes lock on Trey Gardner on the deck, and she's gone again.

"I'll get her," Michaela mumbles, and now it's just me and Sara . . . and her big mouth.

I ease a little closer. "What's happening out there?"

"Trey plagiarized Kathleen's English midterm. Allegedly," Sara adds. An image flashes in my memory: red words, *Kathleen, please see me*, underlined twice. "He obviously did it, but he keeps denying it. Wait, but the worst part"—the big mouth thing really is accurate—"is that Lund threatened to expel them if they get another honor code violation."

I look toward the deck: Kathleen, furious, right in Trey's face. He plays dumb, holding up both hands, and she jabs a finger at his chest. Trey wobbles and tilts backward and, *shit*, we all go silent and still and—he catches himself.

Sara exhales, scrambling onto the deck. I'm over this. All of it. I want Hudson to take me home, now. He's not in the kitchen, so I try the dining room, then the den, then—

I circle back to the den.

Clare O'Mara, Kathleen's sister, stares warily into a plastic cup by the fireplace. She's in thermal pajamas, so I guess the Birds dragged her along? They should be watching her, right?

Ben Sulkin spots her first. He's so drunk that he sways, staggers up to her. "I don't think I know you," he slurs, and slides his hand along her lower back.

Bile shoots up my throat.

"Hey!" I'm yanking Clare's arm, pulling her back from Ben, before I can process it. Her drink sloshes down my jeans, and she gasps, mortified. I say, "It's okay. Let's find your—"

"Clare?" Kathleen nudges me aside. Looks between us, her expression unreadable. Then she takes the cup and her sister's hand and leads her away.

My face goes hot. *Clare Patrol.* But she was only holding the drink; I was the sloppy girl, and I didn't even know it. I hate that. I hate even more how Ben towers over me. There's always been something ghostly about him—translucent pale skin, black eyes.

He grabs my wrist. "What the hell, JoJo?"

"That hurts," I say, and he tightens his grip.

It didn't surprise me how swiftly Ben turned on me after the bonfire. He never liked me all that much, and the guy is just an asshole. At parties, he'd get drunk, then he'd get rough, picking fights and throwing punches, cackling. Sometimes he'd put me in a headlock as a joke—*take a joke*—and I'd wake the next day with bruises on my neck.

He growls, "I was *talking* to her, JoJo. Is that a crime? What did you *think* I was doing?"

I . . . don't know. My chest is so tight. Too tight. The music is too loud, and it's too hot, and it's too much. I wrench my wrist free, push into the hall, almost collide with Hudson. His mouth turns down, brows knitting, but I speak first: "Did you know about Jo Patrol?"

The panicked look on his face tells me all I need to know.

I shove past him and fling open the basement door. Ben deemed the space off-limits after Cody accidentally cracked the plasma TV with a golf club sophomore year. Half the basement is unfinished, strewn with paint cans and free weights. I sink onto the tattered sectional and drop my head in my hands. I can't do this. I can't. I—

"What's up, JoJo?"

Cody. *Shit.* I twist to face him. It might be the single buzzing bulb, but he looks hardened. Older. He's always been boyish: crooked teeth, wild strawberry blond hair.

"Party sucks," he says blandly.

"Yeah, I wonder why."

Cody ignores the comment and wanders over to the foosball table. We've destroyed this thing over the years, splitting the handles, denting the plastic balls. One of us, I can't remember who, scribbled a penis on the goalie's crotch. He digs a ball from the slot return. "Want to play?"

"No."

"Humor me, JoJo."

So, Cody is red. I'm blue.

He drops the ball on the field, and we crouch, getting into position. "I feel like things are weird between us."

"Why do you think that is?" I ask.

Cody never hid what he did to me. Like, his name and number

were *right there*. I was terrified for weeks afterward that I'd get summoned to the office and be forced to admit that, yes, those were my photos. But nothing ever happened.

"I don't want things to be weird, JoJo. Especially if you're with *Hudson*," he says. Maybe I'm stuck on how terse he sounded in their texts, but I could almost swear he spits the name.

"Do you have an issue with him or something?"

"No, I have an issue with *you*." Cody jerks his neck to the left, then the right—his worst nervous habit. "Or with what you . . . know."

"What I know?" I flick the ball to his player instead of my own.

This is what I know about Cody Forsythe: I know that he eats Buffalo wings with ranch instead of blue cheese. I know he believed in Santa until middle school. I know that his favorite birthday gift ever was a karaoke machine from yours truly.

I know Miles Metcalf cheats for him.

"You and Miles," I say. Their stupid arrangement. The secret Cody revealed to me, drunk, which I kept for months until the bonfire, when I threw it back at him, even drunker.

He looks to the ceiling. Like anyone could hear us down here. The stereo is cranked to its max, the bass vibrating the pipes. Something shatters—that handle of watermelon vodka?

"Think I'll rat you out?" It feels good to taunt him.

His player clips the ball, just missing my goal. "I don't think you will. In fact, I know you won't. What you have on me is bad, but what I have on you is worse." His eyes tick to mine, and he smiles, his face hollow under the lights. "Right, *Jolie*?"

Everything stops for a second.

Low, I ask, "What do you want?"

"I want a truce. I'll keep your secret if you keep mine." Because he'd tell in a heartbeat. I threatened him with his cheating, but he got me back first. The photos were a warning shot: *I can do worse, and I will.* Cody extends his hand, his skin cracked, chapped from the cold. "So?"

So, we shake.

And when he lets go, I yank the knob and shoot. *Score.*

"Damn, JoJo." Cody raises his beer at me. "Nice shot."

-16-

Hudson asked for one good reason to end this thing—our fake relationship, the investigation into what the hell happened to Maddie—but I can do better. I've got ten.

1. Cody Forsythe, who's back to being my friend, my bud, my old pal.

   First thing Monday, he finds me and Hudson before first period and yanks me into a hug, his elbow hooked around my neck—not a chokehold but almost. He growls, "Don't forget about our truce, JoJo," his breath hot on my ear.

   "Let me go, or I'll knee you in the balls."

   He releases me with a grin. "I'm glad we're good again," he says, so loud, all eyes on us. Just like he wanted. He wants everyone to know our story: *Jo and Cody are good again, so that means ~~Jo forgave Cody~~ Jo got over it.*

   Teeth gritted, I say, "I am, too."

   I hate myself for it. I hate how the threat of our truce looms like a sky on the verge of a storm. I hate the uneasy way

Hudson says, "That was weird," when Cody departs without a word to him.

I hate that it's another game I'm letting Cody win.

2. Michaela Russell and Sara Caruso, two-thirds of the Birds.

They accost me at my desk—last row, back corner—before AP Econ. (We have a sub, so she doesn't know they don't belong back here.) In absolute, perfect unison, they say, "Hey!"

"Oh, that was creepy." Sara tugs her plastic peach earrings. "Mic, you go."

Michaela faces me straight on. Electric blue liner rims her rich brown eyes. "We wanted to apologize. For Jo Patrol. Even if we had good intentions, it clearly hurt you—"

"Jesus, I wasn't *hurt*." I laugh, the sound scraping my throat.

"It wasn't a judgment against you," Sara says, but it was, wasn't it? My reputation with the guys was almost expected, but I had no clue the girls saw something worse in me.

That to them, I was a dumb drunk girl who needed protection.

I was prey.

Heat blooms up my neck. "I knew what I was doing. Like, I'd never let myself get—"

"Ladies," the substitute says, dropping a pop quiz on my desk.

Two rows up, the Spencer twins frown at the paper, then at each other. Kyle or Tyler raises his hand, and so does that jackass Jack Parker. Someone, somewhere, whispers, "Is this right?"

"We're still sorry," Sara says. "Really."

"I knew what I was doing," I say again, balling my sleeves into my fists. "But thank you. For apologizing." I release my hands. Flex my fingers. "I don't need you to be nice to me."

Michaela flips a hand through her braids. "We've never hated you, Jo."

"Just Maddie and Kathleen?"

The girls say nothing to that.

3. Ben Sulkin, who snaps my locker shut before lunch.

I redial the combination. "Really?"

"Really?" he mimics. (It sounds nothing like me. It isn't meant to.) He slams my shoulder with his, laughing all down the hall, like this is such a clever bit—the joke of a jock bully from a teen comedy. He just needs a letterman jacket.

I touch my wrist. The one he twisted at his party. I've never seen Ben and Maddie speak beyond standard pleasantries: *sorry, thanks, sure.* But he's capable of hurting someone. The way he treats me. The way he looked at—

"Clare."

"Hi. Here." She hands me a sticky note with ten bucks fixed to the adhesive. It reads, *I'm sorry about your jeans.* "I thought you could use the money for, um, dry cleaning."

"You're good, Clare." I hand the bill back. "Are you? Good?"

She gives me a small smile. "I'm good."

"Good." I turn to my locker, but I can't remember what I need. I need to not look at her. I need a . . . library pass. Conti gave me a bunch of blank passes not long into my academic review to reduce my frequent (read: annoying) visits to his office. I fan out the stack and think of Clare's stamp and say, "There is something else you can do for me, though."

4. *I think that I'm in trouble, but I think that you can help me.*
   The words Maddie said to me exactly one week ago.
   But I think she was mistaken.

5. The hottest forum on College Confidential: "NYU Class of 1316!"
   It's almost midnight, and I'm half-asleep, my face pressed to my calculus textbook, when One-L Daniele texts me the link and an *FYI*. I don't get why.
   Not until I navigate to the first post on the first page.

   Welcome! This is the OFFICIAL thread for the 1,316 victims of the NYU ED2 admissions scandal. Feel free to post your stats! Nothing matters!

   "Holy shit," I say, and scare Bay off my bed. I skim the outrage, the heartbreak, the threats to sue NYU, then skip to the most recent page. If this was For My Information, it must mean—
   Have y'all seen this?? Some ED2 girl RAN AWAY???
   The user linked a News 9 article and a screenshot of *that*

post. The one Maddie put on her socials. Like her acceptance solved her troubles, or maybe like there was never any trouble at all.

I scroll through the replies: *How sad. How dumb. Hopefully she's okay. Obviously she's fine. Clearly she just couldn't cut it.*

6. Miles Metcalf, who jogs after me Tuesday morning and shouts, "Jo! Can we please—?"
    "No."

7. The details of the official rank announcement, of which there are currently none.
    "Not even a projected date?" Hudson asks for the third time. He dragged me to the office before lunch, but Mrs. Fitzgerald informed us that Lund and Conti were booked, sorry.
    For the third time, Fitzgerald says, "You'll receive your rank when you receive it."
    "Can I *please* just talk to Principal Lund?"
    Right on cue, her door opens. "I hope this was a learning experience for you both," she says coolly. Kathleen exits first, a rolled paper in her clenched fist, followed by—
    "Oh my God," I gasp, as Hudson says, "What happened to you?"
    Trey Gardner sheepishly lifts his left arm—the one in the sling—and winces. His face is scabbed and bruised. His skin

shines with antibiotic ointment. "I, uh, kind of fell off the deck at Ben's party the other night."

I can see it: Trey drunkenly leaning back on that railing to make the Lourdes girls shriek, a court jester who can't tell the difference between laughing *with* and laughing *at*. I see Kathleen, too, her face furious, her finger jabbing his chest.

Because Trey (allegedly) stole her midterm and could get them both expelled.

"Did you push him?" I ask.

"Nope." Kathleen rips her midterm in half. "But I hope someone did."

8. Mr. Price's ugly midlife crisis car parked across the street. Still.

My mother smokes on the front stoop after dinner. "Do we think Geoff moved back for good?" she calls through the open door. "Or until—?"

"Kate, please," Dad says, but I want to hear the rest.

Until Maddie comes home? Until Maddie is found, alive or—?

9. Hudson Harper-Moore, my horrible fake boyfriend.

Today is Wednesday. It is also Valentine's Day. Kill me.

Just outside the cafeteria, a bunch of juniors in the jazz ensemble hold up cans of orange soda, shouting, "One dollar to send a Crush to your crush!"

"Oh, I'm so getting you one." Hudson drops two bucks

into an empty cheese puffs tub and sifts through the valentines. "Don't look."

"I hate orange soda," I say, not looking.

Not until he slips a heart-shaped valentine—green, my favorite color—into my palm.

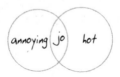

I'm legitimately blushing.

10. My fucked-up sleep schedule. Maddie—*missing, kidnapped, dead*—haunts me when I wake in the night. *Missing, kidnapped, dead. Missingkidnappeddead.* The words beat in my heart like a drum, louder and louder, until I swear I hear—

I *do* hear something. The hum of Lee's voice.

[2:22 a.m.] **JO**: who are you talking to?

He never replies, but everything goes quiet after that.

So, yes, I'm dumping Hudson.

It'd be easier if he were, you know. *Here.*

That noise in his car—metal grinding on metal—has gotten worse, so he ditched to take it to the shop, which means he abandoned me in the cafeteria. It took about two minutes for Ben to "accidentally" shake his leftover Crush and open it in my direction.

Reason #11: I'm scrubbing orange soda from my white sweater.

I'm half-dressed, but I don't cover myself when the bathroom door opens. (I used to wear this bra as a crop top anyway.) Lifting my eyes to the mirror, I say, "Oh, good. It's you."

"I'm just washing my hands." Kathleen pumps a palmful of soap from the dispenser. She glances at me—what I'm doing—but says nothing.

"Any clue how to get orange soda out of a white sweater?" I ask.

"Nope."

"Okay, any clue how to masturbate with a detachable shower-head?" I ask, and she whips her head toward me. "Hudson told me you're the expert, but I don't really get the mechanics."

She smacks off the faucet. "What are you doing?"

"Making casual conversation and trying to get this stain out."

"No, what are you *doing*? You get with Hudson, and now you're buddying up to Sara and Michaela? Trying to bond with me? We're not friends, Jo," Kathleen practically snarls. "I'm not interested in *being* your friend."

Heat crawls up toward my jaw.

How can it still sting this much? That peculiar pang of long-ing. I fell in so easily with the boys, even as a kid, but I couldn't figure out the other girls. Suddenly I'm nine, and I have wood chips in my shoes, and everyone got invited to the roller rink but me.

Or I'm fifteen, and my best friend didn't tell me about her pool party.

The mortifying thing is that the less Kathleen likes me, the more I want her to.

She barely acknowledges me. Rarely speaks to me. She speaks, instead, around me, like the wind will catch her words and blow them toward me. When I look at her for even a second too long, she'll hold my gaze until I break.

I'm always the first to break.

"You don't even know me." It's the exact thing a pathetic, friendless girl would say.

"I know enough."

"Yeah? What did Maddie tell you?"

For the first time ever, maybe, I shut up Kathleen. I don't know when she and Maddie became friends—true, real, actual friends—but on our first day of tenth grade, they walked the halls with their elbows linked, best friends forever. Like I'd never even existed.

Like that one year we were friends meant nothing.

"It's not hard to figure you out," Kathleen says finally. She eases her hip onto the sink. I wonder if she knows I posed like that in one of those six photos. "You're not *like* other girls."

My heart ticks harder. "Excuse me?"

"We're too much drama, and we're shallow, but you get along better with guys, anyway, right? Because you're so cool. That's what they tell you. You're *different*. Is that it?" Kathleen nods, like she knows I have nothing to say. "I thought so."

Even though I watch her leave, I startle when the door slams. I lock eyes with the girl in the mirror. It's the most skin I've shown in months: a strip of midriff, exposed collarbones, nonexistent cleavage.

What the fuck am I doing? Why am I seeking approval from a girl who's clearly made up her mind about me? Waiting for Cody to break our truce? Maddie is gone, and if she ran—which she did—then she probably doesn't want to be found, so the best thing I can do is nothing.

I fling open the door. I'll grab my bag, text Hudson, end this once and for—

"Do you think this is an appropriate outfit, Miss Kirby?" Conti traces the outline of my body with his walkie-talkie. His sneer is less a threat than a taunt. *I'll let you off with a warning, but don't go speeding again, you hear?*

And I don't even fight. I just pull on the damp sweater.

His mustache ticks up. "Good girl."

It makes me want to throw up.

Everyone else in the hall laughs, Ben hardest of all.

"Something funny, Sulkin?" I sidle up beside him. He stops laughing. "From now on, you will not look at or touch or speak to me ever again. Understand?"

Ben sputters out a breath. "Relax, JoJo."

"*Relax, Ben,*" I mimic. "I'm so sick of you. All of you!" I point at Sara and Michaela and say, "You two are okay. But *you*"—I get right in Kathleen's face—"I don't care if you like me. I don't *want* you to like me. You may think I'm a stupid girl who got what was coming for her, but you're no better than me, Kathleen."

Because I changed my mind: I will not be scared off by these assholes.

I throw up my arms. "Anyone else?"

Behind me, a fake cough. Principal Lund. She extends an envelope marked *Jo-Lynn*.

I unseal the envelope and pull out a . . . napkin.

Dear Jo-hyphen-Lynn Kirby,

You're in.

Sincerely,
Tess Spradlin

-17-

Per the guidelines of the Senior Experience, I'll spend five hours a week with Tess Spradlin, plus a half day with the rest of the cohort for site visits to each mentor's place of work. There will be reflections to write, posters to prepare, a capstone to present.

Unfortunately, the program is beyond tedious.

Fortunately, I love dicking around during school hours.

When Principal Lund calls me to her office to sign my contract, she says, "I'm making an exception, but that doesn't make you exceptional, Jo-Lynn. All eyes are on you."

I say, "Got it," and doodle a smiley face next to my signature.

Back home, Dad is so elated that he signs my slips without a glance at the rules—or the terms of my academic probation that I "forgot" to get signed last week.

"*You* got in? Wait." Lee unmutes his laptop, then mutes it again; the kitchen counter is his Italian 201 classroom since *la biblioteca* was too crowded. "How did *you* get in?"

"Dad, Lee is bullying me."

"Stop bullying your sister," Dad says. "This is so fantastic, Jo."

It is, isn't it? I may be hopeless, a lost cause, but Tess Spradlin chose me. *Me.*

The one issue: I have no clue why.

The next day—Friday, my first day—I'm signing my name on the *ROC Weekly* visitor log when Tess emerges from the stairwell.

She spreads her arms wide, a model showing off a brand-new car. "Welcome! It sucks."

I slap my name tag to my chest. "Glad to be here."

"This way. I take the elevator up but the stairs down." Pause. "I have more insight than 'I take the elevator up but the stairs down,' I promise."

The elevator chugs to the fifth floor—the *ROC Weekly* newsroom. Tess explains that the magazine rents space from the local public broadcasting affiliate, then asks, "Is this more or less boring than the elevator thing?"

Still, I whistle when we exit. The newsroom is enormous, open concept with sleek white desks, exposed steel beams, and gunmetal gray walls. I step up to the windows. You can see the minor league baseball stadium and the old Kodak building from here.

"Great view," I say.

"*Gray* view. Follow me." Tess points out the broken copier and the closet full of branded swag, where she grabs me a stress ball, a lanyard, and four foam beer sleeves.

For our last stop, she leads me behind a mesh partition to her messy desk. The surface is stacked with tattered notepads, the pages water-warped. She pulls up a white leather cube for me, then rolls out a yoga ball from under her desk.

"Cool ball," I say.

"Thanks. I turned twenty-eight last month, so now I get back pain when I sit too long."

"This mentorship is so informative."

Tess presses her hands flat to her desk. "I really volunteered to let a teenager bully me."

"This is your punishment for picking me." I say it like a joke, but I'm really asking, *Why did you pick me?* I want to know. I want to know why she picked me and not Maddie, and I hate that it feels like a competition even when Maddie's not here.

Tess undoes her messy bun. "Look, Jo-hyphen-Lynn—"

"Yo, Spradlin!" shouts some guy, flicking a fountain pen on a flimsy suede notebook. He's short, with grayish hair and a baby face. Mid-twenties? Middle-aged? Who can say. He's wearing checkered slip-ons and a T-shirt for a band I've never heard of. "Rad meeting, huh?"

Tess redoes her messy bun. "I'm busy, Justin."

He pretends to notice me for the first time. "Oh, I forgot you had a *visitor* today. Justin Lloyd." He juts out his hand, the pen flinging to my lap. I bypass his handshake to pass it back, and he says, "Can't lose my lucky pen. You go to Spradlin's old high school, right?"

"Did you want something?" Tess asks loudly.

"I want the dead girl. The Price story."

Dead girl. Maddie Price, missing, kidnapped, dead girl. My heart starts, stutters, beats a rhythm to the word—*dead, dead, dead.*

"There's nothing to suggest that Maddie is . . . not alive, and you know it." Tess is looking at him, but she means it for me.

I haven't told Tess about Maddie and me, our ex-friendship, but she saw us in action at the meet and greet. "I thought I made it clear that she's off the pitch list."

"Then what were you writing earlier?" He points to a teal folder under her keyboard.

Tess keeps still. "We'll talk later."

"Fine, fine." He taps his pen on my shoulder. "Later, girl from Spradlin's high school."

"Bye, Jason," I call after him. His steps falter for a second, then he goes for good.

"Brutal," Tess says. "His name is Justin."

Oops. "He said Maddie was—"

"Ignore him. That man is our music writer, and he got the job because his mommy heads our business office. He's not touching this story," Tess says, serious. "It's *not* a story."

"Because she ran away." It comes out hollow.

Tess sighs, readjusting her glasses. "This is a pretty white girl from an upper-middle-class family. If something nefarious happened, she'd be dominating cable news. But she's not. The simplest story is that Maddie ran away." She fusses with a potted cactus, its buds dead, slick with rot. "Except it's those simple stories you risk telling wrong—by not going deep enough, I mean."

I frown. "I don't get it."

"It means you can know *what* happened, but not why." *Why did Maddie run?* "Or how it unfolded." *How did she vanish, and where the hell did she go?* Tess shifts on the ball, searching for her next words. "Maddie struggled with this in her writing sample for the program. She was fine on the line level, but she told her stories wrong."

I still don't get it. "But *she* isn't a story? You're not looking into it?"

"No," Tess says firmly, tucking the teal folder in the top drawer of her desk. "Look, you want to get coffee? I'll expense it to my company card."

I slide my phone onto the leather cube. "Coffee would be cool."

As promised, we take the stairs down. I stop at the second-floor landing and fake a gasp, patting down my pockets. "Shoot, I forgot my phone upstairs. Meet you in the lobby!"

Then I sprint up to the newsroom, grab my phone, try that top drawer.

It's locked. Of course. I feel in my hair for a bobby pin, as if I've ever once picked a lock before, and also, I don't even wear bobby pins. There's an open slat above the lock, and I think my hand can fit if I slide . . .

It can.

Inside the teal folder: a printed email from Maddie, marked up with pen. I angle the sheet and snap a photo with my phone, then return the original to her folder, return the folder to the drawer, start to—

"Tess?"

I drop to the floor. Ease under the desk, ease my face onto the carpet. Peer through the gap under the front panel and—oh, shit. Checkered canvas shoes. *Jason.* Justin?

"Tess?" he says again, all for show. "You back here?"

He lets himself behind her desk, his foot inches from mine. Metal rings. That drawer, unlocking. Justin has a key. Should he have a key? He pulls out the folder, opens it, *hmph*s.

Then—*click*—the shutter sound of his phone's camera.

I count sixty seconds, one minute exactly, before the drawer rolls closed. I watch from the gap again: Justin setting the notebook at a desk before pushing into the bathroom.

Go.

I crawl out from under Tess's desk, run across the newsroom, and steal the notebook. His stupid pen, too. I slip into the stairwell, flip through the notebook pages: grocery lists, half-baked notes about local bands, an ugly sketch of an eye. *Price girl.* I tear out the page and stuff it in my pocket, then I chuck the notebook over the railing.

I'm out of breath when I get to the lobby. "Sorry! I saw Jason. He was looking for you."

Tess frowns. "He was?"

"Yeah, he wanted something from your desk. I think he mentioned Maddie?"

Then Tess Spradlin—who is not looking into Maddie Price—smacks the up arrow at the elevator and mumbles, "Give me a second."

Because I think, maybe, she is.

-18-

The page burns in my pocket. I haven't read it yet. Haven't had a chance. Tess returned from her desk without a word about Justin Lloyd or that teal folder, then treated me to an iced coffee, so now I'm both anxious and very, very caffeinated.

Buzzing, vibrating out of my skin, I text Hudson to meet me in the back stairwell when I get to Culver—and no, not to make out on the fifth-floor landing, which is its typical purpose.

He's sitting on the steps when I kick open the door. "Hey! How'd it—?"

"I have *clues*."

"Clues?"

I sit. "My mentor is an editor, right? Tess. I guess Maddie came up as a pitch." *The dead girl.* I shake my head, then shake out the page, say, "Tess said it's not a story, but she was being weird, and so was this other reporter. Jason or Justin. I ripped this from his notebook."

There are three notes: *fundraiser*, circled; a number with a 212 area code; *RECORDS???*

"Okay, so 'fundraiser' could be that donation page," I offer. "The one that got deleted."

Hudson nods, thinking. "Did her parents make it? Because it feels gross if they knew—or suspected—she'd run away and still asked for donations."

It does. Mrs. Price claims she never saw Maddie's note—where *is* the note?—but even if she did, even if she hid it, she'd taken out photos to make a missing poster. She obviously wants to find her daughter. Then Mr. Price is . . . also there.

"Someone must remember," Hudson says. "Daniele? Daniele knows everything."

I heave a sigh. "Unfortunately, I know who else might."

[1:13 p.m.] **JO:** who created maddie's fundraiser?
[1:14 p.m.] **KATE KIRBY** 👧 🖥️: Her dad's cousin. Why?

Hudson peers at my screen. "Tell Kate hi for me."

"Shut up, Hudson." I look back to the page. "What about 'records'? Medical? Vinyl?"

"Probably not vinyl. Let me see that number." He types in the area code. "Oh, shit. New York City."

"Call it, call it, call it."

Hudson dials. Listens. Pulls the phone from his ear with a frown. "It's the main line for an architecture firm. Should I call back?"

"No!" I surprise us both with the forcefulness of it. I know why Justin-Jason would have that number—know who must work there—but I can't say. My throat tightens, a familiar feeling creeping up my spine. This cannot happen. Not here. Not in front of him. Instead, I say, "I bet he, uh. Messed up a digit. Wrong number, right?" I blink dots from my eyes. "Let's just . . ."

I open my photo of the email from Tess's folder and, cool, another goddamn number with the same 212 area code is scribbled at the bottom. Hudson dials on speaker this time: *Thank you for calling the NYU Undergraduate Admissions Office. If you know your party's extension—*

He hangs up. "That seems straightforward enough."

It's the simplest story: Maddie was sad about NYU, so she ran away.

Hudson nods at my phone. "Can you zoom in on the email?"

DATE: December 12, 10:43 a.m.

SUBJECT: Hello from a Culver journalist!

Hi, Miss Spradlin! My name is Maddie Price. I'm a senior at Culver Honors High School. Your alma mater! I applied to NYU (also your alma mater!) and should hear back mid-February. Until then, I'm hard at work on *The Eagle Eye*! Would you like to meet up? I'd love to pick your brain about something!

Sincerely,

Maddie Price

"That's a lot of exclamation points," Hudson says.

I reread the message. Fix on the date: December 12. The Senior Experience mentors were announced in early January, right after winter break, so Maddie either cold contacted Tess before anything was official—which, why?—or got the list of mentors from somewhere. The paper?

Standing, I say, "Let's talk to Gabe Figueroa," who's the editor in chief.

Hudson makes a face. "I'm not a huge fan of *The Eagle Eye*."

Because of the open letter about his rank. I gasp, "Wait, your rank! We don't know how it fits, right? Maybe Maddie found out something from the paper." I tug his arm. "Maybe she—"

He lets me pull him up. "Lead the way."

The Mr. Coffee in the newspaper lab sounds like it's about to barf. It gurgles, spits—seriously, that machine is ill. It reeks, too, the coffee burned and bitter. I fake a retch when we walk in.

"Out," Gabe says, monotone.

He and I dated for six weeks, which felt like a lifetime in middle school. Gabe wasn't my first kiss—that honor belongs to Isaiah Hilton, a St. Ignatius guy, on a triple-dog dare—but we'd practiced with tongue, like the whole thing was a science experiment.

Then Gabe dumped me over text. For Isaiah Hilton.

"Hello, Gabriel." I roll out a chair and daintily cross my legs.

He immediately stands. "State your business."

I did not think that far ahead. I look to Hudson for a little backup here, but he lowers onto a rolling chair, mumbling, "Sorry, the mechanic is texting about my car."

Gabe tenses the tiniest, tiniest bit when Hudson speaks—and it is exactly what I need.

"Is it awkward if Hudson is here?" I loudly whisper. "After what you did—"

"Oh, please." Gabe crosses to a set of lockers built into the back nook. Fitting a key into the padlock for the one marked Editor in Chief, he says, "*I* was not involved with that mess. It was . . ." His eyes shift to the locker left of his: Managing Editor.

Hudson practically throws down his phone. "Wait, Maddie did it?"

"Yes, and she got us in deep shit." Gabe tugs a tweed coat from the locker. "I told her not to run the letter. Ms. Clay"—the paper advisor—"told her not to run it. Maddie ran it. Snuck it in after both of us had already approved the paper for printing. It's irresponsible journalism." Gabe adds, "Don't get me wrong, I'd totally have run it if I could, but I have actual integrity."

"Why couldn't you run it?" I ask.

"We couldn't verify the sender," Gabe says, buttoning his coat. "It backfired on Maddie, so you get some justice, Hudson." He leans in, like he knows what I'll ask next. "Clay declined to write her a recommendation letter—and she *went* to NYU. For journalism."

I swivel in the chair. "Would that make a difference?"

"Uh, yeah, Jo. It'd certainly help. Like, I was shocked when Maddie posted she got in, so when it came out that she hadn't really, well . . ." Gabe shrugs. "That girl screwed herself over."

I turn to Hudson. He stares back, his arms crossed tight.

Those texts Maddie sent him—she blamed the rejection on him, right? It was obviously misdirected anger, but if he'd forfeited his rank, then she'd have been in the top 10 percent of our class. It must be why she was so desperate to get that letter printed.

Maddie *needed* a higher spot.

But why warn him—*you should've given it up before they take it*—if she was in on it? It makes no sense unless she ran the letter first, then found out . . . something. Something that proves this is about more than the number?

That it's about him?

Hudson's phone rings, and he swears, heads to the back of the lab to take it. Gabe slides his laptop into a neoprene sleeve and says, "Hey, tell your brother to check his damn email."

"Lee?"

"Do you have other brothers? The anniversary of the comeback game is next month, and I'm working on a retrospective with the major players. I need the MVP."

I simultaneously cross and roll my eyes.

The Culver Eagles were a middling team on the cusp of sectionals Lee's freshman year. He played only during garbage time until their starting point guard broke his ankle before the last qualifying game. My brother heeded the call—and nailed nine three-pointers. In a row.

The team immediately lost in the first round of sectionals, but still.

His hero status was locked down.

"Now, if you'll—" Gabe's phone buzzes with a video call from Isaiah. He says, "Both of you better be gone when I get back," and disappears into the hall.

The second he's gone, I go for the lockers in back. *Managing Editor* is marked on a strip of masking tape. A slip of paper pokes out of a slot in the locker door. I tug it out—a torn-off page scrawled with 1211. Her combination? But the small padlock takes a key. I crumple the scrap. "Shit."

"Shit," Hudson echoes, but I don't know if he even heard me.

He drops his head onto the table. "Sorry, I . . . my car is fucked. The shop is towing it back to my place, but—"

I pull out my phone. "What's your address?"

He sits upright again. "What? I don't really have people over. My house is pretty shabby." He runs his finger along a scratch in the tabletop. "And I feel like a dick that I get embarrassed, so."

"Noted. Address?"

Hudson eyes me, still skeptical, but he tells me.

-19-

Hudson doesn't speak on the bus. He also doesn't speak when we walk down his unplowed street or turn up the drive of a small yellow house with a FOR SALE sign staked in the yard.

I point. "You're moving?"

"Um, maybe." He unlatches the chain-link gate and leads us toward his pitiful dead SUV, parked in front of the garage. Popping the hood, he says, "Are you secretly a mechanic?"

"I'm not. But"—I nod at the car pulling in behind us—"he is."

Dad steps out with a grunt. He wears grease-stained jeans and a Carolina sweatshirt, his neck tattoos poking out of the collar. He gruffly says, "Heard there was a sick car out here."

Hudson might truly be speechless.

Maybe that's why I take his hand and say, "Dad, this is Hudson. My boyfriend." Since I can't be sincere for more than five seconds, I add, "And this is his shit car."

Dad shakes his free hand. "Joe."

"No, *I'm* Jo. You're Joseph."

"It's really great to meet you," Hudson says, finally remembering how to breathe.

Dad points to the car. "This the patient?" he asks. Hudson explains, which I tune out until Dad whistles at the mechanic's estimate: $4,000. He peers into the guts of the engine. "Let's see what the problem is. This is also the part where I interrogate you, right? Since you're dating my daughter?"

"I'd sure love it if you didn't, Dad."

He ignores me. "You're Hudson. You're tall. What about school? You applying?"

"No, I'm . . . not." Hudson deflates a little on that last word. I look up at him, but his eyes are downcast, fixed to a pothole in the pavement.

We've never broached the college thing outright. He's *so* smart; he could probably get a full ride to a SUNY school, or at least financial aid. If he'd wanted to apply, he would have, so I guess he just didn't want to. And it's not like I'm going to college, either.

I say, "Dad, Hudson works at Flower City Diner."

This gets Dad's attention far more than academics. "No fucking way! Best diner around."

Hudson scratches the back of his neck. "I'm only a line cook."

"Never say that again," Dad tells him, serious now. "There's no such thing as 'only a line cook,' understand?" Dad waits until Hudson nods, then he nods, too, jutting his chin toward the garage. "Got a stereo in there? Unless it will disturb your folks."

"Oh, no one is home. I live with my grandparents. They work second shift."

"They do?" I ask. If he leaves for the diner at dawn, it's like he functionally lives alone. I dig my hands into my pockets, shivering. "Can I go in? I'm cold."

Hudson holds out the key, too focused on my dad to even look at me.

The back door opens to the kitchen—small but cozy, the fridge humming. I settle at the table, unzipping my coat, rooting in my backpack for my physics homework. (Look at that, Mr. Conti!) I do two whole problems before I rest my head and shut my eyes and accidentally nap for, like, an hour.

Then a car horn blares and gives me a damn heart attack, and my phone is going off, too.

[4:20 p.m.] **UNKNOWN:** Hi! This is Sara. Some of us are going to the Barcade (ugh, I know) but you and Hudson should come 😊

Nice gesture, I guess, but it feels suspiciously like a pity invite.

I force myself up, groggy, and wander into the living room. The walls are bare, marked with pale squares where frames once hung. My steps rattle the photos on the mantel.

Hudson as a toddler looking extra serious.

His kindergarten school picture. He's missing both front teeth, and he wears dorky round glasses. I didn't even know he wore glasses. I linger on the date in the corner. That doesn't work unless he was . . . held back?

The last photo: Hudson at ten or eleven with his mom. She has a cute pixie cut, bleached platinum. She stoops so her chin rests on his skull. He's trying (poorly) not to smile.

The prayer card tucked in the frame reads: *In loving memory of Aubrey Harper-Moore.*

I don't pretend I'm not snooping when the back door creaks open and Hudson comes in.

"You were a cute kid," I say.

"Thanks." He drops onto the couch, fussing with a tear in the fabric. "What did you want to ask about first? Me repeating kindergarten or my dead mom?"

I consider this. "Kindergarten. You'd be young for the grade, anyway, right?" He turned eighteen in September. I remember he bought a bong and a non-winning scratch-off to celebrate.

"Yeah, but I was held back for, uh. Truancy. Our building flooded, so housing was kind of unstable for a few months." Hudson smacks his knees. "Anyway, I have good news and bad news. The good news is that your aunt came over, so she and your dad are going to work on my car until someone from her shop can swing by with a tow truck."

I perk up. "Aunt Leigh?" My brother's namesake.

Hudson combs back his hair, and only now do I notice the slow, lazy way he moves. The unmistakable smell of skunk. "The bad news," he says, "is that your dad's weed is potent."

"You got high with my *dad*?"

"Not on purpose!"

"Oh my God," I say, and then I storm outside. The oldies station blasts from a stereo in the open garage. I shout, "Dad! Also, hi, Aunt Leigh."

She vaguely waves, keeping her head under the hood, rooting around the engine. Beside her, Dad dutifully, uselessly holds a wrench. The man is truly blazed. It took me literal years to realize his glazed, bloodshot eyes were not, in fact, allergies.

I give him my best withering glare.

In return, he gives me a guilty shrug. "Oops?"

But I just hold out my hand and say, "Gimme."

Smoking my dad's weed on my fake boyfriend's twin bed is not how I thought this day would go, yet here we are. Snowflakes flutter through Hudson's open window, so we sit hip to hip.

I take the pipe. "I can't light a lighter, remember?"

"I remember." Hudson flicks the flame and tilts it down, his knuckles grazing my cheek. I must have a contact high because this is kind of . . . hot. (Okay, also, he was *not* kidding about this weed.) His eyes immediately water when I exhale, and he reaches into his nightstand drawer, his shirt lifting, exposing the top band of his boxers. "I need to take my contacts out. One sec."

"Godspeed." I take another hit. Take in his room. Beige paint, whiteish carpet. Matching furniture that requires assembly. It almost looks like a guest room. Like it's temporary.

The flame sputters, so I set the pipe on the nightstand and—*condoms*. My fake boyfriend keeps a strip of condoms in his drawer. It's a simple equation: Hudson + condoms = Hudson has or had or is having sex, and I cannot process that information.

His door opens again, and I sit up, fast, and say, "You sure you're not moving?"

He relights the pipe. "My grandparents are moving to Florida."

"You're moving to Florida?"

"Hopefully not. The market sucks, so their realtor told them to list now." He exhales, sits on his bed, close to me. "Cody actually talked to his parents about it. They said I could take one of their spare rooms to finish the year at Culver if it sells before graduation."

"That's nice of him." I'm not being facetious.

"It was. It is." Hudson takes another hit. "I don't know. I hate feeling like charity. Or like I'm an imposition. Ideally, I'll get my own apartment with—"

"Shit, the scholarship money," I say. "That's why you need it."

"Security deposit, first and last month's rent, furniture, utilities." He ticks off each item on his fingers. "I earn decent money from the diner, and my survivor benefits would cover rent until graduation, but those expire when I turn nineteen and . . . sorry."

I fake cough. "Do you want to talk about your mom? Or we don't have to."

"No. No, I'd like that. Her name was Harper. She was a dental hygienist. She loved estate sales and made-for-TV movies. She had me young, and we were fucking broke, but nothing felt like it was missing." Hudson laughs. "Especially not a dad."

"And he—?"

"Left before I was born," he says with a shrug. "Then when I was in fifth grade, my mom got acute bronchitis. Viral. My grandparents took her to the ER, but she hadn't hit her deductible yet. She made them take her home."

God, I hate that I know how this ends.

Hudson takes a second. "The bronchitis turned to pneumonia, which turned into sepsis, and then she went into septic shock and died." He covers his face but drops his hands when I reach around his waist. "Wait, what're you doing?"

"I'm trying to hug you, asshole."

He relents with an eyeroll. It's an awkward position, but the hug is nice—warm and tight, his heartbeat against mine. "God, sorry for *crying*. I don't really talk about this with friends." He sniffs, kind of laughing. "Although now you'll probably tell me that we're not friends."

"We're not *not* friends."

Hudson props himself on his side. "Your turn. What happened with Maddie?"

My throat goes tight, the smoke choking me. "It's not an interesting story."

"Then bore me."

It's *not* an interesting story. I mean that.

But I say, "Pass the bowl," and take a hit before I begin. "You probably don't remember, but she had a pool party after freshman year. She didn't invite me until after it started. I thought maybe she'd forgotten, or assumed she'd already invited me, but Lee . . ."

I'd been watching the boys play a pickup soccer game at the playground when she finally texted. Back home, I heard the girls shrieking, splashing, singing a song I hated—and Lee said it had been going on for hours.

I blink back the sting. "The Birds were there. One-L Daniele. Honestly, lots of girls were there. I hadn't even known she had other friends." It sounds pitiful like that, so I add, "Then she, um, asked me to invite you guys and—"

"Wait, I do remember!" Hudson says. The boys had been there ten minutes, max, when Mr. Price screamed at them to get out, *now*. Like they were such a danger.

"Maddie had gone inside, so I went to check on her. She was crying to her mom that I'd invited you guys without telling her.

That she only invited *me* to be nice because no one liked me. Including her." I force a laugh. It rips my parched throat. "It's stupid."

"It's not stupid," Hudson says, so serious. "That's awful."

"Yeah, but then I—" I shut my mouth, startled I was about to go there. Explain that I hurt her worse. That I did one of the cruelest things I could ever do to her.

Outside, another horn honks, followed by Dad lazily calling for us. I stand up quick—or it might be very slow; the high is hitting me pretty hard—and we go out.

Lee is just hopping out of the tow truck. (The thing is filthy, dirt streaked along the body, tires caked with mud.) I can't keep track of his schedule. He started helping at the auto shop after his reconstruction surgery, when he could bear weight on his knee.

He says, "You guys smell like weed."

I shoot him a finger gun. "Thanks, it's the weed. Also, check your damn email. For the . . . I'm forgetting words. The story?" Lee frowns, his face unreadable. "The comeback game!"

"Oh." That's all. *Oh.*

"You guys heading out?" Dad asks, and Lee makes his escape, pickpocketing Dad's keys.

I glance at Hudson. "Some people are at the Barcade?"

"Fun! I'll give you bus money."

"Speaking of money," Hudson starts, but Dad shushes him, reaches into his wallet, and extends a bill. "You're paying me fifty dollars for you to fix my car?"

"Buy my daughter a fancy beverage. Nonalcoholic."

"I can't take this," Hudson says, so I snatch the bill and stuff it in my pocket.

"Go." Dad shoos us. "I want nothing to do with either of you."

Hudson is quiet again on our walk, but not for long. "Maddie was wrong, by the way," he says. "Back at the pool party—she said no one liked you, but she was wrong."

"How do you know?"

He stares ahead, but his mouth tilts up. "Because I liked you."

-20-

The Barcade is in this old church, because what's holier than beer and Big Buck Hunter? The bus drops us off on the wrong side of the street, so we sprint, laughing, hand in hand, when there's a gap in the traffic.

Inside, the lights are low, strobing blues and purples. It's crowded, too, teeming with loud nerds hitting up the happy hour and, honestly, I'm too high for this. I feel it even more when Sara abandons the crane machine and bounds up to us. "You came!"

Michaela follows. "And did drugs!"

"Is it that noticeable?" Hudson sniffs his collar.

"Hey!" Cody peers down from the loft, his elbows propped on the railing. There's a Ping-Pong table, Skee-Ball lanes, and a photo-booth up there. He shouts, "I need a partner," and chucks down a paddle, meant for Hudson but aimed at me. I duck before it bonks my head.

Hudson flips it over in his hand, like, *Should I?*

"We'll keep her company," Sara says, taking my hand, guiding me toward the bar.

Kathleen looks up from her seat at the end, dunking a straw in a strawberry milkshake.

"I'm sorry if Kath is more unbearable than usual tonight," Michaela says, then she stage-whispers, "Her ex texted."

Ryan Foley is—was—Kathleen's boyfriend of forever. (Like, two years.) He graduated from St. Ignatius last year, so I mostly knew *of* him. He always seemed fine but boring.

I unzip my parka. "Oh. I'm sorry."

"Thanks," Kathleen mumbles, and this is weird. It's *so* weird. I'm not supposed to talk to these girls, and I'm only doing it because Maddie is gone.

I bring my hand to my forehead. I need sleep. Or water. I'd be a better person with fewer problems if I drank more water. Also, I think I'm very hungry?

Sara sidles up to me, her lip gloss shimmering as she whispers, "See that counter girl?" I look discreetly. She has an undercut and a septum piercing. "I'm in love with her."

"To clarify, Sara is *not* in love with her," Michaela says. "She is, instead, projecting her actual crush onto an unattainable stranger to avoid the risk of rejection."

"I don't know if Daniele is gay!"

"No-H Sara and One-L Daniele?" I glance back to the counter. "Let's test this theory," I add, and drag her to the register. I order Tater Tots (of course a bar/arcade serves tots, not fries) and two sparkling waters, then I break Dad's fifty and say, "Grab my order, Sara, thanks, bye!"

I head toward the bar but slam into someone—a white guy, youngish, average height and weight and build, average in every way. He wears a red sweatshirt, and I'm so certain it's going to say Cornell that the real text—Bard College—blurs.

"Hey, sorry," he says, reaching out a hand, "I didn't see you there."

I jerk back before he can touch me. "I'm fine. It's fine, I mean."

It's *fine*, so I don't know why my heart throbs in my ears.

I look toward the bar. Sara is sprawled across Michaela's lap, minus my order. In the loft, Ben Sulkin tugs at Trey Gardner's sling and Cody rests a hand on Alexis Fitch's hip and Hudson rubs his dry eyes, and then I find that flash of red sweatshirt again. Bard guy is lowering into a booth below the stained glass, right across from—

"Sabrina Kim, News 9," I whisper.

That reporter from school: *I'd love to chat about the missing girl.* Is this a first date? This place reeks of first dates. Both she and Bard College are looking at their phones. Instead of a micro-phone, she holds a very pink cocktail.

I slide into the booth beside her. "Sabrina, right?"

She briefly looks up, then down, then up again. "Hey! Kate Kirby's daughter." Her eyes narrow. "Remember how you told me to fuck off the last time I saw you? Or when you got me kicked out of that stupid holiday party a few years ago?"

"Hmm, I don't think that was me." It was definitely me.

"Uh-huh," she says. Her phone is open to Tinder while her actual Tinder date sits across from her. (I respect the energy.) She swipes left, left, left, left, pauses to read a bio, left.

"I told my mom I ran into you," I lie. "She's been crazy busy with that disappearance—"

Sabrina smacks her phone on the table. "Channel 12 is . . . I mean, your mom . . . ?"

Hook, line, and sinker, baby.

I fake a frown. "Is News 9 not covering it?"

"What is there to cover?" Sabrina says, playing dumb. "I remember how restless I was at her age. *Your* age," she adds, as if she's not midtwenties at most. "I'll bet you anything she was waiting for a reason to run, and now she's off living her best life. I'm sure that girl will post some pretty pictures from a beach soon enough."

That girl. The missing girl. The dead girl.

Like Maddie isn't a person anymore; she's just a story to tell.

"She hates sand," I say, so stoned.

Sabrina shrugs a shoulder, sipping loudly from her cocktail. "Although," she starts, her lips stained pink, "it *is* a bit weird how no one's talking. Not her friends. Her boyfriend. I wonder if I'd change my theory if someone were to speak up."

Hint, hint.

"Maybe I can get your business card?" I offer. "Just in case."

"Just in case," Sabrina says, digging in her purse, pushing aside her phone.

It's still open to Tinder and—wait.

Justin, twenty-six, music writer at *ROC Weekly*, a single dog dad who loves tacos and *The Office* and hiking and is five foot ten, because apparently that matters. (He was not five ten.) I want to see his next picture, so I touch the screen and—

IT'S A MATCH! Oops.

Sabrina flicks out her business card. "Text me anytime."

"I sure will," I say with a wink.

When I stand, I see Hudson sitting at the bar, alone, squinting at the menu like he's never seen the written word before. I step up to him, and he sighs, saying, "I lost."

"I'm shocked." My stomach growls. "Hey, will you grab my tots?" His eyes lower to my chest. "*Tots*, Hudson."

"Oh, that makes more sense." He fetches my order, trying not to laugh when he returns.

I roll my eyes, fake annoyed. "Why would I ask you to do that? Here?"

"It's not like it hasn't happened before."

Something like a spark lights inside me. Like he's flicked open another flame. This is the part where I tell him we don't talk about that, remember? Instead, I say, "Just once." I pop a tot in my mouth. "Also, just one, but it was the left, so you picked well."

"Is that a thing?" Hudson laughs. I like the way he smiles fully when he does. He nods to the token machine and says, "Does your shitty driving extend to fake cars?"

"Have you considered that I choose to fail my road test?"

"Do you?"

"No, I'm a bad driver."

We wind back toward the racing cars. Kathleen stands at the pinball machine beside them, strobes of light streaking her unsmiling face.

I scoot to the edge of the plastic seat and tap the pedal, but it goes nowhere. "Why am I not moving?"

"You're hitting the brake."

"What? No, I'm—" I zoom forward.

Even from down here, I can hear Cody laughing from the loft—so goddamn normal.

"Is it weird for you that I'm friends with him?" Hudson asks, fast. Like he's been holding this in for too long. "I don't know what went on between you—"

"Nothing went on between us." I cut the wheel. "Ever."

The screen reflects blue across his face. "But the . . ."

"I didn't send him those pictures. Cody stole them off my phone."

From the corner of my eye, I see Kathleen jerk her head toward us, the slow ping of the pinball machine wailing when she drops her hands from the controls.

Hudson cranks the wheel, hard, and his car careens around a corner, crashing straight into a fire hydrant. "I didn't . . . I thought you'd . . . I had no clue."

"Now you do." I ease through a narrow bend and bump a coupe. It spins out and smashes into a truck, which smashes into an RV, and somehow I whiz past the collision into first place. I throw up my arms. "Oh my God! See? I'm an *amazing* driver."

Hudson stares at his screen, flashing: LAST PLACE!

-21-

I'm still a little stoned when we leave the Barcade. The good kind—the warm, happy, easy kind. Michaela and Sara both hug me goodbye, but I forget to hug back and just stand there, limp.

Hudson laughs at me before turning to Kathleen. "Hey, can you drive us home?"

She silently winds her scarf around her neck, but it's not a no.

The night is damp and cloudy, like it'll blizzard. Kathleen says, "No shotgun. Clare spilled nail polish on the passenger seat this afternoon."

"Oh, fun," Hudson says, climbing into the backseat. (He might still be stoned, too.) I'm buckling in, closing the door, when something stops it. *Someone* stops it.

"Room for one more?" Cody asks, skin sallow under the parking lot lights.

Kathleen frowns. "Where's your car?"

"Flat tire." He nudges me to the side, so I fumble out of my seatbelt, scoot to the middle seat, and now I'm half sitting on Hudson. I mumble a paltry apology.

It's a quick ride home. Eight minutes, maximum. I can do that.

Cody smells like sweat—salty, sticky, gross. The letter *A* (Alexis Fitch?) pops across his screen, and he tilts the phone toward his chest. "Yo, Hudson, your grandparents have beer?" His eyes drift to me. "Or were you doing something else tonight?"

Something.

Some thing.

"I'm kind of tired," Hudson says dully.

"Cool excuse, man." Cody slides his phone into his pocket, knuckles grazing my hip. I flinch at his touch. The intimacy of it. He holds up his hands. "Don't flatter yourself, JoJo."

Kathleen flicks her eyes to the rearview mirror.

"Wait," Cody says, his teeth extra sharp in the dark. "Remember that game we'd play on the bus?" He demonstrates, his touch light on my knee. "Does this make you nervous?"

I place his hand back in his lap. "I don't feel like playing."

"Come on. Does *this* make you nervous?" His hand eases higher. Hudson glances over at us, his body tensing, jaw grinding, like he wants to say something. He doesn't. Or can't. Just an inch higher, and Cody says, "What about this?"

"Stop." I try to pry him off, but he tightens his grip, fingers sinking toward the inner seam of my jeans. My heart leaps to my throat. "*Cody.*"

"It's just a game, JoJo. Don't be such a—"

The brakes grind, shriek, and the car lurches to a stop. Hudson throws his arm across my chest. Cody's face smashes into the headrest. Rubbing his nose, he says, "What the—?"

"Get out." Kathleen is even. Firm. She twists to face us. "Cody, get out of my car."

His body braces. "It was a game."

"Yeah? Were you having fun, Jo?" Kathleen asks, not taking her eyes off him. She only stops to smack on the hazards, heave open her door, cross to his side.

Cody slowly unbuckles his seatbelt. Steps out even more slowly. I fumble out of my own seatbelt and off the middle seat, off Hudson. Kathleen doesn't back down when Cody gets right in her face. If anything, she stands taller. Cody and Kathleen. The boyfriend and the best friend.

He laughs, mean streak hot. The frigid air scalds his ears. "Her? Really?"

"Yes," Kathleen says, like it's that simple.

I wipe a palm down my thigh. Try to erase Cody's touch with my own. I'm not breathing, and I need to breathe, and we have a truce, remember? *I'll keep your secret if you keep mine.*

He mutters, "Fucking bitch," at me—not her—before he stalks off.

Kathleen leans into the open door, her hair falling into my face. "Hudson," she snaps, and he winces, hesitates before forcing himself to meet her glare. "You're a coward."

"Me?" His voice is low. "What did I do?"

"*Nothing*, Hudson. You did nothing." She punctuates it by slamming the door. When she gets back in the car, yanks the gear out of park, the silence is so unbearable that she turns on the radio. It's disco night on the adult hits station, which might be worse.

It takes only a few minutes for Kathleen to pull down my street, up to my house. I never told her my address. I didn't need to. She stares up at Maddie's darkened window. Hudson keeps his head down and rubs his forehead, eyes shut.

I unfasten my seatbelt. "Thanks, um. For the ride."

"I'm sorry," Kathleen says. I freeze, my hand outstretched, reaching for the handle. "I'm sorry about tonight, and the . . . I didn't know Cody stole the photos."

"I mean, I made it easy. My passcode was my birthday."

"That doesn't make a difference. It's cruel and violating and— Jesus, it's illegal. That was revenge porn, what he did." Kathleen faces me fully. "I really am sorry."

I say something like *thanks*, I think, but the words stick in my throat.

Right as I shut the door, Hudson climbs out his side. "I'll walk you to the door."

"I think I know the way."

He falls into step beside me anyway. "I'm sorry, Jo," he says all in a rush, too fast for me to stop him. "Kathleen was right. She *is* right." Pause. "Please don't tell her I said that." He looks toward her car at the curb, then at me again. "It's not a consolation, but I never . . . like, I didn't . . . I knew those weren't for me, you know?"

My skin heats. "They weren't for anyone. I just felt cute."

God, that really is pathetic, isn't it? It probably sounds so conceited, so fucking foolish to admit I took those photos for me. Because I liked how I looked. Because I looked like myself. I stupidly thought that's how everyone else sees me, too.

But I'm just a body.

"Jesus," Hudson mumbles, so low I barely hear it. "I deleted them, Jo. I promise."

I know that. I'd gotten so drunk at the bonfire, and he was waiting with me for Lee to pick me up when his phone—when every phone—went off one, two, three, four, five, six times. He frowned at the screen like he didn't know what he was looking at, and then, all at once, he did.

It's starting to snow, light and pretty. Hudson looks toward the sky. "I'm done with him, okay? Cody is a monster to you, and I—"

"Hudson, no. It's fine." I'm freezing all of a sudden. "The Forsythes offered you a room if your grandparents move. I don't want you to blow up your life for me."

He keeps quiet for a beat, conflicted. "Then we better get me that ten grand." He looks to the curb again. Exhales. "I don't understand how he could do that to you."

I don't know what to say to this, so I say nothing at all.

The house is quiet tonight.

I gently ease up to my room and shower, lights off, then throw on a T-shirt and crawl into bed. I'm exhausted, but I'm not sure I can sleep. *I don't understand how he could do that to you.*

Neither do I, but sometimes I try.

The night of the bonfire was warm for late October. But there was a brisk undercurrent in the air—a clue the cold would come for us soon.

I'd hitched a ride with Cody, which meant hitching a ride with Miles so that Cody could get obliterated on blue-flavored vodka.

"So, I went to my uncle's cottage earlier," Miles shouted over the open windows. "It's right on the bay. He said I can use it whenever I—"

"How nice," I deadpanned, and dug a Starburst from the seat.

Me and Cody ditched Miles in the parking lot and raced to the beach, but I lost, horribly, because I tripped in the sand and was laughing too hard to get up. It's astonishing I was ever that girl: hot and funny and effortless. What the fuck happened to her? What happened to *me*?

The sun set out of nowhere, or maybe I just didn't see the sky darken since I was buzzed, laughing, hanging with the guys. Hudson, mostly. Things had more or less gone back to normal after our painfully awkward summer, and it was nice. Being friends again, I mean.

Someone by the keg suggested spin the bottle—uh, pass—and I ignored the game until I heard: "Cody, turn?"

He drunkenly spun the bottle, but it was more like a toss— and it landed right on Maddie Price. She'd been hovering along the edge of the game, and she looked up, terrified. Electrified.

"I'm, uh," she started, "I wasn't playing."

"But these are the rules," Cody said, and he kissed her, right there.

Hudson pointed his beer in their direction. "That was a long time coming."

It was, I guess. Maddie and I hadn't been friends for years— almost two and a half, to be precise. Not since everything blew up at the pool party. But it's not like I could get rid of her for good. Our lives ran like parallel lines, rarely intersecting and only ever by necessity. I obviously saw the way Maddie still mooned over Cody, laughing at his worst jokes, staring at him with a dreamy, lovestruck smile.

I rubbed my arms. I'd worn a tank and shorts, which had

been fine until it got dark. But the beer warmed me a bit, and my skin burned when I looked at Hudson. He was much nicer to look at than Maddie and Cody, anyway. I said, "Hey, you look good."

He seemed surprised by the compliment, but he did look good. "So do you," he said, and gently touched the goose bumps on my wrist. "Need a sweatshirt? I have an extra in my car."

The zip-up smelled like him: laundry, a spicy shampoo, general boyishness. I sipped the rest of my beer, too fast. This was another kind of intoxication. I don't know what it was about him now or then or ever, but even though it was nice being his friend, I knew something nicer.

I held out the bottle. "Did you want a turn?"

He eyed me. Rightfully so.

But I wasn't thinking about how this probably wasn't the best way to keep things normal between us, or how this—what I wanted to do—made last summer so awkward in the first place.

I could only think of how badly I wanted him.

Finally, Hudson set the bottle down and spun, the glass ringing, and when I pressed down my foot to steady it, the bottle pointed perfectly at me—right where I wanted it.

That's how I ended up making out with Hudson for roughly four minutes.

Headlights beamed across the lot, and I broke from the kiss, whispering, "Someone might see us," as his mouth dropped to the curve of my neck.

He sighed, like it killed him to let me go. "Maybe we can continue this later?"

"I'd like that." I meant it. "You can go back first if you don't want to be seen together."

Hudson frowned. "Why would I not want to be seen with you?"

So, we walked back, together, and I wore his sweatshirt, and his hand kept bumping mine, but he never pulled away. He fetched me another beer, and I sat on a felled log by the fire. One-L Daniele aimed her camera at me, and I smiled my horrible smile, not knowing his teeth had left a mark. Not knowing this would soon be a clear *before* picture.

Hudson rejoined me a second later, whispering, "Do you see this?"

I blinked it into focus: Maddie and Cody. They sat in the sand, Cody leaning in close, listening. Really listening. Then he looked up, looked across the bonfire to Ben—and he grinned.

It was wolfish and cruel and awful, and that was not my friend.

Maddie kept talking—maybe about NYU or all the words she might write—and he kissed her again, midsentence. Like he wanted to shut her up.

"No," I whispered, looking for the Birds. They needed to stop this, stop him, stop Maddie from getting her heart broken or . . . I don't know. I stood, unsteady.

Hudson caught my hand. "Is everything okay?"

"I'm good. I'm . . . I'll be right back. Maybe then we can get out of here?"

He hesitated. "You're pretty drunk, Jo."

"So?"

"So, nothing is going to happen if you're drunk."

"I'm *fine*," I said, because I was. I just needed space.

I followed the sandy path up to the parking lot, then immediately turned back toward the beach, half-hidden by trees, mosquitoes flitting around my ankles. That's when I heard it: rustling, snapped twigs. Cody's hoarse voice, lazy with beer. His pale face caught in the moonlight.

"You don't understand, man, this bitch is *obsessed* with me." *Maddie.* I pictured her face again, pretty and hopeful when that bottle spun toward her. "I'll get a blow job out of her, right?"

Ben laughed. "Oh, at least."

"At least," Cody echoed. "This girl will do *anything* for me."

I cut them off on the path. "What're you talking about?" I asked, but neither answered; we all knew I'd heard. I gently tapped Cody's sneaker with mine. "Can we talk a sec? Alone?"

Laughing again, Ben said, "Have fun, you two."

Once he was out of earshot, Cody cracked his neck. "What is it?"

"Leave Maddie alone." I tried to act less drunk. From here, I could still hear the bonfire crackling, the kindling cracking, sparks spitting. "You're taking advantage of her—"

"How am I taking advantage of her, JoJo? She *likes* me." Cody jabbed his thumb into my neck, pressing the hickey I didn't yet know was there. "Where'd you get that?"

I brushed him off. "You don't even like her."

He shrugged, not denying it. "Why do you care? It's not like she gives a shit about you."

I folded myself into the hoodie. The beer felt heavy in my stomach. He was right. Maddie didn't give a shit about me, not now, maybe not ever. But that *smile*, and what he'd said—

"I know you cheat." It was all I had. The only thing I could hold over him. Cody frowned at first, confused, so I said, "I know Miles cheats for you."

His mouth opened. Shut.

Then he started to laugh. "You're *blackmailing* me to back off Maddie?"

Hearing him say it like that—I'd made a horrible mistake. This wasn't just about a girl; it was his future. Cody was already deep in the recruitment process, and why would this stop him?

But I needed to stop him. "You're going to hurt—"

"You don't know shit. Not about me or Miles or Maddie or anything." His face had gone dark, burning. "Besides," Cody said, stepping closer, breath hot on my ear, "who'd ever believe you, Jolie?"

Jolie.

The name unraveled me. Sent me back toward the bonfire and off the edge. I didn't think before I chucked that beer can at Maddie. She was already crying before the can hit the ground, and everyone was going *Oh, shit*, and laughing because it's so funny when girls fight, right?

Maddie squeezed the hem of her shirt, sobbing, "What's wrong with—?"

"You told him about Nick?" I didn't know if I was asking or telling her that I knew what she'd done. Maybe if I phrased it like a question, she could prove me wrong.

But Maddie went quiet.

It's funny, sort of. How I stole a handle of vodka and stormed down the beach, far from the Birds fluttering around Maddie; far from Cody, who stood at the outskirts of the bonfire, on his phone; far from all the assholes who saw what I did to Maddie without knowing what she'd done to me first.

Someone—I still don't know who—whispered, "That girl's such a fucking bitch."

How many times have I heard that? Heard worse?

Slut. Whore. Disgusting.

"No." I drop my head in my hands. My ears pound, muffled, until the sound clears—and I hear a door creaking open.

Footsteps, slow and measured, move down the hall, down the stairs.

And I peer through my bedroom window right as my brother disappears outside, into the night.

-22-

I sleep like shit. Mostly I doze, flipping from my side to my stomach to my back to my side. I'm so restless that Bay Leaf abandons my bed in the middle of the night.

All day, I laze around the house. I nap and figure out my birth chart and shave my legs. I'm so bored I do *homework*. My other option is hanging out with my mother, which . . . no.

I'm fast approaching my second nap when my phone vibrates.

[4:17 p.m.] **HUDSON:** you need to get to your aunt's shop

[4:17 p.m.] **HUDSON:** like now

I bolt into the kitchen, where my mother is brewing a cup of decaf.

"I need a ride to the shop." I rephrase, "Can I have a ride?" Pause. "Please?"

"You need your damn license," she says, which means yes.

Today is another gray, gloomy day in a long line of gray, gloomy days. I duck my head to the wind, nearly missing that lilt from across the street: "Kate! Kate, can I talk to you? Please?"

"Oh, Jesus," my mother mumbles, then louder, "Sorry, Lisa, we're heading out!"

"No one wants to talk to me," Mrs. Price says, almost to herself. The family dog, Tanner, paces at her feet, his leash tangled around his paws. "No one wants to hear what I have to say."

Her words reverberate, just like her other words—*you goddamn liar*—in my head.

"I'm sorry, Lisa," my mother says again, unlocking the car, lighting up a cigarette. We're both quiet as she shifts into reverse and starts down the street. Then, like she knows I'm about to ask, she says, "Lisa is upset about Channel 12's coverage of Maddie."

"What coverage?" I snort. That's the point; there *is* no coverage.

The dead girl. That's what Justin Lloyd at *ROC Weekly* called her. Like he wants a brutal explanation. Like the most compelling story is that she's dead. The leads he left—the fundraiser, records (?), the number to the architecture firm (ugh)—lead nowhere I can see yet.

Then there's Sabrina Kim, News 9. In her version of the story, Maddie runs—not from anything, but toward her best life. Hell, maybe Maddie is sipping a frozen drink on the beach, laughing that we were ever worried. Unless someone has more to say . . .

Tess Spradlin thinks Maddie ran, too, because sometimes a story is as simple as that. She was rejected from NYU, her dream school, the only one she applied to, so she left. But Tess lied to me about not investigating, right? Like she didn't want me to know.

I don't know anything, anyway, except that Maddie is in trouble, but she thinks that I can help her, and, no, I still have no clue how or why or—

"What do you know?" I ask, twisting to face my mother. She shakes her head, and I add, "I'm asking as your daughter, not a viewer."

She takes a long drag. "Geoff called the station after the note came out"—again, where *is* that note?—"and he said this is a personal matter and he'd appreciate our discretion. He worries what this will do to her reputation."

"Her *reputation*?" I clunk my head against the window. Immediately sit tall again. "But if he's trying to suppress the story, why does her mom want to talk?"

My mother exits toward the auto shop. "I'm just telling you what Geoff told me. Maddie lied to her parents. Her dad was out of town, so she told her mom she was spending the night at his place. Then she . . ." She sighs, shifts into park. "Look, I'm sure Maddie is fine, Jo-Lynn."

I don't thank her for the ride.

In the waiting room, Hudson is stumped on a crossword puzzle. I tap his shoulder, and he says, "Shit, you scared me," then drags me into the garage. His car looks newish, gleaming.

But that's not what he wants me to see.

"Holy shit," I breathe out. "Is that—?"

Cody Forsythe's car.

Routine maintenance, a flat tire—none of it was true, what Cody told us. The truth is that his car is *wrecked*. The back bumper is smashed, cracked, twisted, the Duke sticker crunched in on itself. I press my fingers to the fender. Trace the white streaks scraped into the red paint.

Hudson says, "He texted me for a ride the morning after

Maddie left, then Ben said he'd been chauffeuring Cody, remember? And I know lots of cars are white, but what if—?"

"Maddie hit his car." Her white Prius. Missing along with her.

The timing is suspect, but white paint isn't enough proof. I need more. I need . . .

My brother steps behind the service desk. He looks ragged—tired eyes, bedhead. I picture him again in the dark night, sneaking out of the house. He unclips a form from a clipboard, sticks it in the filing cabinet, kicks it closed.

"I'll distract Lee so you can steal Cody's intake form," I say, and the look on Hudson's face tells me he hates this plan, but I'm already jogging toward the counter. "Lee!"

My brother sighs, preemptively irritated. "You shouldn't run in here."

"Sorry, I didn't know public pool rules applied," I say, slowing. "I have a question about a car." He doesn't move. "Look, I'm trying to learn about the family business."

He sighs again but follows me onto the floor. I give Hudson a nod, and he goes sweeping past us. I stop at the far end, so Lee does, too, sighing a third time.

"I know you know whose car this is," he says as Hudson dips behind the counter.

"Yeah, and it's not like I can ask Cody what happened."

"Why do you need to know?"

"Because I'm nosy, and he was my friend." *He was my friend.* The words sting in a way I don't expect, especially after last night—his hand on my thigh, sliding up higher. *Does this make you nervous?* It did, and it does, and I'm terrified about our truce, too, because if he tells—

"I just do what Aunt Leigh asks," Lee says. Over his shoulder, I see Hudson roll the first drawer shut and try the next. "You should stay away from Cody, anyway."

I squint at him. "Why?"

"Because all your friends are assholes. Him, Miles—"

"I'm not friends with Miles anymore, either," I say, surprised how that stings, too.

It isn't like we were *that* close. But he always went out of his way to be nice to me, even before we were friends. Even when I was very much not nice to him. I thought Miles enjoyed my company. That he saw me as more than a girl he wanted to—

"Wait, why do *you* think Miles is an asshole?" I'm guessing it's different than my reason.

"Just a vibe," Lee says, and he starts to go, but Hudson is still in those files.

I yank him back by the arm. "Why'd you sneak out last night?"

His mouth drops the tiniest bit. "I had to study. It's probably an unfamiliar concept to you," he says, but I'm done listening. Hudson nods from across the floor, like, *I've got this,* and ducks back under the counter. Lee adds, "Did you actually want something or—?"

"Bye." I quickly walk (*not* jogging, thank you) up to Hudson. He slips me the form.

INCIDENT DETAILS: hit-and-run w/ unknown vehicle; no police report

LOCATION OF INCIDENT: follow up w/ client (bay??)

INSURANCE: n/a

PAYMENT TYPE: visa (out-of-pocket rate)

Cody was in a hit-and-run, but he never filed a police report or got insurance involved because—

"Maddie hit his car," I say for the second time. The words feel heavier. I scan through the form again, stick on the *bay??* jotted beside the location line. "Do you think this means my cat?"

Hudson's eyes light. "No. No, it's *the* bay. Cody has a fishing spot there," he says. I must look confused because he adds, "Cody fishes."

"For what?"

"Uh, fish?"

"Oh." I didn't know that. How could I not know that? I guess I never thought about his life outside our friendship. I never realized there was more to know.

Now I snag Hudson's keys from his coat pocket and say, "Then let's go to the bay."

Hudson drives us toward the south shore. He tells me this, too, like I'd know cardinal directions.

The boulevard dips downhill, the road curving, steep, before leveling with the water. The whole world feels frozen here. Dead. Hudson pulls into a gravel lot at the base of the hill, empty except for a boat draped in tarps, abandoned until spring.

There's a small shack along the water: Ray's Bait & Tackle. The open sign is flicked on, but the windows are darkened. Handwritten signs are duct-taped to the shingles: fishing licenses and kayak rentals and FRESH LIVE BAIT SOLD HERE!!

Beyond the shop, a dock extends into the frozen water, the wood glimmering with ice.

I peer out the car window. "Sorry, just to clarify: Cody comes *here*?"

"It looks less depressing in the summer. He invited me to fish a couple times," Hudson says, stepping out. "We'd park by the tackle shop, but the spot is this way, I think."

Thick swatches of cattails, dead and dried, sprout from the edge of the frozen lake. These things must be a foot taller than me. I step closer, dragging my fingers along the stalks, reaching for one of the fuzzy tails.

"Jo, careful!" Hudson says, and I launch back, stumbling. "I'm sorry, I didn't mean to scare you. But those grow from the water; you were standing on ice."

The wind exhales a frigid gust. I shiver, lifting my hood.

But maybe it's not the cold. Maybe it's the trees stripped of their leaves, that rotten, slimy smell, the overturned buckets and tangled fishing line and broken poles and scattered hooks—

"This is it." Hudson stops at a spot along the shore.

There isn't much to see. The bay empties into the lake, the ice and sky blending into the same dull gray; you can hardly see the horizon. Steep cliffs climb up either side of the water.

Some of these houses go for millions, easy, but there are smaller cottages, too, built into the cliffside, with winding staircases descending down to the docks.

Miles Metcalf, in my head: *I went to my uncle's cottage earlier . . .*

I don't want to think about Miles.

I don't want to think about that night at the beach, period.

I think, instead, about the stories my mother covers sometimes, about lakes and reservoirs and bays being dragged for missing bodies. Here, the ice is intact. But still. *Jesus.*

I turn my back to the wind and the bay. Ahead of us, the gravel path turns to half-frozen mud and disappears behind a thicket of trees. I point. "What's that?"

"Oh. I think it's like a lovers' lane."

"Ew, don't say lovers." I start toward it. "What if they came here the night she left?"

"Presumably you'd carpool to a lovers' lane," Hudson mutters, following me.

Tire tracks overlap, cutting the mud, but nothing looks like a crash—Maddie smashing into Cody, Maddie wrecking his car. *Signs of a struggle.* It hits me from nowhere, those words.

But there are no signs of a struggle. No signs of Maddie.

Nothing.

"Nothing," I say out loud, deflating. "How is there nothing? How did Maddie"—missing, kidnapped, dead—"vanish? Logistically, I mean. Like, doesn't she need money and shelter and a burner, or some shit?" I think of my old flip phone. Buy one, get one. "How did she pull it off?"

Hudson is quiet for a long time. "I don't know."

Me neither, and it's killing me. We head back toward the lot. He unlocks his car, but I go check out the dock. It croaks under my weight, boards creaking, but I take a step, then another.

Then the door to the tackle shop flies open, and a man crashes out. He's old, with the kind of weathered face that comes from years in the sun—and he has a baseball bat.

"Jo!" Hudson shouts, and I scramble off the dock, run toward his side.

The man jabs at the dock with the bat. "How many more

195

fucking signs do you need?" *NO TRESPASSING. KEEP OFF.*
"You trying to get yourself killed?"

"No!" I say, and Hudson says, "We were—"

"I know what you kids do here." *The lovers' lane.* He tilts his
head to get a better look at me. "You one of those girls?"

I shake my head. "What girls?"

But I already know. I'm one of *those girls* who'd come to the
bay, crawl into the back of some guy's car because he asks her to.
Tells her to. I've done it before. Not here, but it doesn't fucking
matter where, and it's nothing, and I—

"I told them to stay away," he says, "and I want you gone, too."

-23-

Monday morning, my mind is still at the bay.

The decrepit tackle shop and the rotted dock and the muted ice and sky and rocks, like it was stuck in grayscale. The muddy lovers' lane. I can't imagine Maddie there. Not to watch Cody fish, which sounds boring, and not to climb into the backseat and—

"Good morning, Miss Kirby," Principal Lund says with a tight smile.

I give her a small salute, which she does not seem to appreciate.

Today is our first Senior Experience site visit, at the George Eastman Museum. But I've been tons of times before. Eastman founded Kodak, the photography and camera company that both built and decimated the city, so our DNA is basically wound with rolls of film.

"This way." Lund ushers me toward the rest of the cohort and their mentors and . . . not Tess. "Ms. Spradlin is running late, so just stand with those girls."

Those girls. It lands differently in this context. That man wielding a fucking baseball bat from the tackle shop told *those girls* to stay away—but what if he didn't mean girls like me?

What if he meant a group of girls? Like the Birds? I mean, it's weird as hell that they'd go to the bay, of all places, but me and Maddie were like that, too, wandering the neighborhood, sitting on a random curb on a random street. Like the whole world belonged to us.

"You can hang with me," Michaela Russell says, making me jump. I knew she was in the program—this is her site visit—but I didn't expect her here, next to me. She cracks a smile. "I'll try not to take that personally."

"Sorry, basic kindness is a real jump-scare for me." I pause. "That sounds depressing."

"Jo, that *is* depressing," Michaela says, but she's laughing.

There are twelve of us total in the cohort. April Kirk lingers beside a woman with a piano broach pinned to her lapel. Miles is here, because of course, standing with a flustered professor-type. Then there's that Frank Hatch, Finance, and—

I freeze when I see Cody. Not just because of what happened the other night—*Does this make you nervous?*—but his car. The smashed bumper. White scrapes in the red paint.

"Come on." Michaela leads me into a conference room. Lower, she adds, "Kathleen told me what happened with him after the Barcade. I'm so sorry."

"I mean, it's fine."

Michaela nods, like she doesn't believe me. "Okay, well, how about some hot goss from the archives?" she asks, unsubtly changing the subject. "Kidding. There's no hot goss. It's a little boring here, but the field itself can be kind of radical." Michaela is almost glowing now. "Black archivists are way underrepresented, so I want to—sorry, I'll shut up."

"No, no, you can keep going," I say. "I know literally nothing about this stuff."

"I actually did this archival camp at the public library a couple summers ago. Me and . . . Maddie." Her name hangs heavy between us. Michaela looks down, picking imaginary lint from her coat. "We were friendly from school, but that was the summer we became friends."

Which means it was the summer that me and Maddie stopped.

Laughing, Michaela adds, "She *hated* camp. We made these personal archives at the end—something to remember the summer we were fifteen—and she put hers inside this ugly pink safe so her mom couldn't get into it."

"Well, her mom *is* a snoop," I say, but the words snag in the back of my brain.

The ugly pink safe. I can almost picture it—small and square and lap-size—but I don't know why I'd know that. The second our friendship ended, it was *done*.

But she lives right across the fucking street, obviously, so it's not like I could escape her for good. Sometimes I'd peer out my window and spot her out in the yard, watering the flowers or digging in the dirt or yanking weeds. She kept to the front garden, mostly, but a few times I caught her in the side yard, jabbing a trowel beneath the lilac bush.

Then I'd pull down the blinds.

Principal Lund steps up to the podium, but I only half listen. *Remember, mandatory Open House is next Monday night.* (I didn't remember.) *Proposals for capstone projects are due this week.* (Ugh.) *Now, how about you introduce yourselves?*

For my turn, I say, "Um, I'm Jo. I'm working with Tess Spradlin. That's it."

Just then, Tess enters. She has an iced coffee in her mittened hand and a pair of oversized sunglasses tangled in her hair. It's like a vision of myself from the future. She mumbles, "Sorry."

"We were just introducing ourselves, Ms. Spradlin," Lund says.

Tess takes the free seat on my other side. "Hey, I'm Tess. I'm an editor at *ROC Weekly*. I'm working with this one"—hi, me—"and that's it."

"Ms. Spradlin is being modest," Lund says, fake smiling. "She's a top-notch journalist."

I whisper, "Top-notch?"

"Yeah, nothing says 'success' like hanging out with a bunch of high schoolers as an adult woman." Her phone lights up with a call: *Justin Lloyd.* She sends him to voicemail.

I tune out the other introductions, but Michaela's presentation is pretty interesting, even if I'm itching to stand when Lund says, "Feel free to take your self-guided tour."

This was my favorite part as a kid: the garish wallpaper, the needless extravagance.

The museum itself is right on George Eastman's estate, and his old mansion has been perfectly restored and preserved, a snapshot of his life until it ended in 1932. (Thanks, Michaela, for the tidbit!) The windows in the atrium open to the gardens, but everything is dead under the snow. There's a fur pelt draped over the couch and an elephant head mounted high on the wall.

Tess says, "I didn't know the elephant wasn't real until five years ago."

I didn't know it wasn't real until five seconds ago.

We pass photos of Eastman in the gardens with Thomas Edison, big game hunting with Teddy Roosevelt. Upstairs, we mess with pinhole cameras and inspect the documents in a glass display case. Early photography patents. His last will and testament. His suicide note.

I think of those Lourdes girls, gossiping about Maddie: *I'd seriously kill myself.* It makes me lightheaded. We got pamphlets in health with the warning signs, but how could I really tell?

Tess nods toward the stairs. "Should we check out the special exhibition?"

The gallery is dark, lit by small spotlights aimed at the photos—self-portraits of half-nude women. I look down. Tuck my hands into my sleeves, cross my arms tight to my waist.

"These are beautiful," Tess says, stopping to read a description.

My skin burns. "Self-portrait seems generous for a glorified selfie."

"That's a bit judgmental."

"Well, that's the trouble with girls like me."

Her steps go quiet. "What did you say?"

"It's a thing my mom says." I search for an example. My mind goes blank and fills up at once. "So, I got fired from Costello's Frozen Custard, right? My mom said the trouble with girls like me is that we always ruin a good thing."

"How come you got fired?"

"Some customer accused me of spitting in his sundae."

"Why would he do that?"

"Because I spit in his sundae."

Tess takes a seat on the bench in the middle of the gallery, waiting for the rest.

I slump down next to her. "We called him Creepy Caleb." I can still picture him: tall, with bug eyes; skin so pale it looked blue. "He was a regular. Hot fudge sundae with five cherries. He made us work for our tips, too. Really suck up."

I wipe off my palms, still feeling the way his fingers lingered on my skin when I handed back his change. "This one day we were extra slammed, and I miscounted the cherries, and he told me I probably had one he'd like more." I can't look at Tess, but I feel her tense. "I texted my manager, but she just laughed. Sent screenshots to the employee group chat. And I know it was a major health code violation and I deserved to get fired, but . . ."

"And you told your mom that?"

I laugh a little too abruptly. "I don't tell my mom anything."

Tess nods, frowning. "I'm sorry that happened to you. It sounds really violating."

"It's whatever." I hate how the portraits stare at me now, like I'm the one who's exposed.

I hate that *cruelviolatingillegal* loops through my head.

Tess picks a fuzz off her knee. "Your capstone project proposal is due this week, right? It seems—and correct me if I'm wrong—that a lot of people tell stories about you. Or for you. So, what if you found a story to tell yourself? In your own words?"

"Like, my side of the story?" My heart patters in a weird way. Maybe I'm dying.

"It seems like you have a lot to say, Jo-hyphen-Lynn. Maybe you should say it."

Her phone chimes with another text. Tess groans, slips it out of her pocket. She types in her passcode—0127—like she has nothing to hide. *Cruel, violating, illegal* fills my head again.

I shake out the words, say, "You an Aquarius?"

"Yes, you snoop."

I peer at the screen. "Is that Jason texting you? How's *his* story?"

"Justin, and yes, and there is no story."

That's a lie. "What'd he say?"

"He said that someone stole his lucky pen last week." Tess shoots me a look, setting her phone on the bench. "I'm running to the bathroom."

I give her a nod, and then I immediately unlock her phone: 0127. I appreciate her trusting me, even if that trust was misguided.

Unless she wanted me to see it? Use it?

[10:15 a.m.] **JUSTIN:** Can I do the story if I get them to talk?
[10:17 a.m.] **TESS:** They're not going to talk. I told you to drop it.
[10:21 a.m.] **JUSTIN:** Just look this up, Spradlin . . .
[10:26 a.m.] **TESS:** It's a bad angle. I told you to drop it.

Justin also sent a photo. It's a screenshot of a code: *SBL* followed by a bunch of numbers.

It means nothing to me, but I scribble it on a piece of paper, because it means something to Justin. To the story Tess told him to drop. Twice. I reposition her phone, like I never even—

"Hey."

"Jesus Christ." My voice echoes in the gallery.

Miles Metcalf jumps, even more startled. "I'm sorry! I'm sorry," he says, blushing, since he's always blushing. "I just . . . I saw you in here, and I wanted . . . like, we never talked about—"

—how he implied my boyfriend (*fake* boyfriend) is only with me because I'm a slut. He didn't use that word, but that's what he meant, all because I picked another guy when Miles was never even a choice. He used my reputation against me, just like Cody had.

"I'm, um. I'm sorry about that," Miles says, not looking at me. "I'm sorry, Jo."

That is . . . nothing like Cody. I'm not holding my breath for that apology because I know it'll never come, and I'd rather not suffocate waiting. But this, from Miles?

"Oh." I don't really know what else to say.

He nods at the paper in my lap. "Why are you looking up property records?"

Records. The word forms in my head, scrawled in Justin's uneven hand. "Wait, this code is for a *property* record? How do you know that?"

"My dad is an assessor for the city, remember?" he asks. I definitely never knew that. He adds, "It's an SBL number: section, block, lot. I can help you look it up if you want?"

I don't know what I want—what to think of his apology, because even if he means it, he meant what he said in the lab, too, didn't he?—but this is a clue, and Tess is opening the gallery door, so I whisper, "Meet me in the design lab when we get back."

I potentially fail to mention Miles when I tell Hudson about this mission.

He looks between us—Miles, me—from his usual seat in the back row.

Too cheery, I say, "Miles is helping us with something."

But also, oops, I forgot to tell Miles about Hudson, too.

I think this might be my personal hell: Miles and Hudson on either side, tension palpable, silence unbearable. Plus, the computer is taking forever to boot up. Hudson stares, unblinking, at the progress bar, but Miles is fidgety.

"Heard anything about rank, Hudson?" he asks, his voice cracking.

Hudson rips his gaze from the screen. "Why?"

"Sorry, I meant, have you heard *anything* about rank? I assumed we'd know by now."

"It's weird, right?" Hudson scoots his chair closer, his knee knocking mine.

"I'm getting nervous, honestly," Miles admits. "None of us at the top have heard."

The progress bar ticks quicker: *92, 93, 94 . . .*

"Do you know who's third, then?" Hudson asks. *97, 98 . . .*

Miles chews his lower lip, the skin flaked, chapped. "Um, it's . . . April."

100.

"Hey, I think the page loaded," I basically shout, shoving the keyboard and mouse toward Miles, ignoring how Hudson stares at me. My phone vibrates in seconds.

[12:43 p.m.] **HUDSON:** HIS EX-GF IS THIRD EXCUSE ME
[12:43 p.m.] **HUDSON:** ??????????????????????
[12:43 p.m.] **HUDSON:** seems like a great motive to want my rank, jo
[12:44 p.m.] **JO:** you're not being subtle!!!

I flip my phone face down.

I mean, *is* it a great motive? Miles is already first, so he doesn't benefit if Hudson loses his rank—but his ex-girlfriend would. Maybe April needs the money? Or Miles thinks it'll get her to . . . get back with him? No, that's too skeevy.

Miles takes the SBL code and types it into the database. The cursor spins, loading, loading, *there.* "Okay, so this is the record," he says, pointing out the obvious. "Looks like this one is a complex. Apartments, condos. Lofts? In that case, if you go here"—he clicks the sidebar—"you can search by the unit."

The desktop goes dark, screen sizzling, staticky.

Miles frowns. "That was weird."

Below the table, Hudson grips the cord in his fist. He shakes his head, just a little.

"Huh, yeah, it was weird." I stand, quick, nearly knocking over my chair. Hudson follows my lead, and Miles does, too, fumbling for his backpack. I say, "I totally forgot I need something from my locker, but maybe we can try again later?"

He trails us into the hall. "I'm actually busy later. Me and some band guys."

"Oh," I say. Not that he isn't allowed to have a social life, obviously, but *I* was his social life for months. Or maybe he was mine. "Uh, thanks for the help, then. It was helpful," I add as Hudson ushers me into the back stairwell. To him, I go, "Thanks, Hudson. Now he's going to think we're in here to make out."

He waits for the door to latch, then says, "The record said Geoffrey Price. Unit 1002."

"Oh, shit." I pull out my phone, find the real estate listing: Riverfront Lofts, Unit 1002. Exposed brick, a decent view of the skyline. "It went off the market in July, so that tracks with when he moved out."

Hudson peers at my screen. "Last sold for $1.1 million? What the hell does her dad do?"

"Finance? I don't know." I need to talk it out. "Justin had 'records' in his notes, then the fundraiser and the"—*architecture firm*—"phone number, but it's nothing." *It's nothing.* "Maybe Justin is thinking, you know, her dad can afford a million-dollar loft, so why ask for donations? Unless they *can't* afford it? Because the Prices are in debt?"

"Because the Prices are in debt," Hudson repeats.

The loft. The mortgage. The midlife crisis car. I get how Justin's clues connect, but not how this works as an angle. Not how it works as a reason for Maddie to run away.

The bell rings, and I rub my forehead. I think I'm getting a headache. "Let's just go."

"But wait," Hudson says, fake serious, "you didn't want to make out?"

My face flushes. "Shut up, Hudson," I say, and I step out of the stairwell, right into—

"Hi! I've been looking for you," Kathleen O'Mara says. I look over my shoulder, because surely she's not talking to me. "Hi, *Jo*."

"Oh. Hi?" I don't mean to phrase it like a question.

She smooths out her already flawless hair. "I wanted to ask if you were busy after school. We're going to Java's—me and Sara and Michaela—and I thought you could come."

My face heats. "I'll pass. I don't want you to be nice just because you feel sorry for me."

"I'm offended that you think I'm being nice," Kathleen says, and I think . . . it might . . . be a joke? Kathleen O'Mara, joking? She fidgets with her cross necklace. "I wouldn't ask if I didn't mean it, Jo." Pause. "Even if I do feel a little sorry for you."

I don't want her pity—I don't want anyone's pity—but at least she's honest. And I need access to *those girls*. I need answers about the bay. What the Birds know. What they're hiding.

So, I slowly nod and say, "I'd love to."

Then someone knocks into me, hard, shoving me into Kathleen.

Fast, so fast I almost don't realize it's happening, Hudson grips Cody, the offender, by the backpack strap and yanks him forward. "Leave her alone," he says, low.

Cody sputters out a laugh. All eyes are on us—just how he wants it, usually. Except now everyone stares the wrong way. He looks to Ben for backup, but Ben is ignoring him. Even that sophomore Alexis Fitch keeps her eyes on her phone.

It's a startling shift—the tides turning toward me, drawn by my magnetic pull, like I'm the moon. Like I'm the brightest thing in the night sky.

Like I'm the one with the power now.

-24-

Something incredible happens: I'm in with the Birds.

Like, I'm *in*.

It gives me whiplash. How, all at once, the girls laugh at my jokes. Partner with me when we have group work in class. The way they include me so effortlessly, like we're . . . friends. But the Birds are not my friends. Like, Maddie will reappear and restart her life, and what'll happen to me then? I need to remember that. Repeat it.

Those girls are not my friends.

Thursday after school, we walk the few blocks to Village Gate, this warehouse converted into shops and restaurants and art galleries. We're in Mythic Treasures, the mystic shop with all the crystals and tarot decks and incense. Us, except Kathleen, who's too Catholic to step inside.

Sara dunks her hand inside a container of crystals. "Jo, you're going to senior bowling night tomorrow, right?"

"Ew, do I have to?"

Michaela props her elbow on my shoulder. "Daniele is taking pictures for the paper, so this is our birthday gift to Sara."

"Birthday *sacrifice*," Kathleen shouts from the doorway, waving away incense.

Sara leads us out of the store. "We'll play, like, one game, and I'll make a fool of myself, and then we'll go back to my house for a sleepover." She turns to me and adds, "Sound good?"

Something warm spreads in my chest. "Sounds great."

"I need an outfit that conveys that I'm bisexual and interested. Probably overalls, right? Or—oh!" Sara presses her palm to the window of Leather & Lace. It sells sex toys and lingerie and porn. "Let's come back on Saturday."

Michaela wipes a fake tear. "I can't believe our favorite Pisces is turning eighteen. Now you can buy your own equipment instead of bullying us."

We go into Second Act, a thrift shop that reeks of mildew. I stifle a sneeze. "Equipment? Oh, like a"—I drop to a whisper—"vibrator?"

"Yes," Sara whispers back, "like a vibrator."

Kathleen nods her chin at me. "Jo doesn't need one. She has a detachable showerhead."

Both Michaela and Sara gasp. *Gasp.*

I hold up my hands. "Okay, can someone please explain this to me?"

"You just, you know." Sara demonstrates, but it only vaguely clarifies things. "You do it the old-fashioned way? Or do you *not* masturbate?" It's so matter of fact, like she's asking why I hate parsley. (Fine garnish, bland herb.)

"Yeah, it's—I tried it a couple times, but I—it's not my thing." I can't believe I'm talking about this with them. I can't believe I'm talking about this at all.

"Really? How come?" Michaela asks.

I've never given it much thought, I guess, which is funny considering how many hours I had to endure the guys joking about jerking off. Or, "joke" isn't the right word; I never laughed.

"You should try it again!" Sara says. "Maybe you'll like it."

Kathleen quickly adds, "But you don't have to."

Michaela shrugs into an oversized denim jacket, faded, frayed at the sleeves. "If you're not getting yourself off, then Hudson better be making you—"

"Why are we talking about this?" I slip on a pair of cat-eye sunglasses.

"I have no evidence to support this theory, but I always thought he'd be generous." She catches my eye in the mirror and blinks. "I'm winking, right?"

Kathleen fits a hot pink cowboy hat on her head. "That's a blink, babe."

"Why can I not wink?" Michaela slips out of the jacket. "So, is he? Generous?"

Sara holds a fringe dress up to her chest. "How big is his penis?"

Pertinent information, I think, and out loud I say, "Uh—"

"Can we change the subject? My innocent ears can't handle it," Kathleen says, but Sara and Michaela have already moved to a different rack. To me, she says, "Sorry about that."

"Sorry about what?"

"You seemed uncomfortable."

"Nope. It's fine."

Kathleen hangs up the cowboy hat. "I guess I misread it."

It's just that I don't talk like this. I have nothing to say that hasn't already been said about me. And sometimes I get so tired of having a body, you know? I don't know how to look at it or touch it or have it be touched, and it gets me so overwhelmed I forget to breathe.

"Seriously, it's fine," I say again, too defensive. "I love talking about Hudson's penis."

Kathleen fixes on something over my shoulder. "That is impressively bad timing."

I twist around, face to face with three Lourdes girls in their uniforms: plaid skirts, white blouses, sweater vests. The girls from Ben's party—the blonde with the beret, the tall one—and another. She's upsettingly pretty, with pin-straight hair and a middle part. She's also pretty upset.

Not like she'll cry. No, this is a hurt she hides behind a fake laugh, saying, "Of course."

Then the girls are gone, just like that.

I slip the sunglasses back onto the rack. "What just happened?"

"Jo, are you serious?" Kathleen hisses. "That was Charlotte Daly." I roll the name in my head, confused. "Hudson's ex."

"Oh. *Oh.* Oh, no."

Hudson dated her most of junior year, and I never learned her name. The filing system in my head deemed her unimportant and, yes, I know that sounds awful. It *was* awful.

Now that I can pair a name—Charlotte—with the beautiful face, I slot her into every memory: Charlotte with her arm around Hudson's waist at a pickup soccer game; Charlotte at prom in a gorgeous navy dress.

Then I see me ruining every moment.

How I wolf whistled when Hudson peeled off his shirt during the game, not seeing her in a lawn chair. How I dragged him onto the dance floor when Earth, Wind & Fire came on since he was born the twenty-first night of September.

"God, no wonder other girls never liked me," I say. "I sucked!"

Sara steps up to us, forcing her wrist out of a plastic bracelet. "Yeah, but you were friends with . . ." She shuts herself up.

"Maddie. I was friends with Maddie." These girls *are* friends with her, present tense. I'm laughing, but I don't know why, and I say, "It's so weird that we don't talk about her. She's just gone, and you guys act like—"

"Maddie asked us to meet that night," Michaela says. Not like how Sara lets things slip; this is deliberate. Kathleen glares at her, but Michaela keeps steady.

My brain buzzes. "You met up with her? Where?"

The bay?

But Michaela says, "The power plant."

"The power plant?" I know the spot; it's not far from our neighborhood. Me and Maddie would pass it on our walks to the ice cream shop the summer we were friends.

"It's walkable for me and Sara," Michaela explains, kind of. "We'd gone to this cupcake place with her after school, and then she got the rejection and wanted to be alone, but she asked to see us again—"

"When?" I'm too desperate.

Michaela frowns. "Nine-ish? She kept saying she had to leave. Get away. I thought she'd be fine by morning, but we got to school the next day and she wasn't there."

"It was horrible," Sara adds softly. "Her mom kept texting me, but it's not like we know anything." Pause. "I mean, I guess we know why, but—"

"We're done here." Kathleen is back to the girl I thought she was. Frigid. Harsh. Jaw set, she says, "I'm not talking about"— *that bitch*; what she called her in the locker room—"Maddie." She turns to Michaela with an even darker glare. "Come with me," she says, and leads her into Leather & Lace, the one place me and Sara can't go.

"Hey!" Sara whimpers, annoyed. "God, we weren't supposed to tell you that."

I gesture her down the hall, past the kickboxing studio. The sick smell of sweat drifts out of its open doors, and so do the grunts and smack of pads on punching bags.

"Kathleen told you not to tell me anything? How come?" I ask, but I know; I'm still on the outside. Sara takes in a breath. I think this is it. I think she'll crack. "Come on—"

"I told you to relax, dude."

My skin pricks at that voice—hoarse, loud. *Cody.* I look toward Sara, and she stares back, eyes huge. I drag her behind the support column, hidden by an overgrown fig tree.

"What're we—?" she starts, but I shush her.

From here, I've got a perfect view: Cody exiting the studio with his phone to his ear. He sips from the water fountain, then swipes his mouth. "I told you I'm working on it." Pause. "Wait, slow down, what happened?" Pause. "Again? Shit."

He disappears back into the studio.

"What the hell was that?" I'm not really asking for an answer.

Sara straightens, swats at the fig leaves. "Who cares? He's just an ass. You know, I never understood what Maddie sees in him," she says. I'm right there with her. "I was so excited when she told us she was breaking up with him."

"Maddie was going to break up with him?" My heart ticks faster. "When did she tell you that? When you met at the power plant? Before she ran away?"

"She was *so* upset," Sara whispers, going so fast she can't stop. "Like, she *snapped*. Her mom and dad refused to speak to each other, you know? So she was in the middle. And the paper kept her so busy, and she was stressed about NYU, and she was super upset about Cody, too, and she told us that he *cheats* on her—"

"He's cheating on her? She said that?"

Sara clamps her mouth shut, then immediately opens it again. "I wasn't supposed to say that. Like, Maddie said to forget it, so I don't know who with or anything, but she swore us to secrecy"— *no one can ever know about this*—"so please don't repeat it, okay? Please."

"I won't say a word," I say, and cross my fingers behind my back.

- *25* -

"Cody was cheating on Maddie."

Hudson jerks his head up from his phone. Blinks. His mouth is twisted into a half frown, more confused than anything. He's picking me up from Village Gate so we can study, but screw studying, sorry. He looks back at his screen, then at me, then says, "He was *what*?"

"Cheating on Maddie." I slam the car door. The mist has become a downpour, the night damp and dark. "The Birds met Maddie that night"—*that night*—"before she left"—*of her own accord*—"and she told them he cheats."

"Who with?"

"Alexis Fitch?" I offer. That pretty sophomore with the lip ring and dyed hair. Except for that hug the day of the press conference, when news broke that Maddie had run away, I've never seen them do more than talk, though.

Hudson looks unconvinced. "We don't know if they're hooking up now."

"I mean, *true*." I bite my cuticle, thinking. "Okay. Okay, how about this: Maddie is into location sharing, yeah? She made me enable it after we became friends." I leave out the part where she also made me add Cody so we could track his very boring daily movements. "What if she sees Cody is at the bay and gets suspicious? Because of the lovers' lane. She goes to confront him, finds him all up in Alexis Fitch—"

"Ew, all up in what?"

"Use your imagination. Maddie gets mad and rams into his car and . . ."

Drives off? His car was smashed; hers would be worse. If she confronted him, he could have done his worst, too, but that would leave Alexis—or whoever—as a witness. *Shit.*

For four steady swipes of the wipers, we're silent.

Then, Hudson: "Look."

Cody is jogging across the parking lot with his Duke umbrella. He unlocks his car (dent-free, like new) and digs a drawstring bag from the trunk before he starts for the road on foot.

"Where's he going?" I whisper, and louder, "Why am I whispering? He can't hear me."

Hudson kills the engine. "I'm tailing him."

"Me too!" I fumble for the handle but immediately jerk back— the seatbelt is child-locked. I half laugh, half choke as he unbuckles me, and we slip outside.

"Keep close," Hudson whispers, reaching for my hand, crouched low. He ducks behind an orange pickup, and I do the same, clinging to his shoulder.

Up ahead, Cody looks both ways (left, right, left) before he steps off the curb and—

"Hey! Cody, right?"

"Holy shit," I whisper. "I know him. That's—"

"Justin Lloyd, *ROC Weekly*."

Cody steps back, a flash of fear on his face. "Did you follow me or something?"

"No! Sorry, didn't mean to scare you." Justin holds up both hands. "I follow your gym on Instagram. They posted a picture of your class from tonight," he says, though it doesn't make his ambush any less creepy. "I thought you might want to chat— you're the boyfriend, yeah? Maddie Price's boyfriend."

Me and Hudson are both impossibly still.

So is Cody, at least until he spits, "I don't want to fucking *chat* with you."

He steps off the curb again, heading toward Bianchi's Old-Fashioned Pizzeria across the street. (Uh, that's all he's doing? Ordering takeout?) He shouts, "Tell that lady to back off, too."

Tess. Tess? She told Justin to drop it, so maybe she wants the story for herself. But how does this—Cody Forsythe, the boyfriend—even work for Justin's angle? Isn't it financial?

Justin watches Cody disappear into the pizzeria, then he sighs and leaves, too.

"One more thing," Hudson whispers, and we dash across the street.

I wait outside, angled beside the restaurant window. The sick smell of burned pepperoni seeps from under the door. I hate their food. I hate the checked tablecloths and red pepper flakes. I hate how Ben Sulkin is in a sauce-stained employee shirt behind the register. He scowls, arms crossed, as Cody counts out cash and a palmful of coins onto the counter.

Neither looks all that happy. Not with each other.

Especially not with Hudson.

I can't hear shit, but I watch: Hudson playing nice, the boys icing him out. Cody fumbles with his bag, his phone jutting from his pocket, and—*his phone.* I blink back the rain as Hudson slides it out of Cody's pocket and into his own and, look at the time, he should get going, bye.

"Hudson!" I hiss when he steps outside.

"Did you know Ben is under academic review?"

"What?"

"Yeah, he was griping about it when I walked in. Also, take this." Hudson presses the phone to my stomach. "Keep it off. We'll crack his passcode after he gets a new one. There are only"—he runs the numbers—"ten thousand possible combinations."

"I don't want this!"

Fast, Cody swivels his head toward the window.

There's no way—no *way*—he heard that, but we bolt, crashing into each other. Hudson pulls me into him, and I'm laughing when we reach his car. I don't know why. I don't know why I feel so warm when the air has only gotten colder.

"Did you still want to study?" Hudson asks, out of breath. His rain-soaked jacket clings to his chest. "Because we could . . . not study."

I let myself fall right into his trap. "What else did you have in mind?"

Hudson insists we get Garbage Plates but nearly revokes the offer when I ask for no onions. The fight continues as we haul our greasy containers up the winding path to the Cobbs Hill Reservoir.

The rain has stopped, so we take an extra jacket from his backseat and drape it across the bench that overlooks the city skyline. Hudson watches me lift the lid and take a slow, small bite.

"This is foul," I say, mouth full. "Wait, it's incredible. But bad?"

"Correct." He jabs a fork at his plate. "This makes you a true Rochesterian."

"You say that as if I haven't lived here my whole life."

"You've lived here, but have you *lived* here?"

I'm honestly not sure anymore. Rochester is a hard place to love, but sometimes I wonder if I haven't tried hard enough. There's so much more to see than I ever looked for.

And I don't know what it is—the glow of city lights or the frozen water in the reservoir or the smell of rain-melted snow—but I can't stop staring at Hudson.

He turns to me. "What is it?"

Suddenly I'm back on Miles's futon, and he's asking me with a flash of the gap between his front teeth. The "nothing" I felt was so immediate I never hesitated. Tonight, I tilt my head toward the dark sky. The clouds have started to part, letting out a scatter of stars.

"Everything," I say.

It's true. I'm thinking about the uneasy way Kathleen looked at me when she asked if I was okay. I'm thinking that of course I'm okay, why wouldn't I be?

I'm thinking about Hudson.

I'm thinking about Cody—*the boyfriend, right? Maddie Price's boyfriend.*

"He told me that he didn't like her," I say, and even without proper nouns, Hudson knows who I mean. "That he knew her better than I thought."

Hudson sets down his fork. "We didn't talk about her a lot, but he seemed pretty into her once they got together, right? He thought she was pretty. Interesting. Smart."

"He did?" My face warms, neck damp with sweat. "I thought he only wanted to get laid."

"Did it work?"

"Nope. Did you and Charlotte bone?"

Hudson lets out a strangled laugh. "I'm shocked you remember her name," he says, and I almost admit I didn't until two hours ago. Low, tentative, he adds, "I've never."

"*What*?" I almost spit out a home fry. "But you have condoms in your nightstand!"

"I mean, I've *almost* had sex." Hudson digs his heel in the dirt. "It seemed inevitable that it'd happen, but we kept . . . not. I think it made Charlotte insecure that we hadn't." He pauses. "I made her feel insecure. Finally, I was like, whatever, so we made plans to do it, um. After prom."

"Prom, huh?" The night we don't talk about, except maybe now. "That's a bit cliché."

"It gets worse. She'd booked us this hotel I couldn't afford and got her friends to decorate it. Flowers. Candles. I didn't even think to do that." He exhales, staring at the ground. "I thought I was nervous about the"—he searches for the word—"*execution.* But sex is big, you know?"

I don't know. I don't say anything.

"As soon as we got there, she went into the bathroom to change into this lingerie, and she was like, 'What do you think?' and I said, 'I think we should break up.'"

"Hudson!"

"I know. I *know*. Charlotte was furious. Justifiably so. So, I got a ride to the after-party everyone else had gone to instead and, you know. Performed oral sex on you."

"Oh my God." I bury my face in my scarf. "Why did you phrase it like that?"

"Did you want me to rephrase it? Because I can." He laughs, and so do I, but it's pained, mortified laughter. "I know we don't talk about it, but do you honestly not even think about it?"

I'm certainly thinking about it now.

The after-party was at this spectacular lake house that belonged to Ben Sulkin's aunt's cousin or something like that.

The night had gotten hazy. I hogged the karaoke machine, flounced around in my perfect dress. Cody kept kissing various Lourdes girls between our duets, which made Maddie upset, so then the Birds had to cheer her up, and the guys got Miles drunk on Keystone and tequila shots.

Late, Cody hooted into the mic, "Look who it is! Hudson and—uh-oh."

But I'd retired to the kitchen to make a gin gimlet from a recipe card I'd found. I dug in the fridge for limes and, when I shut the door, Hudson stood on the other side.

"Hey!" I said, selfishly happy to see him, but confused. "Where's your girlfriend?"

Hudson took a swig of beer, so I thought maybe he didn't hear me. Then he leaned a little closer and said, "What girlfriend?"

"Oh. I'm sorry." I held up my limes. "Want a pity gin gimlet?"

That was the moment I made it my mission to cheer him up. I put on a whole show of my shitty mixology. And he leaned against the counter and watched as I sliced the limes, poured the simple syrup, shook the shaker, passed the glass. "Is this a shot?"

I faked a gasp. "No! You're supposed to savor it." His eyes slid from the bare skin of my sternum to my lips. I said, "Cheers," and clinked his glass with mine.

He finished the drink in one sip. "Want to get out of here?"

I did, very, very badly.

We wandered into the backyard. It was cool but lovely, the sky cloudless and full of stars. The pool wasn't warm enough to swim, but it glowed, water clear and rippling. I lay on a pool chair, and he sat at the bottom, his hand resting by my hip.

"I'm sorry your night went to shit," I said.

"It's better now." Hudson inched up, just a bit. "You look really beautiful, by the way."

Then he kissed me.

It was sudden—a temporary moment of whiplash, a plot twist I didn't see coming.

We'd never kissed before, but I'd thought about it—of course I'd thought about it—and now, with his lips pressed to mine, I wondered what the hell had taken so long. He pulled back and apologized but, holy shit, I wanted to keep doing it.

I *wanted* it.

So, I said, "Shut up, Hudson," and kissed him again.

He leaned on top of me, and the chair slid down a notch. I laughed, let him tug me up and lead me toward the trees, out of the light, out of view.

And I did what I always do: I dropped to my knees.

But Hudson lifted me up by the elbow. "Sorry, did you not want me to?" I asked.

He looked just as surprised. "No, I do. I *really* do. But I think this would end very fast if you did, and I don't want that. I want *you*, Jo."

Me, Jo.

He kissed me again, and I melted into it, dragging him down to the grass with me. I liked his weight on top of me. I liked that our mouths fit so, so perfectly. I liked how he planted his leg between mine, lifted his knee, rocked it against me.

I let out a noise—half gasp, half moan—I didn't know I could make. "Oh my God, I'm sorry. That's so embarrassing."

"Don't apologize for that." He eased his hand into the top of my dress. "It's so hot."

"Oh my God," I said again, even more breathless than before.

My thoughts raced: *I can't believe this is happening. I didn't know I wanted it to happen.*

But I did. Hudson and I orbited each other, drawn by an obvious gravitational pull, never colliding. He was different from those other guys. Kinder and smarter and funnier. More clever. I didn't dare think that, to him, I was different, too. That I might be . . . I don't know. Special.

This, with Hudson—it all felt new. His mouth on mine and his hand on my breast and the knee thing, seriously, *the knee thing.* The hell was that? My breath was growing heavier. Harder.

Then Hudson sat back on his heels.

I propped myself up on my elbows. "Why did you stop?"

His mouth ticked up. "I thought you told me to savor it."

For a third time: "Oh . . . my God."

He laughed, shrugging out of his tux jacket, tugging loose his bowtie. He skimmed his thumb along the hem of my skirt. "Daisies?"

"Uh-huh." I held my breath as his hands slipped under the tulle, slid up my thighs.

"Is that your favorite flower?"

"I don't think I have a favorite flower. How come?"

"I like knowing what you like." His hands landed on my hips. "Can I take these off?"

That wasn't really a thing I did. I was easy, and I'd go far, do everything but, but never for me. My guys-of-the-night had one end goal, so I managed every kiss and touch, deflecting when they pawed at my zipper, slapping their hands when they thought I was kidding.

But I lifted my hips, nodding even as I whispered, "Sorry."

"Why do you keep apologizing?"

"I don't know. Because I'm neglecting your penis."

"This can be about you," he said, a question without asking it.

I nodded again.

Then he hiked up my skirt and I died, I was dead, and I thought of Hudson—what he was doing, which had also never happened before—and what he'd said. I was *beautiful, by the way,* and I felt beautiful and wanted, and I wanted it, too, so much, so desperately, and I *liked* it.

In my brain, "He likes it too" became "He likes doing this to me" which became "He likes me." *Hudson likes me.* But how could it be true when he'd just had a girlfriend hours earlier?

My heart pounded in a different way. I squeezed my eyes tighter as my body shut down, like lights in a building flicking off one by one by one.

"No," I whispered, but it was all me. *No.*

He pulled back. "Hey, are you okay?"

"I'm sorry, I'm . . . I can't." I slid up my underwear. Brushed the dirt from my hips. The moonlight caught the glitter on my dress and shimmered in the dark, dark night.

He shook his head. "Is something wrong?"

Everything was wrong. This thing opened up inside me, a want I didn't know I wanted, and what I wanted was for him to tell me he'd said those things because he meant them. Because he wanted me—Jo—not some girl to heal the fresh wound to his heart.

Because he liked me.

"You just broke up with your girlfriend." I wanted him to read my mind and know the rest without me needing to say it.

But Hudson only said, "Okay."

Here, a flutter of wings rattles the tree branches. I search for the source of the sound, but I stay silent myself. I kind of don't know what to say.

Hudson sighs, his eyes downcast. "I was just confused, I guess. You were so upset—"

"It was nothing *you* did." I stare at the skyline, lit orange against the night sky. "I didn't want to be the girl you went to because you were sad and lonely and horny, and I was . . ." I shut my eyes, just for a second. "Because I was there."

"What?" Hudson shifts to face me. "No, I'm so sorry, Jo. That's not what that was."

"What was it then?"

He looks like he wants to say something—I think I want him to say something—but his phone blares. He fumbles it from his pocket. "Sorry, it's a reminder for bed. I work tomorrow."

I pack up my leftovers. "Then we should go."

On the drive back to my house, I blast my Billy Joel playlist, and he doesn't even make fun of me. He lowers the volume when he parks.

"Thank you. For talking," he says. "Not just about me and Charlotte, but me and you." *Me and you.* "I think about it a lot, so thanks. Seriously."

"It was painless," I half lie, stepping out into the cold. But I hesitate with my hand on the door and turn back to him. "So, you think about performing oral sex on me a lot?"

"Not like that." He rolls his eyes over to me. Takes me in. "I mean, sometimes like that."

Oh my God. "Goodnight, Hudson."

Inside, I stuff my leftovers in the fridge and retreat to my bedroom. I feel . . . weird. So weird that I lie on my bed and stare at the ceiling for ten straight minutes.

The feeling sticks, too, when I pull out my phone.

[9:02 p.m.] **JO:** i have a confession: i didn't remember
charlotte's name
[9:03 p.m.] **JO:** we saw her today

[9:04 p.m.] **HUDSON:** ohhhhh that explains it

[9:04 p.m.] **JO:** uh oh

[9:05 p.m.] **HUDSON:** don't worry about it

[9:06 p.m.] **JO:** i have another confession: i do think about it

[9:06 p.m.] **JO:** a lot

His reply bubble pops up. I bite my thumb, anxiously waiting but too anxious to wait.

[9:07 p.m.] **JO:** that had never happened

[9:07 p.m.] **JO:** so

[9:08 p.m.] **HUDSON:** so?

[9:08 p.m.] **JO:** so . . . i . . . liked it . . .

I throw my phone through the bathroom door with a shriek and immediately fetch it.

His reply doesn't surprise me, but I still gasp.

[9:09 p.m.] **HUDSON:** i really liked it too

I cannot handle this.

I sink against the tub, the tile freezing the backs of my thighs— and I look to the shower.

With the lights still off, I twist the faucet and strip off my clothes, step in the tub, shampoo, condition, cleanse face, think: *what if I hadn't stopped him?* I've never been so close. Not with a guy, not ever. It was overwhelming. It was incredible.

Not thinking, I yank the showerhead from its cradle and

adjust the stream and let myself imagine it: his hand in my dress, the knee thing, *me and you*, his mouth lower and—

"Oh my God," I breathe out, barely. I grip the shower curtain in my fist and bite my lip, my breaths fast and shallow and hard. I get it now. I get it, I get it, I get it.

Once my heart beats its normal rhythm, I rip open the shower curtain. My own reflection in the darkened mirror stares back. So many people have seen this mirror. Me. It feels unfair that I stay in the dark because of what they decided to see in me.

I turn on the light.

-26-

I'm a mess—in a good way, mostly.

Those texts from Hudson fill me with an indescribable feeling each time I reread them. (I reread them a *lot*.) I'll see him tonight at the bowling thing, and then I'm sleeping over at Sara's house for her birthday. I packed my bag last night, then I repacked it this morning since I forgot pants and also deodorant, and no, I'm not nervous for my first birthday sleepover. Not at all.

For now, me and Tess are designing my poster for Open House next Monday in the *ROC Weekly* conference room. I brought a shoebox of photos, so I've been scanning the best (worst?) to paste on the poster. Tess holds up one of me with a silk sash and a small bouquet. Runner-up.

"I did pageants forever ago," I say. "But then I got banned from competing, so."

"Yeah? What happened?"

"I don't remember." I do, duh, but I don't want to talk about it.

Tess flips her laptop open. "I'd love to hear the story if you do."

Tell her. I don't know where the words come from, or even what I'd say. I have nothing to tell. I pick up another picture. Me and Cody in middle school. "See him?" I ask. "My former friend. Cody. He"—*tell her*—"is, uh, dating Maddie. And"—*tell her*—"he was talking to Justin last night. Or Justin talked to him."

Tess frowns. "Justin Lloyd?"

"Yeah, he kind of accosted Cody in the Village Gate parking lot to 'chat' for his story."

"Justin . . ." Tess shuts her laptop. "Excuse me."

"Oh, can I come?" I follow her into the stairwell and down to the third floor.

Justin has overtaken a recording booth near the end of the hall, his laptop illuminating his face, his feet kicked onto the table. He's chewing his headphones wire. Tess flings open the door, and he jolts, yanking off his headphones. "Spradlin—"

"I told you to kill the fucking story," Tess seethes. My first instinct is to laugh, but I force it down, force myself to keep still. "Not only did you not kill the story, you harassed a *minor*?"

"No one in that family will talk! The boyfriend—he must know something." Justin turns to me. "Isn't that what you girls do? Tell your boyfriend your deepest, darkest secrets?"

Tess takes a protective step toward me. "The story is *wrong*, Justin. The angle is *bad*."

"Calm down," Justin says, and I think Tess truly might kill him. "Let me lay it out." He tilts the mic toward his mouth. Shoves it back. "Mom and Dad split up last summer. Mom gets the house; Dad buys a million-dollar loft. How can they afford both on his salary alone? They must be *drowning* in debt, then the girl—"

"Maddie," I say.

"—goes missing, and a *fundraiser* pops up? Is that not shady to you?"

Tess rubs her temples, like she's staving off a headache. "Anyone can create one, Justin."

"It was her dad's cousin," I say.

"See? There you go," Tess says, then turns to me again. "How do you know that?"

I smile innocently. "Know what?"

Justin slams his fist on the table, shouts, "They fucking faked it!" Me and Tess go quiet. Breathing harder, like he knows this is getting good, he says, "This is a get-rich-quick scheme. They're using the disappearance to get out of debt. I'll bet you anything they know just where that girl is so they can 'find' her and pocket the reward."

Low, Tess says, "There is no reward. The fundraiser was shut down."

"That's even better." He nods, not blinking, lost in his new tale. "They use the angle that no one helped; *they* had to save her."

"Save her from what?" Tess says, exasperated. "She left a note, Justin. She ran away."

"You're not listening—"

"Oh, I hear you. I'm telling you that you're wrong. Do you really think her own parents would *abduct* her? Hold her captive?"

"No, Spradlin," Justin says, a sick grin on his face. "I think that girl is in on it. I think she got sad and wanted attention and—"

"Kill the story, Justin. I mean it." Tess motions me out but lingers in the doorway. "And why are you in a recording booth?"

"I, uh. Thought it'd be compelling to explore the story in podcast format."

Tess crashes into the hall.

"Her name is Maddie, asshole," I call behind me.

This time, Tess skips the elevator and guides me into the stairwell, waiting for the door to slam before she says, "Please tell me I'm wrong and you're not playing amateur sleuth."

"You're investigating, too, and *hiding* it."

"I'm not hiding anything!"

"Uh-huh." I kick my foot onto the bottom step and cross my arms, head high, like I can make myself taller. "You want the story for yourself? To get back to New York?"

Tess rips off her glasses, swiping at a smudge. "I have writer's block, remember?" She pops her glasses back on. "I honestly think Maddie ran away." Pause. "But I'd be remiss not to explore all possible angles, and perhaps that involves some light investigation."

"So, what can you tell me? Like, have you seen the note? What does it say?"

"Nothing."

"The note says nothing?"

"No, I don't know what the note says, but I'm not telling you anything."

"Then what do you want to know?"

"We're not doing this, Jo-hyphen-Lynn," Tess says, but it's a lie. I can see it in the way she stares at me, like this is an uneasy alliance. "Don't you have reflections to send me? For the program? Maybe focus on that."

"I emailed them!" It sounds like an excuse—*the dog ate my reflections*—but I did.

Frowning, Tess pulls out her phone. "I keep telling our IT

department that my spam filter is too aggressive." She scrolls through her junk folder. "Here they are."

"Maybe the filter hates my Culver email," I say, mostly joking. Then I go still. Tess is thinking it, too, her finger hovering over the search bar. I whisper, "Maddie emailed you."

"God, you really are a snoop."

I keep going. "Back in December, Maddie emailed you, so what if she—?"

Tess flips out the screen.

in:spam "price"

Dec. 28, 2:11 p.m. — Sorry to bother you! I'm following up on my original email. Would you like to meet? It's winter break, so I have lots of time.

Jan. 10, 6:32 a.m. — Hello! I know you're busy, but I wonder if my emails might be going to spam? I'm actually writing to you about a story I'm working on, and I could really use your help.

Jan. 31, 3:57 a.m. — Please email when you can. I think I'm in over my head.

-27-

It feels so glaringly obvious now. I was too hung up on the stories everyone else tried to tell that I never even considered Maddie had one of her own.

That was unfair. I'm starting over. I'm starting with this: *Maddie was writing a story.*

Hudson rereads the screenshot. "'I think I'm in over my head.' What does that mean?"

"I don't know." I can barely think.

Literally the last place I want to be is *here*, at this bowling alley, even with my very fake boyfriend who brings a very real thrum to my body. Turns out Hudson is terrible at bowling, so we ditched our lane for a green velvet couch by the bar. The TVs above it loop ESPN, News 9, my mother on Channel 12.

Hudson taps his thumb to his scar. "Maddie was writing a story, and she was in over her head, so she was . . . scared?"

It ticks inside me: Maddie, scared. Maddie, in trouble. *I think that I'm—*

"I don't know." I need to use new words, so I add, "Could it be about your rank? Her story? But . . ."

"I'm the only one who'd suffer because of that," Hudson offers.

Something is off about the acoustics in here; each strike and gutter ball and collision of pins is so goddamn *loud.*

I look across the lanes. Trey Gardner, still in his sling, is attempting to bowl left-handed. The ball drops and rolls behind him. Ben Sulkin laughs his horrible laugh and smacks Trey hard on the arm. His smile falls when Cody Forsythe skulks inside the bowling alley. Ben's fist clenches. He beelines over to him, seething. "Dude, why are you fucking ignoring me? You need to fix—"

"I'm not ignoring you." Cody shakes him off. "I lost my phone."

" 'I think I'm in over my head,' " Hudson says again.

I drag my nail across the velvet. "We need to figure out what she was writing—the paper staff must keep a story list, right?" I search for Gabe Figueroa in a perfect cashmere sweater vest, but I guess he has more of a life than us.

"What about Daniele?" Hudson nods toward the bar, where she's capturing an aesthetic shot of a virgin cocktail. One-L Daniele, photo director of *The Eagle Eye.* The reason we came, even if Sara has just stared longingly at her from afar.

Sorry, Sara, but I'm stealing your girl.

"One-L Daniele!" I wave her over. "Hudson wants to see *The Eagle Eye* story list."

He narrows his eyes the tiniest bit, but I don't have a better lie yet. "I wanted to, uh . . . collaborate. I'm in digital design, and we have these portfolios—"

"Sent," One-L Daniele says, and then she's gone again.

"Damn, she's efficient." Hudson opens his email, then the link to the document: "Ideas & Assignments." I take his phone and scroll down, down—

IDEAS

M. PRICE: tips and tricks for senioritis; early action vs. early decision vs. regular decision; healthy cafeteria options (overdone?); personal archive

"Huh," Hudson says, which is about all I have to say, too.

No offense to Maddie, but these seem . . . hollow. Tess even said that, right? That Maddie tells her stories wrong. That she doesn't go deep enough. Except—

Personal archive. That pink safe Michaela told me about from their summer camp at the library. I can picture it so clearly in my mind, but why?

I keep scrolling.

I stop scrolling.

ASSIGNMENTS

COMEBACK GAME (draft due 1/31): Maddie + Lee

I blink, but it's still there: *Maddie + Lee.* But Gabe told me that *he* needed Lee to respond about the story. That he needed the most major of the players to talk, which means my brother.

Maddie + my brother, for a story due five days before she disappeared.

Ran away.

"Did Lee ever mention this?" Hudson asks.

"Never." I hand back his phone. "I wonder if she even contacted him. Maybe she forgot or something. Or she . . ." *I think I'm in over my head.* "I don't know."

What I do know is that I'd absolutely love to leave.

"We're leaving," Kathleen says, dumping my coat over the back of the couch. "Michaela broke the bumper, so we're taking it as a sign from above to get out of here."

"Have *so* much fun without me," Hudson says, fake sad, as if he's not already lacing up his high-tops. He stands, glancing toward the bar. Then he looks again, his face going paler than I've ever seen it. Low, he says, "Jo."

"What?" I follow his gaze to the TV above the bar. "No."

No, no, no, no.

NEWS 9 EXCLUSIVE INTERVIEW!

Kathleen squints. "Is that . . . ?"

Mrs. Price, sitting on the leather couch in her den. She looks beautiful, honestly, which is weird to notice. Beside her, Sabrina Kim is nodding, extra serious. *Tell that lady to back off, too.* That's what Cody said, and I thought he meant Tess, but what if it was Sabrina?

I find him now: Cody Forsythe, slack-jawed and ghostly white, staring up at the screen.

Sara and Michaela nearly crash into us, talking over each other.

Everyone else has gone silent.

I fumble my phone from my pocket, and Hudson fishes out his earbuds, handing me one, leaning into me as I pull up a livestream so we can listen. Mrs. Price is midsentence: ". . . harassed by reporters. I know an upcoming story says *we* hurt Maddie. That we're in debt and—"

Justin Lloyd's story. Someone leaked it, and Mrs. Price is airing it out, beat by beat.

The captions botch her words, so I catch only snippets: "I would never . . . Maddie would never . . . I don't . . . understand she left the note but . . . is such a perfect girl and . . . where did she . . . why . . . vicious attacks . . . vile rumors . . ."

Sabrina comes out clearer. "I'm struggling with the utter lack of interest from her peers. Her friends." Sara covers her mouth. Michaela looks at her shoes. Kathleen stands tall, daring everyone to stare. "Her boyfriend." Cody shoves his way outside, into the cold. "Police are still accepting tips to their nonemergency line. Someone knows something. Someone—"

I rip out the earbud and drop my head in my hands. My brain loops every phrase: *I think I'm in over my head*; *I think that I'm in trouble, but I think that you can help me*; *no one can ever know about this*; *missing, kidnapped—*

"I stole a bottle of rum for tonight," Kathleen says calmly, "and I think we should go."

Because everyone is staring at us. *Them.* I'm not Maddie's friend.

Kathleen nods, and again: "I think we should go."

But her phone starts to vibrate in her hand. Then Michaela's. The jocks', too, and One-L Daniele's, and Hudson looks up at me, his face unreadable. It's just like the bonfire, the photos filtering in, from person to person, and I think I might puke but it can't be me, it can't be—

My phone buzzes, too.

It's a notification from Instagram: **maddie.price_09** posted for the first time in a while.

Finger shaking, heart racing, I open the app and tap the post—a cropped screenshot from a generic notes app.

```
Hi. This is Maddie. I thought I should
set the record straight; I appreciate
that my Mom is concerned (that your all
concerned, and the Police have helped)
but I am ok. I am safe. I said it in my
note.

I just want to be left alone.
```

-28-

Maddie Price didn't write that fucking post.

-29-

"Maddie wrote that post, right?" Sara says it, and so does Michaela. Lots of times, both of them, again and again: *Maddie wrote that post. Maddie is okay. Maddie is safe.*

Right?

They tell this lie until it sounds something like the truth.

Later, after Sara and Michaela have passed out in the den, Kathleen and I sneak outside to split the rest of the rum. It tastes like sunscreen. I'm shivering, freezing, my phone shaking in my hands. I refresh the profile. *I thought I should set the record straight—*

"Maddie didn't write that," Kathleen says, words slurred.

Refresh, reread. *Your* versus *you're. Ok* and not *okay.*

Kathleen peers down at my phone, her chin on my shoulder. Her teeth chatter wildly. "It wasn't her. It was wrong," she whispers. I've never seen her this drunk, but I'm drunk, too. Eyes shutting, she says, "That's not what it said."

"What do you mean?" I turn to Kathleen but there are three of her, and I blink, refresh Instagram—

User not found.

-30-

The next morning, the sky is a startling, cloudless blue, the sun shining bright white. I can't even remember when I last saw the sun. But it is lovely and perfect as we walk, so that's what I think: *I think it is lovely and perfect.*

It's the only way I keep from hurling.

Sara, it seems, is immune to this hangover. "I'm eighteen!"

"I say this out of love," Michaela says, "but shut the fuck up."

I'm a few sidewalk squares behind, but Kathleen waits up. She found a pair of sunglasses in her glovebox; between them and the hunch in her walk, coat tight to her body, she looks like a widow whose husband died a mysterious death.

"You're quiet," she says, raspy.

I'll be way better with food. I want home fries. Eggs over medium. Bacon. Lemon-ricotta pancakes. I want an iced coffee with cream, no sugar, never sugar.

"Last night..." I start, the sentence a fill-in-the-blank. The post, the account—gone again. Maddie is still gone, too, but at least now we know *she is ok; she is safe.* I try again: "Last night, you kept saying 'it' was wrong. The post."

Kathleen stares straight ahead. "I don't even remember saying that."

"But—"

"Beaver whack, no beaver whack back!" Sara shouts, trotting up to us, batting Kathleen on the arm. Kathleen immediately whacks back, hard. "Hey!"

Michaela steps between them. "Use real words, Sara."

"Has no one been on a road trip? You do it when you see those ugly station wagons." She gestures toward the coffee shop across the street, and somehow I know, even before I look, what I'll see parked in front.

That car. A 1996 Buick Roadmaster Estate. White with a stripe of wood paneling. I know nothing about cars but everything about this one: its broken radio; the splinter in the dashboard; how rough the carpet feels against my back, my knees, the side of my face.

"Move it." Kathleen lifts her sunglasses to her head. "Wait, are you okay?"

"I need to—" The vomit burns up my throat. I collapse to my knees, heaving.

"Party foul!" Sara shouts.

Kathleen loops my hair in her fist. "Jo?" I can't speak. I can't—I can't think. I look to the car, and she finds it, too. Her brows knit. "Put our name down, okay?" she calls back to the girls. "I'll take her to get a ginger ale."

She hauls me up by the elbow and drags me down the sidewalk. It's a few blocks to the corner store, but we're fast. Faster than my heart, even, which is beating so fast I think it might rip open my ribs. Break every bone in my body.

I sit on the curb, legs stretched in front of me, as Kathleen disappears inside. She returns with a box of saltine crackers and a can of ginger ale, then she's gone again. I crack the tab and take the tiniest sip. It does little to settle my stomach.

Kathleen reemerges with a coffee for herself. She mixes in two pink sugar packets and a mini creamer. Twirling the stirrer, steam swirling from the cup, she asks, "Whose car was that?"

The air is a crisp kind of cold. The kind that bites. I breathe it in, say, "It was Nick's."

Like a statement of fact. Snow is white. The sky is blue. That was Nick's car.

"Nick?" Kathleen winces when she sips, burned. "Like, Nick Price? Maddie's brother?"

The other name in the Venn diagram between us.

"We had a . . . thing. Barely a thing. It was a stupid summer fling. I can count on one hand the number of times we . . . hung out." I swallow, throat raw. "But it didn't end great, and he was a dick the last time I saw him and, uh. He lives in New York, right? So, I didn't expect to see his car. That's all."

"I'm sorry."

"What's there to be sorry for?"

"You said he was a dick to you. That last time."

"My brother's graduation party," I say with an eyeroll. My parents made me string lights along the fence and prop up childhood photos of Lee. I stole three beers as compensation. "It'd been a year since I'd seen Nick, so I figured we'd, you know, but he—"

"You need to breathe."

"I'm breathing." I'm not breathing.

Kathleen pops the lid onto her cup. "It was the summer before, then? When you . . . hung out?" I nod. Then she nods, too, and we're both nodding until she says, "You can tell me about it, if you want."

"There's nothing to tell."

"Okay." The light at the intersection flips from yellow to red.

I tear at the skin on my lower lip and laugh and say, "It was that fucking pool party."

Right after I heard Maddie sob that she only invited me to be nice. That no one liked me. That *she* didn't even like me. Things had been a little weird since we started at Culver, but just because we never saw each other. Summer was supposed to be different. Better.

It gutted me—clear, undeniable proof that she didn't want to be friends anymore.

I couldn't go back to the party with all those other girls who didn't like me, either, since I was loud and mean and so boy crazy that I invited them to get Maddie in trouble. And I couldn't go home. Not when my brother warned me this would happen.

So, I snuck to the side of the Prices' house and sat in the grass. The sky had just started to darken. Mosquitoes swarmed my ankles. My thighs. I was playing Tetris on the hot pink phone I loved so much until I lost it later that summer when the car—*that* car—parked at the curb.

"Party's out back," Nick said with a nod, cutting across the yard.

"I'm aware."

He stopped. Turned back, slowly, like I was feral. "JoJo, right?"

"You know who I am." Pause. "But it's Jo."

Even if we'd never spoken before, I hated Nick on Maddie's behalf like she hated Lee on mine. It bonded us, being the younger sister. Lee's golden light shined so brightly that it felt like I never did anything right; Maddie, the miracle baby, was so obviously the favorite child, constantly doted on, constantly watched, that she *had* to be perfect at all times while Nick went unchecked.

This, I thought, would be the end of it.

Then Nick said, "You've got a mouth on you," with something like a smile. My face felt hot. I knew, even if I didn't *know*, that no boy had ever looked at me like that before. He nudged my flip-flop with his sneaker. "Want to go for a drive? Tell me what's wrong?"

"Nothing's wrong." I looked down at my phone.

"You're lying."

I looked up again. Started to tell him, uh, this was kind of weird, sorry, and I should get back to the party or go home or something and, anyway, Maddie was my best friend—

But was Maddie my best friend?

It'd make her furious to know I was talking to Nick. Maddie never had anything that was just hers—except for me. Our friendship. I was her one small rebellion, but now I was rebelling, too. I kind of liked it. I liked knowing I could make Maddie mad.

So, I stood. Brushed the grass from my hips.

And I followed Nick to his car.

He reached into the backseat and offered me a hard seltzer—watermelon, like my bikini top—and asked why I was sitting alongside his house. And I told him. For some reason, I told him Maddie hated me now, and I didn't know what I'd done, and none of those other girls liked me, either, but I wasn't that different, was I? Why couldn't they see that?

Why couldn't they see *me*?

Here, back with Kathleen, I rip the tab off the can. "Know what he said? He said, 'You don't want to be friends with my sister, or any of them. You're not like those girls.'" She hisses in a breath, and I say, "It's funny! My whole not-like-other-girls thing. You said it yourself."

"No, I get it, but Nick . . . he's older than us, right?"

My heartbeat trips. I know where she's going with this. I feel myself closing off, like a clenched fist. Like a porcupine curling into itself, spikes extended.

"So, you were fifteen," she says, "and Nick was, what? Twenty-one?"

"It's not a big deal." I knock over the can, soda spilling, bubbling on the pavement.

"You're a June birthday, too, so you'd *just* turned fifteen," Kathleen says, and I don't like this, and I hate it even more when she goes, "Did he, like, try stuff that night?"

"He . . . I . . ." I tilt my face toward the flawless sky. "It just happened."

Because it did. We drove around, talking, and he told me about his architecture program at Cornell, told me Rochester is a hideous city, and then he parked at a park, I think, but I wasn't sure since it was so dark, and I asked where we were, but wasn't it crowded up front, maybe we could pop the trunk and sit in the way back, and did I want another seltzer and, wow, I was so cool and fun and funny, had I ever had a boyfriend, how far had we gone, why did I go by JoJo and I told him it's Jo, just Jo, and he said I should try *Jolie* since it means "pretty" in French and I kissed him—I kissed him, *I* kissed *him*—and I'd never kissed like this and he was heavy on top of me and I felt a little dizzy and then he had a condom and I thought he was showing me, which is funny, like was this show-and-tell or something, and I wanted to tell him how funny it was but then he unzipped my shorts and said, *This is okay, right?* and I sort of didn't say anything, which is also funny—the girl who never shuts the fuck up forgets how to speak—until, after, when Nick said maybe he got carried away, and I told him it was fine, it's fine, it's fine.

I said it was fine.

"Oh my God." Kathleen clasps a hand to her mouth. "Did you ever tell anyone?"

I shake my head. "Tell them what?"

"Do you not . . . ?" She searches my face. I can't read hers. I mirror her—arms tight to my body, shoulders lifting toward my ears—then force myself to stand. To release the tension.

"Our table is probably ready." I start across the parking lot, not waiting up. Not looking when she jogs up to me, coffee sloshing from the lid of her cup.

"Maddie knew." Kathleen doesn't say it like a question.

"I was *her* friend, but I chose Nick," I say. "I knew it'd hurt her, and I did it, anyway."

Quietly, Kathleen says, "I don't think that's what happened, Jo."

What happened is that Nick idled at the end of our street and told me we better not show up together, so I should probably walk the rest of the way. He stroked the inside of my wrist and said, low and serious, "No one can ever know about this."

What happened is that I nodded, dazed from . . . I didn't know what. I started to walk, but my legs felt weird and unsteady and maybe I needed to sit, so I sat, right there, in the middle of the sidewalk, beside the only darkened streetlight on the block.

What happened is that of course Maddie knew.

The other girls were huddled around the firepit when I forced open the gate. Maddie had changed out of her swimsuit, but the smell of chlorine clung to her sunburned skin. Furious, she hissed, "I've been looking all over—wait, are you *drunk*?"

She stepped back. Looked to Nick's bedroom window as the light flicked on. "Where did you—? Who were you—?"

I didn't answer her.

Instead, I dropped onto an empty lawn chair around the crackling fire.

And I looked at those other girls and thought: *I'm nothing like you.*

-31-

My brain won't shut the fuck up about Nick. It's like, *Nick is here. Why is he here? He's here, and he'll probably stay with his parents, so I might see that car again, I might see—*

Him.

The thing is, I try very hard not to think about Nick. Even in the year after our . . . thing or fling or whatever, it's not like I was crying over him. We hung out, like, three or four more times that summer, only late, only in the dark. It was *my* choice to meet up. Hook up. But I never loved Nick, and I knew we'd never be together, and I didn't want that, anyway, so who cared?

Not me.

Then Nick was back for one last night.

Lee's graduation party sucked, so I stole another lukewarm beer and met Nick at his car across the street—two neighbors catching up in the dark. He'd just graduated from Cornell, and he was moving to Manhattan the next day for a fantastic job at a prestigious architecture firm.

I could not care less, sorry. I'd just turned sixteen, and I wanted him to see how much I'd changed since last summer. I wanted him to look at me like I was worth seeing.

Jesus, how mortifying is that?

It gets worse: I leaned against his car in a way I hoped was sexy. I *preened* for him. Told him I was down for anything. Nick laughed at that—*me*—and said, "That's why all the guys like you," and right there, where anyone could see us, he kissed me.

He kissed *me.*

Then he pressed my hand to his shorts.

But I could hear dribbling from my driveway, and a light shone from Maddie's window, and *no one can ever know about this.* I broke from his mouth, said, "Nick, maybe we should—"

"Come on, Jolie," he fake-pleaded, but he let me go, stepped up onto the curb. "Maybe we should what? What did you think was going to happen?"

My throat went tight. "I mean, *this*, but—"

He cut me off with a laugh, short and mean. "What, did you want dinner first? God, you girls always do this shit. You know it was never anything more than *this*, right?"

I shook my head. That couldn't be true. No, it wasn't love between us last summer, but it was something. *I* was something. I was special and different and not like those other girls—he said so—and Nick chose *me*. Jo.

Jolie.

The beer sloshed in my stomach. Slurred my words when I said, "Then why—?"

"Because you were *there*, Jolie." Nick laughed again, then rephrased it: "Because I was bored, and you were there."

Like I was so fucking stupid to think I could ever be anything else.

My hangover lasts to Sunday. Nothing else explains why Nick is poisoning my brain. Every time the door to Java's opens, I hold my breath—but it's always just a white guy with brown hair.

"Is everything okay?" Hudson taps his pen on my physics textbook. We're studying, sort of. I've done, uh. Nothing.

I've been doing so much better recently, turning in my homework on time, passing tests, but I'm unmotivated today. Unfocused.

I stir my iced coffee, spoon clinking the glass. "I'm fine," I say, and I even force a smile, like, *Look how fine I am.* I look toward the counter for a reprieve and gasp, "Tess!"

She heads our way after she pays. "Jo-hyphen-Lynn and friend!"

"This is Hudson. He's my . . ." I choke on the word. "What are you doing here?"

"Trying to keep *ROC Weekly* from totally imploding." Tess sits, sets her laptop onto the table. "I take it you saw the interview?" Then to Hudson: "Should I assume you're in the know?"

He gives her a nod. "I'm in the know."

Tess rolls her neck, stretching out a knot. "There's an internal investigation into the leak. Everyone is thinking that Sabrina passed Justin's story to the Prices, but how did *she* get it?"

Something—a hazy, smoke-filled memory—worms through my brain. I dig into my bag, fish out a business card: Sabrina Kim, News 9. *Hint, hint.* I say, "I got this from her a few weeks ago, at the Barcade. Also, I kind of matched her and Justin on Tinder."

Tess drops her head in her hands. "Do not tell me that man leaked it himself."

Only one way to find out.

The line connects on the second ring. "This is Sabrina Kim."

I put it on speaker and say, "Hey, there, Sabrina," in my best impression of my mother. Tess and Hudson both look equally impressed and horrified. "Yes, this is Kate Kirby. I'm just calling to congratulate you on that Price interview."

"Oh, thank you, Kate! That's so sweet."

Tess types my next line into a new tab. I read, "I'm surprised your sources were so—"

But Sabrina laughs, warbled. "Off the record? I matched some writer on a dating app. His editor killed his story, so he pitched me his 'independent' podcast idea." Tess shuts her eyes. "He sent me all his research so we could 'collaborate.' Can you—?"

"Hang up," Tess says. I do as I'm told.

She's quiet for a very, very long time. Then, finally, she opens up her browser and types *best places to scream loudly rochester ny.*

"I'm sorry," I say sheepishly.

"Not your fault. Never trust a man with a podcast." Tess flips her laptop shut and glances to the pickup counter, then back to us. "It's not like I haven't been through worse. Did I tell you that one of my stories went viral my senior year at Culver? Like, *viral.*"

"What was it about?" Hudson asks.

"Culver had a strong academic reputation, but they wanted to establish their athletics, too. The soccer program was decent. Baseball, track and field—all fine. But they'd never had a winning season in basketball. Ever."

I think of my brother: Lee Kirby, point guard.

"They hired this new health teacher my senior year, and he told them he played a bit of ball in college, so maybe *he* could coach. What do you think happens next?"

"They start winning?" I offer.

"Undefeated. My editor in chief wanted me to profile him, so I started researching before our interview—and turns out, the man lied about *everything*. Faked a master's from a university that doesn't exist. Forged a teaching license. Never even played basketball!"

Hudson leans closer, riveted. "What happened?"

"The administration told us not to run it. The team was winning, so . . ." Tess shrugs. "We still ran it, obviously. It *blew* up. The coach got fired immediately. I got this prestigious award for young journalists, and four internship offers before I'd even moved to New York. It basically got me into NYU," she tacks on, like it's nothing.

Hudson lifts his shoulder. "That sounds great."

"Professionally, yes, but my social life was a fucking nightmare." Tess laughs, but it isn't funny. "My classmates slashed my tires. Filled my locker with death threats."

"Death threats?"

"People like to win, Jo." Tess goes quiet. "Some additional context here is that the coach was my boyfriend's dad." I spit my coffee into the cup. She holds up a hand. "Believe me, no one is more surprised I ever dated men than me."

But that's not the part I'm stuck on.

"Latte for Tess!"

She parts with a salute. "I'll see you both at Open House tomorrow. Nice to meet you, Hudson."

"You too," he says, then to me, "What the hell was that?"

I press my palms on the table. "That story got Tess fame and awards and internships and a spot at NYU," I say breathlessly, waiting for Hudson to catch up. "Maddie knew she fucked up by not getting that recommendation letter, and she wasn't in the top ten percent of our class, but if she had a story—"

"Then she could find another way in," he finishes.

The Senior Experience was more than a bullet point on a résumé; Maddie wanted to work with Tess Spradlin, Culver Class of Whatever, because of what she accomplished ten years ago with her own story. The one that sold out her *boyfriend*.

"I think," I say, "I know what Maddie was writing about."

Ten minutes later, I knock, ring the doorbell, knock again, keep knocking until the door swings open. Miles Metcalf looks between me and Hudson, confused. He wears gray sweatpants and a faded Beatles T-shirt. There's a hole in the heel of his left sock.

He says, "What're you—?"

"I know you cheat for Cody. Now I want to know everything."

Because I misunderstood when Sara said Cody cheats, and so did she. He isn't cheating *on* Maddie; he's cheating, period.

Hudson swivels his head toward me. "What?"

The wind rustles Miles's curls. Pricks goose bumps up his skin. Then he sighs and says, "You guys should probably come inside."

- *32* -

Miles stands in front of the open fridge. Its contents are sparse: milk and butter, soda cans and jars of jam. "Can I get you guys anything to drink?"

I grunt out a no. Hudson says nothing. He's been silent since we came inside. First, his steps dragged the neat vacuum lines in the carpet as he paced. Now, he sits on the stiff recliner, his leg bouncing, rattling the ceramic figurines on the mantel.

Miles returns with a Coke for himself and kneels at the coffee table. He's home alone; his parents are at a movie or something. He sips, coughs on the fizz, says, "How did you find out?"

It's true. I knew it was true, but it feels different coming from Miles. Bigger, maybe. I turn to Hudson to see if he feels it, too, but he refuses to look at me.

I look back to Miles. "Cody told me himself. He was drunk."

"He told you I cheat for him?"

Now I'm confused. "Do you not?"

"No. I do." He rubs his neck, pale skin flushed. "We were, uh. Lab partners sophomore year. He was struggling. If he failed, he'd get cut from the soccer team, so he offered to pay if I let him cheat off our next test." He shrugs. "It went from there."

"Why?" Hudson asks, so much accusation in that one word.

"You guys wouldn't get it." Miles shakes his head, curls unruly. "You're both . . . popular. I didn't even exist to you—to *anyone*—until Cody included me. He'd only include me if I helped him, so I helped him." His face gets even redder. "I was no one without him."

Hudson lets out a cruel laugh. "You think this makes you someone?"

"Maybe not, but at least it gives me a fucking chance to be."

I've never heard Miles swear before.

God, I hate that I get it. I wanted the guys—all guys, any guy—to like me, so I laughed at their unfunny jokes. Let them think they were smarter than me. I became the girl they wanted me to be, but plenty of guys wanted me and still never liked me.

My brain goes: *Nick.*

I'm not thinking about Nick.

"What do you do?" Hudson asks, not trying to hide his disdain. "Take his tests? Write his papers? Or did you hack the grading software?"

His rank. Hudson is trying to connect this, their cheating, to his rank. If Miles can screw with Cody's grades, then what could—would—he do to screw over Hudson?

But why? To help April, his ex-girlfriend, in third? Because Miles is jealous of Hudson? It doesn't make sense to me.

Miles smiles, all smug. "Why? Were you interested?"

If I weren't here, I think Hudson might punch him in the

face. Because it all worked out for Cody and Miles. They'll get what they want—MIT, most likely; soccer at Duke—and he has nothing. No rank, no money. Not yet.

Hudson turns to me, his dark eyes furious, before crashing out the door.

"God, you really are a dick." I stand. "Be better than this, Miles. I know you can be."

His smile crumples. "I was just . . . I didn't mean anything by—"

"Do you know what? You sound *just* like Cody," I say, and I go outside. Hudson leans against his car, arms crossed, head tilted toward the darkening sky.

"Wait!" Miles calls from the porch. He takes the first step, then the next, his socks soaked in the snow. Shivering, he says, "You guys know you can't tell anyone, right?"

"What if someone already did?" I don't care if I'm showing my hand when Miles doesn't care at all. I'm searching for a shimmer of shame that isn't there. "Maddie knew about it, too."

Miles scratches his jaw, frowning. Like he can't make it make sense. "Maddie?"

I go for the jugular. "She was going to expose you, Miles. She was writing a story and . . ."

The whole thing falls apart the second I say it. *People like to win*, Tess said, so Cody and Miles found a way. It's a bit too familiar: the jock and the nerd who made a shitty arrangement.

Hell, I don't even know if this *is* Maddie's story.

But Miles has gone pale. I've rattled the flush from Miles Metcalf and replaced it, I think, with fear. He says, "I didn't know anything about a story," and goes inside. He crosses the window and returns with his hand lifted to his ear.

He must be calling—

—Cody Forsythe, whose old phone is still in my desk.

Hudson nearly rips the drawer off the tracks. "What would his passcode be?"

"His birthday?"

"He's not that stupid." Hudson sits on my bed, cringing. "Sorry, I didn't mean it like that."

It's not Cody's birthday. It's not Maddie's, either. Hudson tries 6969, which isn't a bad guess but isn't right, then 0420, and then a warning pops up: PHONE WILL LOCK FOR 24 HOURS WITH NEXT FAILED ATTEMPT.

"Shit." He chucks the phone to the end of my bed. Overshoots. It slips, smacks to the floor. I don't need to look to know it shatters. He falls against the mattress, and again: "Shit."

"It probably still works."

He stares at a crack in the plaster ceiling. "Do you think Miles will get expelled? Then I'd be first, and *that* scholarship is worth even more than—"

"Wait, why would Miles get expelled?"

"Because we're telling Lund." Hudson sits up, face flushed. "We *have* to tell. I need my rank. I need that money, and you knew our fucking valedictorian was—is!—cheating for one of my friends, and you didn't even *think* to tell me? How could you hide this from me?"

Not breathing, not thinking, I say, "I already confronted Cody about it. At the bonfire. I heard him talking about Maddie, and I thought he . . ." I don't know what I thought. "Cody sent those photos *because* I confronted him. He retaliated against me."

And he threatened me with something worse.

I shake my head, but there it is: Cody, pale under those basement lights, his skin cracked when he extended his hand for our truce. *I'll keep your secret if you keep mine.*

But no one can ever know about Nick. No one can know, but I told Kathleen, and Maddie told Cody, and Maddie knows Cody and Miles cheat, and the story makes no sense, but I still told Miles, and Maddie is gone, and Nick is here, and if Miles tells Cody that I—

"Hey, it's okay," Hudson says gently. I'm breathing too fast. He slips his hands around my waist, his touch tentative, like he's trying not to startle me. "It's okay, Jo."

I cup his face with both hands. "I can't go through that again. I can't have him . . ." I blink hard. "We can't tell. I'm sorry."

It's not enough to be sorry, but he nods, like he isn't devastated. Like I'm not ruining this for him. "Then we'll . . . figure something else out. But I don't want you to keep things from me, okay? You can tell me anything."

"I will," I lie. "I promise."

He looks up at me with those dark, tired eyes. There's something else here. Something that snatches the breath from my throat. This is how he looked at me the second before—

Hudson lifts his mouth to mine, quick. There, then gone.

But I *need* this.

I need to forget and erase and replace everything in my brain with him.

"Hudson." I clumsily straddle him. Kiss his neck, his jaw, his mouth. He's all heat. I am too. He drags my hips higher, against his lap, and I gasp, gasp again when he repeats the motion. I'm dizzy with it, breathing out, "Oh my God."

"Oh my God," Hudson echoes, like he just realized what we're doing. He half shoves me off his lap and stands, fetching his jacket off the floor. "I need to go."

"What? Why?" My eyes lower to the front of his jeans.

He looks down, too, and repositions his jacket. "You should, uh, find a ride tomorrow."

"Hudson, wait!" I follow him downstairs, past Lee at the dining room table, and—

That car. There, across the street, in the Prices' driveway. Hudson finds it, too, staring at it for just a second before climbing into his own. I slowly step away from the door. Lee watches from over his laptop.

Faking a cough, he asks, "You see Nick is back?"

"Yeah." I shut my eyes. "I saw."

-33-

Dad drives me to school the next morning. For some reason, this is the pathetic part to me—that I had to ask my *dad* for a ride. He keeps glancing over like he senses something is wrong, except nothing is wrong, and he only says, "Have a good day, sweetheart."

I'm trudging toward the doors when Kathleen calls my name. I balance on the curb, wait, waving at Clare as she scurries past.

Blinking back snow, Kathleen asks, "No Hudson?"

"Yeah, I don't know."

"Okay." She adds about ten extra vowels to the word. "Well, if you ever need a ride, you can ask me." Pause. "Also, you haven't answered my texts."

The texts asking if I'm all right, telling me that she's happy to listen if I want to talk, but what is there to talk about? I shrug and say, "I forgot. But I did, um. Please don't say anything." *No one can ever know about this.* "About . . . what I told you."

Kathleen stares at me for a long time, but eventually she nods.

The lobby is packed—to set up for Open House later? Beside

the trophy case, black and silver balloons and streamers flank three blown-up senior portraits: Miles and April and Hudson.

"They look dead," I mumble, and then I freeze.

Miles, April, and Hudson, in that order.

Miles, 1. April, 2. Hudson, 3.

One. Two. Three.

"How—?" Kathleen stops herself. *How.* That's all she has to say.

Hudson isn't here yet. He cannot find out like this.

I fumble for my phone. Slam into April Kirk, salutatorian. She stares at herself—poster two of three. If I could find the words, I'd ask what the fuck happened, but I don't know if she knows. No, her face goes too pale; even her lips turn white.

She cranes her neck, scanning the lobby for someone. *Miles.* He grins the same grin from that portrait: gap-toothed, dorky. His gaze shifts to the second spot. The smile collapses.

Miles, valedictorian, and April, salutatorian, and Hudson, here, by the doors.

I force my way toward him. "Hudson, I think—"

"Hey," he says. So blasé. *Hey*, as if we didn't make out on my bed. *Hey*, as if his life isn't about to fall apart. His eyes lift to mine, higher, slightly right. I look down. Let him have this.

One. Two. Three.

Low, he says, "Don't."

I do. "Hudson—"

He ignores the onlookers (*everyone* looks on) and disappears into the main office. He'll get a plaque at Open House later, but who cares about a plaque when he just lost $10,000? He needs the money. Needs it in a very real, very urgent way.

If his grandparents sell their house, find a place in Florida, move—

I need Miles. He stands with his band friends, his smile wobbling the louder they cheer. I latch onto his arm and tug him toward the stairs, whispering, "Did you do something?"

"No! I don't know what happened." Miles looks over my shoulder, his face paling.

Then Hudson yanks him forward by the collar, the striped fabric clenched in his white-knuckled fist. "What the fuck did you do?"

"Nothing!" Miles hisses. Panic lights his eyes. He tries to pry off Hudson's grip and says, quieter, "I don't do stuff like that. I don't have that *access*. I'm old school."

Hudson lets go of his shirt and steps back—right into Cody Forsythe.

Cody claps him on the back and says, "Sorry, man," not meaning it.

My throat tightens. Could *he* have done it? He has no motive or means. He'd been talking to recruiters since junior year; his athletic prowess mattered more than rank.

"Fuck off," Hudson says.

"Relax, bro. I've heard Florida is lovely this time of year," Cody says. Hudson shoves his chest once, hard, and Cody staggers back, holds up his hands. "It was a joke."

"It's never a joke with you." Hudson towers over him. "Not this, not what you did to—"

"Stop," I say, because I know the next word out of his mouth is my name.

Then Ben Sulkin sweeps into frame and shouts, "Hey!" and punches Cody just below the eye. I gasp. Everyone gasps. I mean, these guys are friends and—*are* they still friends? Ben was so pissed at the bowling alley, now this? Cody brings his fingers to his cheek, and Ben lunges for him again. Blocking his face, Cody grunts, "Dude, what—?"

I don't know what Ben says, but it shuts him the hell up.

It's all so chaotic—Mr. Conti trying to pull off Ben; Principal Lund jabbing her walkie-talkie toward them—and Hudson makes his escape. Mr. Chopra whistles for my attention and nods after Hudson, my permission to follow.

"Hudson!" I shout as he crashes through the band doors. "Jesus, tell me what happened."

He won't look at me. "Lund said we can discuss tomorrow. But I'm still required to go to Open House tonight and act so grateful for a *plaque*." He lets out an ugly, bitter laugh. "God, I'm so stupid. The entire point of us pretending to be together was to figure this shit out and to stop it from happening, and instead I got distracted, and look what happened. Maddie was right!" He drags his hands down his face. "I can't do this, Jo. I can't do it anymore."

"What, are you breaking up with me?" I try to say it like a joke. But his silence, the subtle way he shrugs, looking anywhere but me, is my answer. "Oh. Hudson, no, I don't want . . . I don't understand. Like, why can't you do this?"

He forces a laugh. "Because I'm in love with you, Jo!"

"You . . . what?" The cold stings my eyes.

"Don't give me that look," Hudson says. "You must know it.

Everyone knows! Everyone knows that I've been fucking pining after you for *years*."

Did I know? I don't know.

"Charlotte knew better than anyone. She texted me that day she saw you at Village Gate and called me an asshole for stringing her along. And she was right! Prom night—I wanted *you*, Jo." *Me, Jo.* "You're smart and funny and frustrating, and I think about you nonstop, and when I'm not with you, I'm wishing I was." Hudson exhales, his breath fogging. "You've never been just there to me, Jo."

Everything stops. I swear even the snow hovers midair.

This is it. The space for me to say anything. But I can't speak.

Hudson nods. "I'm sorry. I'm done."

I'm losing my mind a little.

The whispers slither into my ear: *Not Hudson. Salutatorian. Ben. Hit. Suspended. Two weeks. Miles. April. Sucks for him. Maddie Price. Gone. That post. Gone. Rank. Gone. Because I'm in love with you, Jo.*

That last one is only in my head.

I pay zero attention in class. My brain is moving too fast, trying to work it out: Maddie told Hudson his rank was at risk. *You should've given it up before they take it.* She wanted him to forfeit his spot, too, so she ran that open letter last fall.

But Hudson refused to give it up, and now he's lost it.

Because someone took it?

Because I'm in love with you, Jo.

During physics lab, I lie that I have cramps and get a pass to the nurse, then I breeze past her office and go straight to the newspaper lab in the basement. The door is locked—of course it is—but the lights are on, so I knock and knock and knock until it opens.

One-L Daniele, photo director. "Sorry, I didn't know it was locked," she says, punching a code (#1310) into the keypad. It beeps, unlatching. "Did you need something?"

I do, obviously, but I hesitate. "Daniele, this has to stay between us, but I need to see that open letter. The original." Pause. "I think something happened with Hudson's rank."

One-L Daniele leans against the doorframe. "If I ask Sara on a date, will she say yes?"

"Uh, yes?"

"Then come on in," she says. Her camera is plugged into a computer, photos uploading to the repository. She pulls a binder from an unlocked cabinet and flips it open.

"What's that?" I roll over a chair and spin, stopping when I face the padlocked lockers in back. The key must be *somewhere*. And what about Maddie's actual locker in the senior wing?

"Password log. Everyone on staff has to provide their login since no one ever remembers to *not* save to their desktop. Here! The staff login," she says. I ease the chair closer, squinting at the page until I see it: MADDIE PRICE. Slyly, I lift my phone and snap a photo.

One-L Daniele logs in and navigates to *The Eagle Eye* inbox.

FROM: anon_rank_throwaway@gmail.com

DATE: Oct. 19, 2:42 a.m.

SUBJECT: AN OPEN LETTER TO HUDSON HARPER-MOORE

"This is bullshit." I take control of the mouse and scroll down to . . . names. There are *names*. It was anonymized in the paper, but the original has the signatures, lots of them.

One-L jabs her finger at the screen. *Danielle de Palma.* Two *L*s. "Hey! I never signed."

I keep scrolling. The Birds are on here and Coach Burke and a teacher who retired last year. Kids two grades below us, people I don't even recognize. *Jolynn Kirby.* Like that hyphen isn't a pain in my ass. Like I don't know how to spell my own goddamn name.

One-L Daniele turns to me, piecing it together, too. I say, "Keep this quiet, okay?"

Because there was no letter. No coalition of students that furious about Hudson's rank, so desperate for him to forfeit. It was *faked.* Maddie ran a fake letter. Maybe she knew it, and that's why she warned him. Maybe she knew it was never about the actual spot.

Maybe this has always been about *him.*

Later, at home, I dig inside my closet for something to wear tonight. The *perfect* thing. I settle on a pink midi-dress—long-sleeved, snug in the hips, the color all wrong for winter.

But I feel so, so pretty in it.

Miraculously, I'm ready early, so I lie on the living room rug and get Bay Leaf stoned on a catnip cigar. My mother watches me—us—and says, "You look beautiful, Jo-Lynn."

I tried. I blew out my hair and finagled my bangs to curtain my face. I even swiped on lip gloss. It's light pink, barely noticeable unless someone leans closer—which I hope Hudson will.

Because I'm in love with you, Jo. Hudson is in love with me. Even if this thing between us started off as fake, his feelings for me never were, and I don't know what the hell I'm doing, honestly. But I do know that it was real when we kissed yesterday. Prom night was real.

How I feel (how he makes me feel) every second I'm with him—that's all real, too.

Hudson deserves that rank and that money, and I'm going to make sure he gets it.

Because I'm not done. I'm just getting started.

- 34 -

We're late, like always. Dad drops me in front of Culver and goes to find parking.

For the next forty minutes, families will explore at their leisure, taking in the fantastic exhibitions from Culver's fantastic students. Then the boring shit, when the parents and/or guardians gather in the auditorium for graduation logistics, et cetera.

The lobby is buzzing when I enter.

I'm buzzing, too.

I search for Hudson—his tall frame, his long hair—but find Tess instead. She wears black trousers, a plaid blazer, a silk blouse. "The woman of the hour!" She looks toward the doors with a frown. "Where are your parents?"

"Oh, just parking."

Lee came, too, mostly because Gabe Figueroa bullied him into the interview about the comeback game. The one Maddie was supposed to do.

Tess frowns again, but not at me—at her phone. "Sorry," she mumbles, and taps out a text. "My editor is blowing up my email."

Too fake, she adds, "I get the absolute privilege of writing the Price redemption arc."

"The what?" I think this dress is too tight; it's suffocating me.

"Her dad is pissed about the News 9 interview, so as penance for Justin going rogue, our editor in chief is giving them the opportunity to 'set the record straight.'" Her phone lights with a call. "One second."

I wait by the trophy case, by those posters: Miles Metcalf, April Kirk, Hudson Harper-Moore. April keeps looking at them, too. No amount of concealer can hide the puffiness under her eyes. Even now, she sniffs hard, like she could cry all over again.

It's weird. It's *weird*. I want to say it—*Uh, this is weird*—but then my parents and Lee approach. Dad is complaining about the parking, and my mother is in full-on Kate Kirby mode, irritated she had to miss the evening broadcast. Lee scans the lobby uneasily.

"What's wrong with you?" I ask.

"Just weird being back," he mumbles, tucking his gloves into his pockets.

Like an angel from above, Tess reappears. "Hi! I'm Tess Spradlin. I'm your daughter's Senior Experience mentor," she says, and gestures us to follow her to the senior wing. "Posters are this way. I know I'm biased, but hers is the best."

There it is, in all its glory . . . right beside my senior portrait. God, that photo is one of the funniest things I've ever seen. I look so *mad*. I look like the girl everyone tells me I am.

There's a tiny card pinned to the bottom of the poster.

A NOTE FROM THE MENTOR: Jo-Lynn is a bright girl with a wholly unique voice—and a lot to say. I can't wait to see what story she tells.

Something warm and lovely blooms in my chest. "That's really nice, Tess."

"It's not nice, Jo-hyphen-Lynn. It's true."

God, I'm dying to see their faces—Dad, my mother, Lee—but they're talking to Coach Burke. He claps Lee on the back, thrilled the basketball star is back, and they all smile. Laugh.

Tess follows my gaze. "I'll get them."

"I don't want you to." I want them to want to see it.

Her phone is ringing again. "But you deserve—"

"You should answer that," I say, and I go.

I have nowhere *to* go, but I don't want to be here. I loop the senior wing twice, climb up and down the stairs, walk until I find him by the open gym doors: Hudson, number three.

No merit scholarship. No honors. Just the privilege of being close, but not close enough.

He sighs when he sees me, but I yank his sleeve before he can walk away, leading him toward the cafeteria. The skylights above show nothing but stars.

"Jo, Jesus, what are you doing?"

I force him to face me. "First, I'm sorry about the scholarship. Your rank. I'm sorry. But I got the original—"

"I don't want to talk about it. Not that, and not . . ." Hudson lolls his head back, his face pained. "You banned prom, so I'm banning *this*."

"Can you shut up for five seconds so I can say none of this"—I gesture between us—"is unreciprocated?" His eyebrows knit together. He's not getting it. But I did use a double negative. "I was . . . confused," I say, and I picture Nick again, but I don't want to picture Nick. "Obviously I like you, Hudson."

His mouth tilts into a smile. "You *like* like me?"

I roll my eyes, but I'm blushing. "Yes, okay? You just caught me off guard. I've never had anyone profess their love for me before, or sound so aggravated by it."

"You're very aggravating," he says, and I want him to kiss me. I think he might—

Except then Sara hugs me from behind. "You look kind of hot in your senior portrait, Jo."

"And your project will be amazing," Michaela says, fixing a flyaway strand in my bangs.

"Thanks." I roll my eyes again, blushing deeper. "Where's Kathleen?"

"Bathroom," Sara says. "Oh, or she's right there."

Right behind me, gripping my shoulder, her nails clawing into me. "The Prices are here. I saw them in the lobby. Jo, *Nick* is here," she whispers. "Talking to Tess."

Everything gets this fuzzy, faded filter on it. Somehow, I say, "It's fine."

Because it is. Maddie may be gone, but they need to keep up appearances, right? She still goes here, even if she isn't *here*. It's fine the Prices are here. That Nick is here, talking to Tess.

It's fine, too, when Clare O'Mara sidles up to us, all moony, her eyes on my brother. He's talking to Lund. Probably detailing his path back to UNC next year.

Flushed, Clare says, "That guy is cute."

"Jo's brother? He's way too old for you," Michaela says, laughing. Kathleen shoots her a look that she doesn't register. Doesn't know she needs to register.

"How old are you anyway?" I ask, chewing my cuticle. "Like, twelve?"

"I'm fifteen," Clare says.

"No, you're not." Everyone has gone quiet around me. "Wait, are you?"

She nervously twirls a strand of hair. "My birthday was in December."

"*You're* fifteen?" I blink again, and it's like I'm seeing her for the first time. Her sweet, round face. The acne dotted along her chin. The way her braces strain at her mouth. I bring my hand to my own face. Run my tongue over the retainer bonded to my bottom teeth.

"Is everything okay?" Hudson asks, and Kathleen says, "Jo, maybe we should—"

"I need a second."

I need more than a second. I need to get the fuck out of here.

I head down the hall, toward the band room door, and sprint into the cold, dark night. My breaths are coming too fast, but I don't know how to make them go slow. I dig my knuckles into my eyes, mascara streaking onto my skin.

In my memories with Nick, the image is me now—Jo at seventeen.

But when I shut my eyes, all I see is me then. Mouth full of braces that glinted in the sun, rubber bands stretching from my canines to my molars; hair crimped from when Maddie and me practiced how to fishtail braid; that stupid, cheap watermelon bikini I stole, ripping the tags with my teeth after my mother refused to buy it for me.

I crouch down and breathe, breathe, breathe until the air cools my scorched skin. When I lift my head, there it is: Nick's car. Thank you, Universe! Solid joke. Except it's not funny, is it?

I'm still waiting for the punchline.

But I'm cold, and I'm tired, and I want to go home. I stand up, step back inside the hallway. The light flickers, almost dead. I start forward and—

"Whoa, watch it." Nick breezes past, digging through his pocket, pulling out a pack of cigarettes. Then: "Holy shit."

Go, I tell myself, but I'm frozen, stuck, even though I want to *go go go go go.*

I turn to face him.

Nick Price, now. He wears corduroy pants and a white button-up. His hair is shorter, too. When I saw him last, it was on the shaggier side, a length that made Mrs. Price nag him to get a haircut. Nick Price, then, wore his Cornell tees until he wore holes in the sleeves.

The slow crawl of a smile spreads across his lips. "Look who it is."

Look. I run my hands down my hips, the fabric clinging. I hate it. I hate this dress. I want to burn it. I want to forget how it feels when he looks at me. I want to know what he thinks.

I want to puke that I'd ever think that.

"How are you?" Nick asks. I say nothing. He cocks his head at me, forces a frown. "What happened to your 'wholly unique voice'?" My poster. He saw it. "Thought you had a lot to say."

It's a joke, but I don't laugh.

He steps closer. "Oh, *I'm* great, thanks for asking. Great apartment, great job at a great firm in the greatest city. Great girlfriend."

I swear he pauses after that last one. "I wish Maddie wasn't putting us through hell, but you know my sister."

I *don't* know his sister. Not anymore. And I don't know why he's here, or why he didn't come when she first disappeared, or how he can be so fucking *great* when Maddie is gone.

Nick nods like he's not annoyed by my silence and turns from me. But his smell lingers: cedar, smoke, something sweet. Bumping open the door, he says, "Good to see you, Jolie."

"Jo." My voice is steadier than I expect it to be. "My name is not Jolie, it's Jo."

Nick stops. Lets the door slowly click shut. "Okay, *Jo*."

I don't look away as he steps up to me again. I can't look away. If I never met Nick and saw him out at the grocery store or something, I'd look right past him. He's just some guy, so I don't know what's fucking wrong with me now or then, when I got into his car.

"What are you doing here?" I ask.

"Damage control. I'm getting us an attorney." Nick swipes his nose with the back of his hand. "My mom is fucking everything up. You see that interview? She made a fool of us. Then Maddie made that stupid post—"

"She did?" I hardly get it out.

"Who else would have?" Nick plucks a cigarette from the pack. "Look, I don't want to talk about my sister. I want to hear about you. It's been forever, right? Let's catch up," he says, and it sounds almost sincere. Innocuous, at least. He goes, "You applying to school?"

No.

"Still friends with those guys?"

No.

"What about that one I saw you with? Long hair? That your little boyfriend?"

"Stop."

Nick laughs. He *laughs.* Up close, he's all chapped lips and dry skin. I do the math: Nick, now, is twenty-four. He is twenty-four and *great* and I am seventeen and no one, and this thing is growing inside me, and I'll scream if I can't get it out.

I need to get it out. "Do you ever think about me? That summer?"

"This again?" Nick lets out a sour laugh. He peers over my shoulder, but the hall is empty except for us. Leaning close, lowering his voice, he says, "I'm sorry you misunderstood what we were, but don't tell me you're still hung up on that."

"I'm not." I'm *not.*

"Because it was nothing."

"It wasn't nothing." Not in the way I've thought for all these years.

"You need to let this fucking go," Nick says. I step back, but he matches it forward, until my body is pressed to the lockers. "The way I remember it, you threw yourself at me, Jolie. It was embarrassing. How you texted me. Flirted with me. You even kissed me first, didn't you?"

"I . . . I did, but I was only—"

"Don't."

"—fifteen."

Nick slaps a hand above my head, his palm flat to the metal. I try to shrink from him, but I have nowhere else to go. "I asked you if it was okay," he says, and it's weird how we talk about that summer but mean just one night. The first night. "I don't know why you're trying to rewrite what happened, but you didn't say no."

"I didn't say anything."

Nick grips my jaw, his palm pressed to my chin, fingers digging into my face. "Don't act like you're some fucking victim, Jolie."

The word rips something inside me.

Nick shoves me back against the locker, the metal rattling my skull. But then he drops his hands, and Michaela and Sara are beside me, and Kathleen is yelling. I look to Sara to see why she's shaking, but it's not Sara; it's me. Nick crashes toward the lobby and slams into—

Lee.

"Did he hit you?" he asks me, serious. I shake my head. (I mean, he didn't.) Lee pushes the girls aside, forcing me to face him. Even lower: "Jo . . ."

I will myself to inhale, to stop shaking, to stand straight.

And I look my brother right in the eye.

Now it's the night of his graduation party, and I'm crushed, humiliated, Nick's words in my head: *Because you were there.* Lee is in the driveway, sipping a beer beneath the basketball hoop. He looks from that car across the street and back to me. I hold his gaze, daring him to say something. Tell someone.

Then, he didn't.

Now, Lee is gone before I can process it. Kathleen calls after me, but Lee left, and I'm running after him. He shrugs out of his jacket and rolls his shoulders and shouts, "Nick," and—

No. No, no, no, no.

Lee's fist connects with Nick's jaw with a sick crack.

He shoves Nick again, and Nick tries to block his face, but Lee jerks his arm back, and finally, finally, finally, I say it: "No."

Two letters, one complete sentence.

Everything comes into focus. Dad and Mr. Price trying to break up the fight. Tess staring at me. My *mother* staring at me. Hudson watches, confused, and there's Cody with a black eye of his own, nudging him, saying, "You didn't know?"

"No," I say again, so low only I hear it.

Then: "Jo-Lynn." My mother steps forward, but I'm already shoving toward the door.

This is the trouble with girls like me. We don't stop, don't listen, don't shut up, don't say the right thing, don't say anything when it matters most.

And we run—always from something, never toward anything.

-*35*-

My sprint slows to a run, a jog, a brisk walk once I reach my street.

The house is dark; we forgot to turn on the porch light. I also forgot my keys. *Shit.* I drop onto the steps. It's not warm out, but it's a different kind of cold—damp, soggy.

The sick split of Lee's fist connecting with Nick's face echoes in my head. I wasn't close enough to smell Nick's blood, but it's all I smell now: metal, rust, salt. I hinge forward, hands on my knees. Mucus coats my throat like right before I puke.

Nothing comes out.

I'm not sure how long it is before the car pulls up to the curb. I blink until the headlights cut and someone steps out and—

"Hudson." *You came.*

"I'm sorry I didn't come sooner." He sits beside me. "Kathleen wanted to, um. Talk."

I slowly nod. I want to ask what she said—the exact phrasing, word for word. I wonder if we'd use the same language.

Jo got a ride with her best friend's older brother.

Jo got drunk on hard seltzer.

Jo got into the way back of his car.

Jo got—

I squeeze my eyes shut. Open them when Hudson gently lifts his fingers to my jaw. Tilts my face up to his. He starts to speak—says my name—but there are more headlights now. Dad's car cuts into the driveway. Lee climbs out before it stops, and my mother is close behind. Next, Dad seethes, "Get inside, Jo. You get out of here, Hudson."

Hudson stands. "Wait—"

I shut the door.

In the foyer, my mother shrugs out of her coat. Dad flips on a light. My brother stalks out of the kitchen with a beer, taking a swig, starting for the stairs.

"Don't you dare!" Dad shouts. He never shouts. But I've never seen him so angry: face plum, fists clenched. "Get your ass in the living room." He turns to me. "Both of you."

Lee sprawls across the couch. His knuckles are bruised, swollen. I perch on the edge of the chair where Bay Leaf snoozes, snoring.

"I don't even know where to start." Dad's volume has returned to a normal decibel. I ball up the hem of my dress in my fists. Dad says, "Think a fucking arrest will get you back to UNC, Lee? You're lucky the Prices aren't pressing charges."

"Real lucky," Lee snorts, ripping the tab off his can. Bay hops onto the floor and trots to the kitchen, slinking between my mother's legs.

My mother, whose eyes bore into me.

Dad, undeterred: "What the hell were you thinking, Lee?"

He drains the beer. "Why don't you ask her?"

They turn to me, all of them all at once. I'm aware, suddenly, of the pain in my head. "I don't know what you're talking about."

Lee laughs, low and mean. "Are you *serious*, Jo?" He crushes the can against the coffee table. "I fucking told you. I told you she was sneaking around with him that summer, and tonight he basically attacked her, so I'm thinking—"

Dad interrupts—"Calm down, Lee"—because Lee is yelling, and my mother is telling them to hush, and everything has fallen away but this one thing.

I told you.

"You knew?" I'm too quiet at first. I need them to hear me. Louder, again: "You knew?"

The room goes quiet. The mantel clock tick, tick, ticks. Bay Leaf crunches dry food in the kitchen. No one else makes a sound.

"Oh my God." I laugh. I don't know why I'm laughing.

Dad tosses his gloves onto the coffee table. "We didn't know it was him. We thought it might be one of Lee's friends."

"But you knew there was someone? You knew something?" All those nights I snuck out of my bedroom, darted across the street to his car, let Nick lead me into the dark.

Nick, then, his touch light on my wrist: *No one can ever know about this.*

Nick, tonight, his hand gripping my face: *Don't act like you're some fucking victim.*

"You knew, and you . . ." I want to laugh again, but my throat has gone tight, choking me. I don't realize I'm crying until a tear splashes onto my knee, but I don't do this. I can't do this.

How could they do this to me?

I swipe under my eye but another tear falls, and another, and then I fold in half, head in my hands, and I start to sob. All the nights I swore I'd never tell—but I never needed to. They knew. They *saw*.

Now they won't even look at me.

I don't want to look at me either.

-36-

Tuesday

My head is killing me. The pain splits my skull when I open my eyes.

5:37 a.m.

God, I feel sick—physically ill, like the time I caught the flu in tenth grade and my body shook, feverish, during a chemistry quiz. I ease into the bathroom. Shake a NyQuil capsule onto my palm and swallow it with a sip from the tap. My throat is parched. If I tried to speak, nothing would come out. I don't even know what I'd say.

I go back to bed.

Dad's voice: "This is Joseph Kirby. My daughter Jo-Lynn isn't feeling too well, so she'll be out today." Pause. "Senior." Pause. "Yes, I hope she feels better, too."

———

Half-asleep, still a little drugged, I turn on my phone. I've got a dozen texts. One new email.

FROM: tspradlin@rocweeklymag.com
DATE: Feb. 26, 9:56 p.m.
SUBJECT: In case you need it

Here's my number, Jo-hyphen-Lynn. I'm just a call away.

I turn the phone off again.

The NyQuil was a mistake. It's almost midnight, but I'm wide awake.

Each time I shut my eyes, I feel a zap at the base of my skull, like the sharp shock of a brain freeze. *Zap.* The shared gasp of breath in the lobby last night. *Zap.* That car. *Zap.* Nick's hand on my face. *Zap.* Nick's hand on my zipper. *Zap.* Nick—

I sit up, nauseated.

Then I create a new note on my phone and type everything, all of it, every detail. I use no punctuation. Make a billion typos. But I need to get this thing out of me so I can read it someday like a story someone else told. Maybe I'll think, *This is what you're so upset about? Lots of girls regret their first time. It's not like you were—*

I press my hand to my mouth. Lower it again. Open a browser and type the words—*was i*—and drop my phone when it auto-fills. Who needs a fucking quiz to know? How humiliating and, okay, I really am going to puke.

My knees crash against the bathroom tile, and I lift the toilet lid and heave, but my stomach is empty; nothing comes out but a string of spit.

It's disgusting.

Wednesday

I'm taking another sick day.

I doze restlessly until noon. I'm sweating, heating pad on high, Bay curled in the bend of my legs, and why did I wake? Doorbell. I head downstairs and unlatch, unlock the door and—

"Hi! You busy?" Sara gives me a once-over. "I'm guessing no."

Michaela holds up a paper bag. "We desperately need an extra mouth for these bagels."

"Shouldn't you be at school?" I ask.

"Shouldn't you? Besides," Kathleen says, gentler, "you're not answering our texts."

They insist I shower—*skip the showerhead*—and after I pile my soaked hair on my head and put on an oversized Buffalo Bills crewneck, Kathleen offers to drive us wherever I want.

I pick High Falls.

The wind is brisk, the sky a muted gray. We claim a bench on the pedestrian bridge. It's kind of incredible—a waterfall rushing against the skyline, right in the middle of the city.

The girls talk about nothing so I don't have to say anything. I've eaten half a bagel when they go quiet. Behind us, a couple walks a wiener dog in a snow vest, its tiny legs toddling.

Kathleen bumps my knee. "Do you want to talk about it?"

"The wiener dog?" My nose fizzes, like before I cry. "I never

287

want to talk about it, but I also don't want to talk about anything else."

"Take your time," Michaela says. "The second you're ready, we'll listen."

Sara nods. "I'm so sorry this happened to you."

Jesus, I know—I *know*—this is the exact right stuff to say, but I hate hearing it, and I hate that I hate it. I abruptly stand. "Is there a trail down to the gorge?"

"I'll look with you." Kathleen shakes her head when the girls try to follow, like, *I got it.*

She leads me toward the snowy terrace at the opposite end of the bridge. The view from this vantage point is even more spectacular. I search for a staircase, but she says, "I'm going to talk, and you're going to shut up and listen, understand?"

I zip my lips.

"I'm not comparing our experiences, but my ex and I had an . . . incident over break. We were about to"—Kathleen vaguely waves a hand—"but he didn't have a condom. I assumed he knew not to . . . but he did, and I know I was stupid, so I don't need you to judge me for it."

Unzip. "I'm not judging you."

"I know you're not," she says quietly. "I'm not on birth control, but Ryan . . . he said if I got pregnant, it was part of God's plan. I thought if I got pregnant, it would ruin my entire life." She exhales, face stung pink. "I'd have to give up everything—the University of Rochester, pre-law, the chance to just be my own person—and he'd lose nothing. But it's complicated for me, you know? My youth ministry protested at Planned Parenthood for years. And I needed to tell someone, so I told Maddie."

The name drags an ache through my chest.

"We drove to a CVS across town for Plan B. She spent the night. We just worked on our English midterms, but it was nice, honestly." Kathleen hesitates. "Then she told her mom."

The wind hisses. "What? Why?"

"Because Maddie can be cruel and careless and a bad friend? I try so hard not to hate her for it because she's also just human." She grips the railing tight. "Maddie's mom told my mom. My mom told Ryan's mom. Who told Ryan. I guess premarital sex is a forgivable sin, but I'm going straight to hell for taking a pill."

"Do you believe that?" It feels like the wrong thing to say. I should tell her I'm sorry (I am) or that this is bullshit (it is) and she deserves better (she does).

Kathleen picks each word carefully. "I liked having such strong convictions. But I needed permission to be wrong—and I *was* wrong, Jo. Especially about things I didn't want to believe."

I breathe out, trying not to cry, crying still. "You're not being subtle."

"I'm not trying to be subtle. Jo, what Nick did—"

"Stop. Please. It feels so . . . bad." Like I'm investigating my own past, reexamining each moment with a magnifying glass. Like I've been hit by a seismic shift no one felt but me. "How is it *so bad* for me, and to everyone else it's just Tuesday?"

"Wednesday."

"What?"

"It's not Tuesday." Pause. "I'm sorry, that was incredibly unhelpful."

But now I can't stop laughing. Kathleen throws her arms

around me, and I half cry, half laugh into her hair. "There's no trail to the gorge, is there?"

"No," she says, "but I thought you'd want to see it for yourself."

Instead of driving me home, Kathleen drops me at Wegmans, just like I ask.

And just like I ask, Hudson waits for me in the parking lot. He leans against his car with his hands jammed in his pockets, head bent against the wind.

"Cutting class?" I call out to him.

He lifts his head and sort of smiles. "I guess I need groceries," he says, following me inside, his hand bumping mine. "It's good to see you, Jo."

I roll my eyes up to him. "I look like shit."

"I didn't say it was good to *look* at you."

"Shut up, Hudson."

"It's pretty good to look at you, too."

Now I shut up. Mist sprays from the produce displays. We pass the florist department, wander toward the cave-ripened cheese. I say, "So, I've been thinking about your rank—"

"I met with Lund on Tuesday. Me being second . . . it was bad math," he says dully.

"I got a copy of the original letter, Hudson. The signatures were *faked*. There was never a group out to get you." I walk past the dairy cases, the craft beer aisle. "I think someone wanted to scare you into dropping out, but you refused."

"So, I got set up?"

"I don't know," I say honestly, "but if you got salutatorian, then you deserve it." I slide my hands around his waist. "And what the hell would I do if you moved to *Florida*?"

He nods, not letting himself hope just yet. His fingers tangle in my still-damp hair. "Jo, I don't know what to say," he admits. We're not talking about his rank anymore. "I, uh. Asked my therapist about it. He said this should be about what you want."

Want. That word again. I'm so bad at knowing what I want. But I draw him closer. "I want *you.*"

"You're sure?"

"I've never been so sure about anything," I say, and I kiss him, the coolers humming. It all seems stupidly romantic.

Thursday

I wake with the sun. Its pale light beams through my ice-webbed window. I yawn, forcing myself up, dressing in layers—cotton leggings and oversized sweatpants, a long-sleeved thermal and my heaviest fleece, two pairs of socks.

Bay Leaf grunts from the bottom of my bed.

"I'm taking a walk," I tell her, and kiss her tiny head.

Downstairs, my mother's voice floats from the dining room— the Channel 12 live stream blaring on Dad's iPad. He's flipping through the newspaper, his readers perched low on his nose. He looks up. "*Jo*," he says, like he might cry at the sight of me. "Did you need a—?"

I'm not going to school. Like, I'll go tomorrow, but I need one last day.

"I'm taking a walk," I say again. I go before he can stop me.

The cold is excruciating. The kind of freezing that takes your breath away. I breathe it in anyway, my throat burning with it— and I look across the street.

My night at the pool party ended not long after I pushed through the gate. I'd snuck sips of beer before—Genny Light, Labatt Blue—but only pretended to be tipsy. But after three hard seltzers, I . . . did not feel good. My legs kept shaking, and I was breathing fast. The girls felt far off and fuzzy, the fire blurring, stars spinning in the sky and—

I threw up.

"Oh, no! Is she sick?" asked one of the other girls, maybe even one of the Birds.

"No," Maddie said, "she's drunk."

I slid off the chair and laid back in the grass for what felt like forever but was more like five minutes before a hand— Mr. Price's—clamped onto my wrist and dragged me to my feet.

Nick touched that wrist, too. *Nick.* I looked to his lit bedroom window right as he slowly lowered the pane.

Maddie. Her name came to me next. The other girls were watching from the firepit, but I needed to find Maddie.

I couldn't find her anywhere.

Mr. Price yanked me forward, toward the back gate, where my mother stood waiting. I caught fragments of their hushed conversation.

"—invited those boys."

"—car unlocked."

"—stole the drinks from Nick."

Stole? I looped my fingers through the fence to stop swaying. "I didn't . . ."

I was too quiet, I guess, because no one heard me.

Back home, I threw up again. I threw up a lot. My mother braided my hair with my head half in the toilet bowl. She kept saying, "What the hell is wrong with you?"

Because something was wrong with me. I felt it, too. This thing beat inside me that went *tell her, tell her, tell her, tell her.* I mean, she was my mom; I was supposed to tell her about the first time I . . . that this happened. Right? I needed to *tell her, tell her.* It beat louder than the part that went *no one can ever know about this.*

I curled my legs to my chest. "Mom?"

"First thing tomorrow, you apologize to that poor girl, do you understand me?"

Tell her. "But—"

"Jesus, what did you do to your top? The straps are all tangled."

Tell her. "Mom, I think—"

"I don't want to hear it, Jo-Lynn."

So, I didn't try to tell her anymore.

The next day, Nick's car was gone from the curb—for now, not forever. Maddie sat on her front steps with a book, so I took three ibuprofen and met her across the street. I glanced at the side yard, quick, but it made me want to hurl again.

"I'm supposed to apologize." My voice had gone hoarse. I'd stared at the glow-in-the-dark stars on my ceiling all night, waiting to pass the hell out, but I never did.

Maddie scratched at a bug bite on her ankle. "For which part? Ruining my party? Or . . ." Her face was a furious red, but her lip trembled. "How could you do this to me? How could you do *that*? And with my *brother*?"

But I never meant for it to happen, and it happened so fast. It was like we were watching a movie he'd already seen, and I looked down for a second—one second—and when I looked up, I'd missed the plot twist. I'd missed everything.

"I didn't—"

"What did you *think* was going to happen?" Maddie shook her head, and she was crying, but I never meant to hurt her like this. I'd just wanted to make her mad because of what she told her mom at the party. I didn't think that . . . I didn't know he'd . . .

Tell her. It thrummed inside me again. "I think that Nick—"

"No," she said, and it seemed so easy. "I'm done with you."

I was crying, too. "Maddie—"

"You're disgusting."

For so long, I've thought about this. The final moment of our friendship. The pain was breathtaking. I felt it every time I saw her that summer, and every day after that. I felt it when Nick messaged me later that night and told me not to save his number. It was *brutal.* Like we were ripped apart, edges torn and jagged. Sharp.

But sometimes I wonder if it was simpler than that.

Like slicing a paper clean in half, Maddie Price wasn't my friend anymore.

I'll freeze to death if I take a walk.

I go back inside.

-37-

Here are all the things I'd rather do than stand outside Culver: cut off my hair and eat it, strand by strand; scrub the locker room with a toothbrush; swallow a mouse.

I'd rather do literally—literally—anything else.

My parents were ready for a fight when they knocked on my door at dawn and told me to get up, get dressed, get in the car, because I cannot keep doing *this*. Like I'm doing *this* to be a brat. I'd already showered and packed my backpack, but neither of them noticed.

Even if I want to stay in bed forever, I've got a physics test and a calculus quiz and three more weeks of academic probation, and the world won't stop spinning for me.

So, I take one step. Then another.

Then a warm hand finds its way to mine.

"Ready?" Hudson asks.

"No," I say, but we go anyway.

One-L Daniele has crafted a compelling story about me being knocked down with a bug. I don't know if anyone believes it. I don't know if I'd believe it, either, but everyone leaves me alone.

Before lunch, Hudson stops in the office to set up a meeting with Lund. He'll show her the open letter. Those fake signatures. If he needs to, he'll wield what Maddie told him in those texts she sent the night she disappeared. Ran off.

I wait for him out in the hall, my back against the wall.

Then, a flash of red hair: April Kirk. She stops dead when she sees me, nearly tripping on her own feet. For a second, she just stares, her eyes huge, posture braced. Panicked. This must be about the salutatorian thing, right? But this is *good* for her, so I don't get why she's still upset or why she reroutes her path from me so fast.

"April, hold on!" I start to follow, but someone—Cody— immediately blocks my path.

"Just the girl I wanted to see," he says, too close. "Got a second, JoJo?"

The bruise below his eye has faded to a sickly yellow-green, curving up his temple like a crescent moon. This is the last stage before it heals; it has to get ugly first.

I tap the same spot on my own face. "I bet Alexis can find you a concealer for that."

Low, words strangled, he says, "Our truce . . ."

I'm slow to get it. The dot, dot, dot in his voice. That nervous neck cracking. I am alone with Cody, but *he's* the frightened one—because there is no truce anymore.

"You have nothing to hold over me," I say.

No one can ever know about Nick Price, but Cody did, and he'd threatened me with it: *Jo messed around with her best friend's older brother.* But that isn't what happened, not like that.

I take a step toward him. "There's nothing stopping me from telling everyone that you and Miles—"

"I wouldn't do that if I were you." He tries to smile, bare his teeth. It wobbles. "I'm doing you a favor here, JoJo. You don't know what you know."

"Is that supposed to be a threat?"

"Only if you take it as one," he says, and shoves open the door to the stairwell, slapping the top of the doorframe—a drawing of a wedge. Conti will flip when he sees that graffiti.

Right before dismissal, I get a text in the family group chat.

[2:27 p.m.] **DAD:** UNC plays @ Syracuse tonight . . . Mom and me driving Lee to meet w/ his coaches now . . . Be home late . . . Love you . . .

I show Hudson the text. "I've got an empty house if you want to study. Or . . . not study."

Hudson, leaning close: "What else did you have in mind?"

- 38 -

I've kissed lots of boys—lots, so many—but the anticipation of kissing Hudson is all new and so, so good. The hum in my body thrums louder on our way to my house, up to my bedroom, on my bed. I wonder if he can hear it. I want him to. I want *him*.

I sit cross-legged, and he mirrors me, our knees touching. "I don't remember what to do," I say. I don't know if I'm kidding, either, so I laugh, warm and flushed and very nervous.

"Maybe we should start slow." Hudson kisses me. "Something like that."

"Something like that is good," I say, and he does it again.

I'm kissing Hudson Harper-Moore again, finally.

That's all at first, but it's everything. I don't know whose hands rove first. His, tracking from my neck to my waist to my hips? Mine, running along the front of his jeans?

I pull back, cupping my hand to my mouth, stage-whispering, "Can I see it?" He rolls his eyes but stops when I shimmy out of my leggings. "It only seems fair."

"Only fair," he says. I watch him undo the button, unzip his zipper, shove his jeans down his hips. His boxer briefs cling to him—*him*—and I stare very obviously.

"You said this wasn't pertinent information." I slip my hand under the waistband.

He laughs. "Why are you just holding it?"

"Was I supposed to do something else?" I tilt my head, like I'm admiring a sculpture in a museum. He laughs again, and I love it. I love when he laughs. It catches when I shove his shirt higher up his stomach, repositioning on my knees. "Can I—?"

"Yes," he says.

It's been a minute since I've done this, so it takes me a bit to find a rhythm, and my hair keeps falling in my face. But it gets better—it gets good, then really good—and that's very true for him, but I like it too. *I like it too.*

And I like it when he lowers his hand to my thigh, so I don't know why I lift my head so fast or say, "Shit, sorry," all frazzled, startling us both.

Hudson snaps his hand back. "It's okay. Are *you* okay?"

"Yes. I'm sorry." I flush as he fixes his waistband. "I can keep, uh. Performing—"

"Nope, you were right. Horrible way to phrase it," Hudson says. There's a weird distance of space between us. Gentle, he adds, "We can slow down if you want."

"I don't want to slow down. I want to . . . start over." I swing my leg over his lap, kiss him again. He slides a hand under my shirt, up my bare stomach, and I flinch.

"Jo, if you—"

"*No.* It's fine. Let me . . ." My elbow catches in my flannel as I shrug out of it, then the tank underneath it. Next—last—is my bralette. It's pink and super cute, and, yes, I wore it hoping he'd see it. "I have lots of layers. I'm an onion."

"Like Shrek." Pause. "I'm sorry I mentioned Shrek in this specific context."

"Keep going, it's so hot."

"Shut up, Jo," he says. I exhale when he lowers one strap, his mouth. Try to *feel*. I reach behind my back and unhook the bralette and let it fall. Hudson gets a goofy look on his face.

"So, these are my boobs." I can't figure out what to do with my arms. "The left is better, as we've established."

"They're both . . ." Hudson fake frowns. "Huh."

"I told you!"

"I'm kidding. You're so gorgeous."

"I mean, you've already seen it," I say, and he really frowns.

But I don't want to think about that, so I kiss him, like we're starting over again . . . again, again? I'm frantic, feverish when he flips me onto my back. His fingers trace the top band of my underwear—*this okay?*—and I nod—*yes, this is okay*—and his hand dips under the fabric.

"What do you like?" Hudson asks.

"I don't know."

"Oh," he says. I hate the twinge of surprise. "You can tell me what feels good?"

It feels experimental, mostly, and it's kind of humiliating. I'm about to tell him to give up and—*that*. That feels good. He can tell, I guess, because he keeps doing *that*, and it keeps feeling very, very good.

I don't know where to look. I try his hand, then his face, but his eyes have drifted down my body. My breath stutters. (Not like that.) I'm so close to being exposed—fully, wholly—and I need him to stop touching me. I don't want to need him to stop touching me.

"Hudson, wait," I say. He's already disentangled himself. He fishes my flannel from the floor and stares at my bedspread as I fold myself into it.

"Did I do something?" He looks so confused.

"This is me. It's me," I say, heart beating hard. I cross into my bathroom and stand at the sink, but I don't want to see myself in the mirror, and I hate it, I hate this, I hate me, and I'm crying. Why am I crying?

I collapse onto the toilet lid. Hudson sits on the edge of the tub. The showerhead tumbles off the hook, but neither of us jokes about it.

"What the fuck is wrong with me?" I ask quietly.

"Nothing is wrong with you. Maybe this is too fast."

"I'm so into you," I say. "I want this. I don't know why my body isn't doing what I want it to. I don't know why you like me."

I don't mean to say that last part out loud.

He's quiet at first. "I like how your eyes get big when you're trying not to laugh—usually at your own joke. I like that you know the lyrics to every Billy Joel deep cut. I like how I never know what you're going to say because it makes me want to tell you everything. You also have a great left boob."

I smack his knee.

"Maybe this"—he gestures between us—"can't happen right now. But if I have to choose between it or you, I choose you, Jo. Every time."

I choke out an ugly sob. Hudson kneels beside me, and I bury my face in his neck and cry and I feel so sad for myself and I say, "I got snot on your shirt," and he laughs.

Then I lift my head. Face him fully.

Say, "I like that you frown when you concentrate. I like that the smell of coffee reminds me of you, so I think about you a lot. I like how you reverse to park and that you're so smart and that you ask what I like and I'm in love with you. I love you?"

"Are you asking me?"

"No, I just know. I just do."

"I obviously love you, too."

"You asked me what I want, and I want *you*, Hudson." I kiss him hard. "I also want you to go down on me again."

He grunts, kind of. "We can make that happen."

I lead him into my bedroom and fall back against my pillows, dizzy as he tugs down my underwear. My skin is hot—burning. I drag my hands over my face; I feel like I'm on fire.

"Why are you covering your eyes?"

"Because I'm mortified."

He unpeels my hands. "Trust me, you have nothing to be embarrassed about." His face is serious. "But this is okay?" I nod. "Tell me if it becomes not okay."

"Okay. Yes. I will."

"Okay." He kisses my neck, my sternum, the soft patch of skin below my belly button. I shut my eyes. Try to breathe out these nerves, try not to think as his arms wrap around my thighs, as his mouth—

My breath hitches. He laughs, like he's so proud of himself.

"Shut up, Hudson."

He does.

I'm bracing for a swell of panic. Waiting for my body to shut down. But something shifts in my brain: Hudson doesn't like me; he *loves* me. I know it's true. Hudson sees me—sometimes the worst of me, always the real me—and loves me still. This knot of doubt unravels, and I focus on this. Him. Me.

Me.

And when my breath goes ragged, when my fingers twist in his long hair, I can't fathom how I ever believed I deserved anything less.

-39-

I'll be honest: I lose myself. I lose myself fully and deeply for two whole weeks. I'm so wrapped up in this thing—love, is that it?—that I float through each day.

Lund cancels on Hudson twice, so he emails the alumni association and explains that the open letter was faked; that his attempts to discuss the matter have thus far been ignored; that he isn't entitled to the spot or the money, and if April earned it, then it's hers, but he'd really, really appreciate a second look.

I mock him about "thus far" for two days, but it's perfect.

He is perfect.

He is perfect, and the Birds are perfect, even if Kathleen is convinced I'm not okay. That I stuck on a bandage without stanching the wound. But I was overreacting about Nick. I was just surprised, is all, and sure, I don't love thinking about him—that night—but Nick is gone.

The Audi across the street is gone, too, replaced with a used Ford.

The deleted Instagram is proof enough that Maddie is *ok, safe,* and the News 9 interview kills the story for good. Kills the good-will toward her parents, too. There is no redemption arc.

They release a statement via their newly hired attorney: *The media scrutiny has taken an immense toll on our family, and we request privacy as we turn toward healing and waiting for our beautiful daughter to come home. Come home, Maddie.*

Sometimes my heart still beats with it—*missing, kidnapped, dead*—but if you forced me to say it out loud, I'd say I believe Maddie Price ran away. I have nothing to suggest otherwise.

Because the simplest stories are often true.

Because I *need* to believe it or else I'll lose my fucking mind.

Is that denial? I'm not in denial about anything.

I am perfect. I am glowing. I am *fine*.

But I'd be better if Tess stopped bailing on me.

Last week she missed the cohort site visit at the music academy where April interns, then she canceled our one-on-one—and apparently, tomorrow's is canceled, too. Lund tells me in the hall before lunch, like it's an afterthought.

Like it's nothing.

"What the hell?" I lean against the windowsill while Hudson digs in his locker. "I haven't seen her in weeks! Not since Open House."

Hudson shuts his locker. "Should you be worried?"

My stomach sways, unsteady. "She sent me her number, so maybe I can call?" I navigate to my Culver email: PASSWORD EXPIRED! I groan. It's a pain in the ass to update anything related to our accounts since it can only be initiated on school servers.

For security reasons, or whatever.

"Let's go to the lab then," Hudson says, slinging his arm around me, and it's so perfect I forget to be annoyed. Then my phone vibrates with a new text, and I'm annoyed again.

[1:02 p.m.] **KATE KIRBY** 👩 📺: Dinner is at seven. You WILL be there, Jo-Lynn.

Hudson reads over my shoulder. "Lee's thing?"

"Unfortunately," I mumble. It's my brother's birthday. Twenty years old.

I've barely seen him or my parents since Open House, either.

But our own house is so old the sound carries: Lee had midterms last week that went fine; his rehab is ahead of schedule; my parents don't know what to do with me. That's how they say it. *What are we supposed to do with her?*

Like I'm a bat infestation in the attic eaves and not their goddamn daughter.

The design lab is crowded; major projects are due next week, so the Spencer twins are in here, a couple of juniors. April, too. She sinks lower in her chair when we enter.

"Just changing my password," I tell Chopra. I'm officially on his good side. I was never on his *bad* side, but he's told me more than once how proud he is, which is kind of nice.

Me and Hudson go to our usual seats, and I boot up my computer. YOUR PASSWORD WAS CHANGED 183 DAYS AGO pops onto the screen after I reset it and . . .

"Hudson," I whisper, gripping his knee. "I have Maddie's login. When One-L Daniele showed me the original letter about your rank, I took a picture of her login info. I totally forgot."

He nervously scans the crowded room. "What would we be looking for?"

I don't know. We've basically stopped looking, period, but I *have* it, so I type it.

YOUR PASSWORD WAS CHANGED 19 DAYS AGO.

Nineteen days ago. Maddie's password was changed nineteen days ago. I count the days; it'd be a Friday. Senior bowling night, the night of the News 9 interview, the night Maddie made that Instagram post. But Maddie wasn't here nineteen days ago.

"What the fuck?" I say, too loud. Everyone glances back at us. But I open Instagram next and input her handle and *a one-click link has been sent to m.price0109@culverhonors.edu* and *this feature was last used nineteen days ago* and—

"Holy shit," Hudson says, also too loud, and now Mr. Chopra, now *everyone*, is crowding behind us, peering at my screen, and they're saying it, too. *Holy shit.*

Because someone changed Maddie's password—and it wasn't Maddie Price.

-40-

The literal last thing I want to do is celebrate my brother's birthday.

All hell broke loose when it came out that someone hacked Maddie's email to make that post. The whispers were relentless. *Maddie. Okay. Safe. Fake. Missing. Kidnapped. Dead.*

Now, after all that shit, the birthday boy refuses to choose a restaurant. Thai? No. Italian? Nope. Mediterranean or Tex-Mex or small plates? No, no, no.

Dad makes an executive decision: a wood-fired pizza place in Village Gate. The pizzas are $26 each, with toppings like honey and hazelnut and lamb. Even the ones on the children's menu are topped with prosciutto instead of pepperoni.

He slips his reading glasses to the tip of his nose. "Do we want an appetizer?"

I rip a hunk of bread from the basket. "Whatever."

"Whatever," Lee echoes.

The silence hangs over us until our waiter appears to take our drink order. "I'd adore a glass of wine," I say with my best Kate Kirby impression.

Dad says, "She'll have a Shirley Temple."

"Dirty Shirley?"

"No," Dad says to me, then to the waiter, "No." He turns back to me. "How do you know what a Dirty Shirley is?"

Lee swishes the plate of olive oil. "Yeah, Jo, how *do* you know?" he asks. I kick his shin under the table. He kicks mine, too, then leans back in his chair, arms crossed. He looks absently toward the window, then frowns. "Is that Cody?"

That sure as hell is Cody Forsythe crossing in front of the glass. His Duke drawstring bag is slung over his shoulder, and he wears basketball shorts, even in the cold. He must have his kickboxing class. His head is ducked, but I slouch anyway, shielding my face behind the menu.

"Hey, I forgot about that kid!" Dad says. "Did you want to say hi?"

Lee shakes his head the tiniest bit. My mother looks between us—Lee, me—and I want nothing to do with Cody, but I say, "Great idea, Dad. I'll be right back."

Most shops are closed for the night, but I'm killing time, so I pull out my phone and—

"Cody, you have to believe me. *Please.*"

I freeze. Ease along the wall toward the kickboxing studio. It's Cody and . . . Alexis Fitch.

Mascara streaks down her face. "I swear I didn't do it."

"Then why did you confess?" he asks, hoarse voice cracking.

"I didn't!" she says, but he's already gone. I should go, too, before she finds me and—

She found me. Like that, she pulls it together—swiping her eyes, calming the rattle in her breath. "I didn't do it," Alexis says again, as if I asked. As if we've ever spoken. "Someone sent Lund a confession saying I hacked Maddie's email to make that post. I *didn't*." She sucks in her lip ring. "I have an expulsion hearing next week for cyberbullying or something."

The pulsing bass from the kickboxing studio thrums louder, ringing in my ears.

Her eyes turn hard. "I see the way everyone looks at me and judges me. How *you* look at me," she says, and I want to deny it. I want to believe I don't look at her the same way they look at me. She says, "Nothing even happened with Cody. I was just trying to be his friend."

"I'm . . . I'm sorry," I say, but I need to go. Now. I head back into the restaurant and find my family's table again. My drink came, so I sip, praying for a bite of booze—but it's a virgin.

"How's your friend?" Dad asks. "He always seemed like a good kid."

Lee stretches his arms above his head. "He's not."

My mother is staring at me again, but Dad is clueless. He asks, "How come he doesn't come around anymore?"

"Because I'm not friends with him," I say, loud enough that the table beside us looks over. "He's not my friend, and he's dating Maddie, so."

"God, who cares about Maddie?" Lee says. "She was a bad friend, Jo."

"How do *you* know?" I snap. Then, again: "How *do* you know?" The two questions are different to me. *Maddie + Lee.*

"You were talking to her. For the story," I say. Lee stares at me. "The comeback game," I add, and he laughs, drops a fork on his bread plate. "She was supposed to interview you—or she did—and you never told me."

"Because it was an *email* about a fucking basketball game I played when I was fourteen."

"Hey!" Dad whisper-shouts. "Language."

"You should've told me."

"Why? She's not your friend." Lee readjusts the candle centerpiece. "Maddie was mean to you, Jo, even back then. But for some reason, you still let her have this weird hold on you. I feel sorry for you, honestly. It's so desperate."

I stand, my chair scraping back against the floor. "Happy birthday, asshole."

The drizzle outside has transformed into a downpour. My throat scrapes with the cold, the rain soaking straight to my bones. Heat radiates out of me as I walk farther, farther.

Only when I reach the end of the block do I look back.

No one's coming after me.

-41-

I'm shivering—hot and sweaty and freezing at once—when I ring Hudson's doorbell two, three, four times in a row. He yanks open the door, already annoyed, then says, "Holy shit."

"I'm choosing not to be offended by that." I step past him. He wears a black T-shirt that looks so soft, sweatpants, his glasses. His hair is damp.

"I thought you had Lee's thing."

"I did." My boots squish when I step out of them. "I left. He . . ." I shake my head, still too furious. "I wish you'd heard what he said to me."

Hudson wrings my sleeve. "You should probably take this off."

"Don't get fresh."

"I didn't mean—"

"I'm kidding. I'm crabby."

The bathroom mirror is still fogged from his shower. He sets a towel on the sink, twists the faucet, tests the water. "I'll put your clothes in the . . ." Hudson looks up as I lift my sweater over my head. He forces his gaze higher. "Did you, uh, need anything else?"

"Nope," I say, and he steps out to let me undress. I dump my clothes in the hall, then pull back the shower curtain. No matter how far I crank the faucet, it never feels hot enough.

I can't get warm.

Hudson is reading for class when I step into his room. The light on his nightstand gives off a low glow. He says, "Your clothes are in the dryer."

"Thanks." I tighten the towel around my chest and drop next to him, combing my fingers through my hair, catching on a knot. "Ouch."

Hudson positions himself behind me, his knees pressed to my back. He drags his fingers through my hair. "Do you want to talk about it?"

"No," I say, then proceed to tell him every horrible detail. "Lee said that I'm stupid to be holding on to Maddie. To *care*. He seems to think she never even liked me. Can you believe it?"

I wait for the indignant yes. I wait for him to match my outrage.

Then he rests his palms on my shoulder blades and says, "What if Lee's right?"

"He's not."

"What if he is?" Hudson asks, and I realize this isn't the first time he's had this thought.

It feels like a betrayal.

I stand. "How long will my clothes take?"

"I'm not trying to be a dick. What if your friendship with Maddie wasn't all you thought it was? That doesn't mean it didn't matter, or can't be meaningful, but I feel like . . ." He takes off his glasses, rubs his hands down his face. "Never mind."

"Clearly you want to say something, so say it."

"Maddie fucking sucks!" Hudson laughs, but it's pure frustration. "You romanticize your friendship with her when, from everything you've told me, it sounds bad, Jo. Toxic. Why does it matter so much to you?"

"Because I thought she saw me!" I almost choke on the words. "I had no friends, Hudson. I didn't know how to *be* friends with other girls, but I wanted it so badly, and then I had Maddie, and all the things that made me feel different or bad or weird were okay with her. So if, after all that, she never liked me, then maybe I'm not worth liking."

My pathetic confession hangs between us for a beat.

"Who are you with me?" Hudson asks, taking my wrist, pulling me back onto the edge of his bed. I refuse to answer, so he says, "I'm asking, Jo. Who are you with me? Kathleen? Or Sara and Michaela, or even Tess?"

"I'm . . . myself." It sounds so small. I rest my head on his shoulder. "Maddie ran away, didn't she?"

That desperate part of me thought Maddie coming to me—*I think that I'm in trouble, but I think that you can help me*—meant she really did need me. *Me.* That I, our friendship, meant as much to her as she did to me. But maybe I'm trying to solve a mystery that doesn't exist.

"I think I need to be done with Maddie," I say.

Hudson nods. "I think that's a good idea."

I roll my eyes and sigh, all dramatic, falling against him. My head knocks into his chin, and my thigh bumps—

"Really, Hudson?"

"Look, I know we're arguing, but you're still naked on my bed."

I roll my eyes again, laugh when he whines that my hand is cold. But it doesn't take long until I'm scorched with a different sort of heat. For the towel to slide to my waist, the floor.

God, I wish I could capture how it feels when he looks at me.

It's more intense now. Urgent. His hands and mine, how we kiss each other everywhere. We feel it the exact same second—a shared static shock, seeing a quick crack of lightning in the sky. He looks down at me, his face flushed and serious.

I press my thumb to the scar on his lip. "How did you get this?"

"I fell off a fence when I was a kid." His breath warms my palm. "Should I get a—?"

"Yes. If you want to."

"I want to." He pulls a foil packet from his nightstand and then, once the condom is on, we both do nothing. "I just got extremely nervous."

"No, same. Uh. Maybe we can . . ." I kiss him again, lying back, and he reaches between us, but my body immediately tenses, breath catching in a way I don't like, so I press my hand to his chest and say, "I'm sorry."

"It's okay."

"I need . . . wait," I say, and he does until I nod again.

It's a lot of talking—*are you okay?* and *is this okay?*—then it's a lot less talking.

Besides, every time the answer is yes.

-42-

I wake in . . . not my bed. Hudson's bed. His arm is draped over my waist, and his chest rises and falls with his deep breaths.

I fumble my phone off the nightstand. I'll either have dozens of furious voicemails from my parents—demanding to know where I am, who I'm with, what the hell is wrong with me—or silence. I'm not sure which is worse.

But my phone is dead. Deader than dead.

"Hudson," I whisper, brushing back his hair. "I should go."

He grunts but keeps his eyes shut. "You should stay."

"It's late."

"What time is it?"

"I don't know."

He reaches over me to check his own phone, also dead. "Then you don't know it's late."

"Compelling argument," I say, and it doesn't take long for us to reach into his nightstand again. After, I say, "Okay, I really do need to go."

My clothes are still in the dryer, so I take his shirt off the floor.

I blink, caught off-guard by the bright bathroom; I guess I left the lights on. Then my vision adjusts, forming my outline in the mirror and . . . the lights are off.

But how?

I yank open the blinds.

"Oh, no, no, Hudson, *no!*" I fling open the bathroom door and scream, face to face with a woman I'm guessing is his grandmother: tired eyes, gray hair in a thick braid. She looks from me to his opening door.

He says, "I'll explain this later," and shoves me into his room. From behind the closed door, I hear, *Culver has been calling— Your grandpa and I need to talk to you about—*

A second later, Hudson returns with my clothes. "I wore this yesterday," I say, popping a stick of gum. "I don't have my backpack and my phone is dead and I . . ."

I didn't go home last night. The thought rattles me.

It's between second and third period when we get to school. Mrs. Fitzgerald sucks on a mint, filling out our late passes. "Hudson, Principal Lund would like to see you."

He looks warily toward her closed door. "But—"

"That was an order, not a request." Fitzgerald turns to me and says, "Get to class, Jo-Lynn. That's an order, too."

I squeeze Hudson's hand and step into the lobby.

Right into Miles Metcalf. His eyes lower, scanning every inch of me—the same clothes, the mussed hair, the late pass. He blushes, like he always blushes, and says, "I've been looking for you! I wanted to tell you something."

"Sorry, but I—"

"I got into MIT." Miles smiles, that blush deepening. "Yesterday, I got my acceptance. They release decisions on March 14. Pi Day. Like, three point one four—"

"Yeah, I get it."

His smile slips. "You're not going to congratulate me?"

"Fine, congrats. You really *earned* it." I'm loud enough to draw stares.

Something else burns behind his flush. "I thought you'd be happy for me."

Somewhere, someone whispers, *Jo, Hudson, late, together, bitch.* Somewhere, I swear I hear Cody laugh. Like I'm slipping lower and lower, right back to where I was before.

I'm summoned back to the office by the end of fourth period.

Principal Lund smiles, cold and terse, when I knock.

My mother does not.

No, she burns. She came from the station—blown-out blonde waves, a fitted blue dress. Blue is her best on-camera color. Really brings out her eyes.

"Kill me," I mumble.

"Miss Kirby, I would not test your luck," Principal Lund says, smile so steady I almost miss the threat. "I was just telling your mom that I'm not sure what to do with you today. The late arrival, the blatant unpreparedness—I fear you're a distraction, and that's not fair to your peers. I propose that your mother take you home."

Three, four seconds of silence pass. "Oh, is that a punishment?"

Because I'd *love* to go home.

"I hope you return to school tomorrow ready to learn. Now,

Kate," Lund says, and flips open a leather-bound planner, "I'd like to set up a meeting to discuss her academic status."

My mother tilts her head. I squeeze my eyes shut.

Lund says, "As I'm sure you're aware"—my mother is not aware—"next week marks the end of her six-week probationary term, so we'll need to determine how to best proceed with her future at Culver. I'm quite open tomorrow, if you're free."

My mother stands, yanking me up. "I'll get in touch."

I don't think she has the power to end this meeting, but no one stops us.

Her heels click on the ice in the visitor lot. This silence is worse than if she screamed at me. My mother never screams at me, not like that, but if she did, I could fight back. Match her rage. Instead, I watch her light a cigarette and wait for the windshield to defog.

Exhaling, she says, "I don't even know where to start."

I crack the window. "Glad you could host the morning show when I was—"

Missing. I was missing last night.

She shifts into gear. "We *called*, Jo-Lynn. You never picked up."

"My phone is dead."

She flicks ash out the window. Her teeth grit, jaw set tight; she must be holding back something brutal. My body is too tense, braced, vibrating with too much . . . just too *much.*

"I'm taking you to Channel 12 with me," she says, stopping at a stop sign. The station is practically walkable from here. "I'm not rewarding you for—"

"For what?"

"For not coming home. Spending the night with your

boyfriend—I assume you were with Hudson. For *failing*." Her concealer has smudged along her chin. "Do you understand how bad it looks that my own daughter is on academic probation, and I have no clue?"

I flip down the visor. "That's what you care about? How bad it makes *you* look?"

"No, I'm concerned that you're flunking. Why didn't you tell me?"

"Why didn't you see it?" The words burn, scorching my throat.

My mother flips on her blinker. "What're you talking about?"

"Nothing."

"Jo-Lynn—"

"I did it on purpose." I choke on the bite of cold in the air. "I did it on purpose because I wanted you to see it—that I was failing, and that I threw away half my clothes, and that I had no fucking friends. But you never asked. You never noticed."

My mother pulls into the parking garage. The lights glow orange. Killing the engine, she says, "What did that boy do to you?"

"Hudson?"

"The Forsythe boy, and do not lie to me."

Tell her. This is all I've wanted. For my mother to see something cruel, violating, illegal happened to me. My voice breaks as I say, "I can't tell you because you'll say the wrong thing. You'll say what I'm already thinking about myself, and it'll kill me." I hate this. I hate that I'm fighting with my mother in the car and *crying.* It's so cliché.

"Whatever is going on here"—she waves her hand toward me—"needs to stop."

"Fine, I'll stop." I fling open the door and head into the station. It's not as good as being home, but I used to love her dressing room; I can take a nap on the pink suede couch, snuggled up against the faux-fur pillows.

Or not. She deposits me in a windowless office off the kitchenette. The ancient desktop hums, its keyboard coated in dust. My mother holds out her hand. "Phone."

"It's still dead."

"Phone," she says again. I hand it over. She types in the intern login on the desktop. "Do your work. Do not make a sound. Understand?"

The second she leaves, I kill the fluorescent lights, blinking against the bright glow of the monitor. I'm caught up on my shit for class, so I play three games of solitaire.

Then I search Maddie Price. It's like autopilot.

The most recent article is the companion piece to News 9's interview with Mrs. Price. It has the details of the Instagram post, too, the account reactivated, then gone again. *Alexis Fitch hacked Maddie.* I test the words in my head, but all I hear is how Alexis cried that she didn't do it—and if she didn't do it, who did?

But I'm done with Maddie, remember?

I'm opening another game of solitaire when the computer chimes with a new notification.

DAILY INTERN REMINDERS!

- Restock coffee pods + sugar packets
- Refill copier w/ paper
- Tip line!!

Tip line. It takes me forever to find the inbox. I sort by the most recent. There was a downed power line causing traffic off the Thruway four days ago. Someone heard a coyote howl in the suburbs.

I scroll back five weeks.

Sat, Feb. 10 at 11:34 a.m. — Hi! My partner lives in the same loft building as that girl Maddie Price's dad, and their doorbell camera caught a pic the night she went missing. Please see attached. (P.S. I'm a BIG fan, Kate!)

That can't be right. Maddie never went to the loft. She lied to her parents about where she was spending the night, then snuck into the house to leave the note before she left.

Except Maddie *was* at the loft.

Maddie was *there.*

I gnaw on my lip, scroll to the attached files—and there are none. But there is a contact number for someone named Tori. I unhook the phone from its cradle. I'll pretend to be an intern combing through old tips and—

"Hi there, is this Tori?" I say in my best impression of my mother. *Shit.* The star anchor wouldn't reach out about a tip. I'm committed: "This is Kate Kirby from Channel 12."

"Oh! Hi! This is so fun, hi. I'm a *huge* fan."

"Isn't that sweet! I'm actually calling about a tip you submitted—"

"The doorbell picture? I don't know how helpful it'll—what?" Tori shouts that last word away from the receiver. To me, she says, "Sorry, I'm on shift. I'm a nurse. You were saying?"

"Yes, so, the photo unfortunately didn't upload."

"I'll resend it after my shift. It'll be after midnight, though."

"Great! You can send it directly to my, uh, personal line." I give her my number—*since it'll be after hours, and all*—and thank her so much for her help. I spin in the chair to face the shut door, like the real Kate Kirby might bust in. "Do you know her father at all?"

"Not really. I haven't seen him in weeks. I never met the girl, either," Tori says, and even now, it gets me. *The girl.* She adds, "I've met that woman, though."

My voice slips. "What woman?"

"His girlfriend. Nice lady," Tori says. Something beeps in the background. "The whole thing is so sad, you know? How that girl thought her only option was running. But I guess you never know what goes on behind closed doors."

"Right. Thank you again." I set the phone in the cradle.

I'm missing something right in front of me. *I guess you never know what goes on behind closed doors.* So, what goes on inside that house across the street? Maddie had to go home that night to plant the note; I want to know what else she left behind.

I told Hudson that I was done and finished and over it, and I will be.

But first, I have to get into that house.

-43-

I'm grounded for not coming home last night. For hiding my academic probation.

For being *completely out of control.*

But Dad's friend is soft-launching her newest restaurant, and Lee booked a study room at the library, so I'm home alone for the evening—and I need Hudson, now. My mother returns my phone before she and dad leave, so I text Hudson to come over as soon as the house empties. Ten minutes later, I rip open the door and say, "I need to talk to you," dragging him up to my room.

"Okay." Hudson sits on my bed. "I wanted to talk too."

"What about? Last night?"

"No! No, that was incredible. Ten out of ten experience."

"For me too. What is it then?"

He hesitates. "You first."

"I think we should break into Maddie's house."

For a second, Hudson stares at me with a whiplashed look on his face. Then he leans forward, his head in his hands, and says, "Go on."

Hudson is not a fan of this mission, even when I tell him we're not breaking and entering since we'll be using a key, so that's technically just entering.

Still, he whispers, "I hate this."

"It'll be quick."

It *needs* to be quick. I don't know where the Prices go on Thursday evenings—a weekly date night or spin class or marriage counseling—but they're never gone long.

I lead Hudson through the back gate. The sky is a dusky, muted pink. The pool is covered for the winter, and the willow tree is bare, its limbs limp. I go straight for the metal frog staked in the earth and reach into its cold mouth, where I know the spare is hidden.

Where the spare *was* hidden.

I crouch, scrape my nails through the frozen dirt. *Shit.*

"What's wrong?" Hudson asks uneasily.

"The key is gone." I look at the windows. The center is unlatched—it goes to the laundry room, I'm pretty sure. "Give me a boost."

"Isn't this breaking?" he asks, holding out his hands. I hoist myself up, shove the window higher and higher, tumble onto the dryer. He looks up at me. "I *really* hate this."

"Relax." I shut the window harder than I mean to. From his dog bed, Tanner lifts his head and stares with clouded eyes. "Hey, it's just me. Remember me?" I let him sniff my hand, and he settles again. It makes me want to cry; the only nice Price is their geriatric dog.

I unlock the back door for Hudson.

He tentatively steps inside. "What are we looking for?"

"Anything. Everything. The note." I open the junk drawer. It's filled with rubber bands, envelopes, pencils and pens, a half-chewed block eraser (ew), stamps, a single Milk-Bone.

Hudson wanders into the hall, nods toward the mess on the dining room table: Mr. Price's de facto office. He wakes the laptop set at the head of the table. "What could his password be?"

"I have no idea." I take his briefcase from the buffet. It requires a four-digit code, but a pen sticks out of the corner, the gap wide enough that I can fit my fingers to pry it open and—

"Did you break it?"

"I don't think so." I definitely did.

I sort through it: to-do lists, boring emails about his boring job, a crumpled yellow sticky note with a password on it. Hudson types it in, and I pull out something else.

VEHICLE BILL OF SALE

I, Geoffrey Price, in consideration of $0, do hereby sell, transfer and convey to Nicholas Price, the following vehicle.

"Mr. Price sold his Audi to Nick," I say, skimming the document. "Gifted it, actually."

"Why would he do that?" Hudson scrolls through Mr. Price's inbox: agenda notes, spam for Viagra, meeting minutes. "That car has to be worth at least sixty grand but he—oh, shit."

FROM: m.price0109@culverhonors.edu
DATE: Feb. 5, 5:14 p.m.
SUBJECT: [NO SUBJECT]

I'm sorry I was upset on the phone, but this is so important to me. Do any of your clients have connections at NYU? Can you please ask around? PLEASE.

FROM: m.price0109@culverhonors.edu
DATE: Feb. 5, 6:05 p.m.
SUBJECT: [NO SUBJECT]

Asshole

Headlights beam through the window, and we drop to the floor, quick. Six, seven, eight seconds pass. I slowly lift my head, whispering, "I think the car was turning around."

"Jo, can we please—?"

"I just want to look in her room." I take the stairs two at a time, and Hudson begrudgingly follows. I brace myself before I turn the doorknob.

It's everything like I remember.

The lime-green walls. The floral watercolor comforter. The standing lamp with its cheap shades. The wobbly vanity we found on the curb and hauled back, block by block, both of us sweating and laughing and taking turns walking backward.

"This is certainly green," Hudson says.

I tug the light chain in her closet. The bulb fizzes before it pops on.

In the corner, angled under her prom dress, is a box labeled LOCKER. The one from the senior wing? It's like a clue marked CLUE. I unfold the flaps and dig inside: a photo magnet of Maddie and Cody where he kisses her cheek, her and the Birds at prom.

There's a pencil sharpener, too, a mug of highlighters, a compact mirror.

"Jo, look. It's you."

"Me?" I join him at the vanity, where photos are tucked into the frame of the mirror.

It's not just me; it's *us*. Maddie and me.

This was her favorite photo of us. We'd spent the day at Seabreeze, riding each ride in the front row, climbing up, up, up the water slides. In the photo, we're sunburned and smiling. Maddie clutches a dolphin plush that I won for her at the water gun race.

I untuck the photo, but another falls out, hidden behind it.

"Is that?" Hudson starts, as I say, "April?"

Maddie Price and April Kirk in their Our Lady of Lourdes uniforms. They smile, posing with their flutes, arms around each other.

Headlights beam up the driveway again, and no—no, no, no—this is not good, this is bad, this is so fucking bad. Hudson looks to me, panicked, and I say, "They'll come in the front, we'll go out the back door."

His foot kicks the compact, sends it skittering. I pick it up, pop it open.

"Jo, let's go," Hudson hisses from the landing.

There's a key. Tiny, gold, hidden—the key to that locker in the newspaper lab?

Again, he says, "Jo, let's *go*," and I follow him downstairs, past the curtainless windows. Tanner howls (at us? At nothing?) but Hudson and I force open the back door as the front swings open. The night has gotten dark, so we dart across the street, unseen.

Pale, Hudson say, "That was—"

"I think this goes to Maddie's locker in the newspaper lab." I hold up the key. He shakes his head, just a little, and I say, "Get your car keys, okay? We need to go."

The doors to Culver are miraculously unlocked for a junior varsity basketball game tonight.

Down in the basement, I punch in the lab code—#1310, thanks, One-L—and beeline right for the Managing Editor locker. The key fits, like I knew it would, and it's . . . empty. I tilt onto my tiptoes, sweep inside the cool metal until my fingers brush something.

"Seriously?" I hold up another key, this one tiny and pink.

"Something is stuck." Hudson reaches over my shoulder and pulls a folded sticky note from the slot. He unfolds it: *m.price0109 pw r7Q_,?k2({4My"V'*

Maddie's Culver login. First initial, last name, four-digit month and day of birth.

"Her new password," I say, ripping the note from him. "This isn't her handwriting. Do you think someone planted it? Or I guess someone might just return it thinking it was hers."

"Try it," Hudson says blandly.

I think he's annoyed with me, but it feels like we're *so* close to uncovering something. I try the password—and it *works.*

Maddie's desktop is neat and organized, her drafts in meticulous order. I click on PRICE_VENDING-MACHINE_0915. It's about the new vending machines.

"Riveting." I right-click, scroll up, down, highlight the text with the cursor—

"Do that again." Hudson scoots his chair up, suddenly interested. He points to the word count: 455 of 458 words. "You're missing three."

I change the font to black and there, at the bottom, in small text: 2-19 = 875.

"I know I failed math last semester, but that's not right, right?"

Hudson jots down the numbers on a scrap of paper. "Try another one."

In PRICE_DRESS-CODE_0923 we find 17-4 = 350. Now that we know what to look for, I'm finding them everywhere: 8-21 = 1250; 9-4 = 600; 11-19 + 20-19 = 1400.

"It has to be a code, right? Equations? Dates? Wait, no, not dates." I rack my brain. Start to write out A = 1, B = 2, C = 3, and so on. It seems so simple—so obvious—but then again, this is Maddie we're talking about. I say, "If this is right, then 2-19 is BS."

"Bullshit?" Hudson offers.

I think for a second. "Ben Sulkin?"

Ben Sulkin, who's back from his two-week suspension for punching Cody, though I still don't know why. He stalks around school with his fists clenched, like he's waiting for a fight.

"What about the second numbers? They're not hyphenated like the others," I say. Hudson stares at the screen, frowning, then angles the keyboard and adds a dollar sign. I blink, say, "Ben Sulkin paid $875 for something."

"Something," Hudson repeats.

I inspect the sticky note again. Flip it over. Freeze. It's a crude pencil sketch—a weird shape, like a wedge, but not really. Hudson looks to me, the same realization crossing his face.

This thing is everywhere. *Everywhere.* Drawn on chairs in the cafeteria, etched on desks, scrawled into the railings, scribbled on doorframes.

"There's one in the locker room," Hudson says, and both of us stand without needing to coordinate. He does a sweep, then motions me inside.

I follow him toward the back row of lockers. "What even is it?"

"We learned about it in AP Art History last year. This piece—it's the last one you add to an arch, yeah? It locks everything in place. It's the keystone."

I stop dead. "Keystone?"

It unfolds at once, so fast and sudden and clear that I know—I *know*—even before I look which locker this will be: #1313.

Neither of us has to say it, but I do: "Miles Metcalf."

Every memory, every moment, forms clearly in my head. Cody looping his arm around Miles's neck, tipping a lukewarm can into his mouth. *You want a sip of Keystone?*

Ben Sulkin, sloppy, clinging to him like a spider monkey. *Keystone, man?*

Every time it happened, a rapid flash of something crossed Miles's face. I thought it was embarrassment. But he wasn't embarrassed by the way those boys treated him. He was *scared*.

He was scared because—

"Miles isn't cheating for Cody," Hudson says. "He's running a whole fucking ring."

-44-

Hudson is beside himself. He paces the length of his car again, again, and I watch, leaning against the hood. He keeps zipping and unzipping his jacket—cold, then hot. *Burning.*

"Those fucking assholes."

"I know." I'm not burning. I'm nothing.

He quits pacing. "Fuck."

I'm trying to unpack it still: Miles lied when we confronted him. I can see that now. How he rephrased my questions not because he didn't understand, but to gauge how much we knew.

Maddie's story—it was about the cheating ring. It was about *Keystone.*

"We need to do something. Tell Principal Lund. Tell Conti. Tell anyone." Hudson tilts his head, searching my face. "Jo, I need you *here*, not wherever your mind is."

"I'm just thinking."

Thinking about how when I threatened Cody at the bonfire, I was really threatening him with Keystone. But Maddie was going to *expose* it. It's not just Cody or Miles who'd want her quiet. Any of those names—the codes—hidden in her files could want her gone.

Gone. I say, "Maddie—"

Hudson laughs, but it's that harsh, bitter laugh. "Do you *really* want to talk about Maddie right now? Then let's talk about how she ran that fucking open letter, Jo, and that she knew about Keystone, and that she did nothing."

"Because she was in over her head! She was scared."

"What if she wasn't?" He lifts a shoulder. "What if this was nothing more than a story to get her into NYU? If she cared that it was unjust or unfair, why did she keep it to herself? Maybe Maddie is just selfish." He shakes his head. "We need to tell."

"What tangible evidence do we have?" I ask, genuinely. "Some stupid codes and a sticky note with a drawing on it?"

Hudson exhales, and with it, his rage sputters like flame. "Know why Lund asked to meet today? To scold me for going to the alumni association. I'm not getting that money, Jo."

"But—"

"I did everything right," he says. "*Everything.* My grandparents unretired for me. Moved school districts. My mom had just died, and even though I was only eleven, I knew I had nothing without my grades."

I can't even bring myself to look at him, so I look toward the intersection instead. The stoplight sways slowly in the breeze.

"I passed the entrance exam to Culver. I got the second-best grades. I joined soccer. I did tech crew." He scrapes a hand through his hair. "I *tried* to apply to college, Jo. I'd come up with a list of schools I liked, but I needed tax forms from my grandparents to get the application fee waivers, and I didn't know what I was doing, and I had no one to help me, so I . . ."

For a second, I think he might cry.

"I did everything right," Hudson says again, "and it was never going to be enough."

I reach for his hand. "Hudson—"

"The house sold, Jo." His voice is dull. "My grandma tried to tell me this morning. They put in an offer on a place in Sarasota, and I'll have to move because I have no place to go and no money to stay, and I'm going to guess a big fucking part of that is because of Keystone."

"*Hudson*," I say again, heart splitting. "Just . . . stay with me, okay?" I know the second I say it that my parents would never go for it. "Or Kathleen." That'll never happen, either. "This can't . . . I can't . . ." I'm frantic now. "I don't want this to be over."

"It's not over, Jo, but I'm fucking mad." Hudson runs his hands over his face. "I tried to tell you when I came over, but you had to break into Maddie's house because you can't let this go. Please let it go." Hudson looks down. "Just let me go."

So, I step back, and he gets in the car—and he goes. I watch until his lights disappear.

Until I'm alone.

He left me *alone*, and I want to be angrier than I am. His house sold, and Maddie knew about Keystone, and—*shit*—a car alarm blares. I spin back.

Cody holds up both hands. "Jesus, JoJo, just hit the wrong button." He drops his hands, keys jangling. "How come you act so afraid of me?"

Because I am afraid. Afraid of what he did to me. Of what

he could've done to Maddie. He asks, "What were you fighting about?"

I breathe out a laugh. "Keystone."

"Like the beer?" he asks innocently. He glances toward school, then back at me. "Team is losing if you want a ride home. I promise I won't hurt you."

Like it's unfathomable that I'd ever be scared to get in a car with a boy. But Hudson left me here, and it's cold and dark and I don't have a bus pass and I want to know what he knows.

Cody opens the passenger door.

I get in.

The interior has a fresh new car smell mixed with something else—sweat, dirt, grass.

"Mind if we stop at McDonald's?" Cody asks. It feels so profoundly familiar. He orders, pays, picks up the bag. He pops a fry between his teeth, then extends the bag to me. "Want one?"

I take two. "This won't distract me."

"Let me nourish my body." He devours half the burger in two bites and swipes a napkin across his mouth. "What do you know?"

Not: *What do you want to know?*

"I don't know what I know," I say, echoing his words. "Miles runs it?"

"He doesn't deserve all the credit."

"You too?" I ask, then again, "You too. You're in on it—in it—together." So, the story that Miles told about him and Cody—it was a little true. "Sophomore year. You asked Miles to help so you could stay on the soccer team, but it never stopped. It just got bigger." I crank the heat. "How does it work? There are those drawings, and the locker—"

"That shit is too clever for my taste. I've got it covered."

"So, Miles does the work, and you, what? Recruit?"

Cody sips loudly from his soda. "I'm more likable." Debatable. "I told a few guys on the team by accident, but they asked if Miles could help them, too. It was a glorious opportunity for us both. I never did shit for class, and Miles got to be *included.*"

It has to be more than that. Neither of them needs the money, and sure, Miles gets social capital, but what about Cody? Power? The thrill of having something to hold over someone?

I take in every freckle on his face. "You have no shame, do you?"

"If people want to pay, who am I to stop them?" Cody parks in front of my house. The Prices' house is all lit up across the street. He never even looks.

"I know something else." I unfasten my seatbelt. Ease my hand toward the handle. If this goes wrong, I'll claw his face, scratch his eyes, run. I will run. "I know that Maddie was going to expose Keystone."

Cody stares at me for a beat. Not horrified or upset or furious, but . . . confused. Then he starts to laugh. *Laugh.* It's a true, honest laugh I haven't heard in years. "Fucking stupid."

"Me?"

"Her."

I shrink against the door. "God, she's your *girlfriend* and you—"

"She's not my fucking girlfriend." Everything is both too quiet and too loud. The tick of his right blinker. My own shallow breaths.

Somehow, I ask, "What?"

Cody crumples the bag. "Maddie asked to talk at the bay," he says. I already feel sick. "I thought she meant 'talk,' obviously. But she *dumped* me, then she up and left, and I've had to pretend we're still together this whole time. Do you know how shady I'd look otherwise?"

I curl my fingers around the handle. "Did you do something?"

"Jesus, JoJo, I didn't do anything. I was going to forgive her—"

"Forgive her?"

"—but she said that she had to get away." He jerks his arm across my body, fast, but he's not going for me. He reaches into the glovebox and pulls out Maddie's garnet necklace.

Dots spot my eyes. I blink hard, blink away the image of his hand on her neck.

"Maddie didn't want this anymore." He traces the delicate gold chain, then drops it into the cupholder. "She didn't want me, either. I loved her, and she broke my heart."

He loved her, and he is using the past tense. I need to go. I need to get out of here, out of this car, and still I say, "But she knew about Keystone and—"

"Maddie would never expose Keystone, JoJo. Trust me." He unlocks the door; I had no clue it was locked. "And I'd never hurt her. Her stupid car was still stuck at the bay when I left."

I cling to it: Maddie's car, stuck at the bay.

The second I step out, shut the door behind me, Cody dumps his backpack on my seat. A #5, his number since he joined the junior soccer league, is peeling off the front pocket. For years, his mom would embroider her sons' numbers on all their bags—the Forsythe Four.

Four numbers.

"Oh, and JoJo?" Cody rolls down the window and leans across the console. "Maybe you should ask your *boyfriend* about Maddie."

Before I can ask what the hell that means, Cody is gone. But what does Hudson have to do with any of this? With her?

I can't even think of him right now.

Besides, I just figured out Cody's phone passcode.

-45-

I sprint upstairs and pull up the old Culver rosters, searching for the Forsythe Four.

Logan, defense: #7. Dustin, center-forward: #8. Parker, midfield: #2. Cody, striker: #5.

I fish inside my desk for Cody's cracked phone and key it in: 7825.

The phone unlocks.

My fingers fumble, sweaty, unsteady as I tap the screen. Texts. I need his texts, to see what he tells Miles about Keystone, what he told Maddie before she—

Zero messages. Call logs, empty. Voicemails, deleted. Email, disabled. He rarely goes on social media; he lives and breathes soccer—strapping shin guards, lacing mud-caked cleats. But I check those, too. Every account has been logged out due to inactivity.

I bite my thumbnail, thinking. Maybe he erased it remotely? But that'd wipe everything on the device; he had to do this manually, *before* Hudson stole it.

"What are you hiding, Cody?" I navigate to his photos. At least he didn't delete these.

Here's a picture of his dog, a sweet lab named Luna, with a slobbery tennis ball shoved in her mouth. A slice of pepperoni pizza dripping in grease. Cody's erection.

"Oh, God." I look up, away, then squint one eye until I scroll past it, scroll to—

Maddie.

Head cropped out, posing on her watercolor comforter in a lacy bra. Her body is rigid. I wonder how Cody got her to take this. *Come on, baby, it's not a big deal. Lots of girls do it.*

Jo did it.

My stomach dips. I know what I'll find when I scroll to September, but I hope—and wish and pray—that I'm wrong.

I'm not wrong.

One.

Two.

Three.

Four.

Five.

Six.

This last one spread the farthest and fastest. It's from the summer, a hot day at the end of August. The boys and I went to the beach but forgot to bring beer, so we splashed in the lake and chucked a Frisbee and ate frozen custard instead. My face hurt from laughing.

In the picture, I pose in my bathroom mirror, the shower curtain drawn behind me. I was about to shower, rinse the sunscreen off my tacky skin, but my bikini had given me a ridiculous tan line around my breasts, so I threw up a peace sign and laughed and snapped.

It's not sexy because it was never meant to be. But it didn't matter to Cody, did it? Not to him, not to any of them.

My head spins: *I think that I'm in trouble, but I think that you can help me.* Did Maddie fear what he'd do to her? That he'd do to her what he did to me?

I want to erase the pictures—mine, hers—but something stops me.

I flip through his apps, looking for *anything,* and . . . huh. Two calculators: the preloaded system app and another with a clip-art icon. I tap it open, but this is not a calculator.

It's a vault.

Inside are hundreds of text threads, encrypted, password protected. Cody isn't tech-savvy enough for this—but Miles Metcalf is. *Keystone.* So, Cody deleted his real texts, but this must be where he talks about Keystone. I need to tell Hudson.

I can't tell Hudson.

Tears prick my eyes. My finger slips, but there, here, is an unlocked thread. Cody and a number with a 585 area code.

Dated two days before Maddie disappeared.

Saturday, February 3

[11:23 p.m.] **CODY:** idk who u are but stay AWAY from my girl

[11:26 p.m.] **UNKNOWN:** ?

[11:27 p.m.] **CODY:** maddie

[11:32 p.m.] **UNKNOWN:** Ah.

[11:33 p.m.] **UNKNOWN:** Don't worry about it, Cody.

[11:34 p.m.] **CODY:** who are u

[11:47 p.m.] **CODY:** WHO ARE U

Stay away from my girl.

This person is . . . seeing Maddie? In all of this, I never considered Maddie could cheat. It ruined her family when her dad had that affair. But Cody caught her with someone, right? Found their texts? He caught her with—

"Hudson," I whisper.

Not because I believe it.

Because Cody does.

Even before Hudson cut contact, Cody had been getting cold and terse and cruel, asking why Hudson was so busy all the time, like he already knew the answer. I shake my head. Force myself not to picture it. Hudson and Maddie's relationship was neutral at best, and he loves *me*.

But I thought Maddie loved Cody.

I find my own phone, hit *67 and dial, hang up immediately. I don't know what I'll say if someone picks up. If *Hudson* picks up.

I redial. The line rings. Rings. Rings. Buzzes.

Buzzes?

I lower the phone from my ear. *We're sorry, but the person you are trying to reach has not set up their voicemail at this time. Please try again.* I do.

Then I step into the hall, listening. Waiting.

Staring at my brother's bedroom door.

Slowly, slowly, I push it open. Kneel beside his bed. Reach

underneath and pull out the phone. I've seen it before. I *had* this phone. The second flip phone from the BOGO deal.

The number Cody messaged; it was *Lee*.

I flip the phone open. There are just two text threads: the one with Cody; the other with a contact marked M. I shut my eyes, so sick and horrified at the thought of what I might find.

I don't want to see this.

I have to look.

Thursday, December 21

[2:23 p.m.] **M**: Only contact me at this number.

Friday, December 29

[8:34 p.m.] **M**: Call me.

Friday, January 12

[11:56 p.m.] **M**: Can we talk?

Monday, January 15

[12:37 a.m.] **M**: Call me.

Saturday, February 3

[10:15 p.m.] **M**: Are we still on for tonight?

Monday, February 5

[11:42 p.m.] **M**: Call me.
[11:43 p.m.] **M**: Pick up.
[11:49 p.m.] **M**: I need you.
[11:53 p.m.] **M**: Please.

[12:01 a.m.] **M**: Please.

"Oh my God." I'm dizzy. Breathless. *I need you, please, please.* Texts sent the night she ran. If he met up with her, that means Lee might have been the last person to see Maddie—

"Jo?"

Fuck.

I stand, drop the flip phone, pick it up, shove it in my pocket. I crash into the hall as Lee reaches the top of the stairs. He frowns. Looks from me to his open door.

"Were you in my room?" He knows the answer. "What were you doing?"

"I . . ." I walk backward down the hall, away from him.

"What were you doing?" he asks again, an edge in his voice. "What did you take?"

I run.

Lee extends an arm to the wall, but I duck under it, scrabbling downstairs, ripping his keys from the console table. He hits the landing and eyes the keys in my fist, his face paling.

I'm already gone—out the door, across the yard.

"Jo!" Lee runs after me, his gait uneven, knee sore. I scramble inside the car and start the engine, yanking the gear into reverse. He slaps his palm to the glass. "Don't you fucking dare."

But I do. I go.

-46-

Tonight, I am a perfect driver. I stop at stop signs. Maintain the speed limit. The last thing I need is to get pulled over without a license in my brother's stolen vehicle.

LEE KIRBY flashes on my phone. I decline the call.

Next, a text: *Jo, wtf?*

I swipe out of my messages and adjust the mirror, drag the seat closer to the wheel. The streets are empty when I end up at Culver for the third time today.

I open a new note on my phone and type:

2:15 pm maddie + me in library

The two of us in that staff bathroom. *I think that I'm in trouble, but I think that you can help me.*

Maddie was in trouble: Keystone and the photos she sent Cody and the texts with Lee.

She left, but she came back for me.

Next, I loop into the senior lot, by the bike rack.

3 pm the birds parking lot

Maddie had been so upset, then she ditched me for the Birds; stood me up (set me up?) like the acceptance changed everything for her.

4 pm maddie rejected from nyu

There are four lost hours between the rejection and her text to Hudson, so where did she go? Her dad's loft—wait, the photo. But I've got nothing from Tori yet.

A call from KATE KIRBY. Decline.

I plug Mr. Price's address into my phone and drive downtown, holding my breath when I merge onto the expressway, letting it out when I see the stunning building. So, let's say Maddie came here because her dad was out of town, and she could be alone.

Four hours later, she texts Hudson that he's going to lose his rank.

8:15ish pm maddie texts hudson

Then she needs to see the Birds.

9ish pm power plant (the birds)

I plug in the ice cream shop two blocks from the plant. Maddie and I walked there weekly that first summer we were friends. The sun melted the ice cream too fast, soft-serve twist dripping down our wrists, sprinkles scattered on our laps.

The towers loom against the dark sky, power lines knotted. I lower the windows to hear the electricity hum. Here, Maddie tells the Birds that she's going to run.

First, she went to the bay.

11 pm ?? the bay w/cody

I ease into the empty lot by the tackle shop. My phone continues to light up with messages. *Jo. Get your ass home, Jo. Jo. Jo, Jo, Jo. I'll call the cops, Jo.* I tuck my phone into my pocket and step outside. It's so dark tonight. So cold. I hug my arms to my waist, shivering. My boots sink in the mud as I search the empty lovers' lane. I don't know what I'm looking for—anything, everything, nothing.

Maybe I just need to retrace Maddie's steps. Is this how it felt for her? Like she might vibrate out of her skin? Like she had so much energy and nowhere for it to go?

Like she, too, hummed with an electric current?

I run it through my head again: Maddie was investigating Keystone, the cheating ring run by Miles and Cody, her boyfriend. The boy who was my friend first.

Cody, who met her here that night.

I feel that other phone in my pocket. The flip phone.

midnight the bay w/lee

Maddie, desperate: *I need you. Please. Please.* My brother acted like he hated Maddie, but he was talking to her. Seeing her?

347

I read their texts again and—wait. This is not Maddie's number. Or it's *hers*, but it's not the one I saved three years ago, when we'd text so much, so often, that my thumbs cramped.

This is a burner, then? It must be.

I check Lee's call logs; the last was February 15, in the middle of the night. That's when I heard my brother talking, I think. Talking to *her*? The call only lasted three seconds, like it was a mistake. I dial the number on my phone, and I don't bother to hide my number because I'm not trying to hide, and it rings.

The phone rings.

Maddie's burner phone rings.

Voicemail for this number has not been set up at this time. Please try again. I do. I try again and again and again. Could it still have a charge after all this time? *Voicemail for this—*

I stare across the bay, at the jagged trees along the cliffs, the steep wooden staircases dipping down to the docks, the perfect ripple of moonlight across the ice. One house along the right side twinkles, smoke pluming from its chimney.

Voicemail—

My flashlight beam guides me back to the lot. I turn on speakerphone just in case Maddie picks up. (She won't.) Dry cattail stalks shake, sigh in the wind. The boulevard is dead except for a black car crawling toward the hill. And then it stops.

Right there in the road, it stops. Reverses so, so slowly.

Pulls into the lot.

I fumble off the flashlight and crouch beside the cattails. *The lovers' lane.* They probably came for the lovers' lane, so once the car's rocking, windows fogged, I'll get the hell out of here.

But the car parks next to mine—to Lee's car, the car I stole.

Someone gets out of the passenger seat. Tallish, dark clothes, hood pulled up. They step to the back window and press their face to the glass, looking for what? For anything?

For me?

I pull the keys from my pocket. My thumb hovers over the panic button.

Then—fuck—I swear they look right at me.

I slam the alarm, and they run to their car. The engine sputters on, and the car peels off. I scared them. I scared me. Breathless, heart thrumming wildly, I sprint across the lot and launch myself behind the wheel. I shift into gear, twist the wheel, and go, go—

No. The tire popped. I hit a decorative rock, and the fucking tire popped. I want to scream or cry or both, but I need to get out of here. I need Kathleen. She told me to call when I need her, and I need her *now.*

I fish my phone out of my pocket and . . . the line is connected.

Five minutes into another call, because Maddie—

"Maddie," I whisper, and lift it to my ear, say more loudly, "Are you there? Maddie?"

It's nothing but dead air.

Voicemail for this number has not been set up at this time. Please try again.

Voicemail for this number—

"You have *so* much to explain." Kathleen is in her pajamas—pink flannel patterned with black cats—when she picks me up.

I fumble into the passenger seat. "Just go," I say, but I can tell by her face that I need to do better than that. "I had a fight with Hudson. I don't want to talk about it. Please go."

She stares a second longer, but at least she drives.

We have to be silent; her parents will flip if they catch us. In her dark bedroom, Kathleen passes me a T-shirt and shorts, then mimes washing her face. I change quick, my skin pink from the cold. Her phone lights on the nightstand.

[12:12 a.m] **HUDSON:** jesus. thanks, kath. i'll let lee know.

Fury flares inside me. I didn't tell her not to tell him, but she should know better.

I sit on the edge of the bed. Exhale, exhausted. My phone has gone silent. I erase every call, text, voicemail notification from Lee and my parents and Hudson and—

Two new messages.

[12:14 a.m] **UNKNOWN:** Hi Kate! This is Tori. Here's that doorbell pic for you. The quality isn't great, but I hope you can still use it!

Kathleen gently shuts the door. "What is it?"

The photo—

"Jo?" she whispers.

There she is. Black wool coat, hood pulled up. Dark, dark hair. Eyes fixed on the doorbell camera, like she knew it took a snapshot. Like she can stare right back at me.

Not Maddie.

Kathleen.

-47-

I don't sleep.

Every time I shut my eyes, I see the clear, startling green of Kathleen's eyes staring back at me from the grainy doorbell photo. I see those texts: *I need you. Please. Please.* I see Cody's penis, which, ew. I see that keystone sketch.

I see Nick, and I don't know if it's from the hall when he gripped my face or in the way back of his car, which makes me want to puke.

I see Hudson, disgusted at me.

I see Maddie staring at herself in the mirror: *I think that I'm in trouble, but—*

I hear nothing but dead air on the line.

I'm staring at the wall when the alarm goes off. Kathleen hits snooze, but I slip out of her bed and into the hallway bathroom. I look like a zombie: bags under my eyes, hair knotted, skin sickly gray. I'm so, so tired.

———

I leave while Kathleen is in the shower. Just sneak downstairs and open the door and go.

It takes me twenty minutes to walk, and I have this thought that maybe I should be afraid, that maybe I was followed last night, but I'm too exhausted to be scared. I barely even care that Dad's car is parked in the visitor lot.

My mother's punishment didn't work yesterday, so it's my kind, sensitive dad's turn.

Hudson is just crossing the street when I do. I pass him without a word.

He jogs after me. "Jo, hold on!"

I do.

"I'm sorry. About last night. I shouldn't have left you alone here—I am so sorry about that—and I don't want us to be over, either." Hudson looks ragged, the skin under his eyes tinted gray. "But we need to do something about—"

"Yeah, no, for sure," I say blandly. "Did you ever hook up with Maddie?"

He stares at me for a long time. "Uh, no."

I nod, so tired my body could melt. "I didn't think so. But Cody does."

"What?" Hudson shakes his head. "Why would he—?"

"I think I have a meeting with Lund," I say, and I leave it at that.

Mrs. Fitzgerald doesn't speak when she points me to Lund's office. Dad stands when I walk in. He's been crying. My sweet dad was crying because of me.

Lund smiles. "Two days in a row, Miss Kirby."

The second day where I am blatantly unprepared, where I will distract my peers, and it's not fair. I hear her words but barely register them. *Erratic. Out of control. Unacceptable.*

Slut. Bitch. Disgusting.

"Did you hear me?" Lund asks. "I merely want to discuss your process."

I missed something. "Process?"

"Your progress over this probationary period has been remarkable. I want to ensure these grades were earned"—Lund pauses, drumming her nails on the desk—"fairly."

"Fairly?" I repeat, and then I choke it out again, laughing. "I didn't fucking *cheat*."

"I'm not accusing you of anything," she says, but she is. Principal Lund is accusing me of cheating when Keystone is *right there*. Miles and Cody, all the names we found written in code.

Those fucking assholes. Hudson was right. He was right, and I let him down. Let myself get so tangled up in Maddie that I ignored what he needs—and he needs us to expose Keystone.

Low, I say, "I did my homework. That was my process. I just did it. But you need to look into—"

"Can you provide some rough drafts? Class notes? Proof?"

"Is my word not good enough?" I know the second I say it that it's not.

My word is not good enough.

"Jo, I'm going to take you home again, okay?" Dad says gently. But Lee is home. I can't be near him, not when he was texting Maddie, not when he . . .

"Go gather anything you need from your locker," Lund says. "I'd like to speak with your father a little longer."

I stand and say, "This is fucking bullshit," before I go.

The bell rings when I step in the hall, force my way to my locker. I spin my combination. Spin it again. Something is stuck. I wrench my fingers into the metal, jiggle it until the door flies open and something falls out at my feet—an envelope.

I tear the seal and pull out five folded pages. There's a handwritten note on the top one: *I thought you might want to see this.*

It takes me a second to figure out what I'm looking at. Screenshots, the image blurred, like the printer ran out of ink. It's a text thread between Cody and—

I shake my head, even though his name is right there.

Even though Hudson is right here, in front of me. "Is something wrong?"

I look down again.

Thursday, February 8

[4:12 p.m.] **CODY:** jojo??????? bro. . . . .

[4:13 p.m] **CODY:** how long did it take before she tried to suck
        your dick

[4:14 p.m] **HUDSON:** like five mins

[4:15 p.m] **HUDSON:** I stopped her tho

[4:15 p.m] **CODY:** good call

[4:18 p.m] **CODY:** u don't know where that mouth has been

It wasn't true then, but it was on prom night. That makes it more humiliating.

Hudson told Cody something true.

I flip through the screenshots: Cody saying something horrible about me—how I'm a bitch, how I must make it worth his time somehow—and Hudson letting him. Not stopping it.

"Jo, what is that?" Hudson asks uneasily.

"Screenshots of your texts with Cody." I hold up a page. "Here's one where he asks if I sent you any recent nudes you could forward."

His face blanches. "No—"

"What the hell, Jo?" Kathleen storms up to us. Her hair is plastered to her forehead. "I get out of the shower, and you're gone? And—wait, what happened?"

I ignore her and keep my eyes trained on Hudson. "You're an asshole," I say, too loud. I toss the pages, let them flutter to the floor. Kathleen picks one up. "You're just like those other guys. God, I'm so stupid for thinking you were different."

For thinking I was different—special—to him.

He's frantic. "I cut off contact, Jo. I stopped when it got real."

Kathleen looks up. Tilts her head. "When what got real?" she asks. We stare at her, and she stares back, realization dawning on her face. "Were you *faking* it?"

"Like you're not hiding shit, too," I say, and that was the wrong thing to say. I can tell when Kathleen steps back, her face twisted. Hudson reaches for me, but I say, "Don't touch me."

"Jo—"

I can't do this. Not with everyone whispering. Not when my brother is home, and Dad is waiting for me in the office, and Kathleen was in that doorbell picture, and Hudson did *this*, and I can't, I can't, I can't. I shove through the hall, toward the band door and—

Miles, saxophone case in hand. He doesn't look surprised to see me so upset. He knows.

Miles, who runs the cheating ring that wrecked Hudson's future.

Miles, who I don't trust, but he's the only one who can give me some answers.

I nod at him and say, "Let's go."

The ride is silent.

I match my breaths with the sound of the windshield wipers. Left, right. In, out.

Miles pulls into a gas station a few blocks from school. The sign on the door promotes a two-for-one hot dog deal. He parks at the pump but keeps his hands on nine and three.

Softly, he says, "I only wanted you to know the truth."

The truth: Hudson let Cody degrade me. He demeaned me, too. Those texts were sick and inexcusable and how the hell could he say that about me? I feel stupid, mostly, that I thought he was different from any of those other guys.

Also the truth: Hudson *was* different. He is. He's proven it time and time again. Pissing off Cody meant giving up a place to sleep. So, in a horrible way, Hudson tried to keep us both.

But in the end, he did choose me.

Miles grips the wheel tighter. "You can do so much better than him."

"No. He's the best I can do." It's not a knock on my self-worth; I do think he is the very best, even if he texted those things to . . . not Miles. Uneasy, I ask, "How did you get the texts?"

"I, uh. Found them on Cody's phone."

But the texts were gone when I went through Cody's old phone last night, and that means they'd been deleted before Hudson stole it weeks ago.

So, what, Miles got the screenshots before then, and just sat on them? Waited until he wanted—needed—to split us up?

To get me alone?

My heart stutters. I think I fucked up. I told Cody that I knew about Keystone, so what if he told Miles? Of course he'd tell Miles. And now I'm alone with him.

I slide my fingers toward the door handle.

Miles is lost in his head. He wipes his palms on his jeans. "You don't realize how special you are." I know where this is going. This is where it always goes. "You're not like other girls."

"How?"

"What?"

"How am I not like them?"

"You're, uh. You know."

"I don't know. I want you to tell me."

Miles fidgets with his glasses, thumb smudging the lenses. "Wait, are you mad? That I showed you the texts? I'm trying to help you, you know."

I can help you, you know. The words smack into me. He said it about my grades, too, and Lund thinks I cheated, and Miles is old school, so what if he got ahold of my work and switched my wrong answers to right? Erased my work and replaced it with his own?

Keystone.

"Miles, did you do something to my grades?" I whisper.

He looks out the windshield, not blinking. Then he winds back his arm, fist clenched, and punches the dash. I heave open the door, scramble outside as he does it again. "What else can I do? Tell me!" he shouts after me. "Tell me why you go for guys who treat you like crap when I've *been* here. I've helped you with your homework. I've driven you around. I'm nice to you!"

"I don't owe you shit." I blink the rain from my eyes. "Jesus, you act like our friendship is a fucking transaction. If you did something to my grades because you think it'll make me—"

"I never touched your grades." He rips a hand through his curls, says, "I never hurt you like those guys. I never tried to get with you. I never called you a slut when you—"

"When I what?"

Miles looks me dead-on. "When you deserved it."

-48-

I have no place to go so I walk—anywhere, everywhere, nowhere. I walk until the rain soaks my hair. Until the cold scrapes my throat. I walk until my legs burn, and then I collapse onto a bench by the art museum. The frozen metal stings my thighs.

I wait to cry.

I don't cry.

This all went so fucking wrong.

That's the trouble with girls like me, right? It always goes so fucking wrong.

Hudson is just as cruel as those other guys. Kathleen was in that photo. Miles was never really my friend. My parents are fed up with me. My brother was seeing Maddie, maybe.

Maddie.

She was a bad friend. I could be a bad friend, too. Everything ended on the night of the pool party, but the cracks were already there. I held onto her so tightly because I thought she saw me, but I couldn't even see myself.

I just believed what everyone else said about me.

Disgusting. Slut. Bitch. You deserved it, you were there, you, you, you, you—

"No." I lift my face toward the big, blank sky. Breathe. Then I find that number I wish I'd used weeks ago. The call connects on the fourth ring, and I say, "Hey. It's Jo-hyphen-Lynn."

Tess pulls up within ten minutes and announces she's taking me to the library.

I follow her upstairs to the children's section. "This is creepy."

"It's not creepy." Tess sounds quite confident for an adult approaching a shelf of picture books with zero children and one teenager. The shelf pushes back and opens into a small, secret room. She says, "Told you it was cool."

"No, you said it wasn't creepy."

That was a lie. Dozens of porcelain dolls line the shelves, which is easily the creepiest thing to display in a secret room. Tess takes a plastic chair at the marker-streaked table. I grab the other seat, my knees bending to my chest.

I skip the small talk. "Why did you ditch me?"

"I got fired," she says bluntly. "I refused to write the Price redemption arc after . . ." Tess lets it end there. "I'm trying to write my own stuff. If I can place a piece in a good pub—"

"Would you move back to the city?" It makes me profoundly sad to imagine.

"Nah. Rochester is good for me, as much as I hate to admit it," Tess says. I think, for the first time, it might be good for me, too. Or at least that I need to give it a try. She adds, "I'm not here with a lesson, Jo-hyphen-Lynn. I'm here to listen." Pause. "Tell me a story?"

There are so many I could tell, but this one I didn't remember until I was waiting for her.

"I used to do pageants. My mom was Miss Tennessee Teen, so it bonded us. I looked like that." I point to a doll with blonde ringlets, wide eyes, and a painted pink pout.

Tess nods. She knows where this is going.

"My last competition was the summer after ninth grade. I'd been seeing this guy. My ex–best friend's older brother." I pick up a crayon and a coloring sheet, absentmindedly doodling to avoid her eye. "Much older. He texted me something—I don't remember what—and I was being annoying, or . . . fifteen. But I remember this journalist backstage saw the texts over my shoulder and told me I never deserved to be treated like that. So, I said thank you and got runner-up and spiked my stupid crown on the ground." I set down the crayon. "That was you. The journalist."

"That was me." She doesn't sound surprised.

"How long have you known?"

Tess grabs a word search. "Since the meet and greet. You seemed *so* familiar. I found a clipping later about a regional pageant you'd won: JoJo Kirby."

"Is that why you chose me?"

"Yes and no. I never even finished the story, but I thought about you for weeks after the pageant. It was so obvious you weren't okay. That you're still not." She hesitates. "Nick Price was the older brother, wasn't he? Will you tell me about it?"

My eyes sting. Even though so many people know—so many people knew—it still feels impossible to say it. To call it what it was.

But I have that note on my phone.

Tess keeps her face utterly blank as she reads. It's excruciating. I imagine her thinking, *This is what Jo is so upset about? Maybe if she hadn't worn that watermelon bikini top, gotten drunk, gotten into the way back, tried to make Maddie mad . . .*

My leg jiggles. I force myself to go still. I bring my thumb to my mouth, yank the cuticle, set my hand back in my lap. I look at Tess. I look at the table. I look at Tess again. I swipe my eye. Swipe the other eye. Bite down, pull up my hood, bury my face in the crook of my arms.

This is the excruciating part. Knowing she believes every word.

After forever, Tess says, "Do you understand what he did to you, Jo?"

I nod, just once.

She taps my elbow with a tissue packet, and I lift my head, say, "If he did that to me—"

"He did."

"—then why did I hook up with him again? I *chose* that."

"He was an adult. You were fifteen. That wasn't a choice you could make."

I rip out a tissue. "It's not fair. It's not fair that I have to be *this* every single day, and he's fine. He's *great*." I barely get out this next part: "And I lost my best friend because of him."

Tess straightens a stack of crosswords. "I'm not defending Maddie," she says tentatively, testing the words, "but this was probably really confusing for her, too. Her brother did a horrible, unforgivable thing to her best friend. This wasn't something either of you could understand."

"But I—"

"No. *Nick* did this," Tess says, forcing me to face her, resting her hand on mine. "Please know I say this with the utmost compassion, but you need a therapist. Like, holy *shit*." I roll my eyes, still crying. "You've been horrifically mistreated, and I don't know if you fully understand it yet. Every adult in your life has failed—is failing—you. Your parents failed you."

I cry harder.

Tess is quiet for a beat too long. "I think it'd be an act of grace to yourself to give up the idea that you'd still be friends with Maddie if this hadn't happened. To imagine instead that you would have grown up and grown apart." Even more gently, she adds, "You're holding on to this friendship, but I don't think it's Maddie you miss. I think you miss *you*."

"Oh my God." I drop my head in my arms. "That's so mean."

And I think, inexplicably, of a photo.

Maddie and me at the pool party, best friends for two more hours. *Those girls used to be friends, you know.* Those girls will never be friends again. I think I've known it, but I wanted so much to believe that maybe we could repair our friendship. That we were worth saving. But it's insurmountable, what happened to us.

What Nick did to me.

I'm done—for good, forever.

Even if we exist solely in the past tense, even if it turns out there was never any trouble at all, she asked for my help. She came to *me*, and I can't turn my back on her. Not when everyone turned their back on me. I want to help her.

But I'm going to need help too.

I wipe a tissue under my eye. "You know, me and Hudson—that guy—were investigating Maddie together. We were in a fake relationship, then it was real, but I think we broke up? Also, we found this cheating ring that Maddie planned to expose before she disappeared. Ran off."

Tess blinks. "What?"

"Do you want her story about Keystone?"

"Like the beer? No, wait, rewind," Tess says. I'm not making any sense, but I try to lay it out the best I can. After, Tess nods and says, "This is a lot. But it gives us a place to start."

"Us?"

"Unfortunately, you still owe me a story."

I rest my head again, too exhausted to function. "What would you do if you were me?"

We're not talking about Maddie anymore.

"I'd go to my mom." Not even a beat of hesitation.

"What'd be your second choice?" I ask, and she gives me a look that makes me want to cry all over again. Heaving a sigh, I say, "How far is the station from here?"

-49-

The Channel 12 visitor's badge dangles from my neck.

My mother is on commercial break, so she lingers behind the anchor desk, half listening to the meteorology intern. Even under her TV-ready makeup—thick layer of foundation, false lashes—I can tell how worn she is.

"Mom?" I call out, and immediately start to cry.

The production assistant looks between me (crying) and her (running, shoeless, across the stage) and says, "Uh, Kate?"

My mother sweeps me into her dressing room and deposits me on the pink suede couch, then she's gone again. Back to set? No, she returns a minute later with a bottled water from the kitchenette. Lowering beside me, she asks, "Jo-Lynn, what're you—?"

"I tried to tell you. I tried to tell you after it happened." *It*. Not the whole summer, but the thing in the car. I clutch a faux-fur pillow to my stomach. "I got sick at the pool party, and then I came home, and I tried to tell you Nick . . ."

That Nick—

He—

My mother rests a palm on her chest.

"I was so confused, and I tried to tell you, and you didn't want to hear it. I *needed* you to hear it. I needed my mom," I say, and it breaks us both. She pulls me into her, my face buried in her shoulder, voice muffled in her silky hair. "I feel like you don't even like me."

"My God, honey. I *love* you." She strokes my hair, her fingers catching in a knot. "I was so terrified to have a girl when I was pregnant, and then I had you—"

"This doesn't sound like the start of a compliment."

"—and you give me hell, but I love that about you. And I . . . I didn't . . . I'm sorry, Jo," she says, crying. My mother never cries. Never calls me Jo. It's always Jo-Lynn, the vowels drawn out. "I'm so sorry that you couldn't . . . that I didn't see it."

I'm a mess. I keep thinking about what Tess said. That my parents failed me. I have food and shelter and love most times, and it feels greedy to want more. But I *needed* more. Something horrible happened to me, and it was impossible for me to say.

I still can't fucking say it.

Mom's phone dings from the vanity. She winces. "I texted your dad to get you. But I'll come, too, okay? We'll all go home."

Home. *Lee.*

"Can Lee not be there?" *Please. Please.* "I need you and Dad. Just us."

Even if she doesn't get it, she nods, looking back to her phone. "Why did Culver call?"

"Oh. I think I'm about to be suspended. They said I cheated—I didn't cheat—and also I used the f-word twice in conversation with Principal Lund, but I promise it was warranted."

"I believe you," Mom says. Tears sting behind my eyes. She turns back to me, cupping my face, and says it again: "I *believe* you, Jo."

Words I didn't know I needed to hear.

Back home, I tell an abridged version of the story to Dad. He cries. Mom cries. I cry. Bay Leaf cries, too, but she wants a can of wet food.

The sky is darkening to dusk when my parents and I leave to pick up Lee's car at the bay, but I warn them in advance not to ask questions. Dad swaps out the spare while Mom angles her phone flashlight toward him.

I wander beside the car. Kick up the gravel, searching for the tire tracks from that black car last night. Shivering at the thought, I look up, toward the sky.

Toward a sign on the light pole: SMILE! YOU'RE ON CAMERA.

Cameras.

"I'll be back," I say, and I jog up to Ray's Bait & Tackle. The sign is flipped CLOSED, but the man from the dock is watching *Jeopardy!* on a tiny TV behind the counter. I knock.

He waits until a commercial break to answer.

"Ray?" I point to the name on the sign. He grunts, so I'll take that as a yes. "I'm sorry I abandoned my car here last night. Thank you for not towing it." I take a breath. "I think I was being followed? And I saw your sign about the cameras."

"Ah, shit." He peers back at a commercial for an injury attorney. "Those are decoys."

"Oh." I deflate. "Okay, one last question." I open Instagram and find a photo of the Birds at prom. "You talked about 'those girls' last time I was here—was it these girls?"

He squints at the photo. "Just the one on the right." *Maddie.* "Her and a redhead."

Redhead? My mind flashes to a photo again, two girls tucked in Maddie's vanity mirror.

April Kirk. *Those girls* I never knew were friends.

"Did they come here a lot?" I ask.

"Just the once. They were yelling their heads off out on the dock. The redhead called that other one a lying you-know-what. Dunno what they were on about, but that one"—Ray points to Maddie—"fell onto the ice. It held, but I wasn't about to have some girl die out here. I made sure she got back on solid ground and told them to get the hell out."

From the TV, a round of applause. Dazed, I say, "I think *Jeopardy!* is back."

He nods at my feet. "You dropped something."

I look down—the envelope Miles put the screenshots in. My boot left a muddy footprint on the front, stamped on my name: *Jolynn.* No hyphen or capital *L.*

Jolynn, spelled just like that. Just like in the open letter.

"Fucking Miles." I shove the envelope back in my pocket. If I weren't so tired, I might laugh about it: Miles Metcalf doesn't know how to spell my name.

Dad is lowering the car jack when I get back, and Mom extends her hand. "Keys, please."

"If I swear not to shred another tire, can I drive? Please? I'll answer my phone if you call, and I won't be out all night."

They exchange a look, clearly not thrilled, but Dad says, "Do *not* get pulled over."

"I'll be home soon," I say. "I promise."

Hudson looks like shit when he opens the door. His eyes are red, swollen behind his glasses.

He also looks deeply confused.

"I'm here to hear your apology." I know he has one. "So, go on."

He launches right into it. "Jo, I'm so, so sorry. I'm *so* sorry. That's not what I think of you. Not at all." Hudson takes in a breath that rattles his chest. "It's not an excuse, and I know it's cowardly, but I didn't know how to shut Cody up without risking the spare room. I just . . . I needed a backup plan." He swipes his hand across his eyes. "I should have put you first—"

"Before food and shelter?" I say. "I hate what you said, but I get why you said it."

"I've loved you forever, and I don't expect us to get back together or—"

"Shut up, Hudson," I say, and I kiss him. I believe him. I'm trying my best, and so is he, and sometimes our best isn't good enough, but I'd rather try and be wrong than never try at all.

He presses his forehead to mine. "I cry so much in front of you, Jo."

With this, I realize Hudson might call me Jo the most—just Jo, just like I want.

"I came here for another reason," I say, and pull out the

envelope addressed to *Jolynn*. "The screenshots were in this—see my name? It was spelled like this in the letter about your rank that Maddie ran. It's from *Miles*. I'm not sure if it was just him or Keystone or what, but I know you got screwed over. That money is yours, Hudson, and we're getting it for you."

He nods, a half smile tilting his mouth. It kills me. I want to stay here, with him, for the rest of the night, for forever. But I say, "I'm so tired that I'm literally about to fall on my face, but I'll call you tomorrow, okay?"

Hudson steps onto the porch. "Wait, did you *drive* here?"

"I sure did." I immediately drop the keys.

"Do you need help?"

"I'm good." I am.

I'm taking the long way home.

Last night, I retraced Maddie's steps.

Tonight, I'm retracing mine.

The road down to Durand Eastman Beach is desolate. The lake runs along my right, the crumbling stone fortress on my left. There are ghost stories about this part of the park, legends about a White Lady trailing the beach on misty nights, wailing into the dark.

Her daughter vanished after she took a walk at the lake.

I think of Mrs. Price, calling out for Maddie.

The story seems more sad than scary.

Just a mile more, and I ease into Lot A, where we parked for the bonfire. I tug the handle but freeze, thinking of that black car from last night, fear catching in my chest. But I fit the keys between my knuckles like spikes, just in case, and take the path down to the beach.

Images from that night superimpose onto this one: Hudson letting his hand brush mine, Cody grinning at Ben over the fire, me dousing Maddie in beer. The wreckage from our bonfire is long gone, but another remains, the charred kindling shimmering, encased in ice.

I look out across the lake, lit by a pale streak of moonlight. Flurries flutter from the sky. I hold out my hand, shivering when the wind gusts and, okay, I'm too cold for this shit.

Back in the car, I warm my fingers on the vent, heat cranked on high.

I've got one last stop.

"Rochester park," it turns out, pulls up 191 million results. Dozens of pins I can drop on a map. I click through the photos, hoping the place Nick drove us might crystalize. They all mostly look the same, with wooden fences and faded signage, but I pause on one: Ellison Park. I used to sled down its steep hill as a kid.

If nothing else, it's on the way home.

Thick woods line either side of the road, streetlights spaced far apart. I pass parking lots for tennis courts, a dog park, an ice rink, and I pull into a lot for a creek trail.

And I step out.

Part of me thought—hoped—I'd be struck with a sure, certain feeling that, yes, actually, this is where it happened. But if this is the place, I can't tell. I'm searching for something I'll never find.

I'm searching for something to undo it when I'm the one who's become undone.

That's the most unbearable thing, I think. Imagining all the girls I could've been if Nick hadn't done this to me.

Maybe I'd be going to college. Maybe I'd have fallen in love with Hudson years ago or had real friends or learned sooner that no one can tell me what to believe about myself.

Nick told me I wasn't like those other girls. He told me I was *there*.

I want him to think I was special. I never want him to think of me again.

I sit on the frozen ground and picture her here beside me: Jo at fifteen in that watermelon bikini top. If she were here, I'd pry the seltzer from her hand. I'd hang the bikini top back on the rack, tell her to ditch the pool party, keep her from getting in that car, keep her from ever asking that girl across the street if she'd like to take a walk.

I'd need to rewind a million of my choices to stop Nick from making one.

Tell me, I'd tell her. Jo at fifteen. Now I'm crying again, because if she—if I—were here, she'd think this was corny as hell. She'd roll her eyes and not cry and flop onto her back and just stare at the sky, and I wish this felt cathartic, but it feels like . . . nothing.

It feels so unfair.

It's not fair that one night derailed my entire fucking life, and to him, it was just another warm summer night.

It was dark.

It was late.

I didn't know where we were or how long we'd been gone or which direction was home.

What did you think was going to happen? Not that.

I was trapped. I was drunk. I was fifteen.

There was nothing I could do.

Tonight, there is.

Tonight, I stand up and go.

- 50 -

I sleep for nineteen hours. It's the deepest sleep I've had in . . . ever?

Then I eat breakfast at three p.m.

My parents told Lee to stay with our aunt again tonight, even if they don't get it. I don't get it either. I get lightheaded when I think about it: Maddie + Lee. *I need you. Please. Please.*

He'll be home tomorrow. I'll have to face him.

For now, I take another nap.

The next day, Sunday, I drag myself out of bed at noon since Tess is picking me up.

We drive to Hudson's house with a whiteboard. He just got home from the opening shift at the diner, so he smells a little like hashbrowns. I'm super hungry all of a sudden.

I dump everything—each clue, all our evidence—onto the carpet. The Keystone codes. The property record for Mr. Price's loft. The hacked social media post. The emails to Tess. The open letter. The phones. The photo of Maddie and April. The sketch of the keystone.

The doorbell photo of Kathleen—actually, I'm keeping this one.

Senior portraits of every major player.

We map it out.

MADDIE PRICE, THE MISSING GIRL

Gone for forty days—it feels biblical, maybe, but I'm not religious.

Tess uncaps a marker and writes *NYU* on the board. "Maddie's motive to run away," she says, and pops the cap back on. "Allegedly."

"Allegedly," I echo.

It's the simplest story: Maddie Price's life kind of sucked, and she was accepted to NYU, her dream school, a dream come true, but it was never hers; it was a glitch. She'd applied to only one school, too, so once she got rejected, she had nothing left.

So, she ran.

I didn't see it before. How Maddie wanted to get out as desperately as I did. We were two girls watching our futures crumbling before us. I was waiting for this nightmare to end; she was waiting for her life to begin.

"But she also had the story," Hudson says. "Maddie was going to expose Keystone."

"It still doesn't work for me." Tess taps the marker to her chin. "It's a big deal—the top magnet school in the city is rife with academic fraud, led by their valedictorian and star athlete. If this was supposed to get her into NYU, then what was she waiting for?"

"She was scared," I say. Scared of Keystone? Scared of *something*. It weighs heavily inside me: Maddie Price, scared, digging deeper, not realizing she was burying herself.

Tess says, "Let's keep going," and starts to write.

CODY FORSYTHE, THE BOYFRIEND

"Ex-boyfriend," I say. The distinction is key.

The night she disappeared, she met Cody at the bay and broke his heart—allegedly. He might not know why, but to me it seems clear: Maddie learned the horrible truth that you can be wrong about someone you love. Maybe Keystone made her end it. His involvement screwed her over in the rankings, I bet, and it revealed the worst of him—the cutthroat, cruel things.

I guess my photos weren't proof enough.

Cody claims he loved Maddie. Past tense. That distinction is key, too.

His motive for wanting her gone—hurting her?—is that she dumped him and she knew too much and she could take Duke from him. *It's always the boyfriend.* The phrase is coy, like you'd wink or tip a drink when you say it. Like it's not absolutely horrifying how often it's true.

"Cody is in Keystone." Tess draws a line from his photo to the sketch. "And Keystone is also connected to—what's his name again?"

MILES METCALF, THE RINGLEADER (?)

Brilliant and brainy and capable of being sweet, but Miles wasn't happy with that; he wanted to get social capital. To be popular. Keystone was his way into the world he thought he deserved.

But those guys weren't his friends. He wasn't my friend either.

"He does the work. He's 'old school' about it." I grab a blanket from the couch and lay it across my lap. "Miles freaked out when I told him about Maddie's story." I pause, thinking. "Just the story part, actually. Not really about her knowing."

Tess uncaps the marker. "So, he'd want to keep her quiet?"

"He's valedictorian, he gets fifteen grand, *and* he got into MIT," Hudson says. "I'd say he has a lot to lose. He faked the open letter, too, telling me to forfeit my rank."

Tess caps the marker again. "If he's first, what would his motive be?"

"He's an asshole?" Hudson offers, only half kidding.

"His ex-girlfriend also benefited from it." I point. "Her. The redhead."

APRIL KIRK, THE FORMER FRIEND

Maddie Price and April Kirk, flutists in the orchestra.
Those girls used to be friends, you know. I had no clue.

378

"They got into a fight at the bay," I tell Tess and Hudson, repeating what the man at the tackle shop told me. "They were out on the dock, and April called her a lying bitch."

Hudson rests his back against the chair. "What if Maddie tried to tell her about Keystone? But April didn't want to hear it. Then our rank got switched, and April realized it was true—and *that's* why she's been so upset?"

Tess erases another line. "So, Keystone is behind the rank swap?"

"Miles is behind it," Hudson clarifies.

"Which means it's personal? Not academic?"

Personal. Miles seemed shocked to see April's face on that second poster. Like he didn't expect it. Like . . .

"It *was* personal," I say. "It was Cody."

Hudson lets out a startled laugh. I can almost read his mind: *Why would he do that? He was my friend.* Laughing again, stunned, he says, "Holy shit. It was Cody."

"He thought you hooked up with Maddie," I say, gripping Hudson's arm. "He found the texts on her burner, and he fucked with your rank to get back at you."

"Texts?" Tess says.

"The texts between Maddie and . . . my brother."

LEE KIRBY, THE SECRET BOYFRIEND (?)

"I found his burner phone. Maddie was texting him. He never replied. He never *liked* her." I don't get it. I don't get any of it. I say it out loud: "I don't get—"

The doorbell rings.

The Birds huddle on the front porch, bodies braced against the cold.

I step outside. "So, you got my text?"

Teeth chattering, Kathleen says, "Why else would we be here?"

"God, could you not?" Michaela shoots back.

Sara, caught in the literal middle, says, "Yes, Jo. We got your text."

The one where I explained everything. *Everything.* Maddie coming to the library and how I thought she set me up, how I needed a way back in, me and Hudson and our investigation.

I fold my arms around my waist, freezing. "I get it if you never want to see me again, or whatever, but I really loved being friends." I refuse to cry. "Questions? Comments? Concerns?"

Sara raises her hand. "Can we *please* come in?"

"Sorry, of course." I open the door and let them inside—except Kathleen. To her, I say, "You're coming with me."

"Where did you get this?"

The photo: Kathleen dressed in black, hood up, green eyes fixed on the lens. The image is grainy, shadowed; I can see how you'd mistake her for Maddie if all you had to go on was that senior portrait on TV.

We're sitting on Hudson's bed. Just us.

"Someone submitted it as a tip to Channel 12," I say.

Kathleen reaches for that cross around her neck. "Maddie

called me after the power plant. Only me." I get the subtext: Michaela and Sara know nothing. "She'd been at her dad's place. He was on a business trip, so he hadn't been expecting her. There was lingerie in the laundry room. I don't think Maddie expected—wanted—her parents to reconcile, but her dad had told her that he and his girlfriend broke up. He *lied*."

"Uh-oh."

She says, "Maddie started to snoop. To see what else he'd lied about. He'd left out this packet on how to prepare a petition for divorce, and a list of questions for his financial advisor about nonqualified withdrawals from a 529 plan."

"What's—?"

"Maddie's college fund," she says. I gasp. "He had this bonus coming, but it got delayed. And he needed money *then*." Kathleen lowers the photo. "She'd written her parents a note about needing to get away, and she didn't want to waste time dropping it off back at her dad's place, so she asked me to plant it there for him to find."

I shake my head. "Her mom got the note."

"No, her dad did."

I remember now: Kathleen, drunk on rum, saying over and over that Maddie's Instagram post, *it was wrong*—she meant the contents of the note. The post got it wrong.

"Maddie tore him apart in that note. She kind of tore his apartment apart, too."

"He knew Maddie ran away from the beginning, and what? Rewrote the note?" Then he let his grieving wife take the fall. That's why he wanted to suppress the story so badly. God, he's a dick. I shake my head, say, "So, wait, you didn't go to her house that night?"

But the spare key in the frog . . .

"No, but Maddie did—before she met us, I think. I guess she'd buried something in her yard?" Kathleen kind of laughs. "God, it sounds deranged. She was going to dig it up, whatever *it* was, but her mom was still awake, so she had to leave without it."

Maddie *buried* something. I think back to all those times I'd see her in the garden.

Kathleen exhales, shutting her eyes. "She kept stalling. Like, 'I need to go, I have to go,' so I told her to just fucking go. Maddie wanted me to make her stay, and I wanted her to leave. After what she did to me, I . . ." Kathleen opens her eyes again. "Maddie may not be my favorite person right now, but I want to help *you*, Jo, because *you're* my friend."

"You're absolutely going to regret that," I say, and I explain everything about Keystone.

Immediately when I finish, Kathleen says, "Yeah, okay, I absolutely regret that."

In the living room, Tess and Hudson have put the girls to work. Michaela is fixing Tess's line system; Sara cracks the codes. *11-19 = KS = Kyle Spencer. 20-19 = TS = Tyler Spencer.*

Kathleen gasps so forcefully that Sara jumps back. *20-7 = TG =* "Trey-fucking-Gardner. So, what, Keystone stole my midterm and sold it to him?"

Hudson makes a face at me. I think we're thinking the same thing: Keystone doing that, stealing Kathleen's midterm, doesn't make sense. Why take that kind of risk? I point all that out to the group and add, "Plus, you guys got caught. Keystone wouldn't have lasted this long if they usually weren't more careful."

Sara gasps, pulling out her phone. "Wait, so Daniele was showing me photos from that party Ben had, and we noticed something—wait."

She turns her screen for us to see. Trey Gardner on the deck railing. He smiles sloppily, mouth wide open and eyes half-shut, arm slung around Ben Sulkin.

Trey and Ben, catcher and pitcher—it doesn't seem that weird to me.

"Now look at this next one," Sara says.

It's an atrocious selfie attempt from One-L Daniele and Gabe, heads turned to the sliding door. I squint. Make out Ben holding a beer, laughing, peering over the railing. Cody standing by the door. The framing is so crooked it almost looks like the camera fell. Like it *fell*.

I say, "This is right after Trey—?"

"There's less than twenty seconds between the time stamps." Michaela toggles between the photos. "Ben *pushed* Trey?"

I hold my wrist to my chest. "Okay, Keystone steals Kathleen's midterm and passes it off to Trey. They get caught, Kathleen confronts him, which brings too much attention. Keystone is scared Trey will rat them out, so they have Ben keep him quiet?"

"Ben is in on it, then?" Michaela asks, unconvinced. "He's the muscle?"

Hudson taps the scar on his lip. "Ben is a bonehead with anger issues. If Cody told him to do something, he'd probably just do it." He hesitates. "But he and Cody aren't friends anymore."

I find 2-19 = BS on the whiteboard. "What if they fought *because* of Keystone? Because they'd been messing up. Kathleen's midterm. And Ben ended up under academic review, too. So *this* is why Cody was on the outs." I frown. "Then it all connects back to Maddie, somehow?"

Tess taps my portrait. "And you."

"Me?"

Except she's right: I'm a common denominator, too.

If I tacked my own portrait to the board, I could loop a strand of twine between me and everyone on here. Cody, the ex-friend. Miles, the nice guy. Lee, the brother. It all leads back to Maddie, but it leads back to me, too. To *us.*

I take a step back. Take in the tangled web.

Then I say, "I want Keystone to fall. I want to find out why Maddie needed me." *If she needed me at all.* "But first"—I point at the board—"I want to take these assholes down."

-51-

Later, Hudson and I go to my house, where we make out and devise our plan of attack. He dozes off after dinner, and I let him sleep, his breaths slow and steady, while I wait.

This last part I need to do alone.

Lee's bedroom door opens a little after ten. I follow him downstairs, then outside. The air is warm, but not really. I guess when you've been freezing so long, anything feels like heat. He's a few houses ahead of me, and I slow. I know where he's going.

The basketball court behind our old elementary school.

Lee fetches a ball from behind the dumpster and dribbles, the ball thwacking against the rain-soaked pavement. He shoots. Misses. Calls out, "You following me?"

I loop my fingers in the chain-link fence. "This is where you sneak out to?"

The ball thuds against the backboard. "Sometimes."

"Other times you met with Maddie?" I offer. He twists back, his knee buckling. "Because you saw her the night she left? You were seeing her?"

"No! Jo, it wasn't like that."

"Then what was it like? Did you do something?" I'm so terrified of the truth that my heart beats in my throat. But I need to know.

"Jesus, *no*." Lee unzips his jacket, face flushed. "That night"—*that night*—"she got in an accident with Cody at the bay. Her car slid in the mud, and it got stuck. She asked me to tow it out." I picture the tow truck, caked in mud, from when he drove it to Hudson's house. "That's it."

"That's not it." I refuse to believe it.

Lee is quiet at first. "She emailed me in December," he says finally, the words slow, "for an interview with *The Eagle Eye* about the dumb comeback game. I thought it could be good for me. Good press, even if it was just my high school paper. We met at Java's, but she didn't want to talk about the game." He shoots. "There was a different story she was writing."

The one about Keystone? But that has nothing to do with him.

Except Lee hangs his head, the ball thudding, and I say, "You cheated."

Shoot. "I was going to fail physics." Miss. "If I failed, I'd lose my spot on the team." Shoot. "If I lost my spot, I'd lose my scholarship to UNC." Miss. "I'd lose everything."

"You *cheated*," I say again, stepping around the fence. This is so not the point, but I have to ask: "I was failing, too. Why didn't you tell me about Keystone?"

"Because you're smarter than that." Lee stares at the hoop. It's busted, hopelessly in need of a new net. "I didn't want you involved with that shit. And"—he dribbles—"I didn't want you to know I'd cheated." He laughs, but it's low. Pitiful. "Know why Maddie wanted me to talk?" Shoot. Miss. "Because I've got *name recognition*."

My brother, the golden boy. The cheater.

Then, all at once, my throat goes tight, words strangled when I say, "Wouldn't you want to keep her quiet? Because if she named you, it could fuck up UNC for you and—"

"I fucked up UNC myself," Lee says, all casual. "I stopped going to class weeks ago. I skipped midterms. I cheated to do the one thing I loved, and now I'm not even doing that."

"Is basketball really what you loved?"

Shoot. "I'm good at it." Miss.

"I beg to differ." I rub my arms. "I'm sorry, Lee."

I don't even know what for.

"I'm sorry, too. I'm sorry that I kept Maddie from you, but I swear I didn't do anything. I don't know anything. I'd tell you if I did," he says, serious. "Like, I called her by mistake—"

"On the flip phone. I know."

This gets a laugh out of him. "So that's what you took."

"Technically, you took it first. That was *my* two-for-one deal."

"Look, when Maddie asked for my number, I sure as hell wasn't giving her my real one." Lee lobs the ball at me. I do not catch it. He hesitates as I fetch the ball, his face pained. "I used to get so mad at you, Jo. Because you were careless, and always got into trouble, and I . . . judged you for it. I'm sorry." He pauses. "I'm sorry about Nick, too."

My nose fizzes, but I'm not going to cry. "You tried, at least." It wasn't enough, but he did the best he could. He was still a kid then, too. He told our parents; *they* should've done more. I dribble once, twice, and step up to the free throw line. I bend my knees. Shoot. Nail the world's worst airball. "Wouldn't that have been amazing if I made it?"

"You were never making it with that form." Lee takes the ball back. "How the hell do you know any of this?"

"I cannot express what a long story it is."

"Try me."

"Me and Hudson were in a fake relationship and—"

"Never mind," he says, and I laugh.

"I've got a hot guy in my room, so I'm out, but *one* more question," I say. "What did you think I took from your room?"

"The stupid USB," he says matter-of-factly, like I should know what it means. "Maddie had everything about Keystone on a USB. I said I'd cut her brakes at the bay if she didn't give it to me." Lee drops the basketball. "I'd never *actually* cut her brakes."

"Can I have it? Please? I think Tess might write about—"

"I'll talk," Lee says. "Yes, you can have it—it's in my top desk drawer—but tell Tess I'll talk. On the record."

I roll the ball to him. "How noble of you."

"It's not noble, Jo. It's just right."

-52-

Hudson is spending the night, which my parents do not and will not know.

But I hate him when his alarm goes off for work at 4:16 a.m.

Neither of us gets out of bed. I scratch the nape of his neck, whisper, "So, we'll take it to Lund." The USB that holds a spreadsheet of hundreds of codes and dollar amounts like the ones we found in Maddie's stories. Two years of transactions. Proof. "If she does nothing, or refuses to believe us, we go big. Take it to the media."

"You mean your mom?"

"My mom *is* the media."

His fingers graze my side. "I'll get my rank and the money—hopefully—and we'll take down Keystone. Take down those assholes, like you wanted."

I'm getting everything I wanted. *Except.*

"What about Maddie? Like, where did she go?" I stare at my starless ceiling. "It feels like we're still missing something key." The word sticks. *Key.* I crawl over Hudson, out of my bed.

He groans, "I think you ruptured my appendix."

I rip open my blinds and look across the street, at the side yard of the Prices' house. I've done this before—standing at my bedroom window, looking outside, finding Maddie digging in the garden. Or that one time, the summer we stopped being friends, when she was digging under the lilac bush in the side yard with something small and pink in the grass beside her.

The *key*. The one from her locker.

"Get ready for work, okay?" I say, shrugging into a zip-up. "I know what's missing."

Maddie collected her life in a safe to stop her mom from snooping, and then to keep it a secret, she went even further. She *buried* it.

I slink along the Prices' side yard with a trowel, find the spot where Maddie sat under the lilac bush, jab at the frozen earth until I hit metal. I kneel and dig and scrape back the dirt, and there, like I knew it would be, is the safe.

Fastened, of course, with a tiny pink padlock.

Flower City Diner won't open for another twenty minutes, but the other cooks let Hudson skip prep when he tells them my dad is Joseph Kirby. We take a vinyl booth in the corner and set the safe between us. My hands shake as I slip the key into the lock.

It clicks. Unlatches.

Opens to an archive of Maddie Price at fifteen.

There's a worn copy of *Pride and Prejudice*, her favorite book at the time. Seashells from a miserable spring break trip to the Outer Banks. A cut corner of her stuffed rabbit's ear. Or was it a pig? A dog? I can see it on her bed—ratty gray when it was once white or cream or pale pink.

Disposable cameras, film undeveloped. I lift one to my eye and squint, finding Hudson through the viewfinder. He holds up a phone—hot pink, very dead.

"Hey, that's mine." I lost it at the end of the summer. *That* summer. I loved that phone, and then it was gone, except not. Maddie had it. Maddie stole it?

Hudson examines its charging port. "Why would she keep this?"

I think about what's on that phone: dozens of texts between me and Nick; quick midnight chats in the call logs where he told me to come outside, come out to his car.

Irrefutable proof that something happened between us.

"Kathleen said Maddie tried to unbury something before she left. This stuff—most of it is hers, but the phone is . . . evidence." I want to vomit at this next thought, but I need to ask it out loud. "Was she blackmailing Nick?"

Hudson stacks mini creamers. "He's in the city, right? Could she want a place to stay?"

"I doubt he'd house her out of the goodness of his heart. He'd want something."

"Like his dad's Audi?"

"Oh my God," I say, so loud that Hudson startles and knocks over his pyramid. "So, we know her dad got the note about Maddie running off. Not her mom. And Maddie found out that he stole from her college fund, so he probably *wants* her to stay gone until after his work bonus clears, right? Then he can replenish the account before Maddie has a chance to tell her mom."

"So, she runs to New York and her dad bribes Nick to let her stay? Maddie is okay?"

Maddie is okay.

"Oh my God," I say again, and I laugh, hard, my head in my hands. I don't have all the proof, but in the end, I think the simplest story really is true: Maddie ran away.

"Get off your ass, Hudson!" one of the line cooks yells from the kitchen.

He looks at the clock. The first customers arrive soon.

"Can you let me out the back?" I ask. "I'll stick the safe in your car."

He pushes open the door for me. "We solved it, huh?"

"I guess." I kiss him, say, "I'll see you soon."

I dump the safe on his passenger seat, then cut across the lot, toward the road. The sun is just starting to rise, a terrific pink, spilled like paint. Red sky at morning—is that good?

No. It's a warning.

My sneakers crunch on the gravel. I picture Maddie in New York City and wonder if she sees the same sunrise. I like the image: Maddie crawling onto a fire escape with a blanket and a coffee mug to warm her hands. Like she got what she wanted.

Maddie's life was falling apart in Rochester, but NYU could solve it. Even after she lost her recommendation and missed out on the top 10 percent, she found a story in Keystone and—

I stop.

How did Maddie find out about Keystone?

I guess I assumed she found out through Cody, that he drunkenly told her like he told me, but when I confronted him about it in his car, he didn't seem surprised that she knew. No, it was the story that got him. *Fucking stupid,* he called her. Same with Miles, right? He only cared—got scared—when I told him about the story. They *knew* she knew about Keystone.

Not because she cheated herself.

Because she was *in* Keystone.

"Maddie Price was a fucking rat," I say, out loud. Maddie was going to expose them, but it meant exposing herself. I need to tell Hudson. I need to—

Wait.

That noise—footsteps? My heart pounds, heavy in my chest. Slowly, slowly, I twist my head back. A squirrel skitters behind the dumpster.

I exhale.

Then I'm on the ground. Pain blossoms in my skull, hot and white.

What the fuck.

Whatthefuckwhatthefuckwhatthefuck.

I stumble to my feet, but I'm dragged down again. My vision blurs, spotted, but I see something—left hand, white skin, dirty fingernails. Whoever it is slaps his palm to my mouth, thumb pressed to my nostrils.

A car peels into the parking lot, and he says, "Help me," and I know that voice. Rough. Hoarse. Like each word hurts.

Cody Forsythe.

There's a second set of hands reaching for me now. They're fighting with each other, and I'm fighting them, and then my head—

-*53*-

My head hurts. It hurts so bad. The pain crackles in my skull, splinters, is that blood? I think it's blood—*my* blood—and the sun is too bright, and everything is moving. *Everything is moving.*

"Look, she's up. She's fine. Fuck."

Someone else: "Crap."

Two of them. Cody and the other one. My head hurts, and I'm in a car, sideways in the backseat, and the freezing morning breeze whips through the windows. I reach (for what?) but my hands fizz with sleep, staticky, and my wrists are . . .

No. I strain against the plastic ties. *Nononono.*

"Left at the light. Thanks for driving, man. I get so woozy when I see—"

"Shut the fuck up."

"Okay."

I brace myself for a swell of nausea. Force my eyes open. I'm facing the seat: faded beige fabric; a tangled seatbelt; blood, *my* blood; something else, tucked in the cushion.

A pink Starburst wrapper.

Cody Forsythe and Miles Metcalf.

Those fucking assholes.

-54-

I'm more alert when the engine cuts. I don't know how long we were driving—fifteen minutes? Twenty? The path up, up, up was winding, and Cody took the curves sharply, even when Miles said, "Be careful, man. Black ice."

I think, *Since when does Miles call Cody "man" so much?*

It's a stupid thing to think, considering.

The door at my feet opens. I hear the word *blindfold*, so I say, "I know who you are, you dumbasses." I don't know if it's the best approach, but my head hurts too much to be scared, like the impact dislodged a bit of my brain—the part that fears.

Cody mumbles, "Told you."

"We're going to help you out, okay?" Miles says. "Just—"

I swing out my leg and connect with a crotch.

"Bitch," Cody groans, jerking me out of the car.

I could try to run, but I can't run. I can't even see straight.

Miles scrambles for my other arm, and they lead me inside. It's dark here—wherever this is—and I'm queasy, uneasy from that drive. Cody drags me forward, toward another door, down a set of stairs, and all at once I am scared. I push my full weight against him and say, "*No*," but he shoves me down the last step.

I land hard. Slowly sit up, dizzy. It's dark, musty—a basement with matted orange carpet and wood-paneled walls. There's a cot in the corner, a TV stand, a door to a small bathroom. No windows. Everything smells damp; a watery mold stain spreads up the corner of one wall. *I went to my uncle's cottage earlier. It's right on—*

The bay.

"Miles!" I shout, because this is his uncle's cottage. Maybe it's the one I saw lit the other night, like Miles was preparing. Like he was waiting.

They talk at the top of the stairs before Miles climbs down. He looks pale. Green. I'm not sure where I'm bleeding from—my face, the crown of my head—but clearly it turns his stomach.

"That wasn't supposed to happen," he whispers, reaching for me. I swat him away with my zip-tied hands. "No. Here." He tears the tie with his key. I'd punch him if I thought I could aim. "There."

"Have you been tracking me? The diner, the bay the other night." I frown. "That wasn't your car at the bay, though. I know your car."

"I borrowed my dad's. And you never disabled location sharing when you got your new phone," Miles says with a shrug. "I, uh, actually need your phone. Please."

"I don't have it. It's probably in the parking lot," I say. At Flower City. *Hudson.* Maybe he'll find the phone. Find *me.*

"Oh," Miles says, quiet. Pain flares behind my eyes. "You're hurt?"

"Cody knocked me out, Miles."

"Can I, like, get you something?"

"*No.*" I want Advil or a pack of frozen peas or my mom. I want to get out of here and go home. I want some fucking answers. "Why are you doing this?"

Miles lowers himself onto the cot, his eyes fixed on the carpet. "Everything was going wrong. You'd been getting in trouble at school. Your new friends were angry at you, and your boyfriend broke up with you." The way he says it, clipped, static—he's rehearsed it. "You saw how everyone cared when Maddie left, and you wanted attention, too, so you ran away. But in two days, you'll come back and apologize for scaring everyone."

My head throbs. "Why?"

"So no one will believe anything you say if you try to expose Keystone."

Tears burn behind my eyes. "You're making me an unreliable narrator?"

"I earned my spot at the top, Jo. I'm valedictorian, and I'm going to MIT, and I . . ." Miles trails off, choked up, not crying. "I have a real future ahead of me. But without Keystone, I lose everything. I *can't* lose everything."

With that, he stands and starts up the steps. He makes it halfway before I shout, "I hope you know how pathetic that is."

Miles pauses for a long time at the top of the stairs.

I fight sleep for as long as I can. That's a thing with concussions, right? *Do not sleep.* Or maybe it's the opposite, and I should sleep more? I guess I sleep anyway because suddenly I'm opening my eyes, and why?

Footsteps. Two sets on the stairs. Miles and—

"Oh my God." April Kirk's pale face twists. I force myself to sit, groggy, but maybe she can help me. Maybe she believes it now, whatever it was Maddie told her at the bay.

Then April turns to Miles and says, "You guys are such idiots."

Uh.

"April, you have to help us here," Miles pleads.

"I don't *have* to do anything. I told you she was messing everything up," April says, and I don't know if she means me or Maddie or both. "I told you she was going to get us caught."

My brain hurts too much for this. "You're in Keystone, too."

April doesn't look at me. "Maddie screwed everything up," she says, like I never spoke. "She *admitted* to stealing that stupid paper, putting us all at risk"—Trey, Kathleen, the English midterm—"and you still didn't believe me."

"Is that why you fought with her?" I ask. "At the bay? That's so weird, by the way. Pick a less creepy place to do your business."

Now April does turn to me, just for a second, but Miles goes, "I'm sorry, April, but—"

More footsteps: Cody, crashing down the stairs, searching for the remote.

NEWS 9 BROADCAST
3:33 p.m.
ROCHESTER POLICE SEARCHING FOR MISSING TEEN

Police are asking the public for help after a local teenager was reported missing. Seventeen-year-old Jo-Lynn Kirby was last seen Monday morning at six a.m. at Flower City Diner. Anyone with information is asked to call 911 immediately.

The TV turns off. Miles holds the remote—I don't know when he grabbed it—and stares at the blank screen. He says, "Okay. Okay, I fear people, uh, might be upset that she's gone."

"Why do you sound surprised?" I ask.

"I'm not surprised! I just . . . didn't . . . think."

"What happened to majority rule?" April asks, furious, her eyes brimming.

Cody grunts. "Two out of three *is* the majority now."

"Because Maddie is gone," I say, but no one looks at me. "So, Maddie asked to get put in the top ten percent of our class, but you said no? It didn't meet the majority rule?" I look toward Cody. "When you changed Hudson's rank—was that majority rule?"

April wipes her eye. "It was not."

"You're both jealous that *I* figured out how to hack the gradebook," Cody says.

"You didn't hack anything; you got lucky that Mrs. Fitzgerald left her password out."

"You do know Maddie and Hudson weren't messing around, right?" I say to Cody. His face falls. "I think you do. I think you were paranoid and insecure and chose to believe the worst in your friend and your girlfriend instead of using your brain for five seconds."

Miles coughs, neck pink with hives. "Guys, we need to figure this out."

This. Me. My head is throbbing again, but my mind is dull. Muted. "This will get worse, you know. People will look for me"— Jo-Lynn Kirby, missing, kidnapped, dead—"and find me. Or they'll find you first. I'm not the only one who knows about Keystone, you assholes."

The three of them go quiet.

Exhausted, dazed, I add, "You're *going* to get caught."

Cody scratches the back of his neck. "Maybe we should just let her—"

"No," Miles says firmly. "Everyone will forget by morning."

NEWS 9 BROADCAST
5:56 a.m.
POLICE SEEK INFORMATION IN MISSING TEEN'S DISAPPEARANCE

In the morning, I wake to April Kirk on the bottom step, her laptop on her knees.

My head hurts worse today. I groan when I sit up.

"I'm making us a schedule," she says, like this is beyond normal. "Mornings are best for me, and then Miles and Cody will alternate the afternoon shift, and we'll regroup at night." She frowns at the screen. "Shoot, but I have a flute lesson tonight."

"Do you not hear yourself right now?"

She must not hear me, either, because she ignores the question. "I think this works," she says, and stands, flipping her laptop toward me.

My chaperones in a color-coded spreadsheet, dated from now until I'm free. April added a comment to the afternoon cells: *I need to let my Mom use my car so your on your own, ok?*

I read it again.

The grammar, that syntax—

"You hacked Maddie's Instagram," I say. April snaps the

401

laptop shut. "You got into her account and made that post. It wasn't Alexis Fitch; it was *you*."

She sticks the laptop in her backpack. "Someone had to take the fall. If you looked deep enough into Maddie, eventually you'd find Keystone. I thought everyone would back off if they thought she was safe. And it worked until *you* found the password change."

"You're getting Alexis expelled, April."

"I did what I had to do to protect us."

I stare up at her: April Kirk, this girl I barely know. Hell, I've barely thought about her, even when our lockers were side by side. "How did you even get wrapped up in this?" I ask. I don't care. Like, I could not give less of a shit, but if she gets talking . . .

"The money. My dad got laid off, and he was going to make me quit flute."

"Then Maddie?"

April pauses. Like she's debating how much to tell, or if she should say anything at all.

Finally, she says, "Keystone was getting too big, and me and Miles needed help with the writing—essays, short answers. I asked Maddie if she'd do it."

I shake my head, and the motion aches, pain throbbing. "Why would she say yes?"

The money is a perk, but she didn't need it, not like April did. Proximity to Cody? It's an enormous risk for, uh. Him.

Another pause, longer. "Maddie wrote for *The Eagle Eye*, but she wanted—needed—to be an editor. To be competitive for NYU. If she helped us, we'd help her," April says. "Half the staff was cheating at the time."

"So, she blackmailed them?"

"She leveraged the information she had to get what she wanted."

"Is that not the same thing?"

"Maddie was my friend first, you know," April says out of nowhere. Her face burns, eyes bright with tears. "I'd gone to band camp"—I hate that my first instinct is to make a joke about band camp, her flute, et cetera—"and you replaced me."

I scrabble to the side of the bed. "I didn't mean to replace you. I didn't know." I take hold of her wrist, but she jerks it free. "April, I'll keep you out of this if you help me, okay? Please."

But she says, "I have to get to school," and leaves without so much as looking at me.

I sleep because I have nothing better to do, and when I can't sleep anymore, I think.

I think about my parents and Lee and if they believe I'd run. I'd *never* run.

I think about Hudson and Kathleen and Sara and Michaela and Tess. They have to know that Keystone did this to me, right? They need to do something. They must be doing something.

I think about Maddie out there somewhere.

I think until I get too tired and fall asleep again.

NEWS 9 BROADCAST
4:57 p.m.
POLICE SUSPECT FOUL PLAY IN DISAPPEARANCE OF LOCAL TEEN

It's dark when Cody Forsythe chucks a McDonald's bag at my head and says, "Eat this."

My stomach growls. I haven't eaten since I don't remember. Sunday night? Forty-eight hours, then. I chuck the bag back at him.

"You need food." Cody digs out a fry.

I curl into myself. "What's happening out there?"

Why has no one followed you? Found me?

He rips a ketchup packet open with his teeth. "It's kind of a shitshow. There are all these news vans outside school. Haven't seen much of your boyfriend, though. Getting questioned at the police station has kept him pretty busy."

It's always the boyfriend. I'm going to be sick. "This is bad for you, Cody. He'll know it was you and Miles. He'll tell the cops and—"

"—they'll think that the paranoid poor kid is so sad about not getting his money that he's making it up to take the heat off himself. Oh, wait. That already happened," he adds with a fake frown. "Seriously, it'll be fine, JoJo. Just chill."

"Just chill? You kidnapped me!" My skin burns, prickling. "God, you're a monster." I laugh, because it's so cliché, what I'm about to say. "You ruined my fucking life, Cody."

He has the audacity to look confused. "What did I do to you?"

"You stole my nudes. Sent them to everyone. Do you not remember this?"

His face blanches. "JoJo, I—"

"But I can never do anything about it because *I'll* suffer for it. They'll blame *me*." My voice is heavy, thick with something I can't place. *Rage.* Pure, absolute fury. I plant my elbows on my knees. "Look at me, Cody." He has a blot of ketchup on his chin. "You'll get everything you want. You'll go to Duke. Play soccer. Join a frat."

I can see it: Cody chugging beer from the keg, taking his hazing in stride.

"You'll latch onto another desperate loser like Miles. Meet a girl. Lots of girls, and you'll treat them like nothing. Maybe you'll do worse. Then you'll graduate and get a fantastic job and marry a woman who doesn't see the real you or, more likely, doesn't care, and you'll be fucking fine the rest of your life."

I try to see him for who he used to be. The untamed bedhead, the smattering of freckles, the impish way he'd grin before we got into trouble.

"When did I stop being a person to you?" I ask, throat tight. "We were *friends,* Cody."

And Cody Forsythe starts to fucking cry.

"Get out," I tell him.

He does.

That night, I wake to talking—Miles, upstairs, alone. (I think?) I ease up the steps. Listen.

"This is going so wrong. I don't know what to do." Pause. "What do I do?"

NEWS 9 BROADCAST
6:17 a.m.
SECURITY FOOTAGE CAPTURES FRIGHTENING ATTACK

I get to witness it. My *frightening attack.*

How I stop in the middle of the lot. Listen. How Cody, dressed in black, slams me to the ground. I've been missing for two days, but I'm getting out today. This morning.

Now.

I hear them upstairs—three sets of footsteps, the TV blasting—and what are they waiting for? I climb to the top of the stairs. Press my ear to the door.

"What do we do?" Miles, frantic. "That's clearly not Hudson in the footage. What if the cops believe him now? And question us? I don't know what to do, I don't—I don't know."

"Just fucking let her go." Cody, hoarse. "We won't even have to talk to the cops then. It was always the plan, right? She won't tell. She'll be . . . it'll be fine."

April: "She'll tell."

Cody: "Then what do you suggest?"

Miles: "Maybe we have to get rid of her."

"What?" Cody, half laughing. "No." Pause. "Guys, no. *No.*"

It goes quiet then.

"No," I say, and I'm panicking. I'm losing it. "You're supposed to let me out. Two days, then I reappear. I'll keep quiet, I swear. I *swear.*" I pound my fist on the door. "Let me *out.*"

No one answers me.

No. I sit on the top step, my head in my hands. My hair is greasy, limp at the roots. I need to shower desperately, but I'm not taking one here. I'll take one when I get out.

They need to let me out.

That was the deal: I'd be gone for two days, then I'd come back and grovel and say how sorry I am for frightening everyone when all I wanted was attention, because that's the trouble with girls like me. All we want is attention.

All I wanted was to copy Maddie Price.

But Maddie was *eviscerated*—by the press, our classmates. The gossip in those first few days was relentless. Cruel. Undeserved. It makes no sense why I'd ever put myself through that after seeing what she endured. The motive is all wrong.

It's *wrong*.

I lift my head. "It's the wrong story."

It's the wrong story, and it doesn't sound like one Miles would ever tell.

It sounds like Maddie.

- *55* -

Maddie Price fucking set me up.

-56-

Alone, when no one can stop me, I throw my weight against the door, rattle the doorknob, claw at the hinges until my nails bleed. Nothing.

Alone, even though no one can hear me, I scream.

Nothing. *Nothing.*

My panic has turned to inaction. I'm frozen. I'm numb.

Maybe we have to get rid of her.

I lie on the cot and stare at the mold-stained ceiling. I turn on my side and stare at the walls, the water splotches on the wood paneling. I turn on the TV and watch the news.

NEWS 9 BROADCAST
11:34 a.m.
SEARCH CONTINUES FOR MISSING TEEN
—disappearance calls to mind that of another local teen, eighteen-year-old Maddie Price. However, authorities insist any similarities are coincidental.

Our senior portraits appear on screen, side by side.

Jo-Lynn Kirby and Maddie Price. The missing girls.

All along, I thought the trouble was with girls like me. That I made myself into a girl who deserved to be horrifically mistreated. I took those photos and set an easy passcode. I wasn't firm enough with a boy who liked me. I fell prey to an older boy.

More stories I've been telling wrong.

Because I can take a stupid picture if I want. I'm allowed to feel cute and capture it and not feel ashamed. It isn't too much to ask that my own friends—that anyone—see me as human.

And I didn't lead Miles on because I never owed him anything more than what I gave. He treated our friendship like a transaction that I could only repay with one thing.

And my impulse to hide what happened with Nick that summer wasn't because no one would understand; it's because *I* didn't understand.

Even now, I'm telling it wrong: *I fell prey to an older boy.*

Nick was an adult. He was twenty-one, and I'd been fifteen a week.

He made me lose my best friend, made me lie and hide. He told me *no one can ever know about this*, and I couldn't find the words, anyway, but maybe I've had them longer than I realize.

That night in the car when *it just happened*—that was sexual assault. Nick raped me. He told me I was special and different and nothing and there, and I believed every word.

But despite all he did to break me, I'm still fucking here.

And I'm getting myself out.

-57-

The garage door grinds open a few hours later.

Next, footsteps. Miles. I recognize his gait now—slow and plodding, feet dragging.

He comes downstairs with a greasy paper bag and a super-sized soda. For me? The smell turns my stomach. "You're early," I say. I don't like that. I don't like that he signed himself out of school or faked sick or slipped out unnoticed.

Miles sighs, his curls falling into his eyes. "Principal Lund got walked out of school," he says, almost monotone. "Mr. Conti, too. I think Keystone is done. I think all of this is—"

I make no plans, and I waste no time.

I slam into Miles Metcalf.

The shock of it knocks him unsteady. He staggers, trips over the TV stand, drops the cup. The soda—cherry-flavored, I think, red and sticky and medicinal—spills everywhere. I scrabble toward the stairs, but he latches onto my ankle, and I pitch forward.

"Stop—"

I kick him in the face.

Blood (*his* blood) drips from his nose. I've shattered his glasses, too. The left lens. He sits back on his feet, his face gone sick-pale. Heart thumping, not breathing, I sprint up the stairs. My nails claw, clip into the wood, and I crash out the basement door and—

"Maddie."

I don't know how I even say her name.

Maddie Price, faded hair cut to her chin, like she hacked it herself with safety scissors.

Maddie Price, clothes rumpled, stinking of stale car smell.

Maddie Price, *here*.

The two of us stare like we've never seen each other before. Then Miles coughs, gagging, and Maddie peers down the basement steps. It's like the sound yanks her back to this moment.

To me.

When she speaks, her voice is steady: "We need to get you out of here."

- *58* -

Maddie Price is here, found, alive, and the very first thing I do is shove her to the ground. "You fucking set me up."

She stares up at me, stunned. "What? Jo, no! I didn't. I *didn't*."

I help her up. "Then how are you here?"

Here, as in Rochester, New York. Here, as in this cottage on the bay.

The room takes shape. Heavy curtains and well-worn furniture and crumbs on the kitchen counter. I look to the door—*how did you get a key*—and out the front window. Her white Prius is haphazardly parked in the driveway, the front bumper destroyed, streaked with red paint.

"Did you call the cops?" I ask.

She goes, "I'll explain everything."

"You said that before." And also, she didn't answer me.

"I *will*. I promise. But we need to go." She lowers her voice. "No one is supposed to be here. The spreadsheet—you should be alone." She takes my hand and drags me toward the door, because Maddie is here to . . . save me? Maddie came back for me.

Then another hand grabs me, wrenching me back.

Miles, pale and sick, his glasses broken. He looks between us: Maddie, me, Maddie, me, Maddie. "What are you doing here?" he asks, confused. *Confused.* Not surprised.

Miles is not surprised to see Maddie Price, and she's not surprised to see him, and he still has my arm in his grasp, and he's blocking the door, and I don't know what's going on and I hate it—I *hate* it—so I rip my arm free and scramble toward the sliding door to the back deck, but there's no way to the driveway from here. *Shit.*

The air is cool under a pale gray sky. Ice melts from the gutters. The cottage is high up on the hill by the bay. Dozens of steps lead to the dock below; the dock stretches along the edge of the water, toward the road.

My heart skips. That's it: I can follow the dock to the road.

Maddie follows me outside, and Miles follows us both. Seeing him, Maddie backs up, her hands raised, until she stands in front of me. "Miles, just let her go, and we won't tell."

"Yes, I will." I push her aside. "Do you *really* think Keystone is worth this? It's pathetic, Miles. You want to be seen as some good guy, but you're just a fucking loser."

He shakes his head, a trickle of blood veering into his eye. "This is my future."

"Why does your future matter so much? What about mine?"

"Because—"

"No!" I say, loud and clear. Then I do the most dangerous thing you can do in front of a guy like Miles Metcalf: I laugh. "Do you know how long I've spent thinking I'm the problem? I was wrong. The trouble is with smug, arrogant, entitled guys like *you*."

He lunges for me, knocks me down. My head hits the deck,

hard, and, God, I see stars, my vision bright, the pain brighter. Miles is heavy but unsteady, woozy when he sees the blood, so I shove him off, shout, "Maddie!"

She helps me stand, both of us reaching for the other's hand. Neither of us lets go as we sprint down the stairs. The wood creaks under our weight.

"Is he—?" Maddie asks.

He is. Running after us, a dozen steps behind. Until the board cracks. *The board cracks.*

Miles clutches the railing, but his leg crashes through. He lifts himself up again. The splintered wood tore his jeans to the knee. Ripped the skin on his shin, exposing tissue. Bone.

Maddie gasps. "Oh my God."

He sways, thinking.

Then Miles starts back up the stairs, away from us.

"Go." I lose track of my steps, think only of the rocks, the ice, the dock that leads toward the road. The boards groan under us. Maddie stops, hesitating, but I pull her onto the dock at the bottom of the stairs, my mind set on going and going and going.

"Jo, careful—"

The board cracks again, and my legs fall through, piercing the ice. The freezing shock of the water knocks me breathless, but then Maddie's hand finds mine again and pulls me up. I gasp, shaking, crying, and she wraps her arms around me and whispers, "I'm so sorry, Jo."

Headlights beam across the twisted road, through the trees, and—sirens. We're not alone anymore. Now there are medics. Cops. Something, somewhere, smells like smoke. Someone (an EMT?) wraps a blanket around me and says, "You're—?"

"Jo. I'm Jo."

"And you?"

"Maddie," she says, dazed, looking toward the cottage. Her own name shocks her back, and she says, "Wait, I went missing, too. I'm Maddie Price. I knew she was in trouble. I knew that I could help her. I—"

She keeps saying it, over and over, so caught up in the story that she doesn't notice when I unhook her hand from mine.

– EPILOGUE –

Things weren't going great for Maddie Price. That part is true.

Her parents split the summer before senior year. Mr. Price was a reckless spender and a cheat and kind of an ass. Mrs. Price was overbearing and a snoop. Maddie—their loved, adored, perfect miracle—was caught in the middle.

Something was off with the Birds, too. Mostly between her and Kathleen. It's like they'd learned new languages and no longer understood each other.

Then there was Cody, the boyfriend who wasn't quite as good as the one she'd created in her head. He was nice to her, which is a low, low bar. And he had those pictures . . .

But it'd be over soon because, soon, Maddie would have NYU. It'd been her dream since forever, so she applied only there, early decision, certain she'd get in.

And she did.

Except she didn't.

It was heartbreaking and devastating and she never planned to run, honestly, but she did everything right and still, after all that, nothing was going right for her.

So, in the end, the simplest story is true: Maddie Price really did run away.

But.

Something is missing from Maddie's motive to run: Keystone.

Most of this I can only assume. Maddie has never denied she was in Keystone, but in every interview, she keeps the details of her involvement vague: *I'd rather not talk about that.*

Keystone was too big for April and Miles, and Cody was no help beyond recruitment, and they needed *someone*. Preferably someone who could write. So, Maddie?

She blackmailed her way to an editor role on *The Eagle Eye*, but she never cheated until, suddenly, she found herself a spot outside the top 10 percent. She'd lost that recommendation to NYU, too, so she *really* needed this—and she asked for a little help.

They told her no. Majority rule. Maddie Price, it seems, was on the bottom.

The story was her revenge on Keystone, and it was also her way into NYU.

But if she exposed Keystone, she exposed herself. It was the wrong angle on the right story, and she couldn't write her way out of it.

Tess Spradlin could help. Or maybe she could get Lee Kirby to talk. Maddie needed a story so good that NYU had no choice but to accept her—even if it was a risk to write it at all.

Because Keystone could be violent. Broken collarbones and expulsions and revenge porn and a cottage at the bay. (Not yet on the last one, but soon.) If they'd do *that* to the people on the outside, just imagine how they'd destroy one of their own.

Then she got rejected, so what the fuck did it matter?

Maddie needed out of Rochester, and she wanted New York City.

She was never close with Nick—blame the age difference—but she hauled her damaged car to the city and pounded on his apartment door in the early hours of the morning and asked to stay, just for a bit, please don't tell.

He told immediately.

But Mr. Price also got that note, and Maddie wrecked his empty loft when she found the divorce papers and the bra and her drained college fund. He asked Nick to please, please let her stay until he got it under control—and got his bonus.

Nick needed compensation.

Like that cherry-red two-seater convertible.

In each retelling, Maddie vaguely mentions that, three weeks after she arrived, she struck out on her own in New York. The truth is, Nick kicked her the hell out. He'd been honest when he told me that he came back to Rochester to do damage control, but the real damage was done the second Lee clenched his fist.

Maddie wasn't just a nuisance anymore; she was a risk to him. *I* was a risk.

Her first night alone, Maddie slept in the stacks at NYU's

library, like a tired student. The next, she rode the train to the end of the line, dozing on the plastic seats. Maddie woke before the morning rush, walked for blocks before she remembered it—her backpack tucked under the seat.

Thousands of dollars, her money from Keystone, gone.

Maddie had nothing.

And Miles Metcalf was calling her burner.

For days, Maddie deleted his calls, texts, voicemails asking if she was going to expose Keystone.

But she was out of money, so the next time he called, she answered.

It terrified him that she was willing to fall with Keystone. In exchange for her silence and the promise that the story was dead, Miles bought her gift cards for a hostel, for groceries, for basic necessities, and he recited the digits over the phone.

And still, he kept fucking calling.

He was panicked that Hudson and I were getting too close to the truth. Petrified that we'd ruin this for him. Them. Maddie told Miles that he needed to keep me quiet, but she never said how—and she'd never have suggested *that.*

It wasn't until the plan was in motion that he told her what he'd done. She weaseled the details out of him: the cottage address, the garage code, the color-coded schedule that decided who watched me when.

That was when she got scared.

So, Maddie came back to save me.

Even with a broken tibia, even woozy, sick from the blood that poured from his torn skin, Miles dragged himself back to the cottage. His car. The lazy warmth of the last couple days had melted the snow on that steep, winding road, then the cold snap refroze it.

Maybe it was the black ice or the sirens approaching uphill or his lightheadedness that made Miles swerve into those trees. He never braked. He never decelerated.

Miles survived for two weeks, and then he was gone, too.

Maddie tells this tale over (*The Today Show*) and over (*Good Morning America*) and over (News 9 exclusive) and over (Justin Lloyd's podcast) again.

The one about the missing girl who saved the missing girl.

The one about us.

In the end, Maddie Price finally got her story.

August: Five Months Later

I'm late for my own graduation party.

Then again, I'm graduating two months late, so I'm on-brand.

It's nearly dusk, the setting sun warm and golden, but the heat is unbearable. Everyone is fighting for shade under the oak tree out back. I watch from the back window—Sara kissing One-L

Daniele's cheek, Michaela crouching to take a photo, Kathleen shielding Clare's eyes.

Like she can feel my gaze, Kathleen finds me in the window— and she flips me off with a perfectly sly smile. I laugh and do it back. I've taught her so well.

All of them (except Clare, obviously) graduated back in June. Culver had already fallen apart by then. Principal Lund and Mr. Conti were forced to resign immediately. Before Alexis Fitch was formally expelled, too. Her name may have been cleared, but last I heard, her parents enrolled her at Our Lady of Lourdes for the fall.

More than a hundred and fifty students were tied to Keystone over its two-year existence. Eighty students were disciplined. Sixteen in my senior class had their college acceptances revoked. Like Ben Sulkin, who lost his baseball scholarship to Vanderbilt and got a misdemeanor assault charge for pushing Trey Gardner off his deck. April Kirk from the SUNY Potsdam Crane School of Music. Cody Forsythe from Duke.

My lawyer—what a deranged thing to say: *my lawyer*—told me to be prepared for a long, painful legal battle. If Miles were alive, he'd bear the brunt of the charges (kidnapping, unlawful imprisonment). But April and Cody took plea deals on reduced charges to spare me a trial.

It's a kindness neither deserves credit for.

Impossibly, it was Cody who cracked first.

Those words—*maybe we have to get rid of her*—unsettled him, and when Miles ditched school, Cody lost it. He told the cops everything, sobbing the entire time.

He found me after sentencing (probation, a fine) and said,

"I'm sorry, Jo," simple as that. His freckled face was pale. It was the first time he'd ever apologized.

The first time he ever called me Jo.

"I'm filing a civil suit," I told him. "For revenge porn. My lawyer will be in touch."

He slowly nodded.

The next day, I found an unlabeled envelope tucked in the mail slot. It was a handwritten letter from his parents. Cody is a good kid at heart, and he just wants to move on, and should his future really be ruined for this? What boy hasn't made a dumb mistake?

Later, my parents helped me light a fire in the yard, and I burned that shit.

"Hey!" I shout upstairs. "Where are the car keys?"

"Console table!" Lee calls back.

He formally withdrew from UNC in April, two months before his clearance to return to sport. Maybe he'll play again. Probably not. He apprentices in the auto shop full-time now.

Then there was his supporting role in Tess Spradlin's cover story about Keystone.

Maddie was right about that: Lee was the biggest name.

The backlash was immediate—the privileged athlete who cheated because he could—but it wasn't exactly wrong, either. Lee knows it. He's trying to be better, which is more than I can say for most people. He's in therapy now. I'm in therapy, too.

Twice a week, down from three, not including our biweekly family counseling sessions.

My therapist's name is Macy. She has gorgeous curls and a lot of linen dresses, and she lets me ramble about nothing until, finally, I give her *something*.

Okay, console table. Me and Lee, our senior portraits side by side.

"The keys aren't here," I say.

Hudson emerges from the kitchen. "Catch."

I do not. "You know I'm a bad catcher."

"You're also a bad driver, but you still got your license." He hands me the keys, then he plants his hands on the console table, on either side of my hips. "Ditching your own party?"

"Oh, great idea." I slide my hands along his waist. "Let's find something better to do."

"What else did you have in mind?" Hudson asks.

I pretend to roll my eyes, but my breath catches like it always does with him, even still.

The second he found my shattered phone in the diner parking lot, he knew something was horribly wrong. He told the police over and over and over that it was Keystone. But they didn't believe him. He'd been too vocal about his rank, and he was the boyfriend, after all.

Except Kathleen corroborated it. Sara and Michaela, too. And Tess told my parents what we'd uncovered, and they took it to Principal Lund, and the police were on their way to Culver when Miles snuck out of school and drove up to the cottage.

Hudson never got an apology from the cops. Not that he expected one. The most he got was a check—a full $25,000—from the alumni association, and then they canceled the scholarship, effective immediately.

His grandparents moved to a retirement community in Sarasota in May. The couple who bought his house planned to rent it out, anyway, and offered him a discount. But Hudson is still at my place all the time to test recipes in our kitchen.

Or to fool around with me. That definitely happens, too.

I'm pulling him down to kiss me when there's a clang from outside, so sudden that Bay Leaf stampedes upstairs. I turn toward the window. Find the moving truck across the street. The house must be empty by now; that truck has been here for hours.

"You're nervous," Hudson says.

"I'm not nervous." It sounds like a lie. "Fine, I'll just feel better once Tess gets here."

It's like my words summon her; she pulls up to the curb and steps out, hauls a cardboard box up the drive. I lead us outside, and Hudson jogs up to her, taking the box, his arms sinking under the weight. I meet the two of them on the grass.

"God, I'm out of shape," Tess says, fanning herself. "C'mere, Jo-hyphen-Lynn. You get to do the honors."

This is the other celebration—the more important one, no offense. I slice the tape with my keys. Unfold the cardboard flaps. My heart beats a wild rhythm when I look inside.

Tess says, "So?"

That damn moving truck bangs again. The movers roll down the back, shouting over the growling engine. Tess gently touches my arm, yelling, "I'll give you a minute," heading for the back-yard right before the truck rumbles away.

It's just me and Hudson now. It feels right. Everything feels right with him—not perfect, because nothing is perfect. *Right.* It felt right when I sprinted into his arms for the first time after everything and sort of headbutted him, and he laughed and said, "Seriously, Jo? Again?"

It felt right that, even though I was sobbing, I choked out, "Shut up, Hudson."

It feels right that I get to love him and let myself be loved by him.

Hudson cups my face, so wonderful, so aggravatingly hot. The sun catches on the gold in his eyes. He asks, "Ready?"

"Yes." I cup his face back. "I'm ready."

Because across the street, just like I knew she would be, is pretty, nice Maddie Price.

She leans against the oak tree by the curb, staring at the house that's no longer hers.

"Maddie!" I shout.

She turns toward me, but she doesn't seem startled today. No, Maddie has a glow to her, something soft and bright, when she steps into the sun to meet me. Her hair is lighter. It falls in loose waves just past her chin. Smiling, sort of, she says, "Jo."

Maddie, Jo. *Those girls used to be friends, you know.*

I nod at the empty house. "Moving day?"

"I guess," Maddie says, but after her reappearance, she never moved back. Her mom filed for divorce when it came out that Mr. Price knew what happened—that he hid it—and it got ugly quick. Maddie has been staying with an aunt, I think.

Hesitant, she asks, "How are you doing, Jo?"

"Oh. You know."

The real answer is that it depends. Some days I feel exceptionally normal. Others I burn with so much rage I forget how to breathe. Every horrible, horrifying thing that happened—my *frightening attack*, the mold-stained basement, the rotted stairs down to the dock—hurts, but it's a duller ache. No one doubts I went through something awful.

I don't doubt myself.

"What about you?" I ask to be polite.

Maddie beams. "I'm really, really good. I appealed my decision to NYU. I got in."

"Wow." I knew that. Michaela and Sara told me. Kathleen tried to see Maddie once—just one time—but it still stings too much. I try to sound more enthused: "Congratulations. Really."

"Isn't it just—?"

"Can I ask you something?" I don't wait for permission. "When you came to me in the library that day"—*that* day—"what did you mean? That you were in trouble?"

The one question that nags me.

For a second, I think she'll lie. I can see it in the way she twitches her nose and stares up at the cloudless sky. Then she says, "Miles had texted us. Keystone. He said you had a meeting with Mr. Conti the next day, and if you failed, he wanted us to intervene."

I exhale. Try to keep steady.

"Me and Cody were at his car, and Cody *flipped*. He was adamant we couldn't do it. That it was too risky since he shut you up once before," she says. *The bonfire.* "I hadn't known that was the reason for it. But I'd sent him some pictures, too. Nothing as revealing as yours—"

"Thanks, Maddie."

"—anyway, it scared me. I didn't want them to get out if we ever broke up or . . ." Maddie blinks back a bead of sweat from her eye. "My story. I needed to write that story, but I was afraid what'd happen if I did. I needed your help, Jo. Because you knew about Keystone."

I shake my head. "I *didn't* know about Keystone."

"But you knew something, and I knew you'd help me. What Cody did to you—we could have used it, you know? To protect us." Maddie absently scratches her shoulder, skin pink under the warm summer sun. "I know this is weird, but do you want to hang out? Before I go?"

I'm quiet a second. "What would you want to do?"

She thinks, then says, "Take a walk? Maybe get ice cream? I liked taking walks with you, and just . . . talking."

Like this, the wind ruffling her hair, I see the girl she was four years ago, when she was my best friend.

Maddie lets out a soft laugh. "It sounds boring, doesn't it?"

It sounds boring because it *was* boring. The things I loved most about her were mundane: sitting on her couch, eating boxed macaroni and cheese from the pan, taking walks, talking. Even when we did nothing, with her, it felt like everything.

Some small, desperate part of me wants this farewell tour to our friendship.

But I say, "I don't think it's a good idea."

"You're probably right." She shivers despite the heat. "Everything between us just ended so badly."

"Because your brother raped me, Maddie."

Nick Price raped me. I practice saying the words in therapy. I practice when I'm waiting in the drive-thru, like the more I say it out loud, the less it'll ache.

It hasn't stopped aching, and I'm terrified it never will, because nothing will ever happen to Nick. I'll never press charges. He'll never suffer, and sometimes I feel evil that I want him to suffer—just a little—and I don't know what justice looks like, but maybe my only justice is that what happened with Nick is over and, God, that's so unfair.

Here, finally, quietly, Maddie says, "You need to be careful with an accusation like that."

They aren't her words. I know that. Maybe her parents fed them to her, or Nick, because Maddie *did* believe it. She does. She filled that safe with proof of what Nick did to me.

I wonder if she planned on giving it to me.

That's what I choose to believe, like an act of grace toward us both.

Whether or not it's true, I believe that someday Maddie will remember the summer we stopped being best friends. That she'll think of me, sneak into her old side yard, and dig up the evidence that isn't there because she wants me to have it.

I wonder if she knows I already do.

"Good luck at school, Maddie," I say. "I'm glad you got what you wanted."

"Wait! I need to tell you something. I've been talking to an editor at *Chirp*." She lifts her chin, the sun shining fully on her face. "They want me to write the story. The editor thinks I can probably leverage it into a book deal. Can you imagine?" Maddie fumbles with her earrings, the diamonds glittering. "I just wanted you to know."

I nod once. Twice. "Of course, Maddie. It's your story."

"I knew you'd—"

"You didn't let me finish."

Her smile falters, just a little. Falls when I drop the magazine at her feet.

"What's this?" Maddie asks quietly.

My unofficial project with Tess. I still owed her a story, after all.

I'm *the other missing girl* in the press, a nameless Jane Doe in court records. Like I'm no longer part of my own story. Tess helped me unravel it all and stitch it together again—the right story, the right way. Then she pitched it to an editor at *New York Magazine* who wanted it for the cover. I even took this photo myself: a self-portrait with my senior portrait.

Maddie slowly lowers to the grass. Picks up the magazine with shaky hands. Low, again, she asks, "What is this, Jo?"

"You have your story," I say, "and I have mine."

With that, I turn my back on Maddie Price.

For good, this time.

And I look at the magazine in my hands—look at that photo— and see me: Jo at eighteen, loud and bright and difficult and here, just like those other girls with stories to tell and, finally, the voice to tell that story herself.

It's what I deserve.

– AUTHOR'S NOTE –

I've never been very good at describing *Not Like Other Girls*.

Seriously, my go-to line used to be, "Oh, yeah, it's a fun little mystery with fake dating," which is technically true but not totally accurate.

So, I tried to get more specific.

This is a book about a friend breakup between two teenage girls and how navigating that loss is so distinctly devastating. This is a book about first love. It's a book about being seventeen and restless in your hometown. It's a book about privilege and power and entitlement.

It's a book about sexual assault.

The thing is, I didn't realize I'd written a book about sexual assault.

Throughout most of *Not Like Other Girls*, Jo refuses to recognize that what happened to her—what Nick, her former best friend's much older brother, did to her—was rape. Recognizing it means reckoning with it, and reckoning with it means saying the words, and Jo isn't ready yet.

In the years I spent writing and rewriting and revising this book, I was often vague about *what happened* with Nick. Most of it—whatever "it" was—occurred off the page, anyway, so I felt justified in my refusal to name it.

And if I called it "rape," what happens to Jo, then what did that mean happened to me?

Late in the summer of 2021, I started thinking about a night I didn't like to think about.

I couldn't stop thinking about it, or dreaming about it, and it was all deeply irritating. I'd complain to my friends, like, *I have no reason to feel weird about this, right? It's been years! It was nothing! It's not like I was assaulted or anything.*

Months went by, summer turned to fall, and I started to see a new therapist over Zoom. In the final minutes of an early session, that night—the one I was still thinking about, still trying *not* to think about—came up. I was super casual when I told her about it. I probably rolled my eyes. I may have laughed.

I was waiting for her to laugh, too, but instead she thanked me for sharing. Told me she was sorry we were ending on such a heavy note. Told me she was sorry this happened to me.

Right after, I logged off and stared at my laptop screen.

And I said, "What the fuck happened to me?"

I didn't realize I'd written a book about sexual assault because I didn't know I'd been sexually assaulted. Or, I knew, but I didn't want to believe it.

Just like Jo doesn't want to believe it.

Before that therapy session—before the start of my own personal reckoning—I'd been in the middle of revising *Not Like Other Girls* to submit to literary agents. But it took me weeks to even open the document again. I knew I'd find so much of myself woven into Jo. Everything on the page, the confusion and rage and devastation and pain—that was mine.

I drafted incoherent, typo-ridden entries in my Notes app about how I probably needed to shelve this book for now, and maybe forever. I cried about it. A lot. It killed me to imagine letting this story go . . . and how the hell was that fair to me?

It felt like another choice I wasn't getting to make for myself.

If all the confusion and rage and devastation and pain were mine, that meant the tiny sliver of hope in Jo's story was mine, too. Instead of shelving it, I wrote *what happened* in the car with Nick. I called it what it was, though I still couldn't say it out loud for myself.

This book is inextricable from my own path toward healing, as messy and nonlinear as it is, and my begrudging acceptance about what happened to me.

But *Not Like Other Girls* doesn't just belong to me anymore. It now belongs to everyone who reads it. I wrote this book because I needed it. If you're reading it because you need it, too, please know I'm sorry. Truly.

Whether you're a survivor—or a victim, if that term feels better—of sexual violence or know someone who is (and statistically, you do), whether you already have the words or you're still trying to find them, I hope you can feel less alone.

I hope you can find some comfort in Jo, a funny, imperfect, sometimes self-destructive young woman who knows what she deserves: Parents who look out for her. Friends who mirror her pain and laugh at her jokes. Healthy, consensual sexual experiences with someone she loves.

Justice, even if she has to define it for herself.

My justice is that I get to tell this story—Jo's and mine.

Meredith

– ACKNOWLEDGMENTS –

For a long, long, *long* time, I was terrified to share this book with anyone else. It was so deeply personal in ways I didn't understand, and the thought of someone reading these words, knowing this story, completely overwhelmed me. I sometimes wondered if I could ever let it go.

But there's a real beauty in letting others in. I know that now. I'm unimaginably grateful for everyone who joined me—guided me, helped me—in making this book a book.

Alex Borbolla, my genius editor and fellow February Aquarius. Your edits are thoughtful and wise and so funny, and during every editorial pass, I'd think: *I am so lucky.* I'm even luckier that you understood the heart of *Not Like Other Girls* from the start and knew implicitly the story I wanted to tell—and you made me feel I could tell mine, too. (That author's note would forever be unwritten without you.) You are the perfect champion for this book, and I'm so thrilled we get to work together on the next one.

The rest of the amazing team at Bloomsbury Children's for cheering on this book since day one. Thank you, especially, to Oona Patrick and Kei Nakatsuka for their input and insight; Yelena

Safronova and Jeanette Levy for their stunning art direction, and Dana Ledl for so perfectly capturing Jo in the gorgeous cover illustration; and Erica Barmash, Lily Yengle, and Lex Higbee for being the most supportive and creative marketing and publicity team I could ask for. Thank you, too, to the incredible folks at Bloomsbury UK, including my editor Alex Antscherl, for their enthusiasm and hard work in bringing this book to even more readers.

Andrea Morrison, who is the absolute best agent. (The *best*.) I'll be forever grateful that you saw potential in *Not Like Other Girls*, and in me as a writer. Not only do I appreciate (and admire) your kindness, patience, and savvy, but your ability to untangle even the messiest plot points with a single suggestion is truly magical. Most of all, I'm so thankful for all the ways you make me feel secure and supported with such a vulnerable book. Thank you for making a tough thing easier. Your unwavering faith in me forces me to have faith in myself.

Everyone at Writers House is not just fantastic at what they do, but genuinely lovely. I'm so happy to have landed here. My endless thanks to Amy Berkower, Alessandra Birch, Cecilia de la Campa, and Hayley Burdett Wilmot.

And thank you, from the bottom of my heart, to Genevieve Gagne-Hawes. Somehow the stars aligned when *Not Like Other Girls* landed in front of you. I'm still so stunned that I got to revise with you and Andrea. Your sharp (and funny!) edits transformed every page of this book, and I learned so much as a writer, too. Thank you for loving Jo first. I could go on, but instead, imagine that I'm passing you a napkin that reads: *thank you for everything.*

Beth Revis and Cristin Terrill and Wordsmith Workshops. I needed this community so badly, and without it—and you, and everyone in it—I'd likely still be netting a negative word count every day. Thank you for making this space for us.

Thank you to my very first readers: Julie, who had an innate sense of this story and never once led me astray; Malice, who always knew how to make the emotional beats shine; and Scott, who not only named Keystone, but soothed my panic many, many times. I'm sorry for making you read this book approximately three times each. I'm grateful that you did.

Thank you to my very last reader, Rachel Rose, who read an absolutely broken version of this book that was missing most of the middle. (I hope you like it, by the way!) Your snark made me laugh out loud, and you were spot-on, too. I'm so happy our R&Rs brought us together.

My friends who excitedly read past versions of this book over the years: Caroline, Jennie, Anna C., Chantal, Eleni, Nicole, Zoe, Sandra, Anna M., Sally, Amanda, Cassandra, Melissa, and Aubrey. I love you all.

And thank you so, so much to my fellow authors who read *Not Like Other Girls* and provided kind blurbs, and to the amazing booksellers who have supported this book since the day it first made its way into the world.

Mr. Craddock and Ms. Gamzon, my creative writing teachers at School of the Arts. They read everything—*everything*—I wrote in middle and high school. My senior year, right before I graduated, they told me I had *something*. Thank you to *all* teachers and librarians who fight for young readers to have access to the books they need.

My therapist for holding space for me each week, especially the tough ones, and learning so much about the publishing industry.

My endlessly talented, brilliantly funny friends. Thank you, too, to friends who changed my life, despite no longer being in it. The Peachies for celebrating with me since the beginning, and to everyone in The Salon for your wholehearted excitement and support, even when we were mostly strangers. I'm lucky I found these weird little corners of the world. To Amanda, Aubrey, Laurel, Rachel, and Rosie: I'd never want to survive being a teenager with anyone else.

Thank you to Wegmans, where I buy all my groceries and revised most of this book.

No thanks at all to my cats, Pearl and Josephine, both of whom repeatedly hindered this process by walking on my keyboard and jumping on my head at four a.m.

My grandmother, the original Jo. It kills me that you'll never be able to read my writing, but I like to think you'd like your namesake. Either that, or you'd say, "Jesus Christ, why does that girl swear so much?"

My mom for letting me pick *just one more* Nancy Drew book (or three) and pretending not to see when my lamp was still on until well after midnight. Thank you for letting me fall in love with books.

And thank you, reader. I'm generally overwhelmed when I imagine *Not Like Other Girls* in the world, and when it feels too daunting, I think of you. I'm thinking of you. For so long, Jo carries her pain alone. If you need someone, you can contact the Rape, Abuse & Incest National Network (RAINN) at 1-800-656-HOPE (4673) or rainn.org.

Thank you, again, for sharing this story with me.